Malcolm Ferguson

Rambles in Skye

With Sketch of a Trip to St. Kilda

Malcolm Ferguson

Rambles in Skye
With Sketch of a Trip to St. Kilda

ISBN/EAN: 9783337101169

Printed in Europe, USA, Canada, Australia, Japan

Cover: Foto ©Andreas Hilbeck / pixelio.de

More available books at **www.hansebooks.com**

A

GENEALOGY

OF

Descendants of John Thomson

OF

PLYMOUTH, MASS.

ALSO SKETCHES OF

FAMILIES OF ALLEN, COOKE AND HUTCHINSON.

————

By CHARLES HUTCHINSON THOMPSON,

OF

LANSING, MICH.

LANSING:
DARIUS D. THORP, PRINTER AND BINDER.
1890.

CONTENTS.

PREFACE.

The basis of this work is a " Genealogy of John Thomson "
by Ignatius Thomson, published in 1841 at Taunton, Mass.
The matter in his book has been rearranged mainly under the
system of the " New England Historic Genealogical Society."
To this has been added names of all other descendants I could
get, and in the later generations have given many families of
daughters and their descendants; which is a variation from the
plan in the edition of 1841.

Some items are gleaned from " History of Bridgewater," by
Nahum Mitchell, also from " Ancient Landmarks of Plymouth," by Wm. T. Davis.

Mrs. Lydia H. Morton, of Halifax, Mass., has given me
valuable information and assistance; in fact, she gave me the
only copy she had of the old Genealogy.

Judge Elijah Hayward, of McCollinsville, Ohio, wrote up a
partial genealogy of the Hayward and Thomson families, from
which I get valuable additions to this work through the kindness of Sarah W. Ames, daughter of Hon. Ellis Ames, deceased,
of Canton, Mass., with whom these papers were left.

Thos. Cushman, of Bridgewater, Mass., gave me the use of
his MSS. of Thomson records.

To Mr. James M. McKinlay, of New York, I am indebted for
the extracts from the Plymouth Colony Records in Astor
Library.

The rearrangement of the names in the old edition has been
done by Mrs. E. G. Thompson, my wife.

From an article by Mr. E. B. Thompson in New Bedford
Mercury of September 24, 1879, I get items of interest.

From Mr. Geo. H. Greene I have received many valuable
suggestions. To all who have responded to requests for information I feel especially grateful. I regret that the record of
many families is imperfect. I could not get more information.

CHARLES HUTCHINSON THOMPSON.

LANSING, MICH.,
312 S. Capitol avenue,
   October, 1890.

DIRECTIONS AND ABBREVIATIONS.

To trace back a name. In the index of Thomsons or those other than Thomsons, as the case may be, find the name desired. The number in the index is the genealogical number which will be found in numerical order at left margin of page in the book. From this number go to number of parent in center of page, then find the parent's number in the left margin; again go to number of parent in center of page as before and so on back to number one, the original emigrant.

The following abbreviations are used herein: b, born; d, died; m, married; dau, daughter.

All the dates in this work are in old style prior to 1752, since then they are in new style.

The full faced numbers indicate that the person has a family which appears further on in regular order, and there the history is given more fully.

The generation of any individual is indicated by the number in small type above and at the end of the name.

The genealogical number is sometimes placed after a name to identify it when out of its regular place.

INTRODUCTION.

The name THOMSON has long been known in England, Scotland and Ireland. The first certain knowledge we have of it is from the records of ancient heraldry, when aristocracy invented badges to distinguish the different degrees of family greatness; each spelled the name differently and were considered distinct families; whether, originally, all who bear this name, however spelled, were of the same family, cannot easily be ascertained.

In the southwestern part of England the name was spelled TOMPSON. Rev. John Tompson, who settled in the ministry at Berwick, on the Piscataqua river, was descended from this family. In Ireland it was THOMPSON, and in the south of Scotland it was THOMSON; of this family were James Thomson, the celebrated poet, and Charles Thomson, secretary of the Continental Congress in Revolutionary days. Born in the northern part of Wales, in the vicinity of Scotland, we are led to consider the subject of our sketch a descendant of the Scottish family. The signature to his will is spelled TOMSON. The circumstance of his youth when he arrived in this country, and the limited means of education which he had, lead us to conclude he did not know his lineage. This may not seem strange or unaccountable when we bear in mind the vast number of persons in Europe who then and even now have no specific knowledge of their grandparents, and in our own country, with all the means of education and records, cases may easily be found where a person could not tell from what nation in Europe his progenitor descended. We naturally look among the best-informed people for correct information: Rev. John Cotton, the first minister in Halifax, Mass., spelled our progenitor's name THOMSON, the records of the town of Mendon spell it the same, and in his deed of Spring-hill it is spelled THOMSON. The letter *p* was not introduced into the name by any of his descendants till a century and a half had rolled away. Judge Hayward says " the name at first was probably Thomasson, originally the son of Thomas; there does not remain a reasonable doubt that the correct spelling is Thomson, the son of Thom, an abbreviation of Thomasson." Mrs. Lydia H. Morton, of Halifax, Mass., whose opinion is based partly on tradition and partly on what she learned from people of forty or fifty years ago, on this subject, says: " The first two generations spelled their names TOMSON, also generally the third generation did so. The fourth generation thought the name should have an *h*, the name did not seem right; probably the first and second generations did not write and spell very well (many deeds and wills are signed with a mark), but when more learning became common, people began to see how much better the name would look with an *h*, and by common consent it was added. I find on the oldest stones in our cemetery the names of TOMSON only in the third generation, but in the fourth the *h* added. My great grandfather spelled the name without the *h*; my grandfather added it, and it is on his tombstone. IGNATIUS THOMSON would not add the *p* to his name. His brothers and many others, however, did so, which he would not acknowledge and never used it when writing to them. They thought the name looked better with a *p* and continued to use it; others followed. I do not know of a family in town who does not use it, although should you look over the old records or walk over the graveyard you would scarcely find a record or stone that has an *h* or *p* on it, and it is only till late in the last century that the name TOMSON was discarded."

In this work the spelling " Thompson " is introduced in the fifth generation, which seems about the time it was adopted.

From Francis' History of Watertown, p. 131–132, is found: The following named persons with others had plough lands allotted to them February 28, 1636, and were the inhabitants of Watertown: John Tomson 2 acres; John Eddy 9 acres; John

Hayward seven acres; William Swift five acres; Abram Shaw ten acres.

The following extracts pertaining to JOHN THOMSON have been taken from Plymouth Colony Records in the Astor Library, New York. The spelling and contractions are as in the original; quotation marks signify exact copy: "li" stands for pounds, "s" for shillings; in many words u is used for v and in others v for u; the original print is followed. As to extract from Vol. VI, page 238, entry is dated May, 1690, and the matter is dated October, 1690; the discrepancy may be in the original printed copy. In Vol. VII, where it says "John Tompson, a juror," it does not necessarily mean in only one case. The spelling of the name is not uniform, it is given as in the record. Parts of the original records were destroyed. The omissions in the entry in Vol. VIII, page 4, are caused by the injury which the original record had received.

Lieut. John Thomson was evidently a man of consequence in the colony, and it is a source of gratification to his descendants that their family has been here long enough to help make all the history this country has.

COURT ORDERS.

Vol. 2, page 80 & 81—"At the Gen^rall Court of o^r Sou^raigne the King, holden at Plym' aforesaid the third Day of March in the XXth Yeare of the now Raigne of our said Sou^raigne Lord Charles by the Grace of God King of England, Scotland, France & Ireland Defendor of the Fayth &c."

3 Mar 1644-5

"John Tompson { bound in tenn pounds a peece vpon the
James Hurst { same condiçon Default p'sently made
{ of this recogñ. Released.

John Tompson { bound in X^li a peece vpon the same
Thomas Willett { condiçon P bona port,
{ for John Tompson. Released."

The condition is for their appearance at the next General Court &c &c to abide the further of the Court & not depart the same without license & in the meantime to be of good behavior toward our Sovrn lord the King & all his liege people.

Vol. 2, p. 87.   4 June 1645.—At the General Court held at Plymouth John Tompson bound in XX^s for good behavior and to appear at next session of Court.

Vol. 2, p. 90. 28 Oct. 1645.—   Bradford Govr.

"The P'porçon & Names of the Souldiers in eich Towne sent forth in the late expedition against the Narrohigansets & their confederates,"

"The first company viz. xvj^{teene} went forth the xvth August 1645.

	John Tompson Richard Foster	
Plymouth viij men: six wth those that went out first and two wth those that went out last.	John Bundy Nicholas Hodges John Shawe Samuel Cutbert	These vj were forth xvij dayes.
	John Jenkins John Harmon	These two were forth xiij dayes "

Then follows a list of six from Duxborrow 4 from Marshfield and then 22 others from four other towns on 23 August.

Vol. 2, p. 94. 26 December 1645.—"John Tompson & Mary Cooke marryed the xxvj Decemb^r, 1645."

Vol. 2, p. 126. In Court 7 June 1648.—"The Court doe al'ow a fine of five pound dew from John Tomson to the towne of Plimouth towards mending of the causway at Joansses River—"

Vol. 2, p. 153. 4 June 1650.—"John Tompson" having been chosen cunstable by the township of Plymouth is p'sented to the Court & sworne.

Vol. 3, p. 63. 7 June 1653.—List of the surveyors for highways including for "Barnsta^r Henry Rowley, John Tompson."

Vol. 3, p. 115. 3 June 1657.—"The names of such as refused to serve on the Grand Enquest" 5 including "John Tompson."

Vol. 3, p. 200. 2 Oct 1660.—"The names of the petty jury or jury of life and death are as follows :—" 12, including "John Tompson."

Vol. 4, p 29. 3 Oct 1662.—"John Tompson warned to attend this Court to serve on a jury ; did absent himselfe, and soe lyable to fine, vnlese hee can satisfy the Court by his defence."

Vol. 4, p. 54. 1 Mar 1663-4.—"This court, taking notice of such evidence as hath bin produced for the clearing of a controversy between John Tompson, plaintiffe, and Richard Wright, in reference to a p'cell of land att Namassakett, doe allow an agreement between the said p'ties, which was ordered here to bee entered as followeth, viz.: that the said p'ties shall have equall share of the land allotted to Francis Cooke at Namasket aforesaid, provided that they bee equal in bearing the charge about the said land."

Vol. 4, p. 61. 8 June 1664.—"John Tompson" and 20 others "Sworne" as "the Grand Enquest."

Vol. 4, p. 112. 2 Dec 1665.—"Att this court Nathaniel Bacon, John Chipman, John Tompson and Trusteeman Hull were approved by the Court to bee the Select men of the towne of Barnstable."

Vol. 4, p. 124. 5 June. 1666.—Same "celect" men for Barnstable approved by the Court.

Vol. 4, p. 150. 5 June 1667.—Names of Select men sworn for Barnstable: "William Crocker, John Chipman, John Tompson, Joseph Laythorp."

Vol. 4, p. 160. 2 July 1667.—" Likewise libertie is granted vnto Will'am Clarke, Joseph Burge, of Sandwich, Thomas Huckens, John Tompson, Edward Dotey and his brother John Dotey and James Cole Juni', to look out for some supplyes of land if it may ⸗ had for theire accomodation."

Vol. 4, p. 182. 3 June 1668.—Five select men named for Barnstable including "John Tompson."

Vol. 5, p. 21. 1 June 1669.—" In reference vnto an attachment served on a p'sell of cedar bolts att the suite of Edward Gray, John Thompson and Benjamin Bartlett, and in reference vnto the complaint of Nathaniel Thomas" and others against Gray, Thompson and Bartlett for vnjust molestation in attaching or causing theire goods to be attached viz: cedare bolts in or near vnto a swamp or swampes lying Northwest or Northerly from Moonponsett Pond, on pretence of great damage done vnto themselves and others, it was agreed by both p'ties " that each pay its own costs and half the marshals fee of 20 shillings in silver, " and that those that cut the bolts shall have liberty to fetch them away "

Vol. 5, p. 22. 1 June 1669.—"The Court hath ordered that on the one and twentyeth of this instant June, the line shalle run between the Namassaketts mens land, called the Major's Purchase, and the townes of Marshfield, Duxburrow and Bridgwater. Mr Will'am Crow and George Bonum were apointed by the Court to doe it with John Tompson and Will'am Nelson for the purchasers."

Vol. 5, p. 35. 7 June 1670.—" John Tompson " one of the 3 Selectmen for Barnstable.

Vol. 5, p. 40. 7 June 1670.—" John Tompson " enters in the sum of £10 as one of two sureties for the good behavior of Samuell Norman, who is to appear at the Oct. term of Court.

Vol. 5, p. 57. 5 June 1671.—" John Tompson " one of the Selectmen for Barnst'.

Vol. 5, p. 62. 5 June 1671.—" The names of the p'sons apointed by the Court to View the Damage done to the Indians by the Horses and Hoggs of the English," for Barnst', five, including " John Tompson."

Vol. 5, p. 90. 5 June 1672.—" John Tompson " a Deputy for a town.

Vol. 5, p. 92. 5 June 1672.—" John Tompson " one of the three Selectmen for Barnstable.

Vol. 5, p. 113. 3 June 1673.—Same.

Vol. 5, p. 114. 3 June 1673.—" John Tompson " a Deputy for a town.

Vol. 5, p. 132. 29 Oct 1673.—" Whereas there hath bin a former graunt vnto John Tompson and Joseph Laythorp and Barnabas Laythorp, to looke out for land which might be purchased of the Indians

that might be convenient for them, and haveing an order to purchase
lands between Assowamsett Pond and Dartmouth bounds, bearing date
the 28th of July 1673, which accordingly they have done, the town of
Middleberry laying claime to a great p'te thereof, this Court orders, that
if Middleberry men recover the lands thuse purchased, the above-men-
sioned p'sons shall have libertie to purchase lands elsewhere."

Vol. 5, p. 135.   15 Sep 1673.—" The names of the Deputies that
served att this Court," 24, including "John Tompson."

Vol. 5, pp. 135, 136.   17 Dec 1673.—" This Court, vpon serious consideration of the injurious actings of the Duch, our naighbours att New
Yorke, in the surprissall of severall vessells and goods of our confeader-
ats, and refusing to make just satisfaction for the same vpon demand,"
etc., declare war against the Dutch.   "The Gouʳ bestowes a drum
towards the expedition. * * * Four halberts; Serjeant Tompson—
one," etc.   The pay of a Serjeant, 3 shillings p' day:

Vol. 5, p. 137.   4 March 1673-4.—" Mr Thomas Hinckley, Mr
Thomas Walley, Will'am Crocker, John Tompson and Thomas Huckens
are appointed by the Court to settle the estate of Mr Nath Bacon
deceased, amongst Mistris Hannah Bacon and her children."

Vol. 5, p. 138.   4 March 1673-4.—" The Treasurer and Serjeant Tompson are appointed by the Court to make purchase of such lands in the
township of Middleberry as the Indians doe or may tender to sell."

Vol. 5, p. 144.   3 June 1674.—" John Tompson " a deputy and one of
the 3 selectmen for Middlebery.

Vol. 5, pp. 146, 147.   3 June 1674.—" Wheras it is ordered by the
Court, in reference vnto a certaine tract of land lying at Middleberry,
that Benjamine Church should purchase it in the behalf of the proprie-
tors and inhabitants of Middleberry aforesaid, and that it doth appear
that the said tract of land is purchased by the said Benjamine Church
and John Tompson, as more fully appears by a deed bearing date the
23 of July 1673; And, wheras, alsoe, wheras the Court have ordered,
that the purchase thereof should be repayed by the last of November
1673, and it not being payed by the time prefixed, it is mutually agreed
by the inhabitants and propriators with them, the said John Tompson
and Benjamine Church, that they should have one-third p'te of the
said land, and to take where they would within the said tract soe as
they take it together for theire purchase and charge, and this to be for
theire cecuritie and evidence for theire said land."

Vol. 5, p. 147.   3 June 1674.—" Weddensday the 24th of this instant,
is appointed by the Court for the inhabitants and purchasers of Dartmouth to meet together for the setteling of the bounds of theire towne,
att which time the Govʳ, Mr. Hinckley, the Treasurer, Mr. Walley
Leiftenant Morton and John Tompson did engage to give meeting with
others to propose and endeauor that some prouision may be made for
the preaching of the word of God amongst them."

Vol. 5, p. 156.   27 Oct 1674.—" John Tompson" named firxt on a jury which found a native named Matthias alias Achawehett "guilty of manslaughter by way of chaunce medley."

Vol. 5, p. 165. 1 June 1675.—"John Tompson" a deputy and one of the 3 selectmen of Middleberry.

Vol. 5, p. 174. 1 June 1675.—"The Councell of War doe impower Serjeant John Tompson and Leiftenant Joseph Howland to keep the Indian prisoners now att Plymouth, and doe allow them two shillings and six pence for every day and night for every man that is or shal be imployed in this p'sent service."

Vol. 5, p. 228. 6 March 1676-7.—In reference vnto a gun pressed for an Indian called Isaacke for the Countreyes service, which gun was pawned by the Indian and since sold to John Tompson by the Treasurer, the Court have ordered the said Indian to pay the sume of ten shillings to the said John Tompson vpon his demand, in silver money, or fifteen dayes worke in deflt thereof."

Vol. 5, p. 229. 6 March 1676-7.—Acct of Sam. Clapp, adm^r of the estate of Eliezer Clapp, late of Barnstable, deceased, shows payment by him "to Serjeant John Tompson last year, 20—00—00; to Sergeant John Tompson the eight of June 20—00—00" and the Court order the adm^r "to pay next year to John Tompson more as appears due by bond—20 —00—00."

Vol. 5, p. 246. 30 Oct 1677.—"Mr John Thompson" named first on a jury to try Ambrose Fish indicted for rape. Verdict, "If one evidence with concurring circumstances be good in law wee find him guilty. But if one evidence, with concurring circumstances be not good in law, wee find him not guilty."

Vol. 5, p. 275. 29 May 1670.—In an exact list of all the names of the Freemen of the jurisdiction of New Plymouth, there are 43 in Barnstable, including "John Tompson."

Vol. 6, p. 35. 1 June 1680.—Selectmen for "Middleberry, Mr. Samuel Fuller Mr. John Thompson Mr. Francis Combe."

Vol. 6, p. 36. 1 June 1680.—"The Deputies of the severall Townes chosen to serve att this Court, and the seueral Adjournments thereof," 23, including "John Thompson."

Vol. 6, p. 59. 7 June 1681.—Select men for Mid': "John Thompson, Mr Francis Combe, John Nelson."

Vol. 6, p. 61. 7 June 1681.—"The names of the Deputies of the severall Townes of this Gou'ment." 22—"John Thompson" is No. 22.

Vol. 6, p. 84. 6 June 1682.—Same Select men for Middleboro.

Vol. 6, p. 85. 6 June 1682.—"John Thompson" a deputy.

Vol. 6, p. 87. 6 June 1682.—"Propounded to take up theire Freedom, if approved." 47 including John Thompson juni^r +

Vol. 6, p. 106. 6 June 1683—John Thompson a deputy.

Vol. 6, p. 112. July 1683.—"Mr John Thompson, Mr William Crow, and John Barker att the Court of his ma^{tie} held att Plymouth the sixt of March 16$^{8}_{3}$ were appointed to be Administrators of the estate of Mr.

Francis Combe late deceased." The entry then recites that they have rendered satisfactory account and they are "discharged from the said Adminestration."

Vol. 6, p. 128. 3 June 1684.—"Mr John Tomson" deputy for "Middlebery."

Vol. 6, p. 128. 3 June 1684.—"Mr. John Tomson" one of the Select Men.

Vol. 6, p. 141. 1 July 1684.—"John Thompson" named first as one of the Grand Jury.

Vol. 6, p. 165.—2 June 1685.—"John Tomson" deputy for "Middlebury."

Vol. 6, p. 168. 2 June 1685.—"John Tompson" one of the 3 select men for "Middleborough."

Vol. 6. p. 178. 27 Oct 1685.—"Memo'. Two of the Celect men of the town of Middlebury viz : Mr. John Thompson & John Nelson, appeared att his maj^ties Court holden att Plimouth on the last Tuesday of October 1685 & according to law complained that John Howard Senr would not depart their town, being warned thereto by s^d select men according to law."

Vol. 6, p. 186. The names of the Town officers—

"Deputies	Celect Men	Constables"
"Mid'lebury Mr Jn⁰ Tompson	Jno Tompson Jno Nelson Isaacke Howland	John Miller"

Vol. 6, p. 238. 20 May 1690.—"By the Councill of war at Plimouth, Octob^r ye 9th 1690. Thomas Tomson of Middleborough being (per order of the major part of the town councill of s^d Middleborough) impressed for the service of their maj^ties at Canada and refusing to attend that service is sentenced to pay a fine of four pounds in money to said town council for the use of s^d town, or be imprisoned till the same be paid with fees &c"

Vol. 7, p. 33. 7 Mar 1642-3.—"John Tompson compl'ns ag^st John Holmes in an action of trespas vpon the case to the dam^r of iiij^li The jury fynd for the pl'tiff 7iii^s x^d debt x^s dam' and charges of the suite."

Vol. 7, p. 54. 7 June 1651.—"John Tompson" a juror.

Vol. 7, p. 80. 5 Oct 1656.—"John Tompson" against James Naighbor ; action of case, damage £10 for not performing agreement about salt and caske & for not paying for 2 barrels of oysters. Verdict and judgment for plaintiff.

Vol. 7, pp. 105, 108. 3 March 1662-3.—"Richard Church and John Tompson complained against Capt. Thomas Willett in an action of the case to the damage of twenty four pounds, for non p'forming an agreement according to covenants about the meeting house att Plymouth." "Find for the defendant the cost of the suite."

Vol. 7, p. 112. 5 Oct 1663.—" John Tompson " a juror in several cases.
Vol. 7, p. 134. 31 Oct 1666.—   do   do
Vol. 7, pp. 143, 144. 5 Mar 1667-8.— do   do
Vol. 7, p. 154. 2 March 1668-9.—   do   do
Vol. 7, p. 157. 29 Oct 1669.—" John Tompson" a juror.
Vol. 7, p. 163. 29 Oct 1670.—   do   in several actions.
Vol. 7, p. 174. 30 Oct 1672.—   do
Vol. 7, p. 181. 4 July 1673.—   do
Vol. 7, p. 191. 7 July 1674.—   do   in several actions.
Vol. 7, p. 194. 27 Oct 1674.—   do
Vol. 7, p. 195. 2 Mar 1674-5.—   do
Vol. 7, p. 196. 27 Oct 1675.—-   do
Vol. 7, p. 197. 7 Mar 1675-6.—   do
Vol. 7, p. 205. 3 July 1677.—" John Thompson " a juror.
Vol. 7, p. 208. 30 Oct 1677.—" Johu Tompson " a juror.
Vol. 7, p. 217. 3 July 1679.—" John Thompson" a juror.
Vol. 7, p. 219. 1 Nov 1679.—" Mr. John Thompson" a juror.
Vol. 7, pp. 231, 233. 27 Oct., 1680.—" John Thompson " a juror.
Vol. 7, p. 275. 5 Mar 1683-4.—-   do
Vol. 7, p. 282. 28 Oct 1684.—John Thompson is mentioned as one of
the persons through whose hands a mortgage passed, as if he had
bought and sold it.

Vol. 7, p. 304. 8 Oct 1689.—" In answer to a petition presented to this
Court by Lieut' John Tompson, in refference to the present want of a
highway viz : A country road from Middlebury, Bridgwater and other
places towards Boston "—Highway ordered to be speedily laid forth by
a jury of 16 named. "The said jury are ordered to meet together at
the house of s^d Tompson " &c. &c.

Vol. 7, p. 305. 6 June 1690.—Five persons added to the jury, and the
jury are ordered to meet at the house of John Tomps. Senr. in Middleborough on the first Tuesday of July next about noone or 12 of the
clock " &c. &c.

Vol. 7, pp. 390 & 310. 7 April 1691.—Report of jury on Boston road
dated 2 July 1690.

Vol. 8, p. 4. 1647.—Plymouth Register of Births, November * * *
John Tompson * * *

Vol. 8, p. 5. 1648.—Plym' Register of Marriages & Burialls "John
Tompson the sonn of John Tompson died the eleventh of Febrewary."

Vol. 8, p. 8. 1649.—Plymouth Register of the Beirth of theire
children. "John Tompson the sonne of John Tompson was born on
the 24th of Nouember."

Vol. 8, p. 136. 7 June 1672.—" John Tompson is one of the 4 who
examine the Treasurers accts.

Vol. 8, p. 189. Aug 1643.—In a list of males in Plymouth from 16 to
60 years able to bear arms " John Tompson " is included.

Copy of Deed from William Weetispaquin and others—Indians—to John Thompson and others.

WINSLOW, GOV'R.

Know all men, Present and to Come, that we William Wetyspaquin, Ananeta Tabyas, O. Benatt, Indians, of the Colony of New Plymouth, in New England, for and in consideration of the full and just sum of ten pounds to us in hand already paid before the insealing hereof by John Thompson, Joseph Laythorp and Barnabas Laythorp, all of Barnstable in the Colonie of Plymouth aforesaid, with which sum we do acknowledge ourselves to be fully satisfied, and thereof do acquit and discharge the said John Thompson, Joseph Laythorp and Barnabas Laythorp, their and every of their heirs, executors and administrators forever, have freely, fully and absolutely given, granted, bargained, sold, aliened, enfeoffed and confirmed, and by these presents for us and our several heirs do give, grant, bargain, sell, alien, enfeoffe and confirm unto the said John Thompson, Joseph Laythorp and Barnabas Laythorp, and to their heirs and assigns forever, a tract of land lying and being in the Colony of New Plymouth aforesaid,—bounded Northerly by * * etquash pond, Easterly by quetoquash River and Snepetuitt pond, and so from the Eastermost end and Southermost side of a little neck of land by the said Snipatuitt pond, and so from the Eastermost side of a little pond on a straight line from thence to Dartmouth path an hundred rod southerly from Dartmouth's now bound tree, and so from thence bounded all along by Dartmouth path until we come within sight of Quetrquas pond, and from the path upon a straight line to the southermost end of the pond, and by the pond.

(In left margin:) PLYMOUTH COLONY RECORDS. Vol. IV. of Deeds. Page 41.

To have and to hold all the above bonded land with all and singular the benefits, profits, privileges and hereditaments whatsoever unto the said John Thompson, his heirs and assigns forever; unto the said Joseph Laythorp, his heirs and assigns forever ; and unto the said Barnabas Laythorp, his heirs and assigns forever. To the onely proper use and behoof of them the said John Thompson, Joseph Laythorp, their heirs and assigns forever.

In witness whereof we the abovesaid William Watuspaquin, Asanetta Tobias and Benatt have hereunto set our hands and seals this first day of November in the year of our Lord God one thousand six hundred seventy and three, 1673.

Signed, sealed and delivered in presence of us, John Bryant, Nathaniel Thomas.

The mark ⍟ of William Weetispaquin &a	(SEAL)
The mark of Asaneta ᵃᴀ	(SEAL)
The mark of Tobias 𝔈°a	(SEAL)
The mark of Benatt ᴮ and a	(SEAL)

This deed of sale was acknowledged by William Tispaquin, Asanetta, Tobias, and Benatt, this first day of November, 1673. As also Old Tispaquin alias the Black sachem and Daniel, alias Pachange, the same day gave up their right in the abovesaid deed expressed before me.

CONSTANT SOUTHWORTH, Assistant.

Another Indian called Acteewanequa, who is said to have right in or to the said lands abovementioned did resign up unto the purchasers abovenamed, his right, title and interest in and unto the lands abovesaid. June the 25th, 74, before   JOSIAH WINSLOW, *Gov'r.*

July the 3, 1675. This Court allow & confirm all the lands contained in the above mentioned deed unto the bove mentioned Mr. Barnabas Lothropp, Capt. Joseph Lothropp, & John Thompson, according to ye order of the General Court to hold to them the said Barnabas Lothropp, Joseph Lothropp, John Thompson, their heirs and assigns forever.

Attest : NATHANIEL CLARK,
Secretary of the Jurisdiction of New Plymouth.

February 4, 1889. The foregoing is a true copy from Plymouth Colony Records of Deeds, Vol. IV., page 41.

Attest : WM. S. DANFORTH, *Reg.*

Copy of the Will of John Tomson.

Know all men to whom these presents shall come, that I John Tomson Senr, of ye township of Middlebury being at this present day weak in body through my infirmities and diseases that are upon me, but of sound and perfect understanding & memory do make and ordain this to be my last will and testament to continue forever firm and inviolable.

Imprimis. I will & bequeath unto Mary Tomson my beloved wife ye use of one half of my house during her widowhood which half she pleaseth, and ye use of all my household goods during her widowhood, and six cows and a score of sheep, and three or four acres of land lying by my house. All these to have and to use during ye time of her widowhood. And also my will is that ye executors shall see that ye said land shall be improved for her, and they shall be paid out of ye estate. And also I will leave her one hundred pounds in money to dispose to her children as she shall see cause, but if in case she should die intestate my will is that this said hundred pound shall be equally divided among them all sons and daughters, that is my own children & hers. Also my will is that she shall have a cow or a steer yearly for her provisions. And if she cannot spare it out of that stock of cattle then it shall be provided for her out of ye estate. Also my will is that whatsoever provisions and clothing is left at my decease shall belong to ye family. And my wife shall have a double part of it at her disposing. And whereas I gave unto my son John half a score of land formerly and he hath nothing to show for it I now give it him by will

3

and he shall have fifty acres of land where his house standeth taking it up the whole length. Also I give and bequeath unto my son Jacob the house wherein he dwelleth, and ye fourth part of ye upland that is of ye two hundred acres of upland. And also I do give and bequeath unto my sons Thomas and Peter the one half of my house wherein I do dwell during their mother's life conditionally that they will agree to keep together and maintain their mother's stock of cattle aforesaid. And they shall have the increase both of cattle and sheep, so that they maintain & make good ye principal. And if they should come to some extraordinary losses so that they are like to be losers by it, they shall be considered in ye estate. And my will is that there shall be meadows set apart to keep those cattle during their mother's life. And I do give and bequeath unto my son Thomas all my house and the barn and ye orchard and ye lands adjacent thereabout after his mother's decease that will amount to a fourth part of two hundred acres, only if my son Peter have not land enough fenced and broken up he shall have ye use of two or three acres of land for two years if he desires it. And also I do give and bequeath unto my son Peter that my fifty acres of upland that I bought of John Morton. And whereas I have given to my sons John and Jacob and Thomas three quarters of this two hundred acres of upland, my will is that in ye division the fourth part be left so as to be most suitably divided amongs them all four. Also I give unto my four sons aforesaid a third part of land that was purchased by Captain Joseph Lothrop and Mr. Barnabas Lothrop and myself. And also I give unto my four sons above written ye one half of that third part of upland that was purchased by Captain Church and myself the one half of that third part next to Snipetrist pond and my one sixteen shilling purchase and that which I bought of John Irish, and that tract of land at Assawamsett that I bought of Felix ye Indian, and that which I bought of William Clark formerly called ye Majors' Purchase lying betwixt the two paths. A fifth part of that tract all which I give to them to divide equally amongst themselves. And also I give unto my four sons aforesaid all that my two hundred acres of upland lying between Monponsett Pond and the Little Herring Pond with my four acres of meadow and my two shares and half in ye Great Cedar Swamp and my two shares and half in ye undivided lands, all which shall be equally divided among my four sons aforesaid. Also my will is that my four sons shall have all my tools of all sorts for Carpentry or Husbandry, and also all my arms all to be equally divided among them. Also I give unto my son Peter twenty pounds in money towards ye building him a house besides four or five thousand foot of boards and plank. Also I do give unto my daughter Mary Tabor thirty and five pounds besides w't is due to me from her husband. Also I do give unto my daughter Esther Read thirty and three pounds besides what is due unto me from her husband. Likewise I do give unto my daughter Elizabeth Swift twenty and five pounds. And also to my grandson

Thomas Swift ten pounds when he cometh to ye age of one and twenty years. And if he should die before then it shall be forthwith paid unto his mother. Also I give unto my daughter Sarah Tomson forty pounds. Also I give unto my daughter Lydia Soul thirty and four pounds besides what she hath had already. Also I do give unto my daughter Mary Tomson forty pounds. Likewise I do give unto my son Jacob a yoke of steers of four years old or upwards or ye value of them. Also I give unto my son Thomas a yoke of steer and two cows or ye value of them. Also I give to my son Peter a yoke of steers and two cows or ye value of them. Also my will is that my four sons John and Jacob and Thomas and Peter Tomson shall be my executors who shall receive what is due unto me and shall pay all my just debts, and shall see that my body be decently buried, and out of my estate to defray ye charges. And whatsoever is left after my and my wifes' decease when all charges is cleared shall be equally divided amongst them, all my children sons and daughters. Thus hoping that this my last will and testament will be kept and performed according to ye true intent of ye same, I commit my body to ye dust and my soul to God that gave it me.

In witness whereof I set unto my hand and seal this twenty third day of April one thousand six hundred ninety and six.

JOHN TOMSON.   [SEAL.]

Witness:
JONATHAN SHAW Junr.
JOSEPH RING his I K mark.
ANNE WATERMAN. her ɔ mark.
Memorandum ye 8th day of July 1696.—That Jonathan Shaw, Joseph Ring and Anne Waterman the witnesses hereto subscribing made oath all of them that they were present and saw and heard John Tomson ye testator here named sign, seal and declare the above written to be his last will and testament, and that to ye best of their judgment he was of sound disposing mind and memory when he did ye same.

Before WM. BRADFORD, Esqr, Judge.
Attest: SAML. SPRAGUE, Register.

A true copy.
Attest: JOHN C. SULLIVAN, Register.

FIRST GENERATION.

I.

JOHN THOMSON was born in the northern part of Wales, in the year 1616. It is said his father died soon after his birth, and his mother married again. "The name of the step-father is concealed behind that impenetrable veil of oblivion which time is spreading over the generations of man." The child lived with and received his scanty education from his legal parents. He came to this country in the third embarkation from England. The second embarkation, which arrived at Plymouth, November 11, 1621, was in the ship "Fortune," Captain Robert Cushman, bringing thirty-five families—the remainder of Robinson's society. The third arrival was two vessels under the patronage of Thomas Weston, a merchant of distinction in London, containing sixty or seventy men; some of them had families, and among the number was JOHN THOMSON, then in the sixth year of his age; they landed at Plymouth early in May, 1622.

The above is taken from Ignatius Thomson's Genealogy of John Thomson. We do not see how this statement can be wholly correct.

The first embarkation, the "Mayflower," arrived in November, and the pilgrims landed on Plymouth Rock December 11, 1620,* O. S.; there were 102 passengers; the second embarkation, the "Fortune," arrived at Plymouth November 23, 1621, with thirty-five passengers; the third embarkation, the "Little James and Anne," arrived August, 1623, with sixty passengers; the foregoing were termed "First comers."

Another arrival was the "Sparrow," in May, 1622, with seven passengers, sent out by Thomas Weston. Still another arrival was the "Charity and Swan," in July, 1622, sent out by Thomas Weston, with sixty colonists for Wessagusset or Weymouth, which visited Plymouth, bringing letters from Mr. Weston to the effect that he had quit the "Adventurers."

We understand that John Thomson came in some one of the above embarkations or arrivals, and landed at Plymouth, but which one is uncertain.

---

* I get the most of these items and dates from Life of Miles Standish by John S¹ C. Abbott, published 1875.

Tradition is silent respecting any incident in his life till he arrived at manhood; then it presents him to us in many events interesting and entertaining. From his will it appears he was a carpenter; besides building houses for others, he built one for himself in each of the places he selected as a settlement, and one for each of his sons, John and Jacob.

Also, with his friend Richard Church, he built the first framed meeting house in Plymouth, in 1637, and sued Thomas Willett, the town's agent, for not complying with the contract. As compensation for his labor the town gave him a deed of a piece of land from the market-house extending back to the herring brook, now called Spring-hill. He was on terms of great intimacy with Richard Church and after his death with his brother Captain Benjamin Church, the Indian fighter.

March 3, 1645, John Thomson purchased of Samuel Eddy a house and garden in Plymouth, near Spring-hill. He married December 26, 1645, MARY COOKE, b. 1626, daughter of Francis Cooke, one of the Pilgrim Fathers who came over in the "Mayflower" in 1620.

His chief business was that of a farmer, and his first appearance in that capacity was at Sandwich. Carpenter work was probably taken up from necessity and not as a trade; being a man fruitful of expedients and of uncommon ingenuity.

He made a purchase in that part of the town called Nobscusset, where he lived a few years, but came to the conclusion that he could better his fortune for himself and children by moving further into the interior. He accordingly selected a place thirteen miles west of the village of Plymouth, on the confines of Bridgewater, Middleborough, and what was then called Plymouth (now Halifax), and purchased land of William Wetis-pa-quin, sachem of the Neponsets, the purchase having been approved by the Court. The deed may be found recorded in Book 4, page 41, in the Registry of Deeds for Plymouth county. The homestead included other purchases than the above deed, in all by estimate more than six thousand acres of land; at the present time it is divided into more than one hundred farms with dwelling houses thereon, commencing at the herring-brook, in the northern part of Halifax, and extending south into Middleborough, the whole distance being nearly five miles. He built a log house in Middleborough, about twenty rods west of the Plymouth line, where he lived until it was burned by the Indians.

It has been handed down by tradition that he first commenced clearing land with reference to locating his house near where the saw mill of Ephraim B. Thompson now stands. After working awhile he became thirsty and went into a valley near by in quest of water, and finding a lively brook of pure water, came to the conclusion that the spring could not be far away. He accordingly followed the brook up about one hundred rods and came to the fountain-head of pure, gushing water. A clearing was here made and a log house built. The importance of locating near a spring of never failing water, instead of attempting to dig wells, at that time, is apparent when we consider that shovels and spades in those times were made of wood instead of iron; wooden shovels were used by the third and fourth generations from John Thomson. When Ebenezer, a grandson of his, had a wooden shovel pointed or shod with iron, it was considered a very great improvement and was borrowed by the neighbors far and near. The ancient practice of building dwelling houses near springs and running water accounts for the very crooked roads in many localities of the old colony.

His settlement amidst a surrounding savage enemy must have been attended with many troubles and fearful apprehensions. He must have felt the need of all the confidence in God that the religion which brought our fathers into this country could afford. He felt the necessity of using every precaution which his ingenuity could suggest or his wisdom dictate. Tradition has given us a few incidents illustrating these characteristics.

An anecdote is related indicating a plan which he adopted for his preservation from Indian surprise. He agreed with a man by the name of Jabez Soule, who had settled in the northwestern part of what is now called Plympton, to entice a young Indian named Pringle Peter to come and live with them and learn to work and live like the English. They succeeded in their overtures—the Indian came and lived with each of them alternately two weeks. They studied to please him by flattery, and in every little competition of strength or agility, by giving him the advantage or yielding to his superiority. When the Indians agreed to make war on their white neighbors this young Indian would secretly steal away and join them; his absence thus became a warning to immediately repair to the garrison. When they had made peace with the English, this young Indian would return and live with them; by this arrangement he ignorantly became their protector. One day, while this young Indian was at work with him, our ancestor observed to the Indian, "I wonder they never attempted to kill me." "Master," said the Indian, "I have cocked my gun many a time to shoot you, but I loved you so well I could not."

As the time drew near when open hostilities were about to commence in the terrible war of King Philip, there was a marked change in the demeanor of the Indians; they were generally morose and sullen; at times, however, the opposite; so uncommonly friendly and helpful as to excite serious apprehensions. At one time three came when Mrs. John Thomson was alone and began to behave rudely, kicking over the chairs. One pulled a fish, which was boiling, out of the pot, for which she reprimanded him, at which he drew a knife and brandished it in a threatening manner. She seized a splint broom and drove them out of the house.

At another time, on a sabbath morning, after his wife and children had gone to meeting, several Indians came into his house in a turbulent manner. He was apprehensive that his life was in danger, and seated himself in the corner of the room with the long gun in his lap, having his brass pistol in his hand. They appeared very friendly at times, patting him on the shoulder, and at the same time making efforts to get possession of the gun, at which he would look sternly at them, holding up the pistol; they would then look at each other and step back. After loitering about the house awhile they returned to the forest. A few days later he was absent from home; when he returned at night he inquired of his wife if she had seen any indians. She replied that there had been a number there, and that they were uncommonly friendly and very helpful, following her to the garden and assisting in picking beans. He replied, "There is trouble ahead; we must pack up immediately and go to the garrison."

The teams were put in readiness and a portion of their furniture and goods were loaded, while a part, together with his money, were secreted in a swamp near the dwelling house, and he and his family started before it was dark. They had not gone more than two miles before the light of the devouring flames made sure to them the fate of their dwelling. On the way to the garrison they passed the house of William Danson, in Middleborough, and urged him to go, but he concluded not to start until early in the morning. Danson had ridden but a short distance in the morning, when, stopping to water his horse, he was shot down by the Indians. The little rill where he was killed is at the present time called Danson's Brook. The next day John Thomson sent one of his sons with two others from the garrison to the deserted farm. On the way they discovered in the horse path a pair of leather shoes and a beaver hat which belonged to Danson; these they considered to be decoys, and put their horses at full speed. When they returned neither of the articles were there.

At the garrison, those capable of bearing arms, sixteen in number, met and chose John Thomson their commander. He applied to the Governor and council for a commission, but considering the small number of men, they gave him a general commission as Lieutenant Commandant, not only of the garrison, but in the field and at all posts of danger.

"He and his men were very active in forcibly contending with the Indians in 1675, and in Philip's war of 1676, braving every danger and meeting the enemy at every point where he could be found. Having associated much with the Indians in early life, he made himself acquainted partially with their language, their habits and customs, and from their manners could discern the motives of their conduct. Often did they attempt to waylay and ambush him, but his vigilance never slept, and his prudence and matured judgment effectually guarded his safety. His stern and positive manner awed them into fear, and his inflexible courage subdued them to cowardice. Whenever he came in contact with them he triumphed and they were defeated, until they believed the Great Spirit protected him and that he could not be killed. Tradition gives him credit for having repeatedly saved the settlements at Halifax and Middleborough by his superior skill and well-timed precaution."

He was equipped with a gun, brass pistol, sword and halberd. The whole length of the gun, including stock and barrel, is seven feet four and one-half inches; length of barrel, six feet one and one-half inches; caliber, twelve balls to the pound; weight, twenty pounds twelve ounces. It is considered to be quite a muscular feat to hold this gun at arms' length and sight an object. The whole length of the sword is three feet five and one-half inches; length of the blade from the guard, two feet eleven and three-eighths inches. Hudibras has described this sword:

> "For want of use it has grown rusty,
> And ate into the blade for lack
> Of something for to hew and hack."

This gun and sword are now in Pilgrim Hall at Plymouth, where are collected many other pilgrim relics.

At the commencement of King Philip's war in 1675, the

Indians became so morose that in the month of June the people from the region around, in all thirty-five families, fled for safety to the fort, which was built near what is called the Four Corners in Middleborough. The Indians would daily appear on the south side of the Nemasket river, opposite the fort, and perch themselves on and about what is called "Hand-rock," and taunt those in the garrison with insulting gestures. Lieut. Thomson ordered Isaac Howland (a distinguished marksman) to take the long gun and shoot one of the Indians. This he did while the savage was on the rock in the attitude of insulting them. The distance from the garrison to the rock was one hundred and fifty-five rods, nearly a half mile. The Indian fell, mortally wounded. Enraged at the fate of their comrade, the others rushed down the hill toward the grist mill (where the Star mills were located). The miller, who was grinding, being signaled from the garrison, placed his coat and hat on a post, which was partially concealed by bushes, as a ruse, and took a circuitous route through the thicket to the garrison. The Indians riddled the coat and hat with bullets and set the grist mill on fire. They carried their wounded companion some two miles to a deserted house on the farm, afterwards owned by Major Thos. Bennet. The Indian died that night and was buried with the usual Indian ceremonies and the house burned. In 1821, one hundred and fifty years after, Major Bennet plowed up some of his bones, a pipe, stone jug, and a knife.

The same year John Thomson, with the other house-holders, was driven back to Plymouth by the Indians, and at the close of the war in 1677, in June, the same families returned and took possession of their estate, accompanied by other families.

In 1677 John Thomson built a frame house near where the former house was burned. It was 38 feet front and 30 feet deep. It had loop holes, and was lined with brick so as to be proof against musket balls. The west front room was 18 feet square, the east room 18 by 12 feet. Each had a fireplace large enough to burn four-foot wood. There was a small window to each room on each side of the house, being seven in front and three in each end. The front part was two stories, the lower story seven feet high ; the back part was one story. The floor was laid under the sills. It was heavily timbered, of white oak; the sills, posts and beams were twelve inches square, and other parts in the same proportion. The boards and joists were sawed by hand in a pit forty rods west from the house; the bricks were made southerly from the house. The outboarding was oak; there was no plastering; the inside finish was largely of cedar; the walls of one chamber were ceiled with cedar seven feet long, curiously wrought and fluted by hand. Here he lived for the remainder of his life. The house was repaired at different times, and was the residence of the fifth generation from John Thomson. It was taken down in 1838, having been inhabited one hundred and sixty years. Nothing remains except a corner stone, a part of the foundation, which has never been disturbed, and is just as it was placed by the workmen over two hundred years ago. The land where the house stood has ever been owned by the Thomson family. On this ancient homestead are standing many of the "high tap" or "summer sweeting" apple trees, which yield now their prolific crop of golden fruit as they did in the earliest days of the colony. Two trees of this variety, set out by a grandson of John Thomson, standing in view from the site of the old dwelling house, produced, by actual measurement, thirty-five bushels of apples in 1876, at which time the trees must have been at least one hundred and forty years old.

So far, we have only viewed the incidents in the life of John Thomson as related to his worldly concerns. We ought not pass by in silence the great object which led him to come to this country. His moral and religious character contains useful instruction to his descendants, and in many respects reproves them for their degeneracy. His customary hour of rising in the morning was at 4 o'clock, especially on Sunday morning. The breakfast must be closed, even in summer, on or before the rising of the sun. He was a regular attendant on the sanctuary, and by his example showed that he felt the sacredness of liberty of conscience, and was determined to improve it as a precious gift of God. After he had made his clearing and moved into his log house, either he or his wife would go every sabbath to the village of Plymouth, the only place where they had an elder to speak to them, a distance of more than thirteen miles, and the members of the family, male and female, frequently walked that distance to attend meeting at Plymouth, returning home the same day. His wife, one year, on two of the Sundays in June, after breakfast, took a child (Elizabeth) six months old, in her arms, walked to Plymouth, attended meeting and returned home the same day. Nor were his children, to the third generation, less zealous of enjoying the happiness of sanctuary privileges. It was a common practice among them to make a cheese on Sunday morning, in summer, provided they could get it under the press before sunrise, and then they would prepare to go to meeting. His grandchildren were regularly found among the worshiping assembly on the sabbath. It is stated the children of his son Jacob started one sabbath morning for Plymouth; they had to cross a dismal swamp which lay between where Amasa Sturtevant now lives and where Caleb Loring formerly kept a tavern. They arrived near the swamp before daylight, and were greatly frightened by the howling of wolves; they climbed a large rock which was near Amasa Sturtevant's and tarried there in fearful suspense till the sun arose.

"Compare their zealous attachment to religious worship with those of the present day, and we should little suspect we were the children of such an ancestor. We certainly do not honor his character or feel zealous to assimilate his piety. We feel it a burden to walk two miles to meeting instead of thirteen."

"This father of warriors and statesmen had but few opportunities for education, and of course his literary acquirements were very limited. Nature, however, had endowed him with a strong, active and vigorous intellect, which he greatly improved by experience and observation. Of many things connected with the times in which he lived, and the well being of society, he seemed to have an intuitive knowledge, but what chiefly supported him in all his trials and privations, and ever sustained him when surrounded by perils, was his firm conviction of the great truths of the Christian revelation, the duties it imposed, the promises it offered and the hopes it inspired. He was pious from a deep sense of his religious obligation. Chastened in his feelings in obedience to the dictates of conscience, he practiced the virtues of humility, meekness and charity from an abiding confidence in the wisdom, justice, and mercy of God. Honesty, integrity and fidelity with him were common and ordinary duties, while those to his Heavenly Father were never avoided or delayed, but with becoming reverence promptly performed. We cannot reflect upon the life of such a man without esteem for his virtues and respect for his character. Greatness was incident to his goodness, and his courage the result of moral rectitude. His example contains the text—it belongs to his posterity to furnish the commentary."

He closed his industrious and useful life June 16, 1696, nearly 80 years old. He was buried in the first burying ground in Middleborough. His grave is marked by a small stone, which is said to be the second one erected. The inscription is as follows:

MEMORANDUM.

In memory of
Lieut. John Thomson, who died June 16th, ye 1696, in
Ye 80 year of his age.
This is a debt to nature due;
Which I have paid and so must you.

Mary, his wife, died March 21, 1714, in the 88th year of her age; buried same place with her husband.

CHILDREN, II. GENERATION.

2. Adam, b. — ; d. when one and one-half years old.
3. John, b. 1648; m. Mary Tinkham.
4. Mary, b. 1650; m. — Taber; settled near New Bedford.
5. Esther, b. July 28, 1652; m. Jonathan Reed; descendants lived in Abington.
6. Elizabeth, b. Jan. 28, 1654; m. Thomas Swift; settled in Nobscusset.
7. Sarah, b. April 7, 1657; unmarried.
8. Lydia, b. Oct. 5, 1659; m. James Soule; descendants lived in Middleborough.
9. Jacob, b. April 24, 1662; m. Abigail Wadsworth.
10. Thomas, b. Oct. 19, 1664; m. Mary Morton.
11. Peter, b. —; m. Rebecca Sturtevant.
12. Mercy, b. 1671; d. April 19, 1756.

SECOND GENERATION.

3.

JOHN THOMSON,[2] (John[1]) b. 1648; son of Lieut. John and Mary (Cooke) Thomson; m. MARY TINKHAM, dau. of Ephraim Tinkham, the emigrant. He was a carpenter. He d. November 25, 1725, in his 77th year. She died 1731 in her 67th year.

CHILDREN III. GENERATION.

13. John, b. —; m. Elizabeth Thomas.
14. Ephraim, b. 1682; m. Joanna Redington.
15. Thomas, b. 1684; m. Martha Soule.
16. Shubael, b. 1685; m. Susanna Parker.
17. Mary, b. —; unmarried.
18. Martha, b. —; unmarried.

19. Francis, b. —; d. July 24, 1734, in the garrison house, Halifax.
20. Sarah, b. —; unmarried.
21. Peter, b. —; m. Sarah Wood. She died Oct. 24, 1742. (See 11.)
22. Jacob, b. 1710; m. Mary Hayward.
23. Ebenezer, b. —; probably died young.

9

JACOB THOMSON,² (John¹) b. April 24, 1662, son of Lieut.
John and Mary (Cooke) Thomson; m. ABIGAIL WADSWORTH.
He held a commission as justice of the peace a number of
years. He d. September 1, 1726, in his 65th year. She d.
September 15, 1744, in her 75th year.

CHILDREN III. GENERATION.

24. Jacob, b. April 17, 1695; m. Elizabeth (Tilson) Holmes.
25. Abigail, b. Feb. 24, 1697; m. Jonathan Packard.
26. Mercy, b. Oct. 13, 1699; m. Nehemiah Bennett. She d. Sept. 4, 1799.
27. John, b. March 19, 1701; m. Joanna Adams.
28. Lydia, b. April 22, 1703; m. John Packard. He d. 1738.
29. Barnabas, b. Jan. 28, 1705; m. Hannah Porter.
30. Esther, b. Feb. 18, 1707; m. Ebenezer Bennett. She d. July 5, 1776.
31. Hannah, b. March 9, 1709; m. Ebenezer Reed. She d. 1787.
32. Mary, b. May 19, 1711; m. Reuben Thomson (34).
33. Caleb, b. Nov. 4, 1712; m. Abigail Crossman.

10.

THOMAS THOMSON,² (John¹) b. Oct. 19, 1664, son of Lieut.
John and Mary (Cooke) Thomson; m. MARY MORTON, b.
1689. He was intimate with John Morton, of Middleborough;
they frequently visited each other. On one occasion Morton
advised him to get married, saying he had arrived at a proper
age, he being then about 25 years old. He replied, "I will
marry that daughter of yours," pointing to the infant child
Mary, who was in the cradel, "when she is old enough." The
father making no objection, he married, in his 50th year, the
said Mary Morton, she being then 25 years old. Thomas
Thomson was a farmer and glazier; he set the diamond glass
in lead, so common in those days, and adjusted it to the window sashes. In the division of his father's estate his share
contained 700 acres of land, including the ancient dwelling
house wherein he lived and died. No man in town was more
highly esteemed; none whose counsels were so scrupulously

observed. Possessing a very large estate, he had the means,
which he frequently employed, to gratify his feelings of benev-
olence and charity. Christianity was his all absorbing object.
It admonished him in prosperity and consoled him in afflic-
tion. Rev. John Cotton, the first minister of Halifax, has
given us the following tribute of him: "Thomas Thomson
was the wealthiest man in town, but what was more to his
honor he was rich toward God. He was just and exact in all
his dealings; he made conscience of all his ways; he was food
to the hungry, a father to the poor, and a harbor even to the
stranger. The two or three last days of his life he seemed to
be upheld only to speak forth the praises of God. This he
kept doing by turns from Saturday to Monday evening; sometimes he would be blessing God for his goodness; sometimes
giving advice to his children and relatives, or to those who
visited him. In short, he seemed to be in heaven while he
was on earth. He had glorious foretastes of the bliss above; he
departed with praises on his lips and with a glorious triumph."
He died October 26, 1742, aged 78. Mary, his wife, died
March 20, 1781, aged 91.

CHILDREN III. GENERATION.

34. Reuben, b. Oct. 11, 1716; m. (1) Mary Thomson (32), (2) Widow
    Sarah Thomson.
35. Mary, b. 1718; m. Samuel Waterman. She d. April 9, 1756.
36. Thomas, b. 1720; m. Mary Loring.
37. Amasa, b. April 29, 1722; m. Lydia Cobb.
38. Andrew, b. 1724; died young.
39. Ebenezer, b. March 22, 1726; m. Mary Wright.
40. Zebediah, b. August 18, 1728; m. Zerviah Standish.

II.

PETER THOMSON[2] (John[1]), b. —; son of Lieut. John and
Mary (Oooke) Thomson; m. REBECCA STURTEVANT. (A will
by Peter mentions a wife Sarah, and children: Sarah, Peter,
James and Joseph, b. respectively 1699, 1701, 1703 and 1706,
which may be the family of this Peter or of Peter (21).

CHILDREN III. GENERATION.

41. Peter, b. 1700; m. (1) Hannah Bolton, (2) Lydia Cowin.
42. Joseph, b. —; m. Betty Bolton. He d. of smallpox.
43. James, b. —; d. Nov. 23, 1737; drowned in Crossman's Pond in
    Kingstʝn.
44. Hannah, b. —; m. Nehemiah Bosworth.

THIRD GENERATION.

13.

JOHN THOMSON[3] (John,[2] John[1]), b. —; son of John and Mary (Tinkham) Thomson; m. ELIZABETH THOMAS. She d. August, 1776.

CHILDREN IV. GENERATION.

45. John, b. Feb. 18, 1725; m. Betty Fuller.
46. Elizabeth, b. August 7, 1726; m. Samuel Fuller. She d. 1794.
47. Lydia, b. August 13, 1730; m. Isaac Soule. She d. August 29, 1771.

14.

EPHRAIM THOMSON[3] (John,[2] John[1]), b. 1682; son of John and Mary (Tinkham) Thomson; m. JOANNA REDINGTON. He d. November 13, 1744, in his 62d year.

CHILDREN IV. GENERATION.

48. Child, b. Oct. 3, 1735; d. Dec. 5, 1735.
49. Joanna, b. July 23, 1738; d. Dec. 17, 1744.
50. Ephraim, b. April 8, 1742; d. Dec. 5, 1743.
51. Ephraim, b. May 8, 1744; d. May 25, 1744.

The father and three children died within thirteen months, leaving the widow alone.

15.

THOMAS THOMSON[3] (John,[2] John[1]), b. 1684; son of John and Mary (Tinkham) Thomson; m. MARTHA SOULE, doubtless a descendant of George Soule of the "Mayflower." He d. March 20, 1781, in his 96th year. She d. 1772.

CHILDREN IV. GENERATION.

52. Peter, b. 1733; m. Rebecca Thomas.
53. Francis, b. March 15, 1735; m. (1) Rebecca Snow, (2) Mary Bumpus.
54. Nathan, b. Dec. 10, 1736; m. Mary Harlow.
55. James, b. Nov. 11, 1739; m. Abigail Allen.
56. Thomas, b. Jan. 1, 1743; d. Sept. 16, 1747.

16.

SHUBAEL THOMSON[3] (John[2], John[1]), b. 1685, son of John and Mary (Tinkham) Thomson; m. Susanna Parker. He d. July 7, 1734, in his 48th year. She d. June 9, 1734, in her 47th year.

CHILDREN IV. GENERATION.

57. Shubael, b. 1715, d. June 9, 1734.
58. Thomas, b. 1720; m. Jane Washburn.
59. Isaac, b. Sept. 14, 1724; d. Sept. 30, 1740.
60. John, b. 1727; m. (1) Lydia Wood, (2) — Soule, widow.
61. Mary, b. —; d. June 28, 1734.

22.

JACOB THOMSON,[3] (John,[2] John,[1]) b. 1710, son of John and Mary (Tinkham) Thomson; m. 1735 MARY HAYWARD, dau. of Nathaniel Hayward. He d. February 17, 1750, in his 40th year. She d. March 18, 1762, in her 44th year.

CHILDREN IV. GENERATION.

62. Jacob, b. July 9, 1736; m. Waitstill Miller.
63. Ebenezer, b. Oct. 14, 1737; m. Elizabeth Besse.
64. Nathaniel, b. July 23, 1740; d. in the service of his country.
65. Mary, b. Sept. 7, 1743; d. August 21, 1747.
66. Martha, b. Jan. 1, 1746; d. Sept. 7, 1747.
67. Ephraim, b. August 1, 1748; m. (1) Hannah Thayer, (2) 1791, Mary Washburn.
68. Daniel, b. Oct. 24, 1850; m. Fear Lyon.

24.

JACOB THOMSON[3] (Jacob,[2] John,[1]), b. April 17, 1695, son of Jacob and Abigail (Wadsworth) Thomson; m. Mrs. ELIZABETH (TILSON) HOLMES, widow of John Holmes. He was a surveyor and scrivener, and was generally known as Clerk Jacob. He d. March 10, 1789, in his 94th year. She d. August 8, 1773, in her 74th year.

CHILDREN IV. GENERATION.

69. Abigail, b. Nov. 26, 1735; m. Seth Miller.
70. Jacob, b. March 28, 1738; m. 1761 Freelove Finney.
71. Elizabeth, b. June 19, 1741; d. Dec. 4, 1747.

5

27.

JOHN THOMSON³ (Jacob,² John¹) b. March 19, 1701, son of Jacob and Abigail (Wadsworth) Thomson ; m. JOANNA ADAMS. He was reported to have had the arms of heraldry of the family. He d. December 6, 1790, in his 90th year. She d. January 10, 1789.

CHILDREN IV. GENERATION.

72. Zaccheus, b. July 22, 1743; d. April 19, 1747.
73. Joanna, b. August 9, 1751; m. Freeman Waterman.

29.

BARNABAS THOMSON³ (Jacob,² John,¹), b. January 28, 1705, son of Jacob and Abigail (Wadsworth) Thomson; m. HANNAH PORTER, dau. of Samuel Porter, of Abington, and sister of Rev. John Porter, of Bridgewater. He served a long time as deacon in the church at Halifax. He d. December 20, 1798, in his 94th year. She d. May 2, 1787, in her 75th year.

CHILDREN IV. GENERATION.

74. Abigail, b. Feb. 12, 1741; d. March 31, 1747.
75. Barnabas, b. Feb. 13, 1742; d. Sept. 7, 1742.
76. Jacob, } Twins, { d. young.
77. Samuel } b. March 14, 1743, { d. April 29, 1747.
78. Jabez, b. March 26, 1744; d. April 8, 1744.
79. Asa, b. Sept. 3, 1745; d. April 5, 1747.
80. Noah, b. March 20, 1747; m. Priscilla Holmes.
81. Hannah, b. May 30, 1748; m. 1781, Elisha Mitchel.
82. Isaac, b. May 29, 1749; m. Huldah Sturtevant.
83. David, b. Sept. 2, 1750; d. Sept. 13, 1750.
84. Olive, } Twins, { d. Feb. 12, 1776.
85. Abel, } b. April 10, 1752, { d. July 28, 1754.
86. Adam, b. April 24, 1754; m. Molly Thomson (117).
87. Ichabod, b. April 23, 1756; m. Lydia Hall.

33.

CALEB THOMSON³ (Jacob,² John¹), b. November 4, 1712, son of Jacob and Abigail (Wadsworth) Thomson; m. ABIGAIL CROSSMAN. He d. January 19, 1787, in his 75th year; she d. November 23, 1791, in her 78th year.

CHILDREN IV. GENERATION.

88. William, b. Feb. 15, 1748; m. Deborah Sturtevant.
89. Nathaniel, b. Sept. 13, 1750; m. Hannah Thomas.

90. Mary, b. —; m. Peter Tinkham.
91. Hannah, b. —; unmarried.
92. Sarah, b. —; m. Frederick Miller.
93. Abigail, b. —; m. John Thomson (176).
94. Caleb, b. —; m. Mary Perkins.
95. Silvia, b. —; m. Elias Thomas.

34.

REUBEN THOMSON[3] (Thomas,[2] John[1]), b. October 11, 1716, son of Thomas and Mary (Morton) Thomson; m. (1) MARY THOMSON (32), (2) SARAH (SOULE) THOMSON, widow of John Thomson (60). He d. September 28, 1793, in his 77th year; first wife d. July 19, 1769, in her 59th year; second wife d. August 20, 1805.

CHILDREN BY FIRST WIFE IV. GENERATION.

96. Deborah, b. July 27, 1740; m. Micah Reed.
97. Andrew, b. Jan. 18, 1741; m. Judith Noyes.
98. Mercy, b. Sept. 21, 1745; d. Sept. 1, 1774, in her 29th year.
99 Abigail, b. Oct. 25, 1748; d. April 2, 1757.
100. Lucy, b. Dec. 4, 1755; m. Thomas Drew. She d. Jan. 5, 1818.

CHILD BY SECOND WIFE IV. GENERATION.

101. Joanna, b. Jan. 19, 1772; m. Dr. Nathaniel Morton.

36.

THOMAS THOMSON[3] (Thomas,[2] John[1]), b. 1720; son of Thomas and Mary (Morton) Thomson; m. MARY LORING. He d. September 14, 1769, in his 50th year. She died May 17, 1802.

CHILDREN IV. GENERATION.

102. Joshua, b. July 22, 1746; d. July 27, 1747.
103. Asa, b. March 15, 1748; m. (1) Rebecca Campbell, (2) Widow Priscilla Phillips.
104. Ignatius, b. August 24, 1750; d. Jan. 22, 1770. He commenced a concordance to the Bible; did not live to finish it.
105. Sarah, b. April 5, 1752; d. Nov. 27, 1769.
106. Mary, b. Sept. 16, 1754; m. 1774 (1) Abijah Tyrrel, (2) Job Chamberlain, (3) Asa Coburn. She lived in Abington.
107. Loring, b. April 25, 1756; m. (1) Mary Whitton, (2) E. Swinnerton, (3) Rachel Whitton.
108. Lois, b. April 12, 1758; m. Eliab Knapp.
109. Seth, b. June 18, 1760; m. Mary Waterman.

110.   Thomas, b. May 27, 1762; m. Ruhamah Barrows.
111.   Bezer, b. Feb. 27, 1765; d. March 24, 1773.
112.   Caleb, b. March 23, 1767; m. Eunice King.
113.   Sarah, b. Jan. 12, 1770; m. Ford Bryant.

37.

AMASA THOMSON[3] (Thomas,[2] John[1]), b. April 29, 1722, son
of Thomas and Mary (Morton) Thomson; m. LYDIA COBB.
He d. May 7, 1807, in his 85th year. She d. August 22, 1809,
in her 92d year.

CHILDREN IV. GENERATION.

114.   Ruth, b. Jan. 14, 1745; m. Simeon Sturtevant. She d. May 8,
       1831.
115.   Zadock, b. May 11, 1747; d. Dec. 4, 1786, in his 40th year.
116.   Lydia, b. May 9, 1752; m. Oliver Holmes and had Molly (242).
117.   Molly, b. Dec. 13, 1756; m. Adam Thomson (86).

39.

EBENEZER THOMSON[3] (Thomas,[2] John[1]), b. March 22, 1726,
son of Thomas and Mary (Morton) Thomson; m. MARY
WRIGHT. January 2, 1775, he was chosen a member of the
Provincial Congress to be held at Cambridge February 1; also
May 29, 1775, chosen for the same body to be held May
31 at Watertown, and July 26 was chosen to represent the
town in a convention to be held at Cambridge 1st of September following. May 13, 1784, he was chosen a representative
of the general court to be held at Boston; was also representative in 1789 and 1792, and held a commission as justice of the
peace for twenty-one years. He d. September 10, 1813, in his
87th year. His wife d. November 29, 1804.

CHILDREN IV. GENERATION.

118.   Susanna, b. June 4, 1749; m. Stephen Ellis. She d. March 24,
       1834, in her 86th year. He d. March 5, 1824, aged 76 years.
119.   Josiah, b. June 9, 1751. He enlisted as lieutenant in the Revo-
       lutionary army. He was one of those rare persons who refuse
       promotion when offered to them. His reply was, " I am satis-
       fied with my office; I engaged to serve my country and not
       for promotion." After his father through weight of years
       declined holding the office of justice of the peace, he was
       commissioned and regularly held the same till near the close
       of life; was town clerk of Halifax many years. He d. July 23,
       1828, in his 78th year.

120. Ebenezer, b. Oct. 18, 1753; m. Deborah Prior.
121. Mary, b. April 28, 1757; m. 1785 Elijah Hayward, of Bridge-water, b. June 18, 1741, father of Hon. Elijah Hayward, of McCollinsville, Ohio, one of the Supreme Court judges of Ohio ; also commissioner of general land office under General Jackson, and who at his death left a partial genealogy of the Hayward and Thomson families, extracts from which are included in this work. She d. Sept. 21, 1846.
122. Eunice, b. Sept. 10, 1765; m. James Soule. She d. Aug. 18, 1811.

40.

ZEBADIAH THOMSON[3] (Thomas[2], John[1]), b. August 18, 1728, son of Thomas and Mary (Morton) Thomson; m. 1745 ZER-VIAH STANDISH, dau. of Ebenezer, who was son of Alexander, the son of Captain Miles Standish of the Mayflower. Ebenezer m. Hannah Sturtevant, Alexander m. Sarah Alden, dau. of John and Priscilla (Mullins) Alden, of the Mayflower. He d. September 30, 1775, in his 48th year. She d. July 25, 1769.

CHILDREN IV. GENERATION.

123. Rebecca, b. March 5, 1746; m. Francis Woods. She d. August 17, 1813, in her 67th year.
124. Rachel, b. Jan. 22, 1748; d. May 7, 1751.
125. Zerviah, b. March 17, 1750; m. Ephraim Fuller. She d. March 19, 1783, in her 33d year.
126. Zebadiah, b. Dec. 17, 1752; d. Nov. 7, 1753.
127. Thomas, b. Nov. 17, 1754; d. Dec. 10, 1837, in his 83d year.
128. Mercy, b. Oct. 28, 1756; m., 1780, Mathew Parris.
129. Zebadiah, b. Dec. 15, 1758; m. (1) Clarissa Sturtevant, (2) Phebe Curtis.
130. Moses, b. July 1, 1762; m. Abigail Sampson.
131. Rachel, b. Oct. 22, 1767; m. Eliab Thomson (147).

41.

PETER THOMSON[3] (Peter,[2] John[1]), b. 1700, son of Peter and Rebecca (Sturtevant) Thomson; m. (1) HANNAH BOLTON, (2) LYDIA COWIN. He d. November 2, 1791, in his 91st year. His first wife d. July 6, 1755, in her 35th year; second wife d. May 12, 1800, in her 75th year.

CHILDREN BY FIRST WIFE IV. GENERATION.

132. Hannah, b. Dec. 12, 1741; d. July 28, 1747.
133. Peter, b. April 27, 1747; d. March 2, 1750—drowned.

42.

JOSEPH THOMSON[3] (Peter,[2] John[1]), b. —; son of Peter and Rebecca (Sturtevant) Thomson; m. ELIZABETH BOLTON, dau. of John and Ruth (Hooper) Bolton. He d. July 1, 1778, of smallpox.

CHILDREN IV. GENERATION.

134. Betty, b. —; m., 1762, Nicholas Wade; lived in Halifax. She d. 1828.
135. Joseph, b. —; m. Jerusha Wood.
136. John, b. Oct. 14, 1737 m. Martha Bisbee or Elizabeth Bisbee..
137. Sarah, b. April 17, 1744; m. 1767, Luther Keith of Bridgewater, son of Ebenezer Keith. He and his family moved to Pelham, thence to Sangersville.
138. Hannah, b. May 19, 1748; d. March 7, 1755.

FOURTH GENERATION.

45.

JOHN THOMSON[4] (John,[3] John,[2] John[1]), b. February 18, 1725. son of John and Elizabeth (Thomas) Thomson; m. BETTY FULLER. He was frozen to death January 18, 1777, in coming home from Plymouth, near Nathan Perkins' in Plympton.

CHILDREN V. GENERATION.

139. Susanna, b. May 12, 1763.
140. Thaddeus, b. July 1, 1765; m. Ruth Tilson.
141. Nathan, b. March 17, 1769, m. Elizabeth Eaton. He was deaf and dumb. He d. Sept. 24, 1831.
142. Zaccheus, b. March 17, 1769; m. Jennet Atwood.
143. Elizabeth, b. Oct. 24, 1770; m. William Wood. She d. Nov. 11, 1810.
144. Stephen, b. April 10, 1774; m. Nancy Hastings.

52.

PETER THOMSON[4] (Thomas,[3] John,[2] John[1]), b. 1733, son of Thomas and Martha (Soule) Thomson; m. REBECCA THOMAS. He d. June 21, 1800, in his 67th year. She d. October 16, 1792, in her 56th year.

CHILDREN V. GENERATION.

145. Levi, b. Jan. 6, 1764; m. Betty Snell.
146. Ezekiel, b. May 4, 1766; m. Mary Bosworth.
147. Eliab, b. Dec. 8, 1768; m. Rachel Thomson (131).
148. Asaph, b. Sept. 6, 1771; m. Mary Wood.

53.

FRANCIS THOMSON⁴ (Thomas,³ John,² John¹), b. March 15, 1735, son of Thomas and Martha (Soule) Thomson; m. (1) REBECCA SNOW, (2) MARY BUMPUS. He d. December 17, 1798, in his 63d year; second wife died December 17, 1829, in her 85th year.

CHILDREN BY FIRST WIFE V. GENERATION.

149. Zilpha, b. June, 1763; m. Noah Cushman. She d. June 23, 1806
150. Rebecca, b. —; d. young.
151. Elias, b. 1766; m. Elizabeth Hoisington. He d. Sept. 1839.

CHILDREN BY SECOND WIFE V. GENERATION.

152. Thomas, b. Oct. 1, 1770; m. Wealthy Whitmore.
153. Cynthia, b. Nov. 8, 1773; m. John Cox.
154. Reuel, b. Jan. 4, 1777; m. Thankful Wood.
155. Mary, b. March 4, 1781; m. Jabez Vaughan.
156. Francis, b. April, 1785; d. young.

54.

NATHAN THOMSON⁴ (Thomas,³ John,² John¹), b. December 10, 1736, son of Thomas and Martha (Soule) Thomson; m. MARY HARLOW. He d. in 1802.

CHILDREN V. GENERATION.

157. Sarah, b. August 16, 1762; m. (1) John Finney, (2) Ezra Holmes.
158. Susanna, b. May 16, 1764; m. Daniel Tucker.

55.

JAMES THOMSON⁴ (Thomas,³ John,² John¹), b. November 11, 1739, son of Thomas and Martha (Soule) Thomson; m. 1765 ABIGAIL ALLEN, b. 1743, dau. of Nathan and Rebecca (Read) Allen, of Bridgewater, Mass., a descendant of Samuel Allen (1635) of Braintree, Mass. He removed from Halifax to Brookfield, Mass., and in 1796 settled in Salem, N. Y. He and his wife are supposed to have died there.

CHILDREN V. GENERATION.

159. Phebe, b. Oct. 11, 1766; m. Dennison Ruggles
160. Abigail, b. Nov. 20, 1767; m. Stephen Estee.
161. Cyrus, b. Dec. 21, 1774; m. Polly Waterman.
162. Bela, b. March 16, 1779; m. Diadamia Kellogg.
163. Belinda, b. 1790; m. Abiather Blowers.
164. Azor, b. —; m. Mrs. Hannah (Cutler) Hall.
165. Nathan, b. —; m. Ellis or Phebe Blowers.
166. Rebecca, b. —; m. James Shearer.

58.

THOMAS THOMSON[4] (Shubael,[3] John,[2] John[1]), b. 1720, son of
Shubael and Susanna (Parker) Thomson; m. 1745 JANE
WASHBURN, dau. of John and Margaret (Packard) Washburn.
They lived in Bridgewater. He was a shoemaker. He d.
February 8, 1756. She d. March 22, 1773.

CHILDREN V. GENERATION.

167. Mary, b. 1746; m. 1796 Edmond Alger, of West Bridgewater
(2d wife). She d. Feb. 22, 1798.
168. Abisha, b. 1747; m.; went into the Revolutionary army and died
in the service of his country.
169. Jane, b. 1749; m. Nathaniel Bolton. She d. May 8, 1814, in
Oakland, Mass.
170. Peggy, b. Sept. 30, 1750; d. Oct. 15, 1750.
171. Margaret, b. 1751; un-m.; d. Dec. 17, 1815, aged 63.
172. Bethiah, b. Nov. 15, 1755; m. Thomas Cushman.

60.

JOHN THOMSON[4] (Shubael,[3] John,[2] John[1]), b. 1727, son of
Shubael and Susanna (Parker) Thomson; m. (1) LYDIA
WOOD, (2) WIDOW SARAH SOULE. He d. June 22, 1776. His
first wife d. January 28, 1761 in her 39th year; second wife d.
August 20, 1805.

CHILDREN BY FIRST WIFE V. GENERATION.

173. Shubael, b. March 11, 1742; m. Ruth Hall.
174. Susanna, b. Nov. 1, 1743; m. Sylvanus Thomas. She d. Sept. 4,
1822.
175. Isaac, b. Feb. 1, 1746; m. Lucy Sturtevant.
176. John, b. May 6, 1748; m. Abigail Thomson (93).
177. Ezra, b. July 4, 1750; d. 1778, in his 28th year.
178. Lydia, b. June 21, 1752; m. (1) Thomas Gifford, (2) — Sheldon.

179. Sarah, b. Oct. 6, 1754; d. Nov. 10, 1777.
180. Uzza, b. Dec. 10, 1756; d. June 11, 1758.
181. Fear, b. Nov. 6, 1757; m. Abraham Perkins. She d. Nov. 10, 1796.
182. Priscilla, b. April 11, 1760; m. Lemuel Sturtevant.

CHILD BY SECOND WIFE V. GENERATION.

183. Mary, b. —; m. Dr. Penuel Hutchins.

62.

JACOB THOMSON⁴ (Jacob,³ John,² John¹), b. July 9, 1736, son of Jacob and Mary (Howard) Thomson; m. WAITSTILL MILLER. He was deacon of a church in Halifax a number of years; also served in the French war. He d. November 12, 1815. She d. July 18, 1807, aged 67 years.

CHILDREN V. GENERATION.

184. Huldah, b. May 17, 1757; m. Ephraim Tinkham. She d. Feb. 26, 1810.
185. Ezra, b. April 14, 1760; m. Sarah Whitton.
186. Jennet, b. June 28, 1763; unmarried; d. July 16, 1830.
187. Martha, b. Dec. 20, 1764; m., 1782, Jonah Benson of Bridgewater, d. March 9, 1822.
188. Jacob, b. Oct. 25, 1769; m. Lucina Keith.
189. Margaret M , b. April 22, 1771; m. Elkanah Thomas; d. March 17, 1837.

63.

EBENEZER THOMSON⁴ (Jacob,³ John,² John¹), b. October 14, 1737, son of Jacob and Mary (Howard) Thomson; m. ELIZA-BETH BESSE, of Wareham. They lived together sixty years. He served in both the French and Revolutionary wars; d. May 10, 1832, in his 95th year. She d. August 31, 1820, in her 80th year.

CHILDREN V. GENERATION.

190. Nathaniel, b. May 11, 1761; m. (1) Sarah Thayer, (2) Mary (Hall) Foster.
191. Rebecca, b. June 20, 1764; m. 1793 Lewis Chamberlain, of Bridgewater. They lived in Halifax.
192. Aseneth, b. Sept. 3, 1767; unmarried; d. Sept. 10, 1842.
193. Elizabeth, b. June 28, 1771; m. Asaph Bosworth, of Halifax.
194. Charity, b. June 24, 1775; m. (1) Isaac Chamberlain; he d. Nov. 2, 1806; (2) 1809 Daniel Bryant. She d. July 23, 1866.

67.

EPHRAIM THOMSON[4] (Jacob,[3] John,[2] John[1]), b. August 1, 1748, son of Jacob and Mary (Howard) Thomson; m. (1) HANNAH THAYER, (2) January 12, 1791, MARY WASHBURN, dau. of Josiah and Phebe (Hayward) Washburn. Lived in Marlow, New Hampshire.

CHILDREN BY FIRST WIFE V. GENERATION.

195. Ephraim, b. Nov. 2, 1771; m. Lucy Thomas.
196. Hannah, b. Jan. 23, 1773; m. Abner Barrows. She d. Oct. 17, 1835, aged 62.
197. Silas, b. April 3, 1778; m. Catharine Beal.
198. Rhoda, b. Oct. 27, 1780; m. Daniel Wood. She d. July 9, 1833.
199. David, b. April 11, 1783; drowned in Connecticut river.
200. Francis, b. August 2, 1785; m. (1) Jane Beal, (2) Sally Beal.

CHILDREN BY SECOND WIFE V. GENERATION.

201. Bethiah, b. July 19, 1793; m. Jason Ware.
202. Polly, b. —; m. John Wench. Moved to Marlow, N. H.
203. Phebe, b. —; m. —.
204. Sally, b. —; m. —.

68.

DANIEL THOMSON[4] (Jacob,[3] John,[2] John[1]), b. October 24, 1750, son of Jacob and Mary (Howard) Thomson; m. FEAR LYON.

CHILDREN V. GENERATION.

205. Samuel, b. Dec. 9, 1773; m. Mary Kingman. Lived in Burlington, Vt.
206. Molly, b. August 20, 1778; m. Enos Eaton.
207. Phebe, b. Jan. 17, 1781; m. Israel Thomas.
208. Fear, b. Jan. 27, 1785; m. Alfred Thomson (271).
209. Daniel, b. April 27, 1787; m. 1813, Sybil Horton.

70.

JACOB THOMSON[4] (Jacob,[3] Jacob,[2] John[1]), b. March 28, 1738, son of Jacob and Elizabeth (Tilson) Thomson; m. October 27, 1761, FREELOVE PHINNEY, dau. of Pelatiah and Mercy (Washburn) Phinney. He was chosen captain of a military company, and was distinguished from others of the same name by the title of his commission. He d. November, 1806. His wife d. November 7, 1826, in her 86th year.

CHILDREN V. GENERATION.

210. Solomon, b. June 7, 1762; m. Lydia Murdock.
211. Benjamin, b. March 39, 1764; m. Mary Bourn.
212. Mercy, ⎱ Twins b. ⎰ m. Thomas Gage.
213. Elizabeth, ⎰ June 17, 1766, ⎱ m. (1) Josiah Barker, (2) Daniel Wild.
214. Ruth, b. July 7, 1768; m. Major Thomas Bennet.
215. Jacob, b. Nov. 4, 1771; m. Mercy Waterman.
216. Freelove, b. Oct. 8, 1780; m. Perez Crocker.

73.

JOANNA THOMSON[4] (John,[3] Jacob,[2] John[1]), b. August 9, 1751,
dau. of John and Joanna (Adams) Thomson; m. December
18, 1766, FREEMAN WATERMAN, b. 1748, son of Robert, who
was son of John, who was son of Robert and Elizabeth
(Bourne) Waterman of Plymouth, 1638. Joanna d. September
10, 1833.

CHILDREN V. GENERATION.

217. Thomas, b. 1769; d. 1770.
218. Rebecca, b. 1771; d. 1839.
219. Mercy, b. 1774; m. Jacob Thomson (215).
220. Jonathan, b. 1776; d. 1784.
221. Joanna, b 1780: d. 1820.
222. Priscilla, b. 1782; m., 1800, Josiah Marshall.
223. Abigail, b. 1784; d. 1784.
224. Abigail, b. 1786; d. 1786.

80.

NOAH THOMSON[4] (Barnabas,[3] Jacob,[2] John[1]), b. March 20,
1747, son of Barnabas and Hannah (Porter) Thomson; m.
PRISCILLA HOLMES.
An incident relative to this man is worthy to be left on
record.
At the commencement of the Revolutionary troubles, a man
by the name of Taylor deserted the British army, and hired
himself to his nearest neighbor. A British sergeant, with a
file of men, came to take him; they arrived about mid-day.
As the officer was entering the front door Taylor passed out
the back way and escaped to a thick swamp. After a fruitless
search they concluded Taylor was concealed in the neighboring house. Accordingly they entered Thomson's house, finding him at dinner; they demanded Taylor, threatening to

shoot him if he did not comply. On this he laid down his knife and fork and opened the bosom of his shirt to the officer, who exclaimed, "Deliver up Taylor or I will shoot you," placing his hand to his pistol. "Will you?" says Thomson, rising from the table and taking his gun which hung over his head, "We will see who will get the first fire." This brought the Britisher to his senses, "I do not wish to harm you," he said, "all I want is Taylor." "Taylor is not in my house to my knowledge," said Thomson. The officer replied, "I shall search the house," turning to the door of a room. "Stop!" says the owner, "I have no objection to your searching my house, but you must first ask my leave." After the Revolution closed he settled with his family in the town of Bridgewater, in the state of Vermont. He was a justice of the peace, and died March 5, 1813. His wife died April 9, 1839, in her 89th year.

CHILDREN V. GENERATION.

225. Barnabas, b. Nov. 20, 1769; m. Sarah Fuller.
226 David, b. March 16, 1772; m. Betsey Leach.
227. Noah, b. July 3, 1774; m. Lydia Smith.
228. Abel, b. Oct. 3, 1776; m. Polly Stacy.
229. John H., b. Sept. 16, 1779; m. Betsey Churchill.
230. Priscilla, b. Sept. 19, 1781; d. Nov., 1821.
231. Betsey, b. Feb. 16, 1784; m. Artemas Walker.
232. Cromwell, b. April 27, 1786; m. Abigail Boyce.
233. Elihu, b. August 1, 1789; m. Hannah Phelps.
234. Charles, b. April 23, 1792; m. Sally Shaw.

82.

ISAAC THOMSON[4] (Barnabas,[3] Jacob,[2] John[1]), b. May 29, 1749, son of Barnabas and Hannah (Porter) Thomson; m. HULDAH STURTEVANT. He d. December 6, 1782. She d. March 16, 1839.

CHILDREN V. GENERATION.

235. Jabez, b. Nov. 3, 1772; m. Betsey Wood.
236. Isaac, b. Nov. 17, 1774; m. (1) Phebe Soule, (2) Mrs. Lucy (Copeland) Holmes.
237. Olive, b. March 17, 1777.
238. Abigail, b. Sept. 26, 1779; m. Obadiah Lyon. (See 380.) She d. March, 1808.
239. Jacob, b. June 26, 1782; m. (1) Sally Sturtevant, (2) Esther Shaw.

86.

ADAM THOMSON[4] (Barnabas,[3] Jacob,[2] John[1]), b. April 24, 1754, son of Barnabas and Hannah (Porter) Thomson; m. MOLLY THOMSON (117). He d. August 20, 1821. She d. June 12, 1835.

CHILDREN V. GENERATION.

240. Samuel, b. Sept. 24, 1778; m. Clara Sturtevant.
241. Adam, b. May 27, 1784; m. Salvina Wood.
242. Ward, b. Sept. 4, 1786; m. Molly Holmes.
243. Zadoc, b. Jan. 4, 1790; m. Deborah Bosworth.

87.

ICHABOD THOMSON[4] (Barnabas[3], Jacob,[2] John[1]), b. April 23, 1756, son of Barnabas and Hannah (Porter) Thomson; m. LYDIA HALL. He was a deacon in the church at Halifax; d. August 31, 1821. His wife d. April 20, 1821, in her 74th year.

CHILDREN V. GENERATION.

244. James, b. April 13, 1780; m. Deborah Washburn.
245. Hannah, b. Oct. 14, 1782; m. Asa Thomson (285).
246. Sarah, b. March 1, 1785; m. George Drew.

88.

WILLIAM THOMSON[4] (Caleb,[3] Jacob,[2] John[1]), b. February 15, 1748, son of Caleb and Abigail (Crossman) Thomson; m. DEBORAH STURTEVANT, b. September 30, 1748, at Halifax, dau. of Lemuel and Deborah (Bryant) Sturtevant, a direct descendant of Peter Sturtevant, the Dutch governor of New York. "A beautiful woman; the portrait painted by her son Cephas shows an admirable face." He was a captain of militia and had command of a company at the battle of Bunker Hill; he was very zealous among that band which braved British aggression. In the latter part of his life he was honored with the commission of justice of the peace. He was a farmer and large land-owner. He d. March 14, 1816, in his 69th year. She d. December 25, 1842, at Middleboro, at family residence erected by her husband.

CHILDREN V. GENERATION.

247. Oakes, b. July 31, 1771; m. Hannah Bisbee.
248. William, b. April 11, 1773; m. Susanna Wood.

249. Cephas, b. July 1, 1775; m. (1) Olive Leonard, (2) Lucy Thom son (475).
250. Lucy, b. Sept. 25, 1776; m. Abner Wood.
251. Sophia, b. —; m. Eliab Thomson (286).
252. Ira, b. August 3, 1780; m. Sophia Drew.
253. Galen, b. Oct. 27, 1782; m. (1) Susanna Porter, (2) Fanny Marble.
254. Deborah, b. —; m. Lemuel Harlow.
255. Arad, b. Dec. 30, 1786; m. Mercy Bourne.
256. Boadice, b. Feb. 17, 1789; m. Simeon Leonard.
257. Irene, b. May 12, 1791; m. Daniel Warren.

89.

NATHANIEL THOMSON[4] (Caleb,[3] Jacob,[2] John[1]), b. September 13, 1750, son of Caleb and Abigail (Crossman) Thomson; m. HANNAH THOMAS. He d. January 31, 1833, aged 83 years. She d. April 10, 1823, aged 73 years.

CHILDREN V. GENERATION.

258. Otis, b. Sept. 14, 1776; m. (1) Rachel Chandler, (2) Charlotte Fales.
259. Sally, b. March 5, 1778; m. June 7, 1784, Captain Joseph Cush- man. She d. Feb. 28, 1841.
260. Sybil, b. April 27, 1780; m. (1) James Daniels, (2) Nathan Bas- sett, of Bridgewater. She d. March 4, 1860.
261. Polly, b. April 2, 1782; m. Crocker Cobb..
262. Nancy, b. Sept. 2, 1784; m. 1807, Caleb F. Leonard. She d. Sept. 7, 1863.
263. Sabina, b. 1786; d. Sept., 1790.

(93 *see* 176.)

94.

CALEB THOMSON[4] (Caleb,[3] Jacob,[2] John[1]), b. —, son of Caleb and Abigail (Crossman) Thomson; m. MARY PERKINS. She had fifteen children. He d. February 9, 1821. She d. Decem- ber 9, 1816.

CHILDREN V. GENERATION.

264. Gains, b. March 18, 1777; m. Olive Tarbox.
265. Sylvia, b. April 5, 1778; m. Jacob Cushman.
266. Jonah, b. April 23, 1779; m. Patience Cushman.
267. Ansel, b. Sept. 2, 1780; d. Sept. 29, 1782.
268. Nathan, b. Nov. 6, 1781; d. Sept. 17, 1782.
269. Abigail, b. Feb. 8, 1783; m. Nelson Wood.

270. Serene, b. March 27, 1784; m. Paul Leonard.
271. Alfred, b. Sept. 20, 1785; m. Fear Thomson (208).
272. Mary, b. March 31, 1787; d. June 8, 1788.
273. Eliza, b. Jan. 25, 1789; m. (1) Eleazer Jones, (2) Nathan Keith.
274. Caleb, b. Nov. 30, 1790; m. (1) Lydia Russell, (2) — Field. He
    d. June 22, 1837.
275. Nathaniel, b. July 28, 1792; m. Susanna Field.
276. Joanna, b. August 20, 1794; m. Pelatiah Reza.
277. Sabina, b. Feb. 9, 1796; m. Chester Field.
278. Frederick M., b. June 20, 1797; m. Susanna Cheesman.

97.

ANDREW THOMSON[4] (Reuben,[3] Thomas,[2] John[1]), b. January
18, 1741, son of Reuben and Mary (Thomson) Thomson; m.
JUDITH NOYES. He d. May 23, 1773. She d. April 1, 1832,
aged 91 years.

CHILDREN V. GENERATION.

279. Abigail, b. March 26, 1766; m. Nehemiah Noyes. She d. Dec. 2,
    1820.
280. Reuben, b. May 9, 1768; m. 1791, Eunice Whitman.
281. Abel, b. July 15, 1770; m. Elizabeth Leach.
282. Andrew, b. August 28, 1772; d. May 23, 1773.

103.

ASA THOMSON[4] (Thomas,[3] Thomas,[2] John[1]), b. March 15,
1748, son of Thomas and Mary (Loring) Thomson; m. (1)
REBECCA CAMPBELL, (2) Widow PRISCILLA PHILLIPS. His
first wife died October 23, 1808, in her 69th year. He served
in the Revolutionary war.

CHILDREN V. GENERATION.

283. Ignatius, b. March 11, 1774. He graduated at Brown univer-
    sity in 1796, and settled in the ministry at Pomfret, Vermont.
    Some years after his dismission he joined the Methodist Epis-
    copal church. He is author of the Patriot's Monitor; also com-
    piler of a Thomson Genealogy (the basis of the present work).
    He has been a member of the Legislature of Vermont, a mem-
    ber of the convention of censors under a former constitution,
    and a justice of the peace. He d. Sept. 11, 1848.
284. Nehemiah, b. May 9, 1775; m. Experience Curtis.
285. Asa, b. August 17, 1776; m. Hannah Thomson (245).
    Eliab, b. Dec. 8, 1775; m. Sophia Thomson (251).
    Rebecca, b. March 15, 1782; m. Samuel Ramsdel.

107.

LORING THOMSON[4] (Thomas,[3] Thómas,[2] John[1]), b. April 25, 1756, son of Thomas and Mary (Loring) Thomson; m. (1) MARY WHITTON, (2) April 20, 1788, MRS. ELIZABETH (HALL) SWINNERTON, b. February 21, 1750, in Sutton, Mass.; (3) RACHEL WHITTON. Loring went to Cornish, N. H., when 18 years old, bought a large farm of Gen. Jonathan Chase; afterwards enlisted in the army and was one of Lafayette's picked men when he crossed the Schuylkill. He was knocked down by the wind of a cannon ball and taken up for dead, but revived. He was taken prisoner and retaken, and came home at the end of the war sound and hearty. Second wife d. October 21, 1821.

CHILDREN BY FIRST WIFE V. GENERATION.

288.   Bezer, b. —; settled in Ohio and there died.
289.   Mary, b. —; m. in Vermont.
290.   Lydia, b. —; m. in Vermont.
291.   Zadoc, b. —; settled in Ohio and there died. He was a colonel of militia.

CHILDREN BY SECOND WIFE V. GENERATION.

292.   Samuel Hall, b. Nov. 19, 1789; m. Mary Wright.
293.   Sarah Hall, b. Nov. 26, 1792; m. Jesse Tracy.
294.   Stephen Hall, b. Oct. 26, 1795; m. Sarah Allen.

109.

SETH THOMSON[4] (Thomas,[3] Thomas,[2] John[1]), b. June 18, 1760, son of Thomas and Mary (Loring) Thomson; m. MARY WATERMAN; served in the Revolutionary war; settled in Ohio, where he died.

CHILDREN V. GENERATION.

295.   Sylvia, b.—; m. and settled in Vermont.
296.   Seth, b. —; settled in Ohio.
297.   Apollos, b. —; m. and settled in Vermont.
298.   Mary, b. —; settled in Ohio.
299.   Zebadiah, b. —; killed by a falling tree.
300.   Thomas, b. —; settled in Ashtabula county, Ohio.
301.   Hannah, b. —;   "   "   "
302.   Deborah, b. —;   "   "   "
303.   Robert, b. —;   "   "   "
304.   George, b   "

110.

THOMAS THOMSON[4] (Thomas,[3] Thomas,[2] John[1]), b. May 27, 1762, son of Thomas and Mary (Loring) Thomson; m. RUHAMA BARROWS. He settled in Vermont and died there. He served in the Revolution.

CHILDREN V. GENERATION.

305. Deborah, b. —; m. — Stevens.
306. Lois, b. —; m. Stacy Bingham.
307. Thomas, b. —.
308. Moses, b. —.

112.

CALEB THOMSON[4] (Thomas,[3] Thomas,[2] John[1]), b. March 23, 1767, son of Thomas and Mary (Loring) Thomson; m. EUNICE KING. He settled in Ohio.

CHILDREN V. GENERATION.

309. Bezor, b. —

(117 see 86.)

120.

EBENEZER THOMSON[4] (Ebenezer,[3] Thomas,[2] John[1]), b. October 18, 1753, son of Ebenezer and Mary (Wright) Thomson; m. DEBORAH PRIOR, b. 1751. He served in the Revolutionary army. He died March 11, 1841, in his 88th year. She d. April 9, 1817.

CHILDREN V. GENERATION.

310. Jabez P., b. Jan. 15, 1787; m. Sally Briggs.

129.

ZEBADIAH THOMSON[4] (Zebadiah,[3] Thomas,[2] John[1]), b. December 15, 1758, son of Zebadiah and Zerviah (Standish) Thomson; m. (1) CLARISSA STURTEVANT, (2) PHEBE CURTIS. He was engaged in the Revolutionary war, was a captain in a volunteer company, a member of the legislature and a justice of the peace. He d. November 4, 1840, in his 84th year. His first wife d. December 31, 1781, in her 24th year. His second wife died January 14, 1833, in her 75th year.

CHILD BY FIRST WIFE V. GENERATION.

311. Clarissa, b. —; d. Feb. 4, 1782, aged 3 months.

7

CHILD BY SECOND WIFE V. GENERATION,

312. Zebadiah, b. May 16, 1784: m. Martha Briggs.

130.

MOSES THOMSON[4] (Zebadiah,[3] Thomas,[2] John[1]), b. July 1,
1762, son of Zebadiah and Zerviah (Standish) Thomson; m.
ABIGAIL SAMPSON. He served in the Revolutionary war; was
a member of General Lafayette's regiment of 1,000 young men
which was drilled by Baron Steuben. When Lafayette visited
this country in 1825 Moses went to Boston to see him, and was
very cordially received, but the General did not seem to recol-
lect him in particular, and said to him, "Can't you call to
mind some incident which occurred while you were in the regiment?" Moses said, "Do you remember, General, our regiment being detailed to watch the movements of Lord Cornwallis, and of fording a creek near the Brandy-wine river; the
current was rapid and our regimental drummer, being a small
man, floated down stream with the drum, and was rescued by
one of the tall soldiers?" The General patted him on the
shoulder and said, "You were there, you were there; I remember the circumstance." Lord Cornwallis, writing home,
mentioned this occurrence and said, "I thought I was sure of
the little Frenchman, but he gave me the slip." Moses d.
December 2, 1858, aged 96 years, 5 months. His wife d. July
21, 1857, aged 92 years.

CHILDREN V. GENERATION.

313. Zerviah, b. June 24, 1784; m. Timothy Smith.   •
314. Nancy, b. Sept. 29, 1793; m. (1) William Soule, (2) Isaac Soule.
315. Mercy, b. Feb. 24, 1800; m. Consider Fuller.

(131 *see* 147.)

135.

JOSEPH THOMSON[4] (Joseph,[3] Peter,[2] John[1]), b. —, son of
Joseph and Betty (Bolton) Thomson; m. JERUSHA WOOD. He
d. August, 1778, of small-pox at Cambridge, a soldier of the
Revolution. His wife d. December 16, 1808.

CHILDREN V. GENERATION.

316. Joseph, b. April 28, 1763; m. Priscilla Ripley.
317   Hannah, b. Nov. 5, 1766; d. Dec. 31, 1771.
318. Timothy, b. Jan. 29, 1769; m. Susanna Cushing.

319. Amos, b. —; d. young.
320. Hannah, b. March 23, 1774.

136.

JOHN THOMSON[4] (Joseph,[3] Peter,[2] John[1]), b. October 14, 1737, son of Joseph and Betty (Bolton) Thomson. According to Ignatius Thomson, "m. MARTHA BISBEE, who d. February 10, 1778; he d. January 19, 1776. The names of the children are lost to us; one is supposed to have been among the first settlers of Mendon; the rest went into the western part of Massachusetts. It is said they named the place where they settled Petersham in grateful remembrance of their great-grandfather, Peter Thomson." In Giles' Memorial, page 198, a John Thomson is mentioned who lived for awhile at Halifax, Mass., removed to Springfield, Vt., thence to Kingsborough, N. Y.; m. ELIZABETH BISBEE, b. September 20, 1741, dau. of John and Abiah (Bonney) Bisbee of Pembroke, Mass., a lineal descendant of Thomas Bisbee, who came from Sandwich, England, with six children, and settled in Scituate, Mass., as early as 1634. The records of the town clerk of Pembroke show the following: "John Thompson of Bridgewater and Elizabeth Bisbee of Pembroke was married April ye 13th 1762 by ye Rev. Mr. Gad Hitchcock." It seems very probable John Thomson mentioned first above is the same who m. Elizabeth Bisbee. Their children are as follows:

CHILDREN V. GENERATION.

321. John Bisbee, b. —; d. in Vermont after removal of his parents to New York.
322. Peter, b. —; unmarried; joined the Society of Friends.
323. Cynthia, b. —; unmarried.
324. James, b. —; unmarried; d. in middle age.
325. William, b. —; m. Belinda Reeve.
326. Barzillai, b. —; went west, perhaps to western New York. No issue.
327. Calvin, b. —; settled in western New York.
328. Joseph, b. —; " " "
329. Sarah, b. —; m. Elijah Foster; lived in Sherburne, N. Y.; had two daughters.
330. Elizabeth, b. —; m. Peltiah Shepard.
331. Lucinda, b. —; m. Jacob Mead.
332. Chloe, b. —; m. Richard Horth; had four sons and two daughters. Lost her husband, and in 1862 was living with her children in Cattaraugus county, N. Y.

FIFTH GENERATION.

140.

THADDEUS THOMPSON[5] (John,[4] John,[3] John,[2] John[1]), b. July 1, 1765, son of John and Betty (Fuller) Thomson; m. RUTH TILSON. He removed from Halifax, Mass., to Sumner, Maine; d. April, 1832.

CHILDREN VI. GENERATION.

333. Betty, b. May 26, 1787; m. Levi Cushman; d. 1835.
334. John, b. March 31, 1789; m. Margaret Robinson.
335. Ammiel, b. April 18, 1791; m. (1) Fear Tilson, (2) Hannah Waterman.
336. Ruth, b. March 30, 1793; m. (1) Nathaniel Glover, (2) Joshua Glover.
337. Thaddeus, b. July 16, 1795; m. Dolly Bisbee.
338. Olivia, b. Sept. 10, 1806; m. Paul Dolan. She d. Jan. 18, 1832.
339. Orpha, b. March 22, 1808; m. (1) Jesse Morse, (2) Zenas Stetson.
340. Hannah, b. —; d. young.
341. Mary, b. —;   "
342. James, b. —;   "

142.

ZACCHEUS THOMPSON[5] (John,[4] John,[3] John,[2] John[1]), b. March 17, 1769, son of John and Betty (Fuller) Thomson; m. JENNET ATWOOD. He was deaf and dumb; settled in Reading, Vt.

CHILDREN VI. GENERATION.

343. Susanna, b. April, 1797.
344. Laura, b. 1799.
345. Abigail, b. 1801.
346. Zaccheus, b. —.
347. Jane, b. —.
348. Betty, b. —.

144.

STEPHEN THOMPSON[5] (John,[4] John,[3] John,[2] John[1]), b. April 10, 1774, son of John and Betty (Fuller) Thomson; m. NANCY HASTINGS; settled in Thomastown, Maine. He d. 1833. She d. August 13, 1842.

CHILDREN VI. GENERATION.

349. George L., b. Nov., 1801.
350. Henry, b. 1804.
351. William H., b. August, 1805; m. Mary Washburn.
352. Susanna, b. March 8, 1808; m. John Peters.
353. Elizabeth B., b. May 27, 1810.
354. Andrew L., b. June 17, 1812.
355. Nancy H., b. June 7, 1815.
356. Samuel, b. 1817.
357. Mary, b. August, 1819; d. one and one-half years old.

145.

LEVI THOMPSON[5] (Peter,[4] Thomas,[3] John,[2] John[1]), b. January 6, 1764, son of Peter and Rebecca (Thomas) Thomson; m. BETTY SNELL; lived in Woodstock, Vt. He d. April 6, 1844.

CHILDREN VI. GENERATION.

358. Rebecca, b. —; m. John H. Palmer.

146.

EZEKIEL THOMPSON[5] (Peter,[4] Thomas,[3] John,[2] John[1]), b. May 4, 1766, son of Peter and Rebecca (Thomas) Thomson; m. MARY BOSWORTH; moved to Vermont and there died.

CHILDREN VI. GENERATION.

359. Polly, b. August 20, 1791.
360. Peter, b. August 1, 1793; went to the state of New York.
361. Harriet, b. —.
362. Levi, b. —; d. Dec. 4, 1808.

147.

ELIAB THOMPSON[5] (Peter,[4] Thomas,[3] John,[2] John[1]), b. December 8, 1768, son of Peter and Rebecca (Thomas) Thomson; m. RACHEL THOMSON (131). He d. October 2, 1835.

CHILDREN VI. GENERATION.

363. Clarissa, b. July 19, 1792; m. Jeremiah Sampson.
364. Eliab, b. Feb. 22, 1795; m. (1) Lavina Washburn, (2) Lydia Thompson (503).
365. Rachel, b. Sept. 6, 1799; m. Leavitt, son of Judah Wood, of Halifax, Mass.

148.

ASAPH THOMPSON[5] (Peter,[4] Thomas,[3] John,[2] John[1]), b. September 6, 1771, son of Peter and Rebecca (Thomas) Thomson; m. MARY WOOD. He graduated at Brown university, 1795, and was the first of the family name to receive a collegiate degree; studied theology; then medicine; settled in Maine. He d. March, 1834.

CHILDREN VI. GENERATION.

366. Hadassah, b. —.
367. Mary, b. —.
368. Persis, b. —.
369. Silas W., b. —.

152.

THOMAS THOMPSON[5] (Francis,[4] Thomas,[3] John,[2] John[1]), b. October 1, 1770, son of Francis and Mary (Bumpus) Thomson; m. WEALTHY WHITMORE. He d. December 9, 1806.

CHILDREN VI. GENERATION.

370. Betsey, b. Nov. 30, 1794; m. Isaac Packard.   She d. Nov. 10, 1858; he d. May 7, 1860.
371. Venus, b. May 18, 1796; m. Jane Southworth.
372. Francis, b. Sept. 8, 1797; m. Miranda Barney; settled in New York.
373. Deborah, b. April 2, 1799; m. Caleb Alden. She d. June 18, 1836.
374. Philander, b. Sept. 8, 1800; m. Eliza Giles.
375. Cynthia, b. May 13, 1802; m. John Perkins.   She d. August 29, 1840.
376. Thomas, b. Feb. 25, 1805; m. Rebecca Voluntine.

154.

REUEL THOMPSON[5] (Francis,[4] Thomas,[3] John,[2] John[1]), b. January 4, 1777, son of Francis and Mary (Bumpus) Thomson; m. THANKFUL WOOD.

CHILDREN VI. GENERATION.

377. Israel W., b. Oct. 8, 1803; m. (1) Betsey W. Perkins, (2) Lydia Lyon.
378. Reuel, b. Sept. 21, 1806; m. Sarah T. Wood.
379. Ivory H., b. April 1, 1808; m. Jerusha B. Sparrow.
380. Priscilla W.,) Twins,   { m. Henry C. Lyon.
381. Benjamin F.,) b. June 24, 1810,   { m. (1) Sarah Wood, (2) Mary Abby Carr.

382. Martson, b. Sept. 28, 1812; m. (1) Harriet G. W. Bumpus, (2) Mary A. Wilbur, (3) Mary Anderson.
383. Anna T., b. August 14, 1814; m. Isaac Thompson (639).
384. Mary F., b. April 26, 1817; m. Cyrus Fuller.

157.

SARAH THOMPSON[5] (Nathan,[4] Thomas,[3] John,[2] John[1]), b. August 16, 1762, daughter of Nathan and Mary (Harlow) Thomson; m. (1) 1780, JOHN FINNEY, (2) 1799, EZRA HOLMES. John Finney, b. December 6. 1760; d. April 2, 1785. The family lived in Winthrop, Maine. Sarah d. April 17, 1838.

CHILDREN BY FIRST HUSBAND VI. GENERATION.

385. Sarah, b. Jan. 1, 1781; m. Isaac Babbitt.
386. John, b. Sept. 8, 1783; m. —.
387. Zeruah, b. Dec. 15, 1784; m. Ebenezer Packard.

158.

SUSANNA THOMPSON[5] (Nathan,[4] Thomas,[3] John,[2] John[1]), b. May 16, 1764, daughter of Nathan and Mary (Harlow) Thomson; m. DANIEL TUCKER, b. May 19, 1760. She had seventeen children. He d. June 22, 1842. She d. February 25, 1850.

CHILDREN VI. GENERATION.

388. William, b. Oct. 9, 1783; m. Rebecca Child. He d. Dec. 24, 1835.
389. Daniel, b. Jan. 7, 1785; m. Mary Tarbel. He d. August 14, 1863.
390. Woodward, b. Sept. 8, 1786; m. Elizabeth Cressy.
391. Mercy, b. Feb. 20, 1788; d. Oct. 1868.
392. George, b. May 4, 1789; m. Roxelana Drake. He d. March 4, 1858.
393. Susanna, b. Oct. 9, 1790; d. Oct. 9, 1810.
394. Darius, b. Feb. 9, 1792; d. March 5, 1829.
395. Nathan Thompson, b. August 25, 1793; d. August 29, 1831.
396. Cyrus, b. Feb. 29, 1795; d. July 4, 1803.
397. Betsey, b. June 16, 1796; m. John Soule. She d. August 27, 1864.
398. Jehiel, b. July 29, 1798; d. Nov. 26, 1862.
399. Mary, b. April 26, 1800; d. Oct. 14, 1819.
400. Nancy, b. Feb. 24, 1802; d. August 29, 1819.
401. Almon, b. March 6, 1804; d. Nov. 6, 1805.
402. Mandana, b. Oct. 6, 1807; unmarried; lives in Beverly, Mass.
403. Hadassah, b. August 8, 1811; m. Charles Packard. She d. March 8, 1842.
404. Infant, b. —. No record.

159.

PHEBE THOMPSON[5] (James,[4] Thomas,[3] John,[2] John[1]), b. October 11, 1766, daughter of James and Abigail (Allen) Thomson; m. DENISON RUGGLES. He was b. July 9, 1767; he d. July 2, 1839. She d. January 3, 1857.

CHILDREN VI. GENERATION.

405. Docia, b. May 31, 1794, in Brookfield, Mass.; d. Nov. 9, 1873.
406. Clarissa, b. Sept. 17, 1795, in Brookfield, Mass.; d. Dec. 23, 1873.
407. Allen, b. Oct. 6, 1796, in Brookfield, Mass.; d. Oct. 1797, in Salem, N. Y.
408. James, b. Feb. 7, 1797; d. April, 1798.
409. James. b. April 1, 1798, in Salem, N. Y.; d. June 21, 1806.
410. Abigail, b. Dec. 27, 1799, in Salem, N. Y.; d. March 12, 1861.
411. Allen, b. March 28, 1802, in Hampton, N. Y. Lived in Euclid, O., Feb. 1882.
412. Martha, b. Sept. 18, 1804, in Hampton, N. Y.; d. Oct. 19, 1870.
413. Ruel, b. Oct. 19, 1808, in Hampton, N. Y.; m. Celesta Perkins.

160.

ABIGAIL THOMPSON[5] (James,[4] Thomas,[3] John,[2] John[1]), b. November 20, 1767, daughter of James and Abigail (Allen) Thomson; m. February 7, 1790, STEPHEN ESTEE, b. October 21, 1767. He d. March 18, 1831.

CHILDREN VI. GENERATION.

414. Galen, b. Jan. 31, 1791; d. April 2, 1827.
415. Ansel, b. Feb. 7, 1793; m. Olive Tyler.
416. Azor, b. June 10, 1795; d. Sept. 12, 1796.
417. Hollis, b. June 28, 1797; d. August 6, 1798.
418. Rebecca, b. July 29, 1798; m. May 13, 1819, —.
419. Clark K., b. March 31, 1801; m. April 15, 1826, —; d. June 3, 1849.
420. Azor, b. June 30, 1803; m. March 29, 1827, —.
421. Hollis, b. May 21, 1806.
422. Sidney A., b. April 5, 1808.
423. Stephen, b. Jan. 1, 1812.

161.

CYRUS THOMPSON[5] (James,[4] Thomas,[3] John,[2] John[1]), b. December 21, 1774, in Brookfield, Mass., son of James and Abigail (Allen) Thomson; m. January 12, 1800, POLLY WATERMAN, b. February 9, 1779, in Brookfield, dau. of The-

·ophilus and Lydia (Allen) Waterman. In 1802 Cyrus removed to Salem, N. Y., and in 1803 to Verona, N. Y., and about 1837 to LeRoy, N. Y. He was a farmer. He and his wife were members of Presbyterian church. He was chosen deacon several times, but declined to serve. He died September 26, 1840, in his 66th year, at South LeRoy, Genesee county, N. Y. She d. August, 1850, in Clarendon, Orleans county, N. Y.

CHILDREN VI. GENERATION.

424. Elvira, b. Oct. 1, 1801; m. Joseph Root.
425. Cyrus, b. May 23, 1803; m. Charlotte H. Mead.
426. Lucy, b. Jan. 21, 1805; m. Luman Stevens.
427. Martha, b. Sept. 30, 1806; m. (1) Arza Brown, (2) Paul B. Hutchinson.
428. Theophilus W., b. Oct. 29, 1808; m. Ruth Maria Watkins.
429. Edwin A., b. Feb 2, 1811; m. Julia A. Sutton.
430. Nathan, b. June 1, 1813; m. Clarissa E. Hutchinson.
431. Daniel W., b. March 14, 1815; m. Lydia Jones.
432. Mary, b. May 20, 1817; m. (1) Harvey Root, (2) Abell Woodhull.
433. Eusebia, b. May 23, 1821; never married; d. 1840, at LeRoy, N. Y.

162.

BELA THOMPSON[5] (James,[4] Thomas,[3] John,[2] John[1]), b. March 16, 1779, in Brookfield, Mass., son of James and Abigail (Allen) Thomson; m. April 7, 1805, by Rev. Mr. Hall, to DIADAMIA KELLOGG, b. November 4, 1784, at Hampton, Washington county, N. Y. They lived later in Attica Center, N. Y. He d. March 8, 1863. She d. Feb. 23, 1847.

CHILDREN VI. GENERATION.

434. Harriet, b. June 5, 1806, Poultney, Vt.; d. July 19, 1811, in Hampton.
435. Jason K., b. Feb. 18, 1808; m. Eliza A. Frisbie.
436. James A., b. April 13, 1810; m. Eunice A. Benedict.
437. Bela D., b. March 16, 1812; m. Charlotte O. Sutton.
438. Loren, b. July 1, 1813; m. August 29, 1844, by Rev. Chas. G. Finney of Oberlin, O., to Nancy M. Griffin of Syracuse, N. Y. He was for twenty years a missionary at Jamaica, W. I. He died June 8, 1865.
439. Harriet M., b. Sept. 14, 1815; m. John Paine.
440 Lucinda, b. June 2, 1818; m. Seth W. Paine.
441. Dennis R., b. Oct. 24, 1820; m. Maria H. Knight.
442. Martha, b, Sept. 22, 1823; m. Heman R. Dewey.

443. Diadamia, b. April 23, 1826; m. (1) Dexter C. Johnson, (2) Matthew Morehouse.
444. Abigail, b. Oct. 26, 1829; d. June 18, 1831.

163.

BELINDA THOMPSON[5] (James,[4] Thomas,[3] John,[2] John[1]), b. 1790, dau. of James and Abigail (Allen) Thomson; m. ABIATHER BLOWERS, b. 1790. She d. 1850. He d. 1856.

CHILDREN VI. GENERATION.

445. Phebe, b. 1809.
446. Obed, b. 1811.
447. Azor, b. April 12, 1813.
448. David, b. June 28, 1814; m. Clarissa, dau. of Elijah Mattison of Shaftsbury, Vt.
449. James, b. April 12, 1816; m. Matilda Myers.
450. Ansel, b. March 27, 1818.
451. Henry, b. 1824.

164

AZOR THOMPSON[5] (James,[4] Thomas,[3] John,[2] John[1]), b. —, son of James and Abigail (Allen) Thomson; m. MRS. HANNAH (CUTLER) HALL of Brookfield, Mass., b. March 15, 1769, widow of Sewell Hall, b. April 15, 1767, in New Braintree, Mass. Azor had no children. His wife d. October 25, 1846, in Jackson, N. Y. PATTA HALL, b. January 2, 1793, in New Braintree, daughter of Sewell and Hannah (Cutler) Hall; m. January 1, 1810, James Tefft, b. June 6, 1787, in Greenwich, N. Y. Lived in Jackson, N. Y., also Ticonderoga, where he d. December 30, 1863. He was an hotel-keeper. His wife d. August 13, 1825, at Ticonderoga, N. Y.

CHILDREN OF JAMES AND PATTA (HALL) TEFFT.

Henry, b. Nov. 17, 1811, at Battenville, N. Y.; a school teacher; d. June 6, 1833, at Salem, N. Y.
Edwin N., b. Dec. 2, 1813, at Battenville, N. Y.: m. Sept. 20, 1841, Jane A., dau. of Joel and Jennette Rich, and had Pliny C., b. Dec. 24, 1843, and Eliza Amanda, b. May 28, 1846. Residence, Cambridge, N. Y.
James Cutler, b. March 4, 1816, in Bolton, N. Y.; m. (1) Nov. 5, 1850, Eliza Benton of Guilford, O. She d. June 10, 1851, at Mendi Mission, Africa; m. (2) Oct. 31, 1854, at LeRoy, N. Y., Lovina R. Saxton of Morgan, O. He d. Oct. 16, 1855, at Mendi Mission.

Eliza, b. April 16, 1818, at Ticonderoga; m. Sept. 26, 1839, Samuel W. Warner, at Cambridge, N. Y., and had Charles D., b. July 18, 1840, and William H., b. July 6, 1850.

Martha, b. Nov. 3, 1820, at Ticonderoga; m. James T. Estee (954).

William, b. March 3, 1823, at Ticonderoga; d. August 20, 1839, at Salem, N. Y.

Martin, b. April 1, 1825, at Ticonderoga; m (1) June 8, 1852, Ann Maria Scott of Poultney, Vt. She d. Sept. 30, 1855; m. (2) March 3, 1857, his brother's widow, Lovina R. (Saxton) Tefft. He d. 1881, in the West Indies.

165.

NATHAN THOMPSON[5] (James,[4] Thomas,[3] John,[2] John[1]), b. —, probably at Brookfield, Mass., son of James and Abigail (Allen) Thomson; m. Phebe Ellis (?) Blowers; they lived in Poultney, Vt.

CHILDREN VI. GENERATION.

452. Cyrus, b. —.
453. Abigail, b. —.
454. Sylvia, b. —.
455. Caroline, b. May 5, 1811; m. Daniel Heath.
456. William, b. —.
457. Edwin, b. —.
458. Polly, b. —; m. Reuben Brown.
459. Emily, b. —; m. Russell Warren.

166.

REBECCA THOMPSON[5] (James,[4] Thomas,[3] John,[2] John[1]), b. —, dau. of James and Abigail (Allen) Thomson; m. JAMES SHEARER.

CHILDREN VI. GENERATION.

460. Malinda, b. —; m. Nathan Root.
461. Abigail, b. —; m. Nathan Root.
462. Emily, b. —.
463. Sarah, b. —.
464. Bela, b. —; m. —.
465. Milton, b. —.
466. Harvey, b. —.

172.

BETHIAH THOMPSON[5] (Thomas,[4] Shubael,[3] John,[2] John[1]), b. November 15, 1755, dau. of Thomas and Jane (Washburn)

Thomson; m. June 25, 1794, CAPT. THOMAS CUSHMAN of
Bridgewater, b. in 1736, and who was a soldier at the reduc-
tion of the stronghold of Ticonderoga in 1759 and a minute
man at Roxbury in 1775. She d. November 28, 1822. He d.
October 15, 1820.

CHILDREN VI. GENERATION.

467. Thomas, b. Nov. 2, 1795; m. Lucy Pratt.

173.

SHUBAEL THOMPSON[5] (John,[4] Shubael,[3] John,[2] John[1]), b.
March 11, 1742, son of John and Lydia (Wood) Thomson; m.
RUTH HALL, b. 1747, dau. of Reuben and Ruth (Gilbert) Hall
of Bridgewater. He d. December 3, 1770.

CHILDREN VI. GENERATION.

468. Susanna, b. July 11, 1767; m (1) William Sampson, (2) Ezra
    Thompson (483).
469. Shubael, b. —; d. May 1, 1770, nine months old.

175.

ISAAC THOMPSON[5] (John,[4] Shubael,[3] John,[2] John[1]), b. February 1, 1746, son of John and Lydia (Wood) Thomson; m.
LUCY STURTEVANT. He was a justice of the peace until his
death. Represented the town of Middleborough in the state
legislature several years; also he represented the county of
Plymouth in the senate till his weight of years called him to
retire from public life. He was in this public employment
sixteen years. He was a man of integrity and of gratuitous,
arduous labors. During the Revolutionary war his attachment
to the cause of liberty was ardent and unabated. As a magis-
trate he was a peace-maker. In the legislature he was placed
in situations of labor and responsibility; was distinguished for
his industry, fidelity and uprightness of purpose. As the head
of a large family, few were more respected and beloved. His
piety was a leading trait in his character. In company and
in conversation with his friends, he was cordial and happy.
He d. December 21, 1819, in his 74th year. His wife d. November 4, 1834, in her 81st year.

CHILDREN VI. GENERATION.

470. John, b. March 22, 1775; m (1) Sarah Austin, (2) Belinda Dean,
    (3) Jane Richardson. Settled in Maine.

471. Cyrus, b. Dec. 23, 1776; m. Rebecca Robinson. Lived in Maine.
472. Lydia, b. March 1, 1779; m. Rev. Elijah Dexter of Plympton (second wife). She d. 1861.
473. Isaac, b. Nov. 7, 1781; m. Abia Haskell.
474. Uzza, b. August 23, 1784; m. Abigail Elliot. Settled in Maine.
475. Lucy, b. Oct. 1, 1786; m. Cephas Thompson (249). She d. in North Bridgewater.
476. George, b. August 12, 1788; m. Deborah P. Clark.
477. Mary, b. April 14, 1790; m. Robert Capen. She d. March 8, 1822.
478. Ezra, b. March 8, 1792; m. Cynthia Gifford.
479. Harriet, b. Dec. 19, 1795; m. Solomon Thompson (563).

176.

JOHN THOMPSON[5] (John,[4] Shubael,[3] John,[2] John[1]), b. May 6, 1748, son of John and Lydia (Wood) Thomson; m. ABIGAIL THOMPSON (93). He settled in Lime on the Connecticut River in New Hampshire. He served in the Revolutionary war. He d. August 4, 1817.

CHILDREN VI. GENERATION.

480. Abigail, b. —; m. Richard Dame.
481. Lydia, b. —; m. — Sawyer.
482. Sarah, b. —; m. — Freeman.
483. Ezra, b. —; m. Widow Susanna (Thompson) Sampson (468).
484. John, b. —; went west.
485. Jennet, b. —.

185.

EZRA THOMPSON[5] (Jacob,[4] Jacob,[3] John,[2] John[1]), b. April 14, 1760, son of Jacob and Waitstill (Miller) Thomson; m. SARAH WHITTON. He d. March 27, 1827. She d. May 25, 1841, in her 81st year.

CHILDREN VI. GENERATION.

486. Sarah, b. June 25, 1782; d. Oct. 17, 1808.
487. Charles, b. April 12, 1784; m. (1) Sarah Darling, (2) Widow Hannah Pratt.
488. Abraham, b. June 12, 1786; m. Mary Sampson.
489. Ezra, b. April 12, 1789; m. Mary Bates.
490. James, b. Jan. 6, 1791.
491. Drusilla, b. Jan. 23, 1792; m. Nehemiah Thomas. She d. 1860.
492. Experience, b. April 22, 1794.
493. Peleg, b. May 25, 1797; m. Freelove Washburn.

494. Margaret, b. June 14, 1799; m. Perez Robinson of North Bridge-
      water.
495. Elkanah, b. Oct. 22, 1803; m. Rachel Bump.
496. Levi, b. Feb. 12, 1806; m. Elsadah Raymond.

188.

JACOB THOMPSON[5] (Jacob,[4] Jacob,[3] John,[2] John[1]), b. October
25, 1769, son of Jacob and Waitstill (Miller) Thomson; m.
LUCINDA KEITH, b. 1768, dau. of Isaac and Mary C. (Randall)
Keith of Easton. He d. May 11, 1818. She d. April 10, 1833.

CHILDREN VI. GENERATION.

497. Polly Keith, b. Oct. 29, 1795; m. (1) Isaac Lyon, b. March 31,
      1793, son of Obadiah Lyon, (2) George Gross (second wife).
498. Lewis, b. August 17, 1797; m. (1) Huldah Wood, (2) Mrs.
      Hannah Holmes.
499. Lucina, b. Dec. 22, 1798; m. (1) March 27, 1823, Cornelius Pratt,
      b. April 20, 1795, son of Cornelius Pratt of Bridgewater; he d.
      May 30, 1836; m. (2) Capt. Seth Benson of Plymouth, b. Nov.
      3, 1790; he d. June 2, 1877. She d. May 22, 1884.
500. Jennet, b. Nov. 8, 1800; m. Francis W. Bourne, b. May 9, 1796,
      son of Newcomb Bourne; he d. 1869.
501. Jacob, b. Nov. 30, 1802; m. Emeline Bent.
502. Lucia, b. Jan. 27, 1805; d. young.
503. Lydia, b. May 20, 1806; m. (1) Eliab Thompson (364), (2) Jacob
      Soule.
504. Waitstill, b. Sept. 29, 1809; m. Charles E. D. Purcheron from
      Canada; he d. March 27, 1865.
505. Lysander, b. Sept. 14, 1811; m. Abigail Thompson (636).

190.

NATHANIEL THOMPSON[5] (Ebenezer,[4] Jacob,[3] John,[2] John[1]),
b. May 11, 1761, son of Ebenezer and Elizabeth (Besse)
Thomson; m. (1) 1785, SARAH THAYER, dau. of David
Thayer, (2) MRS. MARY FOSTER, dau. of Jabez Hall. She
was b. 1777. He lived in Halifax, Mass.; held a commission
as major in the militia. First wife d. December 18, 1810, in
her 47th year; second wife d. April 13, 1839, in her 63d year.
He died January 13, 1843.

CHILDREN BY FIRST WIFE VI. GENERATION.

506. Polly, b. Dec. 2, 1785; m. Melvin Crooker. She d. Nov. 4, 1811.
507. Lucy, b. Sept. 30, 1787; m. Joshua C. Lyon, son of Obadiah
      Lyon. She d. Jan. 18, 1817.

508. Nathaniel, b. Nov. 19, 1789; d. August 26, 1811.
509. Seth, b. Sept. 6, 1791; m. Bethiah Benson.
510. Elizabeth, b. Sept 30, 1793; m. Melvin Crooker (second wife). She d. May 27, 1816.
511. Charity, b. Jan. 12, 1796; m. 1835, Thomas Rogers of East Bridgewater.
512. Ebenezer, b. Jan. 17, 1793, m. Louisa Eldridge.
513. David, b. Jan. 29, 1800; d. young.
514. Sarah, b. Oct. 30, 1801; m. Sept. 20, 1821, Capt. Charles Rogers of East Bridgewater. She d. August 8, 1872.
15. Welcome, b. Feb. 27, 1805; d. Jan. 12, 1833.
516. Almira, b. Feb. 3, 1807; m. Sidney Packard. She d. June 3, 1826.

195.

EPHRAIM THOMPSON[5] (Ephraim,[4] Jacob,[3] John,[2] John[1]), b. November 2, 1771, son of Ephraim and Hannah (Thayer) Thomson; m. LUCY THOMAS.

CHILDREN VI. GENERATION.

17. Bathsheba, b. —; d. in infancy.
518. Lucy, b. Feb. 17, 1794; d. April 28, 1795.
519. Bathsheba, b. April 18, 1796; m. (1) David M. Gifford, (2) John B. Taber.
520. Abner, b. Oct. 9, 1797; m. Nancy H. Gifford.
521. Alva, b. March 2, 1801; m. Lydia Chase.
522. David, b. July 30, 1803; m. Judith Snow.
523. Lucy, b. April 30, 1805; m. Obed Sherman.
524. Jeremiah F., b. June 26, 1807; m. Sarah Ann Case.
525. Joseph, b. —; m. Caroline Little.

197.

SILAS THOMPSON[5] (Ephraim,[4] Jacob,[3] John,[2] John[1]), b. April 3, 1778, son of Ephraim and Hannah (Thayer) Thomson; m. CATHARINE BEAL.

CHILDREN VI. GENERATION.

526. Martin, b. July 31, 1801; m. Amanda Thompson (772).
527. Jane, b. Feb. 15, 1803; m. Joel Finney.
528. Rhoda, b. Sept. 12, 1807.
529. Joanna, b. April 3, 1810; m. — Fletcher.
530. Nancy, b. March 25, 1813; m. Daniel Garland.
531. Silas, b. Jan. 22, 1815; d. April 12, 1815.
532. Daniel W., b. Dec. 21, 1817.
533. Silas B., b. May 11, 1820.

200.

FRANCIS THOMPSON[5] (Ephraim,[4] Jacob,[3] John,[2] John[1]), b. August 2, 1785, son of Ephraim and Hannah (Thayer) Thomson; m. (1) JANE BEAL, (2) SALLY BEAL. First wife d. September, 1811; second wife d. April, 1833.

CHILDREN BY FIRST WIFE VI. GENERATION.

534. Edmund, } Twins,
535. Edward, } b. August 15, 1811; Edward m. Mary H. Bryant.

CHILDREN BY SECOND WIFE VI. GENERATION.

536. Gilman, b. 1814; m. Lucinda Dunbar.
537. Lyman, b. May 2, 1817.
538. Francis, b. June 28, 1823; m. Dorlisca Vinica.
539. George, b. —.
540. Franklin, b. —.
541. Grenville, b. —.
542. Sumner, b. March, 1833.

206.

MOLLY THOMPSON[5] (Daniel,[4] Jacob,[3] John,[2] John[1]), b. August 20, 1778, dau. of Daniel and Fear (Lyon) Thomson; m. ENOS EATON.

CHILDREN VI. GENERATION.

543. Betsey, b. —.
544. Charity, b. —.
545. Phebe, b. —.
546. Albert, b. —.
547. William, b. —.
548. Ralph, b. —.

207.

PHEBE THOMPSON[5] (Daniel,[4] Jacob,[3] John.[2] John[1]), b. January 17, 1781, daughter of Daniel and Fear (Lyon) Thomson ; m. ISRAEL THOMAS.

CHILDREN VI. GENERATION.

549. William, b. —.
550. Ralph, b. —.
551. Albert, b. —.

(208 see 271.)

209.

DANIEL THOMPSON[5] (Daniel,[4] Jacob,[3] John,[2] John[1]), b. April 27, 1787, son of Daniel and Fear (Lyon) Thomson; m. 1813, SYBIL HORTON, b. 1788, dau. of Barnabas Horton of Bridgewater. Lived in Maine.

CHILDREN VI. GENERATION.

552. Israel T., b. Jan. 20, 1813.
553. Horatio, b. Jan. 1, 1815; m. Silvina Jane Harlow, and had Silvina.
554. Harriet, b. March, 1817; m. Seth Horton.   She d. June 2, 1841.
555. Jane, b. 1819; m. Seth Horton after Harriet's death.
556. Daniel, b. April 17, 1822.
557. Mary, b. 1824.
558. Verres, b. Feb. 18, 1826.
559. Greenleaf, b. —.
560. Francis, b. Oct., 1830.

210.

SOLOMON THOMPSON[5] (Jacob,[4] Jacob,[3] Jacob,[2] John[1]), b. January 7, 1762, son of Capt. Jacob and Freelove (Finney) Thomson; m. LYDIA MURDOCK, b. December 8, 1766.   He was a Baptist deacon for a long time.

CHILDREN VI. GENERATION.

561. Lucy, b. Oct. 1, 1787; m. 1810, Charles Shaw.   She d. Oct. 19, 1847.
562. Lydia, b. Oct. 2, 1789; m. Timothy Drew.   She d. Feb. 7, 1870.
563. Solomon, b. Sept. 25, 1791; m. (1) Harriet Thompson (479), (2) Widow Mary Simmons.
564. Mercy, b. June 15, 1794; m. George Atwood.   She d. Nov. 13, 1873.
565. Calvin, b. Oct. 29, 1796; m. Margaret Richardson.
566. Jacob, b. Oct. 3, 1801; m. (1) Nancy Tinkham, (2) Joann Benson.

211.

BENJAMIN THOMPSON (Jacob,[4] Jacob,[3] Jacob,[2] John[1]), b. March 30, 1764, son of Capt. Jacob and Freelove (Finney) Thomson; m. MARY BOURN.   He served in the Revolutionary war.

CHILDREN VI. GENERATION.

567. Betsey Wild, b. Nov. 20, 1789; m. Hon. Wilkes Wood.
568. Mary B., b. Nov. 4, 1792; m. Ebenezer Pickens.

9

569. Sally,   } Twins,   { Sally m. James M. Leonard. She
570. Benjamin,   } b. May 22, 1795, { d. Nov. 16, 1822.
                                     { Benjamin d. June 13, 1795.
571. Abner B., b. Sept. 22, 1797; m. Eliza Williams.
572. Freelove, b. Dec. 21, 1800; m. Gamaliel Rounseville.
573. Benjamin, b. Nov. 25, 1803; m. Margaret Lindley.
574. James D., b. Oct. 31, 1807; m. (1) Abigail Kendrick, (2) Louisa
     H. Farnham.

215.

JACOB THOMPSON[5] (Jacob,[4] Jacob,[3] Jacob,[2] John[1]), b. November 4, 1771, son of Capt. Jacob and Freelove (Finney)
Thomson ; m. MERCY WATERMAN, b. 1774, dau. of Freeman
and Joanna (Thomson) Waterman (73). She d. 1860.

CHILDREN VI. GENERATION.

575. Abigail, b. August 17, 1797; d. young.
576. Freeman, b. April, 1799; drowned while passing Cape Horn.
577. Eliza Ann, b. Dec. 18, 1805; m. Rev. Joseph F. Phillips.
578. Adaline, b. 1806; d. young.
579. Julia, b. April 3, 1807.
580. Mercy F., b. July 7, 1815; d. March 5, 1842.

(219 see 215.)

222.

PRISCILLA WATERMAN[5] (Joanna,[4] John,[3] Jacob,[2] John[1]), b.
1782, daughter of Freeman and Joanna (Thomson) Waterman ;
m. 1800, JOSIAH MARSHALL. She d. 1860.

CHILDREN VI. GENERATION.

581. Sabina, b. 1801; d. 1803.
582. Josiah T., b. 1803; d. 1875.
583. Almira, b. 1805; d. 1863.
584. Emily, b. 1807; d. 1836.
585. Priscilla, b. 1808; d. 1841.
586. Henry, b. 1810; d. 1835.
587. Marian, b. 1812; m. 1844, J. G. Holbrook. Live at Athens, Pa.,
     and had (1) Charlotte M., b. 1845; (2) Stephen, b. 1846; (3) Mar-
     garet M. R., b. 1849; d. 1852; (4) George O., b. 1850.
588. Charlotte, b. 1819; m. June 10, 1846, Horatio Bridge, Paymaster
     General, U. S. N., now retired (1888), living at Athens, Pa.
     Had (1) Marian, b. Oct. 3, 1851; d. March 29, 1855.

225.

BARNABAS THOMPSON[5] (Noah,[4] Barnabas,[3] Jacob,[2] John[1]), b. November 20, 1769, son of Noah and Priscilla (Holmes) Thomson; m. SARAH FULLER. He was a captain of militia. He d. March 20, 1838.

CHILDREN VI. GENERATION.

589. Barnabas, b. Sept. 24, 1793; m. Hannah Shaw.
590. Zadoc, b. May 23, 1796; m. Phebe Boyce.
591. Sally, b. March 1, 1799; m. Moses Shaw.
592. Salmon, b. March 11, 1803; m. Sylinda Boyce.
593. Eliza, b. Jan. 7, 1810; m. Jesse T. Shurtleff.

226.

DAVID THOMPSON[5] (Noah,[4] Barnabas,[3] Jacob,[2] John[1]), b. March 16, 1762, son of Noah and Priscilla (Holmes) Thomson; m. BETSEY LEACH. He was a captain in the militia, a justice of the peace, a member of the legislature of Vermont, and a member of the convention to change the constitution in 1836.

CHILDREN VI. GENERATION.

594. Alvinzy, b. March 23, 1797; m. Emily Seabury.
595. Eunice, b. Oct. 1, 1798.
596. Edwin, b. August 26, 1800; m. Wealthy Cox.
597. Calista, b. April 16, 1803; m. John Seabury.
598. Ovid, b. August 27, 1805; m. Waitstill Shurtleff.
599. Roxelona, b. August 10, 1808; m. Henry W. Leach.

228.

ABEL THOMPSON[5] (Noah,[4] Barnabas,[3] Jacob,[2] John[1]) b. October 3, 1776, son of Noah and Priscilla (Holmes) Thomson; m. POLLY STACY. He d. September 25, 1852. She d. December 2, 1850.

CHILDREN VI. GENERATION.

600. Patty, b. June 17, 1801; m. (1) — Walker, d. —, m. (2) — Wilder, d. —. She d. Oct. 15, 1884.
601. Hosea B., b. August 19, 1803; m. Sarah P. Barrows.
602. Anna, b. March 16, 1806; m. John Harris.
603. Oliver Holmes, b. April 1, 1809; m. Melinda Harris.   He d. March 17, 1871.   She d. Jan. 24, 1882.
604. Noah, b. March 15, 1812; m. Oratio Dawley.
605. Elihu, b. Dec. 25, 1814; m. Phebe S. Macomber.
606. Polly, b. Dec. 19, 1820; m. Phineas Hammond.

229.

JOHN H. THOMPSON[5] (Noah,[4] Barnabas,[3] Jacob,[2] John[1]), b. September 16, 1779, son of Noah and Priscilla (Holmes) Thomson; m. BETSEY CHURCHILL.

CHILDREN VI. GENERATION.

607. Alpheus, b. March 9, 1804; d. March 26, 1813.
608. Tabitha, b. Dec. 2, 1805; m. Jeremiah R. Lewis.
609. John C., b. Jan. 4, 1816.
610. Betsey, b. June 26, 1820.
611. Melvina, b. June 11, 1826.

232.

CROMWELL THOMPSON[5] (Noah,[4] Barnabas,[3] Jacob,[2] John[1]), b. April 27, 1786, son of Noah and Priscilla (Holmes) Thomson; m. ABIGAIL BOYCE.

CHILDREN VI. GENERATION.

612. Almon, b. July 23, 1809.
613. Mary Ann, b. Nov. 10, 1812; m. Stillman Atwood.
614. Abigail A., b. Jan. 2, 1817; m. Norman W. Henley.
615. Fanny M., b. Oct. 24, 1820; m. George W. Huntoon.
616. Orlando C., b. Oct. 27, 1822.
617. De Algeroy, b. April 8, 1826.
618. Lorena P., b. April 5, 1828.

233.

ELIHU THOMPSON[5] (Noah,[4] Barnabas,[3] Jacob,[2] John[1]), b. August 1, 1789, son of Noah and Priscilla (Holmes) Thomson; m. HANNAH PHELPS. He d. February 8, 1814. She d. June 21, 1813.

CHILDREN VI. GENERATION.

619. Delight, b. Nov. 26, 1811; d. March 30, 1812.
620. Adrastus, b. Jan. 13, 1813; d. same day.

234.

CHARLES THOMPSON[5] (Noah,[4] Barnabas,[3] Jacob,[2] John[1]), b. April 23, 1792, son of Noah and Priscilla (Holmes) Thomson; m. SALLY SHAW.

CHILDREN VI. GENERATION.

621. Emily C., b. July 2, 1814; m. Tracy Wade.

622. Eveline A., b. March 5, 1817; m. Elisha Bowman.
623. Marinda, b. Feb., 1820; d. March 1, 1820.

235.

JABEZ THOMPSON[5] (Isaac,[4] Barnabas,[3] Jacob,[2] John[1]), b. November 3, 1772, in Halifax son of Isaac and Huldah (Sturtevant) Thomson; m. December 31, 1799, BETSEY WOOD of Middleboro, b. October 3, 1775. She d. March 16, 1839, in Plympton. He d. February 7, 1845, in Plympton.

CHILDREN VI. GENERATION.

624. Huldah, b. Oct. 10, 1800, in Plympton; d. July 22, 1822.
625. Arioch, b. June 22, 1802; m. Adaline D. Virgin.
626. Ichabod Wadsworth, b. April 29, 1804, in Plympton; m. Susannah Churchill of Plymouth. She d. April, 1837. He went to Galena, Ill., where, in Nov., 1837, he m. Amelia Babcock; had one son, who d. when one and one-half years old. Ichabod W. d. May 12, 1846, in Galena.
627. Isaac, b. April 27, 1806, in Plympton; went south and d. there.
628. Simeon, b. June 13, 1808; m. (1) Abigail W. Churchill, (2) Sarah Faulkner.
629. Samuel V., b. July 20, 1810; m. Betsey Nash.
630. Josiah, b. Sept. 8, 1812; m. Jane Ann Shaw.
631. Betsey Wood, b. Dec. 15, 1814; m. Otis Thompson (659).

236.

ISAAC THOMPSON[5] (Isaac,[4] Barnabas,[3] Jacob,[2] John[1]), b. November 17, 1774, son of Isaac and Huldah (Sturtevant) Thomson; m. (1) PHEBE SOULE, (2) LUCY HOLMES, b. 1784, widow of Ellis Holmes, and dau. of Dea. Joseph Copeland of West Bridgewater. First wife d. December 8, 1823, in her 46th year. He d. 1858.

CHILDREN BY FIRST WIFE VI. GENERATION.

632. Sabina, b. May 3, 1801; m. Martin Willis.
633. Roxanna, b. Nov. 15, 1802; m. Samuel Jewett.
634. Deborah, b. Oct. 6, 1804; m. Albert Thomas. She d. July 1887.
635. Christopher C., b. June 5, 1807; m. (1) Almira Dunlap, (2) Mary A. Strong.
636. Abigail, b. April 10, 1809; m. Lysander Thompson (505).
637. Phebe, b. April 1, 1811; m. Nahum Bailey.
638. Mary, b. May 17, 1813; m. Ichabod Sampson.
639. Isaac, b. July 17, 1815; m. (1) Anna T. Thompson (383), (2) Lydia R. Thomas.

640. Hiram, b. April 7, 1818; d. August 30, 1845, in Thompson, Ill.
641. Joseph S., b. Dec. 1, 1823; m. Melissa Pingrey.

239.

JACOB THOMPSON[5] (Isaac,[4] Barnabas,[3] Jacob,[2] John[1]), b.
June 26, 1782, son of Isaac and Huldah (Sturtevant) Thomson;
m. (1) SALLY STURTEVANT, (2) ESTHER SHAW. First wife d.
December 1, 1805, aged 24 years. Second wife d. November
7, 1832. He d. February 6, 1856.

CHILD BY FIRST WIFE VI. GENERATION.

642. Maria, b. July 31, 1802; d. Nov. 12, 1805.

CHILDREN BY SECOND WIFE VI. GENERATION.

643. Hosea V., b. Jan. 23, 1808; m. Susan M. Maynard.
644. Jacob, b. August 8, 1809; m. Adnie V. Booth.
645. Marcia V., b. June 22, 1811; m. Moses Titcomb.
646. Sally, b. Feb. 10, 1813; m. Charles Chipman.
647. Betsey, b. August 7, 1815; m. Simeon C. Clark.
648. George M., b. Jan. 29, 1817; m. Caroline E. Hyde.
649. Lewis S., b. Nov. 10, 1819; m. Mary W. Macomber.
650. Sumner S., b. April 12, 1823; m. Harriet S. Wiley.
651. Huldah V., b. Sept. 10, 1825; m. Silas D. Newcomb.
652. Caroline M., b. Nov., 1828; m. Stephen Hersey.

240.

SAMUEL THOMPSON[5] (Adam,[4] Barnabas,[3] Jacob,[2] John[1]), b.
September 24, 1778, son of Adam and Molly (Thomson) Thomson; m. CLARA STURTEVANT, dau. of Samuel Stafford Sturtevant. He was captain of a volunteer company, and representative in the legislature of Massachusetts in 1835 and 1836
from the town of Middleboro; also a justice of the peace. He
was a teacher of music and taught several singing schools in
Halifax. When he was married, his father, Adam Thomson,
built him a large, two-story house in the northerly part of the
town, the raising of which brought together a large company.
Everything passed off well, and after the raising they decided
to have a sing. Boards were laid on the lower flooring, where
the company assembled, and under the lead of their old master
began singing one of Dr. Watts' old hymns in these words:
"Ye tribes of Adam join with heaven and earth and sea;"
suddenly the flooring gave way and they were all promiscuously
landed in the cellar.

CHILDREN VI. GENERATION.

653. Amasa, b. Sept., 1802; m. Betsey M. Eddy.
654. Lydia C., b. Sept. 11, 1804; d. May 29, 1870.
655. Matilda, b. Nov. 23, 1808; m. Abiel Wood. She d. Oct. 26, 1886.
656. Maria P., b. March 30, 1812; d. Oct. 16, 1834.
657. Clara S., b. July 8, 1816; m. William, son of John Tilson of Halifax.

241.

ADAM THOMPSON[5] (Adam,[4] Barnabas,[3] Jacob,[2] John[1]) b. May 27, 1784, son of Adam and Molly (Thomson) Thomson; m. SALVINA WOOD, dau. of Timothy and Salvina (Soule) Wood. He d. April 22, 1867. She d. June 10, 1856.

CHILDREN VI. GENERATION.

658. Molly, b. March 14, 1811; d. Feb. 13, 1853.
659. Otis, b. May 1, 1813; m. Betsey W. Thompson (631).
660. Albert, b. Oct. 9, 1815; m. Charlotte M. Warren.
661. Shepard, b. Nov. 2, 1820; m. Priscilla T. Wiswell.

242.

WARD THOMPSON[5] (Adam,[4] Barnabas,[3] Jacob,[2] John[1]), b. September 4, 1786, son of Adam and Molly (Thomson) Thomson; m. MOLLY HOLMES (116), dau. of Oliver and Lydia (Thomson) Holmes. He was captain of a volunteer company. He d. Feburary 17, 1871. She d. February 21, 1859.

CHILDREN VI. GENERATION.

662. Mary H., b. June 8, 1819; d. August 27, 1824.
663. Ward, b. May 6, 1826; m. Marcia Wright.

243.

ZADOCK THOMPSON[5] (Adam,[4] Barnabas,[3] Jacob,[2] John[1]), b. January 4, 1790, son of Adam and Molly (Thomson) Thomson; m. DEBORAH BOSWORTH, dau. of Sala Bosworth. He was captain of a volunteer company. Was chosen in 1831 representative to the General Court for the winter session, also chosen in 1832 and 1833. He held a commission as justice of the peace. He d. January 18, 1879. His wife d. July 26, 1868.

CHILDREN VI. GENERATION.

664. Rebecca P., b. Feb. 29, 1816; m. Samuel S. Inglee.

665. Cyrus, b. July 16, 1819; m. (1) Mercy O., b. Feb. 10, 1819, dau. of Stafford Sturtevant; (2) Clara G. Daland. He d. Nov. 13, 1864, of exposure in war of Rebellion. No children.

666. Amanda, b. March 15, 1821; m. Ebenezer P., b. Jan. 18, 1820, son of Cyrus and Fear (Waterman) Richmond. She d. Feb. 13, 1842.

667. Zadock, b. Sept. 2, 1826; m. (1) Lydia S. Pope, (2) Mary E. Bosworth.

668. Salina F., b. Feb. 20, 1831; m. Simeon H. Williams.

244.

JAMES THOMPSON[5] (Ichabod,[4] Barnabas,[3] Jacob,[2] John[1]), b. April 13, 1780, son of Ichabod and Lydia (Hall) Thomson; m. DEBORAH WASHBURN. He graduated at Brown university in 1799, and settled in the ministry at Barre, Mass.; received degree D. D. from Harvard university. He d. May 14, 1854. His wife d. May, 1836.

CHILDREN VI. GENERATION.

669. Louisa W., b. March 23, 1804; m. James W. Jenkins.

670. James W., b. Dec. 13, 1805; m. Mary James.

671. Charles C. P., b. July 11, 1808; he was editor of a public paper; d. May 7, 1838.

672. Philo H., b. Dec. 17, 1810.

673. Lydia, b. March 18, 1813; m. Walter A. Bryant.

674. Leura Ann J., b. Sept. 13, 1817; d. Oct. 4, 1833.

675. Elvira, b. May 13, 1820; d. Feb. 24, 1827.

676. Alexander Y., b. Oct. 24, 1824.

(245 see 285.)

246.

SARAH THOMPSON[5] (Ichabod,[4] Barnabas,[3] Jacob,[2] John[1]), b. March 1, 1785, dau. of Ichabod and Lydia (Hall) Thomson; m. GEORGE DREW, son of Thomas Drew (100). She d. July 13, 1886, 101 years, 4 months and 12 days old, retaining her faculties of mind and body until a short time before her death. Her husband d. January 19, 1866.

CHILDREN VI. GENERATION.

677. George, b. August 28, 1811; m. Lucy Lewis.

678. James Thompson, b. April 18, 1813; m. Georgiana F. Tuttle.

679. Lydia Hall, b. Feb. 17, 1815; m. Dr. Cyrus Morton, son of Nathaniel (101).

680. Steven, b. July 16, 1817; m. Jane W. Soule.
681. Cyrus, b. April 11, 1820; m. Evelina Donaldson.
682. Mary Jane, b. Jan. 4, 1823; m. Adoniram Soule of Plimpton. She d. Sept. 30, 1865.
683. Julia A. W., b. April 21, 1826; m. Charles L. Winslow of Rockland.

247.

OAKES THOMPSON[5] (William,[4] Caleb,[3] Jacob,[2] John[1]), b. July 31, 1771, son of William and Deborah (Sturtevant) Thomson; m. April 21, 1796, HANNAH BISBEE, b. April 2, 1774, a descendant of Thomas Bisbedge, who came from Sandwich, England, in the ship "Hercules," with his wife and six children and three servants, landing at Scituate Harbor in the spring of 1634. He was a man of wealth and position in England. His son was called Bisbee. In 1797 Oakes Thompson left Middleboro and went to the District of Maine to survey, sell, and settle a large tract of wild land of several thousand acres, which had been purchased by his father and called "Thompson's Grant," situated in that part of the District embraced in the towns of Hartford and Peru, in Oxford county. In September following, having abandoned the idea of a permanent settlement in Maine, he was one day "packing up" to return to Middleboro, when, to his surprise, there arrived his father, his brother Cephas, together with his own wife and child Lucy, six months old, who had come with their pots and kettles and household goods for their future home. She had performed the last twelve miles of the journey on horseback with her child in her arms through an unbroken forest, guided only by spotted trees. They erected a frame house and barn in North Hartford on the northwest shore of Whitney Lake, and later a saw-mill. They cleared land and raised crops, which were sometimes destroyed by early frost. In the year 1816 there was a partial famine, and they subsisted chiefly on potatoes and milk; at one time they gave a fine two-year-old heifer for two and one-half bushels of smutty wheat. Their secluded but busy life was not altogether monotonous; the wild Indians, whom they were glad to feed and send on their way as quickly as possible, were wont to visit their house. Around the cheerful hearthstone at night occurred many a scene of gayety, and many a story was there told of personal experiences in trapping wild animals, and in startling adventures with bears. With other pioneers, he established a Baptist church, of which he was a deacon for many years—up to

the time of his death. His son Oakes refers to the regular
attendance of his father and mother on Sunday at religious
meetings at Livermore Corners, ten miles distant, on horse-
back, he sitting in the saddle, while she sat sidewise on the
horse behind. He also cites an instance of his father's
punctuality in devotional exercises. It was his custom to
have family prayers every morning, but says that "on one
day when my father was engaged in haying on the meadow,
half a mile away from the house, I (being only four years
old), noticing that there had been no prayers that morning, mentioned the fact to my mother, who at once sent me
down to remind him of his omission. He thereupon returned
to the house with me, read a chapter, and offered a prayer,
and then returned to his work." He d. August 31, 1829.
His wife d. October 18, 1860.

CHILDREN VI. GENERATION.

684. Lucy Wood, b. May 20, 1797; m. Noah Bosworth.
685. Mary, b. March 23, 1800; m. James Brown.
686. Oakes, b. Oct. 20, 1802; m. Livonia Banks.
687. William, b. Jan. 18, 1805; m. Jan. 27, 1859, Mrs. Lucy (Wins-
       low) Tilson. He resided for many years at Canton, Me.; was
       successively teacher, surveyor of land, merchant, and legal
       counsellor, and for several years was a prominent member of
       the Maine legislature, in the house and senate. He later re-
       moved to Rockland, Me., where he engaged in the lime rock
       business.
688. Philander,) Twins.
689. Philena,   ∫ b. March 7, 1810; d. March 19, 1810.

248.

WILLIAM THOMPSON[5] (William,[4] Caleb,[3] Jacob,[2] John[1]) b.
April 11, 1773, son of William and Deborah (Sturtevant)
Thomson; m. SUSANNA WOOD. They settled in Maine; about
1832 moved to Quincy, Ill., and soon after to Farmington,
Iowa. She d. 1839.

CHILDREN VI. GENERATION.

690. Roxellana, b. March 29, 1803; m. Henry Moulton.
691. Florinda S. W., b. May 31, 1806; m. Daniel Torrey.
692. Otis, b. April 17, 1809; m. (1) Clarissa A. Wing, (2) Martha
       Laycock.
693. Hiram, b. May 13, 1811; m. Eliza Pottle.
694. William Augustus, b. July 29, 1813, in Livermore, Me.; m.
       June 7, 1847, in Payson, Ill., Maria S. Stewart. No children.
       Reside in Payson.

695. Deborah Wood, b. May 16, 1816; m. Benjamin F. Cate.

249.

CEPHAS THOMPSON[5] (William,[4] Caleb,[3] Jacob,[2] John[1]), b. July 1, 1775, son of William and Deborah (Sturtevaut) Thomson; m. (1) 1802, OLIVE LEONARD, dau. of Daniel and Mary (Hall) Leonard of Bridgewater; m. (2) LUCY THOMPSON (475). He fitted for college, but instead of entering, took up portrait painting. His field of labor was in the south, where he remained winters, painting in many cities from Philadelphia to New Orleans. His patrons were the leading men of the country. He was a man of strict integrity and courteous manners. His home was Middleboro, Mass. First wife d. May 22, 1819.

CHILDREN BY FIRST WIFE VI. GENERATION.

696. Marietta T., b. Feb. 27, 1803; unmarried. An artist in oil painting. Residence, Raynham, Mass.
697. Elvira S. T., b. July 3, 1804; m. George Bonney.
698. Cordelia, b. May 1, 1806; m. Benjamin A. Bryant.
699. William Henry, b. Nov. 17, 1807; m. Mary Miller.
700. Cephas G., b. August 8, 1809; m. Mary G. Ogden.
701. Floranthe, b. May 14, 1811; m. Grenville Sproat.
702. Jerome B., b. Jan. 30, 1814; m. (1) Louisa Colden, (2) Marie May Tupper.
703. Charles Frederick, b. June 2, 1816; unmarried. In 1834 he had been three years in Amherst college; d. Sept. 3, 1839, in the South.

CHILD BY SECOND WIFE VI. GENERATION.

704. Julius, b. Oct. 21, 1824; m. Bathsheba T. Warren.

250.

LUCY THOMPSON[5] (William,[4] Caleb,[3] Jacob,[2] John[1]), b. September 25, 1776, dau. of William and Deborah (Sturtevant) Thomson; m. ABNER WOOD, b. April 6, 1775. He d. April 24, 1852. She d. March 18, 1856.

CHILDREN VI. GENERATION.

705. Deborah, b. May 16, 1798; m. Nathan Sherman. She d. —.
706. Citoyenne, b. Oct. 25, 1799; unmarried. She d. —.
707. William T., b. July 11, 1801; m. Amanda Sampson. He d. —.
708. Lucy T., b. May 7, 1803; m. Lewen Barrows. He d. —.
709. Louisa, b. May 15, 1805; m. Edrick Clark. She d. —.

710. Emily K., b. July 21, 1807; m. John Bennett. She d. —.
711. Julia A., b. Sept. 23, 1809; m. Abner Harlow. She d. —.
712. Boadicea T., b. March 24, 1812; m. Willard Clark.
713. Marcia, b. May 12, 1815; unmarried. She d. —.

(251 *see* 286.)

252.

IRA THOMPSON[5] (William,[4] Caleb,[3] Jacob,[2] John[1]), b. August 3, 1780, in Middleboro, Mass., son of William and Deborah (Sturtevant) Thomson; m. September 25, 1802, in Kingston, Mass., SOPHIA DREW, b. October 15, 1782, in Duxbury, Mass. In 1801 Mr. Thompson removed from Middleboro, Mass., to Hartford in the District of Maine, where his father had received a grant of land. After staying there a year, he returned to Massachusetts and married his wife. They went by packet from Boston to Portland, and were two weeks on the way. From Portland they went to Buckfield, and from the latter place they traveled to Hartford, Me., on horseback, finding their way by spotted trees, the bride riding on a pillion behind her husband. After living in Hartford a year and a half, Mr. Thompson exchanged his farm for one in the town of Livermore, where he remained until his death, bringing up a large family of children. During his long residence in Livermore, he enjoyed the respect and confidence of all who knew him, and was often chosen to fill positions of honor and responsibility. In 1812 he was chosen captain of militia. He was one of the building committee of the first church built in Livermore, was a deacon of the Baptist church there for a great number of years, and served as one of the selectmen of the town. In 1816 he was elected representative to the general assembly of Massachusetts from the District of Maine. He drove to Boston, where it was held, with his own horse and carriage. The suit he wore was made of merino wool, sheared from his own sheep, spun and woven in his own house, and sent to Fayette to be colored dark blue and pressed. In this year, 1816, was built the large and roomy house which is still the Thompson homestead, and is owned and occupied by Job Drew Thompson (1888). Something should be said of the mother of this large family. Mrs. Sophia (Drew) Thompson was a woman of great energy and resolution, and of such excellent judgment that her husband was always accustomed to consult her, even in matters of business. These parents lived to see all their children grown up and married, having families of their own, and all honorable and useful members of society. There have been three reunions of this large family, where all the children and many of the grandchildren were present—the first at the homestead, when forty-five were present; the next, October 29, 1863, at the same place, when fifty-five were present, twenty-six more being unable to attend. Several of the absent ones were in the army, and letters full of affection and encouraging words were sent to them at that time. The third family reunion was held at Skowhegan, Me., on the occasion of the golden wedding of the eldest daughter, Susan D., who married Rev. Charles Miller. Ira Thompson d. February 13, 1857. His wife d. January 29, 1856.

CHILDREN VI. GENERATION.

714. Ira D., b. Sept. 25, 1803; m. Lydia Hathaway.
715. Susan D., b. Sept. 25, 1805; m. Rev. Charles Miller.
716. Elbridge G., b. June 29, 1807; m. Sarah Ballou.
717. Clarinda M., b. March 16, 1809; m. John Monroe.
718. Arad, b. Jan. 24, 1811; m. (1) Margaret L. Cole, (2) Louisa M. Baldwin.
719. Boadicea L., b. May 5, 1813; m. (1) Abner S. Aldrich, (2) George W. Pierpont.
720. Erastus, b. April 24, 1815; m. (1) Catherine W. Oakes, (2) Mary C. Cummings.
721. Abby S., b. Feb. 2, 1818; m. Joseph S. Monroe.
722. Job Drew, b. March 30, 1820; m. Ruth W. Winslow.
723. Charles O., b. April 8, 1822; m. Nancy Marsh.
724. Mary S., b. June 6, 1827; m. William K. Wyman.

253.

GALEN THOMPSON[5] (William,[4] Caleb,[3] Jacob,[2] John[1]), b. October 27, 1782, son of William and Deborah (Sturtevant) Thomson; m. (1) SUSANNA PORTER, (2) FANNY MARBLE. Settled in Maine. He d. April 21, 1871. First wife d. January 16, 1808. Second wife d. October 15, 1864.

CHILD BY FIRST WIFE VI. GENERATION.

725. Susan Porter, b. Oct. 23, 1807; m. Solomon Beals.

CHILDREN BY SECOND WIFE VI. GENERATION.

726. Fanny M., b. March, 1810; unmarried; d. May 26, 1847.
727. Galen M., b. March 23, 1812; m. Myrtilla Harlow.
728. Alonzo, b. —; m. Mary J. Dolly.
729. Cephas, b. Sept., 1816; d. March 23, 1838.

730. Loammi B., b. Sept. 5, 1819; m. Laura J. Dolly.
731. Rodolphus P., b. Sept. 29, 1825; m. Abbie L. Wadsworth.
732. Don Carlos d'Vaudrille, b. July 4, 1833; m. Elmira A. Atwood.

255.

ARAD THOMPSON[5] (William,[4] Caleb,[3] Jacob,[2] John[1]) b. December 30, 1786, son of William and Deborah (Sturtevant) Thomson; m. December, 1816, MERCY BOURNE. He graduated from Dartmouth college in 1811; studied medicine and practiced with success in Middleboro the remainder of his life. He d. April 23, 1843. She d. June 5, 1843.

CHILDREN VI. GENERATION.

733. Mary W., b. Sept. 22, 1817; d. Oct. 20, 1848.
734. Ellen, b. Jan. 9, 1821; m. Nathan King.
735. Lucy Ann, b. Oct. 23, 1823; m. William A. King.
736. William Arad, b. June 21, 1835; m. Ella Mason Williams.

256.

BOADICE THOMPSON[5] (William,[4] Caleb,[3] Jacob,[2] John[1]), b. February 17, 1789, dau. of William and Deborah (Sturtevant) Thomson; m. May 5, 1817, SIMEON LEONARD. Lived in Middleboro. She d. December 26, 1871, at home of Thomas Kent.

CHILDREN VI. GENERATION.

737. Boadicea T., b. March 22, 1818; d. June, 1885.
738. Rachel Stone, b. May 31, 1819; m. Dexter Marvel.
739. Fanny, b. March 19, 1821; m. Thomas Kent.
740. Eliza,   } Twins,
741. Eloisa,   } b. Oct. 30, 1823; d. in one week.
742. Sarah Louisa, b. Nov. 17, 1825; d. 1832.
743. Mary, b. Dec. 3, 1827; d. about 1833.
744. Simeon, b. Jan. 7, 1831.
745. Hermon, b. Oct. 1, 1833; m. —; has three children; resides at Elmswood, Mass.

257.

IRENE THOMPSON[5] (William, Caleb,[3] Jacob,[2] John[1]), b. May 12, 1791, in Middleborough, Mass., dau. of William and Deborah (Sturtevant) Thomson; m. October 1, 1815, at Middleborough, DANIEL WARREN, b. October 29, 1788, son of Nathan and Keziah (Weston) Warren. She d. November 23, 1869, at East Boston, Mass. He d. June 2, 1838.

CHILDREN VI. GENERATION.

746. Royal Friend, b. —.
747. Irena Maria, b. May 26, 1820; m. Dexter Phillips; have two married daughters; resides with one of them at Middleborough.
748. Elizabeth Barker, b. —; m. James Coggeshall; have several daughters, who are teachers; all reside in Bristol, R. I.
749. Daniel Frederick, b. —.
750. Juliet Harlow, b. June 23, 1827; m. Alanson C. Keen.
751. Edwin, b. —; address No. 5 Grape street, Cleveland, Ohio.

258.

OTIS THOMPSON⁵ (Nathaniel,⁴ Caleb,³ Jacob,² John¹), b. September 14, 1776, son of Nathaniel and Hannah (Thomas) Thomson; m. (1) RACHEL CHANDLER, (2) CHARLOTTE FALES. He graduated at Brown university in 1798. Settled in the ministry. His first wife d. September 16, 1827, aged 47 years. He d. June 26, 1859, in Abington, Mass.

CHILDREN BY FIRST WIFE VI. GENERATION.

752. Sabina, b. 1803; m. William Carpenter.
753. Lucina, b. 1804; m. James Carpenter.
754. Fidelia, b. 1805; m. Rev. Tyler Thatcher. She d. 1838.
755. Rachel C., b. 1806; m. Lewis Kent.
756. Charlotte, b. —; m. Cyrus Batchelder.
757. Chandler, b. —.
758. Josiah, b. —.
759. Lucius, b. —.
760. Nathaniel, b. —; scalded to death.

264.

GAIUS THOMPSON⁵ (Caleb,⁴ Caleb,³ Jacob,² John¹), b. March 18, 1777, son of Caleb and Mary (Perkins) Thomson; m. OLIVE TARBOX. He was drowned May 19, 1806.

CHILDREN VI. GENERATION.

761. Ansel, b. —.
762. Albert, b. —.
763. Gaius, b. —.

266.

JONAH THOMPSON⁵ (Caleb,⁴ Caleb,³ Jacob,² John¹), b. April 23, 1779, son of Caleb and Mary (Perkins) Thomson; m.

PATIENCE CUSHMAN, dau. of Robert and Lucy (Thomas) Cushman of Hartland, Vt., b. March 11, 1782.

CHILDREN VI. GENERATION.

764. Ira, b. March 21, 1803; d. March, 1811, of spotted fever.
765. Robert Cushman, b. July 26, 1804; d. March, 1811, of spotted fever.
766. Mary Perkins, b. July 12, 1806; d. March, 1811, of spotted fever.
767. Lucia Ann, b. August 31, 1808; m. Rev. Benjamin Noyes, a Methodist minister. She d. August 18, 1831.
768. Polly Perkins, b. Oct 11, 1811; m. Richard Williams. Lived in Palmyra, Wis.
769. Ira Robert, b. May 18, 1814; m. Louisa Labaree of Hartland, Vt.
770. Lavina Thomas, b. —; m. Henry W. Hayes, a cabinet maker, of Palmyra, Wis.
771. Lucy Cushman, b. —.

271.

ALFRED THOMPSON[5] (Caleb,[4] Caleb,[3] Jacob,[2] John[1]), b. September 20, 1785, son of Caleb and Mary (Perkins) Thomson; m. FEAR THOMPSON (208). He d. February 10, 1841.

CHILDREN VI. GENERATION.

772. Amanda, b. Oct. 2, 1808; m. Martin Thompson (526).
773. Elbridge G., b. March 28, 1810; m. Nancy Spaulding; had a family; lived in Vermont; d. in the army.
774. Harriet, b. Jan. 13, 1812; m. (1) Asel Thomas, (2) Ruel Eaton.
775. Israel T., b. Feb. 6, 1814; m. Joanna Town.
776. Sabina, b. Jan. 26, 1816; m. James Leland, who d. —.
777. Lucy, b. May 9, 1818; d. —.
778. Eveline, b. Sept. 24, 1822; d. —.
779. Mary Eliza, b. Oct. 12, 1826; m. David Wilder.

275.

NATHANIEL THOMPSON[5] (Caleb,[4] Caleb,[3] Jacob,[2] John[1]), b. July 28, 1792, son of Caleb and Mary (Perkins) Thomson; m. SUSANNA FIELD.

CHILDREN VI. GENERATION.

780. Ambrose, b. —.
781. Mary P., b. —.

278.

FREDERICK MILLER THOMPSON[5] (Caleb,[4] Caleb,[3] Jacob,[2]
John[1]), b. June 20, 1797, in Middleboro', Mass., son of Caleb
and Mary (Perkins) Thomson ; m. September 8, 1819,
SUSANNA CHEESMAN of Braintree, Mass., b. January 31, 1796.
He d. August 21, 1880. She d. October 10, 1874.

CHILDREN VI. GENERATION.

782. Susanna, b. Sept. 15, 1820, in Braintree; d. July 16, 1821.
783. Infant daughter, b. June 22, 1822, in Braintree; d. June 22, 1822.
784. Sarah, b. June 17, 1823, in Braintree; m. John Wales.
785. Frederick M., b. May 9, 1825, in Braintree; d. Oct. 22, 1847,
    unmarried.
786. Charles Perkins, b. July 30, 1827, in Braintree; m. Abby Her-
    rick.
787. Caleb, b. Feb. 18, 1832, in Braintree; m. Sarah Jane Waite.
788. Elizabeth Moore, b. Dec. 10, 1838, in Braintree; unmarried.

280.

REUBEN THOMPSON[5] (Andrew,[4] Reuben,[3] Thomas,[2] John[1]),
b. May 9, 1768, son of Andrew and Judith (Noyes) Thomson;
m. 1791, EUNICE WHITMAN, dau. of Nicholas and Mary
(House) Whitman of Bridgewater. She d. 1837, in her 68th
year.

CHILDREN VI. GENERATION.

789. Andrew, b. July 24, 1791; m. Mercy Tilson.
790. Thomas, b. Feb. 7, 1793.
791. Reuben, b. Oct. 24, 1795; m. Sally Washburn.
792. Bela, b. March 28, 1798.
793. Clarissa, b. Nov. 7, 1800; m. Nathan Perkins.
794. Mary W., b. March 29, 1805; m. Jason Perkins. She d. March
    23, 1838.
795. Josiah, b. Sept. 10, 1807; d. April 27, 1838.

281.

ABEL THOMPSON[5] (Andrew,[4] Reuben,[3] Thomas,[2] John[1]), b.
July 15, 1770, son of Andrew and Judith (Noyes) Thomson;
m. ELIZABETH LEACH, dau. of John Leach. She d. January
9, 1841, in her 83d year.

CHILDREN VI. GENERATION.

796. Abigail, b. May 11, 1791; m. Harvey Kimball.
797. Giles, b. June 2, 1794; m. Fanny Waterman.
11

284.

NEHEMIAH THOMPSON[5] (Asa,[4] Thomas,[3] Thomas,[2] John[1]),
b. May 9, 1775, son of Asa and Rebecca (Campbell) Thomson;
m. EXPERIENCE CURTIS. He d. January 21, 1844. She d.
June 16, 1849, aged 74 years.

CHILDREN VI. GENERATION.

798. Phebe Waterman, b. Sept. 15, 1797; d. April 19, 1840; unmarried.
799. Dexter C., b. April 11, 1800; m. Harriet Bosworth.
800. Joshua C., b. Dec. 26, 1801; m. Lucy C. Weston.
801. Experience C., b. Feb. 16, 1806; m. Capt. George Waterman.
    She d. May, 1885.
802. Mary Morton, b. July 4, 1810; m. Ebenezer T. Soule.   She d.
    August 7, 1832.
803. Joan W., b. March 21, 1814; m. Benjamin W. Harlow.   No
    children. She d. 1888.

285.

ASA THOMPSON[5] (Asa.[4] Thomas,[3] Thomas,[2] John[1]), b. August 19, 1776, son of Asa and Rebecca (Campbell) Thomson;
m. HANNAH THOMPSON (245). He was a captain of a volunteer company. He d. February 21, 1862. She d. August 22,
1861.

CHILDREN VI. GENERATION.

804. Learned H., b. Sept. 24, 1807.
805. Stella, b. March 29, 1809.
806. Hannah Mitchell, b. Jan. 14, 1811; m. Ebenezer Wood, Jr.
    (Second wife.)
807. Ichabod, b. April 27, 1813; m. Lucy Standish.
808. Mahitabel, b. March 9, 1815.
809. Lucy C , b. Feb. 1, 1818; m. Ira Bailey.
810. Sarah W., b. June 13, 1820; m. Samuel B. Carver.
811. Rebecca L., b. August 2, 1826.

286.

ELIAB THOMPSON[5] (Asa,[4] Thomas,[3] Thomas,[2] John[1]), b.
December 8, 1778, son of Asa and Rebecca (Campbell) Thomson; m. SOPHIA THOMPSON (251). Settled in Indiana; d. of
small-pox March, 1818.

CHILDREN VI. GENERATION.

812. Sophia, b. April 17, 1804; m. John Moore.
813. Fidelia, b. —; m. Joab Bullard.

814. Rebecca, b. —; m. Samuel Olmsted.
815. Deborah, b. —.
816. Irena, b. —; m. Samuel Inglerite.
817. Elmira, b. —.
818. Eliab M., b. Feb. 21, 1816.
819. Ira W., b. 1818.

292.

SAMUEL HALL THOMPSON[5] (Loring,[4] Thomas,[3] Thomas,[2] John[1]), b. November 19, 1789, son of Loring and Elizabeth (Hall-Swinnerton) Thomson; m. MARY WRIGHT of Grantham, N. H. He enlisted in the late war—probably war of 1812.

CHILDREN VI. GENERATION.

820. Chloe Hall, b. —.
821. James Riley, b. —.
822. Mary Whitten, b. —.
823. Sarah Western, b. —.
824. Susan Emilie, b. —.
825. Caleb Loring, b. —.
826. Martha Elizabeth, b. —.

293.

SARAH HALL THOMPSON[5] (Loring,[4] Thomas,[3] Thomas,[2] John[1]), b. November 26, 1792, dau. of Loring and Elizabeth (Hall-Swinnerton) Thomson; m. JESSE TRACY of Plainfield, Conn.

CHILDREN VI. GENERATION.

827. Thomas Thompson, b. —.
828. Samuel Morey, b. —.
829. Timothy Nutting, b. —.
830. Elizabeth Quinton, b. —.
831. Lucy Stone, b. —.

294.

STEPHEN HALL THOMPSON[5] (Loring,[4] Thomas,[3] Thomas,[2] John[1]), b. October 26, 1795, in Cornish, N. H., son of Loring and Elizabeth (Hall-Swinnerton) Thomson; m. (1) June 5, 1816, SARAH ALLEN, b. September 1. 1799, dau. of John and Sarah Allen, son of William, son of William, son of Joseph, son of Ralph, son of GEORGE, the Emigrant of Lynn, 1636; m. (2) HANNAH C———. First wife d. July 16, 1836, at

Windsor, Vt.; second wife d. August 4, 1880, aged 77, in
North Charlestown, N. H. He d. August 11, 1880, in North
Charlestown.

CHILDREN BY FIRST WIFE VI. GENERATION.

832. Allen Dinsmore, b. October 26, 1817, in Cornish; m. Louisa
Bancroft; d. in Windsor, Vt.
833. Marshall Ellery, b. April 27, 1820, in Corydon; m. Hattie J.
Bemis.
834. Eliza J., b. Feb. 22, 1822, at Windsor, Vt.; m. (1) Oct. 21, 1840
John Reed, (2) Daniel Raymond. She d. August 3, 1878, at
Chelmsford.
835. Lafayette, b. May 14, 1824, at Windsor; m. Alice Clay in Boston.
836. Louisa P., b. May 20, 1826, in Windsor; d. June 27, 1839, in
Claremont.

CHILDREN BY SECOND WIFE VI. GENERATION.

837. Stephen, b. —.
838. James, b. —.

310.

JABEZ PRIOR THOMPSON[5] (Ebenezer,[4] Ebenezer,[3] Thomas,[2]
John[1]), b. January 15, 1787, son of Ebenezer and Deborah
(Prior) Thomson; m. SALLY BRIGGS, b. January 25, 1788,
dau. of Rev. Ephraim and Rebecca (Waterman) Briggs. He
was captain of a volunteer company; a representative in the
legislature of Massachusetts for the years 1831, 1834, 1835,
1836, and 1837, and a member of the senate in 1851. Also
held a commission as justice of the peace fifteen years; was
selectman of town of Halifax many years, and employed much
in settlement of estates of deceased persons. He d. August
10, 1852, aged 65. His wife d. September 5, 1857, aged 69.

CHILDREN VI. GENERATION.

839. Ephraim B., b. Nov. 11, 1813; m. Eliza R. Soule.
840. Deborah Prior, b. Feb., 1815; m. George Hart.
841. Edwin, b. —; d. young.

312.

ZEBADIAH THOMPSON[5] (Zebadiah,[4] Zebadiah,[3] Thomas,[2]
John[1]), b. May 16, 1784, at Halifax, son of Zebadiah and
Phebe (Curtis) Thomson; m. MARTHA BRIGGS, b. April 2,
1784, dau. of Ephraim and Rebecca (Waterman) Briggs. He
was a delegate to a constitutional convention in 1820, also

member of the legislature and justice of the peace. He d.
June 23, 1853, at Halifax. She d. May 31, 1844.

CHILDREN VI. GENERATION.

842. Clara S., b. Oct. 27, 1806; m. Rev. Thomas A. Spilman.
843. Clarinda Morton, b. Dec. 1, 1807; d. Feb. 8, 1810, aged 2 years
6 months.
844. Martha Briggs, b. Sept. 6, 1809; m. John B. Atwood.
845. John T. Z., b. Sept. 3, 1811; m. Sagie B. Tilden.
846. Rebecca Waterman, b. Oct. 3, 1813; d. Jan. 27, 1830.

316.

JOSEPH THOMPSON[5] (Joseph,[4] Joseph,[3] Peter,[2] John[1]), b.
April 28, 1763, son of Joseph and Jerusha (Wood) Thomson;
m. PRISCILLA RIPLEY. He d. December 30, 1808, aged 45.
She d. August 9, 1800, aged 30.

CHILD VI. GENERATION.

847. Priscilla, b. Sept. 18, 1797: m. James A. Bourne.

318.

TIMOTHY THOMPSON[5] (Joseph,[4] Joseph,[3] Peter,[2] John[1]), b.
January 29, 1769, son of Joseph and Jerusha (Wood) Thom-
son; m. SUSANNA CUSHING. He and his family moved to
Connecticut and there died.

CHILDREN VI. GENERATION.

848. Isabella C., b. Jan. 26, 1803.
849. Timothy, b. June 17, 1805.
850. Sarah C., b. August 18, 1807.
851. Joseph, b. Sept. 15, 1809.
852. Susanna, b. —.
853. Sofrona, b. —.
854. Columbus, b. —.

325.

WILLIAM THOMPSON[5] (John,[4] Joseph,[3] Peter,[2] John[1]), b. —,
son of John and Elizabeth (Bisbee) Thomson; m. BELINDA
REEVE, a relative of Topping Reeve of Litchfield, Conn., chief
justice of Connecticut. He lived in Kingsborough, N. Y.

CHILDREN VI. GENERATION.

855. Sarah, b. —; m. — Rowe. Removed to the Black River country, near east end of Lake Ontario; d. soon after.

856. William, b. —; went to the far West.
857. John, b. July 17, 1799, in Kingsborough; m. Ruth Bateman Johnson.
858. Abner, b. —; d. in Florida, N. Y.
859. Belinda, b. —; m. Aaron Smith.
860. Mary, b. —; lived in Ohio.
861. Eliza, b. —; m. Josiah Houghton; lived in Ohio.
862. David, b. —; lived in Ohio.

330.

ELIZABETH THOMPSON[5] (John,[4] Joseph,[3] Peter,[2] John[1]), b. —, dau. of John and Elizabeth (Bisbee) Thomson; m. PELTIAH SHEPARD of Kingsborough, N. Y. Removed to Wisconsin.

CHILDREN VI. GENERATION.

863. Elizabeth, b. —; un-m.; d. aged 30.
864. Stephen, b. July 26, 1800, at Kingsborough; m. Margaret C. Slow of Champion, N. Y.; left two children. He was a missionary printer in the Sandwich Islands, where he d. July 6, 1834.
865. John Bisbee, b. —; m. Rachel Willis; lived in Delevan, Wis.; had four or five children.

331.

LUCINDA THOMPSON[5] (John,[4] Joseph,[3] Peter,[2] John[1]), b. —, dau. of John and Elizabeth (Bisbee) Thomson; m. JACOB MEAD. Settled in Palatine, N. Y.

CHILDREN VI. GENERATION.

866. Isaac, b. —.
867. Charles, b. —.

SIXTH GENERATION.

334.

JOHN THOMPSON[6] (Thaddeus,[5] John,[4] John,[3] John,[2] John[1]), b. March 31, 1789, son of Thaddeus and Ruth (Tilson) Thompson; m. MARGARET ROBINSON. He d. September 17, 1876.

CHILDREN VII. GENERATION.

868. Deborah, b. March 28, 1809; m. Sylvanus R. Bosworth.
869. Hannah, b. April 8, 1811; m. Ephraim B. Gammon.
870. Ammiel, b. Feb. 12, 1815; m. (1) Harriet Holmes, (2) Lydia J. Thompson, (3) Martha A. Record.
871. Abigail Robinson, b. Dec. 19, 1818; m. America Bonney.
872. Lydia, b. Dec. 24, 1822; m. Thomas Bonney.
873. John, b. Nov. 28, 1827; m. Mahala J. A. Burnham.
874. Lumira, b. June 28, 1829.
875. William Hastings, b. August 1, 1833; m. Cornelia A. Fuller.

335.

AMMIEL THOMPSON[6] (Thaddeus,[5] John,[4] John,[3] John,[2] John[1]), b. April 18, 1791, son of Thaddeus and Ruth (Tilson) Thompson; m. (1) FEAR TILSON, dau. of Ephraim and Fear (Waterman) Tilson; m. (2) Feb., 1858, MRS. HANNAH PERKINS, b. March 1, 1792, dau. of Dea. Ichabod and Parthenia (Carter) Waterman, and widow of Orman Perkins. First wife d. April 17, 1855. He d. July 1, 1862, in East Abington.

CHILDREN BY FIRST WIFE VII. GENERATION.

876. Lucius, b. July 28, 1819; m. Lydia Ryder.
877. Ammiel, b. Dec. 13, 1825.
878. Edward Franklin, b. Sept. 4, 1827.

337.

THADDEUS THOMPSON[6] (Thaddeus,[5] John,[4] John,[3] John,[2] John[1]), b. July 16, 1795, son of Thaddeus and Ruth (Tilson) Thompson; m. DOLLY BISBEE.

CHILDREN VII. GENERATION.

879. Charles B., b. Jan. 25, 1824. Address, North Attleboro, Mass.
880. George W., b. August 10, 1825.
881. Harriet W., b. March 20, 1827.
882. Benjamin F., b. Jan. 28, 1837.
883. Leander G., b. March 2, 1838.
884. John Bisbee, b. May 13, 1840.

364.

ELIAB THOMPSON[6] (Eliab,[5] Peter,[4] Thomas,[3] John,[2] John[1]), b. February 22, 1795, son of Eliab and Rachel (Thompson) Thompson; m. (1) LAVINA WASHBURN, dau. of Salmon and Hannah (Orcut) Washburn, (2) LYDIA THOMPSON (503). He

d. February 24, 1834. His first wife d. April 3, 1824, aged 29. His widow m. Jacob Soule. She d. November, 1874.

CHILD BY FIRST WIFE VII. GENERATION.

885. Hannah W., b. 1820; d. March 30, 1841.

CHILDREN BY SECOND WIFE VII. GENERATION.

886. Edwin, b. June 23, 1829; m. Olive T. Pratt.
887. Asaph P., b. Jan. 2, 1832; m. (1) Lydia C. Atwood, (2) Betsey A. Baker.

371.

VENUS THOMPSON[6] (Thomas,[5] Francis,[4] Thomas,[3] John,[2] John[1]), b. May 18, 1796, son of Thomas and Wealthy (Whitmore) Thompson; m. JANE SOUTHWORTH. He d. January 24, 1875. She d. February 3, 1875.

CHILDREN VII. GENERATION.

888. Clarinda, b. Nov. 29, 1823; m. Lewis Thatcher.
889. Franklin S., b. Sept. 15, 1825; m. Lucy M. Putnam.
890. Venus, b. June 29, 1832; m. Georgie Sawin.

374.

PHILANDER THOMPSON[6] (Thomas,[5] Francis,[4] Thomas,[3] John,[2] John[1]), b. September 22, 1800, son of Thomas and Wealthy (Whitmore) Thompson; m. ELIZA GILES, b. January 5, 1813.

CHILDREN VII. GENERATION.

891. Angelina Frances, b. Sept. 12, 1835; m. Charles F. Cornish.
892. Henry Austin, b. March 16, 1837.
893. Mary Elizabeth, b. Feb. 4, 1839.
894. Philander Williams, b. Nov. 30, 1840; m. Lucy A. T. Cushman.
895. Charles L., b. July 7, 1842; m. Lillian Lines.
896. Anne E., b. May 17, 1844; m. Alfred Wood Thompson (907).
897. Catharine Lawton, b. Oct. 12, 1846; d. Sept. 9, 1847.
898. Ellen Whitmore, b. Oct. 13, 1847; m. Amasa Gray, Jr.

376.

THOMAS THOMPSON[6] (Thomas,[5] Francis,[4] Thomas,[3] John,[2] John[1]), b. February 25, 1805, son of Thomas and Wealthy (Whitmore) Thompson; m. REBECCA VOLUNTINE.

CHILDREN VII. GENERATION.

899. Voluntine, b. Sept. 20, 1840.
900. Anne B., b. 1841.

377.

ISRAEL WOOD THOMPSON[6] (Reuel,[5] Francis,[4] Thomas,[3] John,[2] John[1]), b. October 8, 1803, son of Reuel and Thankful (Wood) Thompson; m. (1) BETSEY W. PERKINS, (2) LYDIA LYON.

CHILDREN BY FIRST WIFE VII. GENERATION.

901. Leander, b. Dec., 1836; d. 1842.
902. Elvina W., b. Sept. 10, 1844; m. Wm. H. Bennett.

CHILDREN BY SECOND WIFE VII. GENERATION.

903. Allerton, } Twins,   { m. Ella Jones.
904. Arabella, } b. June 18, 1850; { m. Samuel S. Bourne.

378.

REUEL THOMPSON[6] (Reuel,[5] Francis,[4] Thomas,[3] John,[2] John[1]), b. September 21, 1806, son of Reuel and Thankful (Wood) Thompson; m. SARAH TINKHAM WOOD, b. May 11, 1811.

CHILDREN VII. GENERATION.

905. Sarah Jane, b. Sept. 15, 1840; d. Oct. 7, 1841.
906. Reuel Francis, b. August 20, 1842; m. Eliza Shaw.
907. Alfred Wood, b. March 19, 1844; m. Annie E. Thompson (896).
908. Leroy, b. Jan. 10, 1846.
909. Lucia Ann, b. July 20, 1847; m. Alanson Washburn.
910. Rhoda Ella Sparrow, b. Dec. 2, 1849; m. Albert J. Wood.
911. Sarah Evelyn, b. Nov. 24, 1851.

379.

IVORY HOVEY THOMPSON[6] (Reuel,[5] Francis,[4] Thomas,[3] John,[2] John[1]), b. April 1, 1808, son of Reuel and Thankful (Wood) Thompson; m. JERUSHA B. SPARROW. He d. November 3, 1887. She d. December 22, 1887.

CHILDREN VII. GENERATION.

912. Ivory B., b. October 14, 1836; d. August 10, 1866.
913. Jerusha Almeda, b. August, 1840; d. Sept. 16, 1842.
914. Francena, b. July 3, 1844; d. young.
915. Marcena, b. —; d. young.
916. Francena, b. —; d. young.

380.

PRISCILLA WOOD THOMPSON[6] (Reuel,[5] Francis,[4] Thomas, John,[2] John[1]), b. June 24, 1810, dau. of Reuel and Thankful (Wood) Thompson; m. HENRY C. LYON, son of Obadiah Lyon of Halifax. She d. July 19, 1850. He d. March 18, 1888.

CHILDREN VII. GENERATION.

917. Henry Clinton, b. May 17, 1838, in Halifax; m. Weltha Gilmore.
918. Celeste Molena, b. Oct. 2, 1840, in Bridgewater.
919. Algernon Sidney, b. October 3, 1843; m. Louisa Frances Copeland.
920. Priscilla, b. Jan. 9, 1850, in Bridgewater.

381.

BENJAMIN FRANKLIN THOMPSON[6] (Reuel,[5] Francis, Thomas,[3] John,[2] John[1]), b. —, son of Reuel and Thankful (Wood) Thompson; m. (1) SARAH WOOD, (2) MARY ABBY CARR.

CHILDREN BY FIRST WIFE VII. GENERATION.

921. Mandana A., b. July 2, 1843.
922. David W., b. Nov. 26, 1846; m. Clarissa B. Finney.

CHILD BY SECOND WIFE VII. GENERATION.

923. Benjamin F., b. July 28, 1861.

382.

MARTSON THOMPSON[6] (Reuel,[5] Francis,[4] Thomas,[3] John,[2] John[1]), b. September 23, 1812, son of Reuel and Thankful (Wood) Thompson; m. (1) HARRIET G. W. BUMPUS, (2) November, 1844, MARY ANN WILBUR, (3) MARY ANDERSON. First wife d. May 7, 1842; second wife d. November, 1851.

CHILD BY FIRST WIFE VII. GENERATION.

924. Harriet M. V., b. Sept., 1839.

CHILDREN BY SECOND WIFE VII. GENERATION.

925. Herbert M., b. May 26, 1847; m. Sept. 3, 1879, Addie R. Thomas.
926. Horace G., b. June 8, 1850; m. Dec. 25, 1881, Annie E. Staples.

CHILDREN BY THIRD WIFE VII. GENERATION.

927. Miner, b. —.
928. Reuel, b. —.
929. Everett, b. —.

(383 *see* 639.)

384.

MARY FRANCES THOMPSON[6] (Reuel,[5] Francis,[4] Thomas,[3] John,[2] John[1]), b. April 26, 1817, dau. of Reuel and Thankful (Wood) Thompson; m. CYRUS FULLER, son of Cyrus Fuller of Halifax.

CHILDREN VII. GENERATION.

930. Mary Ann, b. Sept. 1, 1842; m. Obed Ripley of Kingston. She d. March 28, 1878.
931. Laura Frances, b. Feb. 24, 1845.

385.

SARAH PHINNEY[6] (Sarah,[5] Nathan,[4] Thomas,[3] John,[2] John[1]), b. January 1, 1781, dau. of John and Sarah (Thompson) Finney; m. March 13, 1806, ISAAC BABBITT, b. September 1, 1781. She d. March 17, 1844. He d. February 8, 1858.

CHILDREN VII. GENERATION.

932. Isaac Thompson, b. December 21, 1806; m. Ann Packard.
933. Irene Adeline, b. April 30, 1809; m. Cyrus Lovell.
934. Harrison Willard, b. March 31, 1812; m. Marilla T. Converse.
935. Pliny Henry, b. June, 1818; m. Lydia Perry.
936. Charles Albert, b. 1821; m. (1) May 15, 1845, Charlotte Eaton, (2) Cornelia Crosby. He dropped the name Babbitt, calling himself Charles Albert. Lived in Jamestown, N. Y.

386.

JOHN PHINNEY[6] (Sarah,[5] Nathan,[4] Thomas,[3] John,[2] John[1]), b. September 8, 1783, son of John and Sarah (Thompson) Finney; m. —. Lived in Middleboro, Mass.

CHILDREN VII. GENERATION.

937. John, b. —.
938. Sylvanus, b. —.

387.

ZERUAH PHINNEY[6] (Sarah,[5] Nathan,[4] Thomas,[3] John,[2] John[1]), b. December 15, 1784, dau. of John and Sarah (Thompson) Finney ; m. EBENEZER PACKARD. Lived in Winthrop, Maine. She d. May 20, 1871.

CHILDREN VII. GENERATION.

939. Ebenezer, b. —; m. —. Lived in Winthrop, Maine.
940. Charles, b. —.
941. Albert, b. —.
942. Ann, b. —.
943. Daughter, b. —; m. — Parlin.

390.

WOODWARD TUCKER⁶ (Susannah,⁵ Nathan,⁴ Thomas,³ John,²
John¹), b. September 8, 1786, son of Daniel and Susannah
(Thompson) Tucker; m. ELIZABETH CRESSY. He d. July
4, 1857.

CHILDREN VII. GENERATION.

944. Elizabeth Woodward, b. April 14, 1837; d. Dec. 13, 1858.
945. Nathan Thompson, b. Oct. 20, 1839; d. Nov. 18, 1864.
946. Nancy Sophia, b. March 10, 1842.
947. Susan Hadassah, b. March 28, 1844; m. John W. Pickett.
948. Mary Bachelder, b. Nov. 6, 1847; d. August 12, 1864.

413.

RUEL RUGGLES⁶ (Phebe,⁵ James,⁴ Thomas,³ John,² John¹),
b. October 19, 1808, in Hampton, N. Y., son of Denison and
Phebe (Thompson) Ruggles; m. CELESTA PERKINS, b. January 20, 1811, in New Haven, Conn. Address Fort Edward,
N. Y.

CHILDREN VII. GENERATION.

949. Chancey Allen, b. Nov. 18, 1833, in Hampton, N. Y.; d. March
21, 1834.
950. Phebe Abigail, b. April 7, 1835, in Hampton. N. Y.
951. Julia Charlotte, b. May 1, 1837, in Hampton, N. Y.
952. Amelia Augusta, b. March 13, 1842, in Hampton, N. Y.; m.
Sept. 18, 1867, Rollin B. Jones of Rutland, Vt.; they have dau.
b. May 30, 1868, and son b. March 5, 1877.
953. Edson Delos, b. Sept. 3, 1844, in Hampton; m. Nov., 1871, Anna
Case of Maine; have two sons, born, respectively, July, 1872,
and June, 1877.

415.

ANSEL ESTEE⁶ (Abigail,⁵ James,⁴ Thomas,³ John,² John¹),
b. February 7, 1793, son of Stephen and Abigail (Thompson)
Estee; m. October 12, 1819, OLIVE TYLER, b. May 22, 1794.

CHILD VII. GENERATION.

954. James T., b. March 11, 1821; m. Martha Tefft. See 164.

424.

ELVIRA THOMPSON[6] (Cyrus,[5] James,[4] Thomas,[3] John,[2] John[1]), b. October 1, 1801, in Brookfield, Mass., dau. of Cyrus and Polly (Waterman) Thompson; m. January 29, 1827, in Verona, JOSEPH ROOT, b. March 12, 1801. She d. November 25, 1864, in Clarendon, Orleans county, N. Y. He d. June 13, 1871, in Clarendon.

CHILDREN VII. GENERATION.

955. Joseph Sidney, b. Dec. 5, 1828, in Verona; d. Feb. 11, 1835.
956. William Clark, b. August 17, 1831; m. Mary A. Williams.
957. Lucy E., b. Feb. 9, 1835; m. (1) George W. Clark, (2) N. Atwell.
958. Mary Eusebia, b. July 5, 1841; m. Chauncey Burnham.
959. Daniel Thompson, b. Sept. 19, 1844; m. Ettie Reynolds.

425.

CYRUS THOMPSON[6] (Cyrus,[5] James,[4] Thomas,[3] John,[2] John[1]), b. May 23, 1803, in Verona, N. Y., son of Cyrus and Polly (Waterman) Thompson; m. March 23, 1830, CHARLOTTE HAMLIN MEAD, b. February 27, 1811, dau. of Samuel L. Mead of Litchfield, Conn., and Aurora (Norton) Mead of Roxbury, Conn.; m. January 30, 1806. Samuel L., b. November 13, 1783; d. February 13, 1868. Aurora, his wife, b. January 30, 1785; d. February 27, 1876.

Cyrus resided in Verona till 1832, when he removed to Le Roy, Genesee county, N. Y., where he remained till 1846; then he removed to the farm in Carlton, N. Y.

He was educated in the common schools of Oneida county and at Hamilton academy, and read law for two years with Jenkins & Hinman at Vernon, but was obliged to relinquish the profession on account of temporary failure of health. In the earlier years of his manhood he was very much interested in the subject of education, and taught twenty terms of district school, besides teaching English grammar by lectures several years when not otherwise engaged in teaching, and was one of the town inspectors of schools both in Oneida and Genesee counties, and town superintendent of schools for one or two terms after taking up his residence in Carlton. He was also a justice of the peace for many years, both in Genesee and Orleans counties.

He was editor and proprietor of the LeRoy Gazette during the years 1839 and 1840, and became warmly attached to the editorial profession, but very much to his regret, was compelled to abandon it in consequence of the business failures of others, and losses which he sustained by reason thereof, and start life anew on the then uncleared and unimproved farm in Carlton, where he spent the last forty years of his long and useful life.

He was a pioneer in the anti-slavery cause, and a delegate from Genesee county to the first anti-slavery state convention, held at Utica, where the convention was broken up by a mob —the members rotten egged out of the city, and compelled to adjourn to, and re-organize at Peterboro, under the protection of Gerrit Smith, who had educated his people to a degree of toleration which enabled them to endure even the then hated abolitionists. He rejoiced that he lived to see the institution of slavery uprooted and annihilated, even though at so great a cost of treasure and life as it involved.

He was honest and upright in all his transactions with his fellow men, a kind husband and indulgent father. A great reader and thinker, he taught his children far more than they ever learned in the schools, and they, though themselves advanced in years and mostly gone out from the old roof tree, will greatly miss the wisdom and instruction which, till sealed by the death stroke which came upon them, ever fell from his lips.

He died at his residence in Carlton, April 24, 1886, of disease of the heart and paralysis, in the eighty-third year of his age.

His funeral took place at his late home, conducted by the Rev. N. Foster Brown, and the large concourse in attendance as well as the words of the preacher, attested the respect in which he was held by his long-time neighbors and friends.

With him, earthly toil and cares have ceased, and the new life in which he so firmly believed, has begun. Loving, grateful hearts appreciate his life labors, and cherish his memory.

His wife d. March 14, 1888, in Carlton, aged 77. Her funeral was conducted by Rev. N. Foster Brown, assisted by Rev. Mr. Strasenberg.

Equable in disposition, faithful to duty, kindly and true to her friends, devoted to her family and self sacrificing always,

> "None knew her but to love her,
> None named her but to praise."

Years will come and go ere the fragrance of her memory will vanish from the hearts of her neighbors and friends, and her children with their latest breath "will rise up and call her blessed."

CHILDREN VII. GENERATION.

960. Irving Mead, b. March 15, 1831; m. Melissa Warner.
961. Mary Aurora, b. April 14, 1833; m. Emery H. Simpson.
962. Martha M., b. Feb. 12, 1835; m. Mather P. Godfrey. Address Carlton, N. Y.
963. Lloyd Garrison, b. Feb. 5, 1837; m. (1) Mary L. Thompson (1006) (2) Ellen Easter.
964. Ellen E., b. Dec. 16, 1838; m. Edward Mosher.
965. Wendell Daniel, b. March 6, 1842; d. June 11, 1853; run over by a land roller.
966. Cyrus Samuel, b. April 8, 1845; d. August 4, 1849.
967. Edwin Delos, b. Feb. 10, 1849.
968. Carrie Waterman, b. Sept. 16, 1854; m. Charles Bronson.

426.

LUCY THOMPSON[6] (Cyrus,[5] James,[4] Thomas,[3] John,[2] John[1]), b. January 21, 1805, in Verona, dau. of Cyrus and Polly (Waterman) Thompson; m. March 10, 1832, LUMAN STEVENS. Lived for many years on a farm in Manchester, Washtenaw county, Mich. Were members of Baptist church. She d. about 1850, on her knees at family worship. He d. about 1870.

CHILDREN VII. GENERATION.

969. Thomas, b. —; m. Zilpha ———.
970. Cyrus Thompson, b. about 1837; d. Feb. 11, 1880, in Manchester.

427.

MARTHA THOMPSON[6] (Cyrus,[5] James,[4] Thomas,[3] John,[2] John[1]), b. September 30, 1806, in Verona, dau. of Cyrus and Polly (Waterman) Thompson; m. October 24, 1829, ARZA BROWN, b. December 22, 1803, in Salem, N. Y. He d. August 13, 1843. She lived for some years at Pearl Creek, Wyoming county, N. Y. About 1852 she m. PAUL B. HUTCHINSON and removed to Orangeville. This union proving uncongenial, a separation took place, she removing to Warsaw, N. Y. Later she moved to LeRoy, Genesee county, N. Y., where she d. October 23, 1882. She lived a faithful Christian life—Baptist.

CHILDREN BY FIRST HUSBAND VII. GENERATION.

971. Emma, b. July 30, 1833, in Salem, N. Y.; m. August 23, 1876,.
      Reuben Glass, in LeRoy, N. Y.
972. Cyrus T., b. Sept. 19, 1835, in Salem, N. Y.; was a carriage
      trimmer; became insane; d. August 15, 1876, in LeRoy, N. Y.
973. Eusebia M., b. March 20, 1841, in Pavilion Center, N. Y.

428.

THEOPHILUS WATERMAN THOMPSON[6] (Cyrus,[5] James,[4]
Thomas,[3] John,[2] John[1]), b. October 29, 1808, in Verona, son
of Cyrus and Polly (Waterman) Thompson; m. April 25,
1839, RUTH MARIA WATKINS, b. February 6, 1819, dau. of
Royal and Sarah (Carpenter) Watkins of Walpole, N. H.,
and grand dau. of Benjamin and Ruth (Howard) Carpenter
of Keene, N. H.   Prior to 1850 Waterman, as he was usually
called, removed to Michigan, settled on a farm near Brooklyn,.
Jackson county, where he lived until his death.   Industrious,
energetic and successful in business, acquiring a valuable
property; a prominent and valuable man in the township and
a leading member of the Presbyterian church.   He d. October
3, 1887.   His wife d. February 2, 1888.

CHILDREN VII. GENERATION.

974. Lucius Freeman, b. August 16, 1843, m. Theresa M. Minton.
975. Edwin Clarence, b. Sept. 6, 1851; m. August 19, 1875, Hattie P.
      Murdock of Dexter, Mich.   He is a prominent and successful
      school teacher; was superintendent of schools in Albion,
      Mich., for some years; at present (1890) superintendent of
      schools in Saginaw, Mich.; publisher of Morning Exercises for
      Public Schools.

429.

EDWIN ALLEN THOMPSON[6] (Cyrus,[5] James,[4] Thomas,[3] John,[2]
John[1]), b. February 2, 1811, in Verona, son of Cyrus and Polly
(Waterman) Thompson; m. August 20, 1834, JULIA ANN
SUTTON, b. August 4, 1812, in Pompey, N. Y., dau. of Ros-
well Sutton of Vermont, b. February 22, 1773.   Removing to
Western New York, he lived for a time in Pavilion, Wyoming,
LeRoy, Clarendon and Farewell's Mills.   In the fall of 1845
he with his family moved to Michigan, making Paw Paw, Van
Buren county, his home until 1857, except a year or so spent
in Berrien county.   From 1849 to 1855 he was foreman in the
boot and shoe manufacturing establishment of A. Sherman &

Co. In his early manhood he was profoundly impressed with the enormity of the crime of human slavery, and very naturally espoused the anti-slavery cause. He rejoiced at the events that brought about a political revolution in Michigan in 1854, and contributed not a little with tongue and pen to bring about that result. He was elected in that year register of deeds of Van Buren county, which office he filled two years, when he was appointed deputy secretary of state by John McKinney, which position he held for four years, serving during the last term of Mr. McKinney and the first term of Hon. Nelson G. Isbell. His family removed to Lansing during his stay there. Retiring from the secretary of state's office, he held a clerkship in the auditor general's office for nearly four years, and until, at the earnest solicitation of Hon. E. J. House, then assessor of internal revenue, he with his family returned to Paw Paw and accepted the office of assistant assessor of internal revenue for Van Buren county, in which position he continued for several years. Was partner with Mr. A. H. Herron in a claim agency for a few years. At the republican state convention in 1866, he was quite a prominent candidate for the office of secretary of state; and was enrolling clerk of the house of representatives of Michigan during the session of 1869, following which and for about two years he filled a clerkship in the census bureau at Washington; this practically ended his public life. He was never found wanting in ability, or in any of those elements that go to make up a popular and efficient public officer. He was never a policy man. In all his dealings he was honest and faithful to his convictions of right.

Though not a member of any Christian society, he was a man of deep religious convictions, and of high moral attainments, and sought to live a life void of offense to God and man. He gave liberally for the support of the gospel, and for several years was one of the trustees of the Methodist Episcopal church in Paw Paw. Amid the trials and afflictions of this life he manifested a firm trust in God. When his soul was well nigh overwhelmed, he was wont to repeat that matchless poem of Whittier's, entitled "Eternal Goodness." Intellectually he was far above the average, and could he have had in early life that thorough education which was the ambition of his life to give to his children, he might have held high rank in the field of letters. He had a wonderful memory; he loved the companionship of our standard poets, and had a large portion of the writings of Scott, Whittier and others at

13

his tongue's end, some of which he has been known to recall and repeat though he had not seen them for twenty or thirty years. He was afflicted with paralysis the last few years of his life. His end was peaceful; without a struggle he passed to the better land. He d. January 10, 1883; his wife d. July 7, 1885; both buried in Paw Paw.

CHILDREN VII. GENERATION.

976. Bryant Sutton, b. August 20, 1835, in Pavilion, N. Y.; d. June 3, 1848, at St. Joseph, Mich.

977. Ellen Elizabeth, b. July 19, 1837, in Pavilion, N. Y., d. August 28, 1838, at Wyoming, N. Y.

978. Frances Ellen, b. July 11, 1839, in Wyoming, N. Y. Studied for three years at Oberlin College; an excellent school teacher; taught for many years in Paw Paw, Mich., and Indianapolis, Ind.; later went to Pasadena, California.

979. Celia Maria, b. June 27, 1841, in LeRoy, N. Y. She was a genius in writing poetry; wrote many short poems of merit. Taught a district school in Windsor, Eaton county, Mich.; also taught a while among the Indians of Isabella county; d. Sept. 22, 1863, in Lansing, Mich.

980. Herrick Adelbert, b. Sept. 10, 1844; d. Feb. 22, 1854, in Paw Paw.

981. Edwin Warren, b. June 3, 1848; m. August 27, 1871, May Wright, dau. of Philander Wright of Massachusetts. He was a fine student and school teacher; taught some in Michigan, also held high position as a teacher in Indianapolis, Ind.; held a diploma from Hillsdale College, Mich.; d. August 19, 1875, of consumption, in North Carolina.

982. Carrie Bell, b. March 24, 1855. Graduated at Paw Paw high school; also studied a while at state normal school at Oswego, N. Y.; a good school teacher; went to Pasadena, California.

430.

NATHAN THOMPSON[6] (Cyrus,[5] James,[4] Thomas,[3] John,[2] John[1]), b. June 1, 1813, in Verona, son of Cyrus and Polly (Waterman) Thompson; m. January 31, 1838, at Pavilion, N. Y., CLARISSA ELMER HUTCHINSON, b. April 22, 1817, in Western, Oneida county, N. Y., dau. of Dr. Zenas Hutchinson. He learned the wagon-maker's trade and worked some time for Warren Tompkins at Pavilion; then lived a short time on a farm in Clarendon, Orleans county; later put a little property into the "Fourrier Society," and with his family moved to a place in Clarkson, near Lake Ontario, called the "Domain." Becoming dissatisfied with this plan of living and business, he

returned with his family to Clarendon, lived awhile at Morgan-
ville, later in Albion, working at wagon making for a Mr.
Dana; from here he went to Farewell's Mills, near Clarendon.
From here, in 1845, he removed to Jackson county, Mich.,
living awhile at his brother Waterman's. He soon moved
to Jefferson and worked at his trade for a Mr. Pickett; again
moved to Brooklyn, working for a Mr. Stanley; after shaking
with fever and ague for about two years, he returned to New
York, engaging work of a Mr. Crittenden, near Wyoming;
remaining here a year or two, he removed to Warsaw, where
he found work in the wagon shop of C. T. and T. H. Buxton.
About 1850 he bought, on credit, a farm of eighty acres of Mr.
Allen Redish in East Orangeville. After about four years the
farm was sold and he returned to Warsaw. In 1856 he removed
to Berlin Heights, Ohio, near his cousin, Jason K. Thompson,
and in the same year went to Van Buren county, Mich., staying at Paw Paw with his brother Edwin. In the fall of 1856
he bought a farm of eighty acres in the town of Keeler of Mr.
S. S. Abbott, hoping in this then new country to make a home
for himself and family, and in this he succeeded, for the farm
has continued in the family since then.

He was an industrious and skillful mechanic, a man of san-
guine temperament, cheerful in every trial or perplexity,
always hoping for the best, a kind husband and indulgent
father, his memory will long be cherished by those who knew
him. He was a firm believer in the Christian religion and for
about forty years had been a member of the Methodist Episcopal church. He d. February 7, 1877, in Lansing, Mich.;
buried in Keeler. His wife was a faithful and industrious
helpmeet, kind and willing, never weary of helping those who
needed assistance, never thinking of self if she could do a
kindness for others, a true and faithful mother, ever striving
to bring up her children in right paths. For about fifty years
she lived a Christian life, a member of the M. E. church.
She d. March 29, 1885, in Keelersville, Mich.

CHILDREN VII. GENERATION.

983. Charles Hutchinson, b. Nov. 29, 1838, in LeRoy, N. Y.; m.
Elizabeth Giles Sutton.
984. Albert Cyrus, b. Oct. 24, 1840, in LeRoy, N. Y. He left western
New York in 1856; came to Michigan with his father. Sept.
23, 1861, he enlisted in Co. F, Birge's sharpshooters, afterwards
known as Co. D, 66th Ill. Inf., or Western Sharpshooters;
after being in the service about a year and a half he was

made first sergeant. He was in the battles of Fort Donelson, Shiloh, siege of and second battle of Corinth; was also in several engagements in the Sherman campaign in Georgia, in one of which, the battle near Dallas, he was captured and taken to the prison at Andersonville, where he stayed three months, when he was removed to Charleston and later to Florence, S. C.; at this place he was held for nearly three months more; while here he came near dying from starvation and exposure. Dec. 23, 1864, a mere skeleton, he was paroled and returned to Michigan. Was discharged Feb. 11, 1865, having served a few months over his term of enlistment. After passing a few months in school, he secured a position as teacher in the State Reform School at Lansing, where he remained two years; after this he studied a year or more in Albion College, then worked a few years on a farm with his father and brothers. In the spring of 1875, returned to the Reform School as a teacher, where he has remained until this time (1890.) Bold and independent, ready to approve the right and condemn the wrong, nothing would swerve him from what he believed to be his line of duty. Fearless on the battle field he would take his chance of life or death with the foremost, trusting fully in an overruling providence. He regarded the Christian religion a never failing source of help in times of danger or hardship in the army or in prison. He has been a member of the Methodist Episcopal church since 1856.

985. Geraldine, b. August, 1843, in Clarendon; d. Jan. 18, 1844, in Clarendon.

986. Edwin Arthur, b. June 20, 1847, in Brooklyn, Mich. Became insane and in 1880 was taken to Michigan Asylum for Insane at Kalamazoo.

987. Nathan I., b. August 1, 1850, in Warsaw, N. Y.; m. Ella Aida Tuttle.

988. Frank Zenas, b. June 6, 1853, in Orangeville, N. Y.; a thorough and energetic man.

989. Sarah Cornelia, b. Nov. 16, 1855, in Warsaw; d. Oct. 12, 1856, in Kinderhook, Mich.; buried in Paw Paw, Mich.

990. Clara Gertrude, b. August 25, 1858, in Keeler, Mich.; m. William E. Bass.

431.

DANIEL WEST THOMPSON[6] (Cyrus,[5] James,[4] Thomas,[3] John,[2] John[1]), b. March 13, 1815, in Verona, son of Cyrus and Polly (Waterman) Thompson; m. September 5, 1837, in LeRoy, by Rev. Gideon Osborn, LYDIA JONES, b. March 5, 1817, in LeRoy, dau. of Silas Jones, b. December 13, 1778. Daniel d.

January 11, 1841, in South LeRoy. She d. September 29, 1888.

CHILDREN VII. GENERATION.

991. Elizabeth Permelia, b. Jan. 27, 1839, in LeRoy, N. Y. Removed to York, Washtenaw county, Mich. The widow of Daniel m. May 6, 1847, in Saline, Mich., Ebenezer Brown Conde, b. Feb. 1, 1810, in Charlton, Saratoga county, N. Y. He d. April 27, 1869, in Saline. Their children were:

Susan Louisa, b. July 21, 1848; m. July 3, 1871, Walter M. Culver, and had Alva Roy, b. 1875, and Fred Arthur, b. May, 1879.

Ellen Eusebia, b. Nov. 12, 1850; m. Dec. 23, 1875, Hiram D. McBride, and had Adna K., b. May, 1880.

Arthur Daniel, b. August 28, 1856.

432.

MARY THOMPSON[6] (Cyrus,[5] James,[4] Thomas,[3] John,[2] John[1]), b. May 20, 1817, in Verona, dau. of Cyrus and Polly (Waterman) Thompson; m. (1) January, 1844, HARVEY ROOT, br. of Joseph; (2) ABELL WOODHULL, whose ancestor's name formerly was Flanders, but attaining to the baronetcy of Woodhull, England, retained the latter name. They left England in the reign of Queen Anne. Her first husband d. about 1849. She lives now (1889) in Oak Orchard, N. Y.

CHILDREN BY FIRST HUSBAND VII. GENERATION.

992. Cyrus, b. Jan. 23, 1845, in Clarendon. Enlisted in Orleans Battery for service in the war of the rebellion; d. April 12, 1864, at Alexandria, Va., before reaching his regiment.

993. Adelbert, b. Jan. 5, 1847, in Carlton, N. Y. Scalpers induced him to enlist, was taken prisoner, and the last heard of him he was in Danville prison in 1864.

CHILDREN BY SECOND HUSBAND VII. GENERATION.

994. Wendell Thompson, b. Nov. 20, 1855.
995. Eugene Nathan, b. Nov. 14, 1857; d. Nov. 5, 1885.
996. Edwin E.,   ⎱ Twins,
997. Ellen Eusebia, ⎰ b. Jan. 26, 1861.

435.

JASON K. THOMPSON[6] (Bela,[5] James,[4] Thomas,[3] John,[2] John[1]), b. February 18, 1808, in Poultney, Vt., son of Bela and Diadamia (Kellogg) Thompson; m. January 2, 1830, by

Rev. Mr. Cochrane, ELIZA ANN FRISBIE of Poultney, Vt., b.
March 17, 1808. Lived at Berlin Heights, O. She d. February 23, 1875. He d. July 7, 1885.

CHILDREN VII. GENERATION.

998. James D., b. Jan. 7, 1832; m. Marion E. Webster.
999. Emily, b. Oct. 16, 1834; m. Nov. 18, 1851, Norman Allen. She d. July 2, 1853.
1000. Franklin D., b. Dec. 13, 1835; m. Abby N. Price.
1001. Frederick F., b. Sept. 18, 1838; m. Georgia Price, sister of Abby.
1002. Amos Francis, b. March 10, 1844; m. Clara Daniels.

436.

JAMES ALLEN THOMPSON[6] (Bela,[5] James,[4] Thomas,[3] John,[2] John[1]), b. April 13, 1810, in Hampton, N. Y., son of Bela and Diadamia (Kellogg) Thompson; m. October 18, 1838, by Rev. Mr. Haines of Perry, N. Y., EUNICE ANN BENEDICT, b. November 12, 1818. He d. January 30, 1866.

CHILDREN VII. GENERATION.

1003. Ellen Amelia, b. May 20, 1840; m. Albert Strong.
1004. Celia Benedict, b June 5, 1843; m. (1) Albert Strong, (2) David Powell.
1005. Irving Graham, b. Jan. 29, 1845; m. Martha E. Butler.

437.

BELA DEWEY THOMPSON[6] (Bela,[5] James,[4] Thomas,[3] John,[2] John[1]), b. March 16, 1812, in Hampton, N. Y., son of Bela and Diadamia (Kellogg) Thompson; m. October 2, 1836, by Rev. Mr. Osborn at LeRoy, N. Y., CHARLOTTE OLIVIA SUTTON, b. 1817, in Pompey, N. Y., dau. of Roswell Sutton. He was a student three years at Oberlin College, and taught school fifteen or twenty years. His wife also taught school. They lived awhile in Ohio and later in Paw Paw, Mich. He d. November 24, 1878. The widow removed to Kalamazoo, Mich., and subsequently to California, with her daughters, Julia and Josephine.

CHILDREN VII. GENERATION.

1006. Mary Lucretia, b. March 31, 1839; m. Lloyd G. Thompson (963).
1007. Herrick Adelbert, b. Nov. 13, 1841; d. Feb. 13, 1842.
1008. Julia Lettice, b. April 10, 1844; m. Albert B. Thompson (1018); he d. Nov. 30, 1872.

1009. Josephine Cutler, b. May 30, 1848.
1010. Bela Dewey, b. Nov. 23, 1850. Killed March 2, 1881, by a log rolling on him.
1011. Lottie Minniehaha, b. June 7, 1857; m. Oct., 1883, William Buckley. Has a son b. —, 1890. Address, Paw Paw.

439.

HARRIET MARIAM THOMPSON[6] (Bela,[5] James,[4] Thomas,[3] John,[2] John[1]), b. September 14, 1815, dau. of Bela and Diadamia (Kellogg) Thompson; m. February, 1836, by Rev. Mr. Scovel, JOHN PAINE of Covington, N. Y. Address, Covington, N. Y.

CHILDREN VII. GENERATION.

1012. Olimena L., b. May 31, 1832; m. Jan. 20, 1874, Albert Sprague.
1013. Curtis A., b. Jan. 6, 1845; m. Nov. 28, 1867, Mary A. Tompkins.
1014. Clinton T., b. Feb. 19, 1847; d. Oct. 6, 1864.
1015. Cornelia L., b. April 11, 1849; d. Feb. 2, 1867.

440.

LUCINDA THOMPSON[6] (Bela,[5] James.[4] Thomas,[3] John,[2] John[1]), b. June 2, 1818, dau. of Bela and Diadamia (Kellogg) Thompson; m. December 26, 1837, by Rev. Mr. Bridgman, SETH W. PAINE of Covington, N. Y. She d. December 4, 1862.

CHILD VII. GENERATION.

1016. Lyman T., b. Oct. 13, 1838; m. July 10, 1859, Nellie Beal; he d. July 16, 1865.

441.

DENNIS ROCKWELL THOMPSON[6] (Bela,[5] James,[4] Thomas,[3] John,[2] John[1]), b. October 24, 1820, son of Bela and Diadamia (Kellogg) Thompson; m. May 1, 1843, by Rev. Mr. Preston, MARIA H. KNIGHT of Attica, N. Y. Lived in Oconomowoc, Wis. He d. January 6, 1882.

CHILDREN VII. GENERATION.

1017. Arthur Dewitt, b. May 25, 1844; d. Sept. 1859.
1018. Albert B., b. March 25, 1846; m. June, 1872, Julia Lettice Thompson (1008); he d. Nov. 30, 1872.
1019. Ernest D. R., b. June 18, 1857; m. Carrie L. Streeter.

1020.   Carrie Lucinda, b. May 7, 1866; m. June 10, 1888, Frank D. Merwin.   Lives in Somonauk, Ill.

442.

MARTHA THOMPSON[6] (Bela,[5] James,[4] Thomas,[3] John,[2] John[1]), b. September 22, 1823, dau. of Bela and Diadamia (Kellogg) Thompson; m. HEMAN R. DEWEY.   She d. April 6, 1865.

• CHILDREN VII. GENERATION.

1021.   Ida, b. —.
1022.   Charles, b. —.
1023.   May, b. —.
1024.   Bela, b. —.
        Four more children d. in infancy.

443.

DIADAMIA THOMPSON[6] (Bela,[5] James,[4] Thomas,[3] John,[2] John[1]), b. April 23, 1826, dau. of Bela and Diadamia (Kellogg) Thompson; m. April 23, 1846, by Rev. Mr. Kidder of Attica, (1) DEXTER C. JOHNSON of Orangeville, N. Y ; m. (2) August 6, 1870, MATTHEW MOREHOUSE.   First husband d. July 3, 1866, in Fenton, Mich., aged 41.   Second husband d. November 9, 1885, at Holly, Mich.   In 1847 she moved west, spent a few months in Wisconsin, afterwards locating in Fenton, Mich. In 1852 she moved to Berlin Heights, O., and in 1858 to Lawrence, Ind.   In 1862 she returned to Fenton.   She d. February 8, 1888, in Holly, and was buried in Oakwood Cemetery, Fenton, Mich.   She was a life-long earnest christian woman, having united with the Congregational church before her first marriage.

CHILDREN BY FIRST HUSBAND VII. GENERATION.

1025.   Burdette Loren, b. Oct. 22, 1849; m. Jannett McMillan.
1026.   Herbert Raymond, b. Sept. 11, 1857, in Berlin Heights, O.; m. Oct. 3, 1885, Ida Hoffman.

449.

JAMES BLOWERS[6] (Belinda,[5] James,[4] Thomas,[3] John,[2] John[1]), b. April 12, 1816, in Greenwich, N. Y., son of Abiather and Belinda (Thompson) Blowers; m. MATILDA MYERS in Ohio. Later he lived in Michigan.

CHILDREN VII. GENERATION.

1027.   Ellen, b. 1848.
1028.   Phebe, b. —.

1029. Marion, b. —.
1030. Augusta, b. —.
1031. Eugene, b. —.
1032. Jerome, b. —.

455.

CAROLINE THOMPSON[6] (Nathan,[5] James,[4] Thomas,[3] John,[2] John[1]), b. May 5, 1811, in Poultney, Vt., dau. of Nathan and Phebe Ellis (?) (Blowers) Thompson; m. August 25, 1831, DANIEL HEATH, b. June 17, 1809, in Washington county, N. Y. He d. November 18, 1885. She d. May 21, 1872.

CHILDREN VII. GENERATION.

1033. William A., b. Jan. 4, 1833; m. Phebe Ayres in Manchester, Mich.
1034. Mary J., b. August 31, 1835; m. Atilla G. Wilson.
1035. Nathan T., b. Oct. 1, 1836; m. Mari White.
1036. Amarilla O., b. March 14, 1838; m. Wellington C. Page.
1037. Daniel F., b. Jan. 2, 1855; m. Ann North.

459.

EMILY THOMPSON[6] (Nathan,[5] James,[4] Thomas,[3] John,[2] John[1]), b. —, dau. of Nathan and Phebe E. (?) (Blowers) Thompson; m. RUSSELL WARREN. They lived for many years in East Orangeville, Wyoming county, N. Y.; later removed to Sauk Center, Minn.

CHILDREN VII. GENERATION.

1038. Susan, b. —.
1039. Albert, b. —.
1040. Martha, b. —.
1041. Harriet Diadamia, b. —.

460.

MALINDA SHEARER[6] (Rebecca,[5] James,[4] Thomas,[3] John,[2] John[1]), b. —, dau of James and Rebecca (Thompson) Shearer; m. NATHAN ROOT, brother of Joseph Root (424).

CHILDREN VII. GENERATION.

1042. Caroline, b. —; m. Charles Chase.
1043. Rhoda, b. —; m. David Chase.
1044. Erastus, b. —; m. —.
1045. Abbie, b. —; m. Uri Mason.

461.

ABIGAIL SHEARER[6] (Rebecca,[5] James,[4] Thomas,[3] John,[2] John[1]), b. —, dau. of James and Rebecca (Thompson) Shearer; m. NATHAN ROOT, brother of Joseph.

CHILD VII. GENERATION.

1046. Mary, b. —.

464.

BELA SHEARER[6] (Rebecca,[5] James,[4] Thomas,[3] John,[2] John[1]), b. —, son of James and Rebecca (Thompson) Shearer; m. —. Lived in Clarendon, N. Y.

CHILDREN VII. GENERATION.

1047. Hiram, b. —.
1048. Emery, b. —.
1049. Gustavus, b. —.
1050. Datus, b. —.
1051. Frank, b. —.

467.

THOMAS CUSHMAN[6] (Bethiah,[5] Thomas,[4] Shubael,[3] John,[2] John[1]), b. November 2, 1795, son of Capt. Thomas and Bethiah (Thompson) Cushman, a lineal descendant from Robert Cushman, the emigrant who came to Plymouth in the ship Fortune, 1621.

Thomas became a soldier in Capt. Sears Washburn's Bridgewater company stationed at Plymouth in 1814 and was connected with the old Bridgewater Cadet Rifle company, organized in 1819, of which Mr. Thomas Hooper was afterwards a member. At the age of 21 Mr. Cushman began his career as a teacher and for more than thirty years, with slight interruptions, he continued to be an instructor of youth in Bridgewater and neighboring towns, deeply devoted to his calling and laying deep and broad the foundation of good order and sound morals in the community.

In 1849 and 1850 Mr. Cushman represented his native town in the General Court, and has ever manifested an intelligent interest in public affairs.

Mr. Cushman was the last of the original members of the Church of the New Jerusalem in Bridgewater, and upon the fiftieth anniversary of its organization, in 1883, presented a paper descriptive of the planting of the church and the formation of the society.

In his declining years Mr. Cushman has enjoyed the full possession of his faculties; he has devoted much attention to genealogical research and has welcomed with avidity the publications of the day. In the death of this aged man the town has lost an esteemed citizen, the church an efficient and revered member, and his family circle a devoted father and friend.

He compiled a brief genealogy of descendants of John Thomson (many items from which are in this work). He m. October 5, 1823, LUCY PRATT, b. April 20, 1799, dau. of Cornelius and Martha (Leonard) Pratt. She d. July 21, 1863. He d. August 20, 1889.

CHILDREN VII. GENERATION.

1052. Edwin, b. July 11, 1824; d. Sept. 21, 1826.
1053. Franklin, b. Oct. 23. 1825; d. Sept. 29, 1826.
1054. Albert, b. Oct. 12, 1827; m. Mary Ann Jeffery.
1055. Charles, b. Jan. 20, 1829; m. Eliza Jane Kelsey.
1056. Darius, b. July 21, 1830; m. (1) Elvina Thompson (1124), m. (2) Widow Jane Frances (Fuller) Pratt.
1057. Bethiah, b. Dec. 15, 1831; m. (1) Abram G. J. Spooner, (2) Philander Pratt.
1058. Martha, b. April 18, 1833; m. August 19, 1863, Joseph E. Carver.
1059. George, b. July 11, 1837; d. Oct. 23, 1854.
1060. Julius, b. Sept. 30, 1843; d. April 5, 1844.

470.

JOHN THOMPSON[6] (Isaac,[5] John,[4] Shubael,[3] John,[2] John[1]), b. March 22, 1775, son of Isaac and Lucy (Sturtevant) Thompson; m. (1) SARAH AUSTIN, (2) BELINDA DEAN, (3) JANE RICHARDSON. He was a physician. Lived in Maine.

CHILDREN BY FIRST WIFE VII. GENERATION.

1061. Isaac, b. April 14, 1802. Was a physician; m. Emily Voluntine; had three children.
1062. Peter A., b. August 10, 1803; m. Wealthy Stephens; had three children.
1063. Leander, b. June 14, 1807.
1064. Sewell, b. March 25, 1810.
1065. Deborah, b. Sept. 3, 1811.

CHILD BY SECOND WIFE VII. GENERATION.

1066. John D., b. Dec. 30, 1817.

CHILDREN BY THIRD WIFE VII. GENERATION.

1067. Robert, b. Dec. 7, 1821.
1068. Sarah J., b. March 23. 1824.

1069. Belinda, b. Dec. 7, 1826.
1070. Margaret, b. April 23, 1829.
1071. Thomas E., b. April 1, 1831.
1072. Charles, b. June 7, 1835.

471.

CYRUS THOMPSON[6] (Isaac,[5] John,[4] Shubael,[3] John,[2] John[1]), b. December 23, 1776, son of Isaac and Lucy (Sturtevant) Thompson; m. REBECCA ROBINSON, b. March 18, 1785. Said to be first white girl b. in Sumner, Me. He was a justice of the peace. Lived in Middleboro at one time. He bought a farm of Oakes Thompson (238) in the Thompson Grant in that part of Maine afterwards called Hartford, Oxford county He was a successful farmer. He d. April 27, 1851. She d. March 17, 1871.

CHILDREN VI. GENERATION.

1073. Joseph R., b. Nov. 21, 1804; m. Martha C. Rogers.
1074. Cyrus, b. Dec. 24, 1805; m. Marenda Pitts.
1075. Lydia, b. August 20, 1811; d. July 19, 1814.
1076. Martha S., b. April 30, 1814; m. Stillman Read.

473.

ISAAC THOMPSON[6] (Isaac,[5] John,[4] Shubael,[3] John,[2] John[1]), b. November 7, 1781, son of Isaac and Lucy (Sturtevant) Thompson; m. ABIA HASKELL. He d. March 26, 1835.

CHILDREN VII. GENERATION.

1077. Joanna H., b. Oct. 3, 1809; m. Israel T. Haskell.
1078. Lucia C., b. Feb. 3, 1811; m. Robert C. Randall.
1079. Zebulon H., b. Jan. 20, 1813.
1080. Abigail H., b. Oct. 16, 1814.
1081. Ezra, b. Nov. 29, 1817.
1082. Jane N., b. Oct. 15, 1819; m. James M. Leonard.
1083. John, b. Jan. 14, 1824.

474.

UZZA THOMPSON[6] (Isaac,[5] John,[4] Shubael,[3] John,[2] John[1]), b. August 23, 1784, in Middleboro; son of Isaac and Lucy (Sturtevant) Thompson; m. ABIGAIL W. ELLIOTT of Rumford, Maine, b. May 13, 1785. They settled on a farm in Hartford, Maine, purchased from the Thompson Grant. He d. January 5, 1849. She d. October 28, 1864.

CHILDREN VII. GENERATION.

1084. Lucy S., b. Sept. 22, 1808; m. 1835, James B. DeCoster of Buckfield, Me. Had one dau. d. in infancy. She d. Jan. 8, 1837. He d. in Illinois.

1085 Mary Ann, b. May 8, 1810; m. Hiram Hall. Lived in Ohio.

1086. Louisa, b. March 12, 1814; m. Veranus DeCoster of Buckfield.

1087. Ezra, b. May 4, 1816; d. May 30, 1816.

1088. Charlotte, b. Oct. 6, 1817; d. Dec. 10, 1836.

1089. Abigail E., b. June 3, 1821; m. (1) Alanson Bradford, (2) William R. French.

1090. George C., b. Oct. 15, 1827; m. Feb. 14, 1856, Harriet B. Bisbee. He d. August 17, 1863. Had a son who d.

1091. Isaac H., b. Jan. 3, 1831; m. Hattie E. Bray.

(475 see 249.)

476.

GEORGE THOMPSON[6] (Isaac,[5] John,[4] Shubael,[3] John,[2] John[1]), b. August 12, 1788, son of Isaac and Lucy (Sturtevant) Thompson; m. DEBORAH P. CLARK.

CHILD VII. GENERATION.

1092. George Edward, b. Dec. 15, 1828; d. —.

478.

EZRA THOMPSON[6] (Isaac,[5] John,[4] Shuabel,[3] John,[2] John[1]), b. March 8, 1792, son of Isaac and Lucy (Sturtevant) Thompson; m. CYNTHIA GIFFORD.

CHILDREN VII. GENERATION.

1093. Anna S., b. July 25, 1821.

1094. Isaac, b. Jan. 14, 1823.

1095. Rouesette S., b. April 7, 1827.

1096. William G., b. —.

1097. Almeda R., b. August 5, 1831.

1098. John A., b. Dec. 30, —.

(479 see 563.)

487.

CHARLES THOMPSON[6] (Ezra,[5] Jacob,[4] Jacob,[3] John,[2] John[1]), b. April 12, 1784, son of Ezra and Sarah (Whitton) Thompson;

m. (1) SARAH DARLING, dau. of Daniel Darling of Middleboro,
(2) MRS. HANNAH PRATT, dau. of John W. Bates and widow
of John Pratt. He d. January 11, 1833. First wife d. December 26, 1814.

CHILDREN BY FIRST WIFE VII. GENERATION.

1099. Naomi, b. August 7, 1808; m. Alden Beal.
1100. Marshal, b. Feb. 13, 1811; m. Lurania Howard.
110i. Catharine, b. June 8, 1812; m. Josiah Tilson.
1102. Charles, b. Dec. 7, 1813; m. Mary Ann Curtis.

CHILDREN BY SECOND WIFE VII. GENERATION.

1103. Sally, b. Jan. 23, 1817; m. Samuel Beale. She d. May 26, 1844.
1104. Levesta, b. 1819: m. Robert Curtis.
1105. Ezra, b. March 12, 1822.

488.

ABRAHAM THOMPSON[6] (Ezra,[5] Jacob,[4] Jacob,[3] John,[2] John[1]),
b. June 12, 1786; son of Ezra and Sarah (Whitton) Thompson; m. MARY SAMPSON. He d. December 21, 1869. She d. 1858.

CHILDREN VII. GENERATION.

1106. Ephraim, b. July 1, 1811; d. July, 1836.
1107. James, b. May 15, 1813; m. Polly Simmons.
1108. Mary S., b. Sept. 17, 1821; m. June 23, 1842, Ezra Lambert.
1109. Henry L., b. Feb. 19, 1828 ?); m. Mary Simmons.
1110. Robert, b. July 27, 1833; d. March 17, 1840.
1111. Laura T. Ann, b. Oct. 19, 1841.

489.

EZRA THOMPSON[6] (Ezra,[5] Jacob,[4] Jacob,[3] John,[2] John[1]), b.
April 12, 1789, son of Ezra and Sarah (Whitton) Thompson;
m. MARY BATES, dau. of John W. and Lois Bates. He d.
April 17, 1815.

CHILD VII. GENERATION.

1112. Sally, b. Jan. 29, 1815; m. Reuben Hollis of Weymouth. She
       d. May 26, 1844.

493.

PELEG THOMPSON[6] (Ezra,[5] Jacob,[4] Jacob,[3] John,[2] John[1]),
b. May 25, 1797, son of Ezra and Sarah (Whitton) Thompson;

m. Freelove W. Washburn, dau. of Zenas and Lydia Washburn, b. September 16, 1805. He d. April 1, 1872.

CHILDREN VII. GENERATION.

1113. Amanda Washburn, b. Jan. 18, 1828.
1114. Addie Esther, b. Oct. 5, 1844; m. Nov. 20, 1864, Minot Shaw Curtis.

495.

Elkanah Thompson[6] (Ezra,[5] Jacob,[4] Jacob,[3] John,[2] John[1]), b. October 22, 1803, son of Ezra and Sarah (Whitton) Thompson; m. June 1, 1823, Rachel Bump.

CHILDREN VII. GENERATION.

1115. Caroline Frances, b. Feb. 25, 1824.
1116. Olive S.,) Twins,   ) Olive m. James Ramsdell.
1117. Oliver,   ) b. April 20, 1829.)
1118. William H., b. July 10, 1835.

(479 *see* 563.)

496.

Levi Thompson[6] (Ezra,[5] Jacob,[4] Jacob,[3] John,[2] John[1]), b. February 12, 1806, son of Ezra and Sarah (Whitton) Thompson; m. Elsadah Raymond. He d. June 14, 1864.

CHILDREN VII. GENERATION.

1119. Rosza Ann, b. Sept. 21, 1830; m. Floyd Robinson. She d. June 7, 1865.
1120. Rinaldo Benoni, b. April 11, 1836.
1121. Leonard Spooner, b. March 15, 1841; d. Jan. 23, 1861.

498.

Lewis Thompson[6] (Jacob,[5] Jacob,[4] Jacob,[3] John,[2] John[1]), b. August 17, 1797, son of Jacob and Lucina (Keith) Thompson; m. (1) Huldah Wood, b. March 30, 1795, dau. of Timothy Wood; m. (2) June, 1860, Mrs. Hannah Holmes, widow of Charles Holmes and dau. of Seth Conant. She was b. April 7, 1805. He d. February 13, 1872. First wife d. November ?, 1858.

CHILDREN VII. GENERATION.

1122. Marietta, b. Feb. 15, 1824; m. Oct. 29, 1843, Samuel Goodwin.
1123. Lewis Henry, b. Nov. 23, 1826; m. (1) Hannah Holmes, (2) Mary Holmes.

1124. Elvina, b. Oct. 14, 1830; m. Sept. 19, 1859, Darius Cushman (1056). She d. Jan. 2, 1867.
1125. Matilda, b. June 5, 1834.
1126. Marcus Morton, b. April 14, 1840; m. (1) Susan M. Nichols, (2) Mary A. Barlow. First wife d. June 20, 1882, aged 40 years, 10 months and 23 days.

501.

JACOB THOMPSON[6] (Jacob,[5] Jacob,[4] Jacob,[3] John,[2] John[1]), b. November 30, 1802, son of Jacob and Lucina (Keith) Thompson; m. EMELINE BENT, b. October 23, 1804, dau. of Francis Bent.

CHILDREN VII. GENERATION.

1127. George Williams, b. Sept. 26, 1828.
1128. Franklin Watson, b. June 6, 1830; d. Nov. 10, 1847.
1129. Mary Jacobs, b. May 1, 1835; m. Nov. 25, 1859, Daniel Thrasher. She d. April, 1860.
1130. Vernon Messenger, b. March 16, 1837; m. July 10, 1869, Rebecca C. Silsby, widow of Samuel T. Silsby, and dau. of Zeno Laurence of Sandwich. He d. May 13, 1875. No children.
1131. Frances Maria, b. Jan. 24, 1839; m. Henry Bradford of Plympton.
1132. Jacob Perkins, b. Oct. 31, 1841.
1133. William McLeod, b. August 22, 1843; d. Oct. 18, 1853.
1134. Minerva Williams, b. July 16, 1846; d. March 7, 1854.

(503 *see* 364.)

505.

LYSANDER THOMPSON[6] (Jacob,[5] Jacob,[4] Jacob,[3] John,[2] John[1]), b. September 14, 1811, son of Jacob and Lucina (Keith) Thompson; m. ABIGAIL THOMPSON (636). He d. January 1, 1860. She d. December 10, 1863.

CHILDREN VII. GENERATION.

1135. Lysander M., b. Sept. 2, 1834; m. (1) Marietta Hathaway, (2) Sarah A. Hathaway.
1136. Soranas, b. Nov. 12, 1836; m. Lucinda Sears.
1137. Sidney W., b. July 8, 1841; d. June 27, 1847.
1138. Sidney Herbert, b. Feb. 27, 1850; m. Mary E. Churchill.

509.

SETH THOMPSON[6] (Nathaniel,[5] Ebenezer,[4] Jacob,[3] John,[2] John[1]), b. September 6, 1791, son of Nathaniel and Sarah (Thayer) Thompson; m. January 1, 1815, BETHIAH BENSON, b. July 3, 1793, dau. of David and Charity Benson. In 1840 they lived in Sandwich. She d. October 16, 1887. They lived together in the marriage relation 72 years and 9 months. He d. November 20, 1888, in East Bridgewater. At the time of his death he was believed to be the oldest man in the county. For a great many years he was a consistent member of the M. E. church.

CHILDREN VII. GENERATION.

1139. David, b. Dec. 1, 1815; m. Jan. 1, 1844, Ann Fernetta Collins. He d. Oct. 21, 1869.
1140. Martin Benson, b. Nov. 25, 1819; d. Dec. 8, 1826.
1141. Nathaniel, b. Feb. 16, 1822; d. July 18, 1840.
1142. Mercy W., b. Oct. 26, 1824; m. June 6, 1844, James W. Fish, son of Abraham and Eunice Fish.
1143. Julia Ann, b. August 22, 1828; d. August 26, 1829.
1144. Seth, b. August 27, 1830; m. Nov. 21, 1855, Ann Jennette Reynolds.
1145. Martin Van Buren, b. May 24, 1833; d. April 22, 1854.
1146. Frances Maria, b. Oct. 8, 1835; m. Albinus O. Hamilton.

512.

EBENEZER THOMPSON[6] (Nathaniel,[5] Ebenezer,[4] Jacob,[3] John,[2] John[1]), b. January 17, 1798, son of Nathaniel and Sarah (Thayer) Thompson; m. LOUISA ELDRIDGE. Lived in New Bedford in 1841.

CHILDREN VII. GENERATION.

1147. Charles H., b. Nov. 16, 1827.
1148. Elizabeth E., b. July 26, 1832.

519.

BATHSHEBA THOMPSON[6] (Ephraim,[5] Ephraim,[4] Jacob,[3] John,[2] John[1]), b. April 18, 1796, dau. of Ephraim and Lucy (Thomas) Thompson; m. (1) DAVID M. GIFFORD, (2) JOHN B. TABER.

CHILD BY FIRST HUSBAND VII. GENERATION.

1149. Lyman W., b. —.

15

CHILDREN BY SECOND HUSBAND VII. GENERATION.

1150. Lucy, b. —.
1151. Mary, b. —.
1152. James, b. —.
1153. Harriet, b. —; m. (1) William Hested, (2) Josiah G. Childs.

520.

ABNER THOMPSON[6] (Ephraim,[5] Ephraim,[4] Jacob,[3] John,[2] John[1]), b. October 9, 1797, son of Ephraim and Lucy (Thomas) Thompson; m. NANCY H. GIFFORD.

CHILDREN VII. GENERATION.

1154. John H., b. Dec. 4, 1824; m. Harriet Robertson.
1155. David W., b. Sept. 11, 1832; d. Sept. 19, 1837.
1156. Pardon G., b. July 3, 1836; m. Theresa Gifford.

521.

ALVA THOMPSON[6] (Ephraim,[5] Ephraim,[4] Jacob,[3] John,[2] John[1]), b. March 2, 1801, son of Ephraim and Lucy (Thomas) Thompson; m. LYDIA CHASE.

CHILDREN VII. GENERATION.

1157. Rebecca F., b. Oct. 31, 1829; m. George Davis.
1158. Eveline C., b. Sept. 16, 1831; m. Aaron Besse.
1159. Ephraim, b. Dec. 1, 1833; d. —.
1160. Amanda M., b. Dec. 26, 1835; d. Sept. 1839.
1161. Lucy T., b. June 27, 1838; d. Sept., 1839.
1162. Henry C., b. July 26, 1840; d. —.
1163. Amanda, b. —; m. James Whelan and had children.
1164. Elizabeth, b. —; m. Stephen Tripp; had two sons and three daughters.
1165. Charles, b. —; m. Adaline Barker.
1166. Francella, b. —; m. — Briggs; had two children.
Three other children d. young.

523.

LUCY THOMPSON[6] (Ephraim,[5] Ephraim,[4] Jacob,[3] John,[2] John[1]), b. April 30, 1805, dau. of Ephraim and Lucy (Thomas) Thompson; m. OBED SHERMAN.

CHILDREN VII. GENERATION.

1167. Susan, b. —; m. Sylvester Crandall.
1168. Julietta, b. —.

1169. Job, b. —.
1170. Lucy, b. —.

524.

JEREMIAH F. THOMPSON[6] (Ephraim,[5] Ephraim,[4] Jacob,[3] John,[2] John[1]), b. June 26, 1807, son of Ephraim and Lucy (Thomas) Thompson; m. SARAH ANN CASE.

CHILDREN VII. GENERATION.

1171. Mary C., b. June 13, 1835; m. John Cornell.
1172. Marcus M., b. Jan. 25, 1840; m. Ellen Jennings.

526.

MARTIN THOMPSON[6] (Silas,[5] Ephraim,[4] Jacob,[3] John,[2] John[1]), b. July 31, 1801, son of Silas and Catharine (Beal) Thompson; m. AMANDA THOMPSON (772).

CHILDREN VII. GENERATION.

1173. Henry N., b. Feb., 1836; d. —.
1174. Amanda M., b. June 20, 1840; d. —.
1174½. Alfred P., b. —; m. Maria Sampson; had two children, d. in infancy; the mother also dead.

535.

EDWARD THOMPSON[6] (Francis,[5] Ephraim,[4] Jacob,[3] John,[2] John[1]), b. August 15, 1811, son of Francis and Jane (Beal) Thompson; m. MARY H. BRYANT.

CHILDREN VII. GENERATION.

1175. Amos E., b. Feb. 11, 1834.
1176. Henry F., b. Feb. 27, 1838.
1177. Drusilla J., b. June 29, 1840.

536.

GILMAN THOMPSON[6] (Francis,[5] Ephraim,[4] Jacob,[3] John,[2] John[1]), b. —, 1814, son of Francis and Sally (Beal) Thompson; m. LUCINDA DUNBAR.

CHILD VII. GENERATION.

1178. Charles G., b. Oct. 16, 1837.

538.

FRANCIS THOMPSON[6] (Francis,[5] Ephraim,[4] Jacob,[3] John,[2] John[1]), b. June 28, 1823, son of Francis and Sally (Beal) Thompson; m. January 1, 1843, DORLISCA VINICA, b. April 15, 1820, dau. of David and Rachel (Vaughan) Vinica.

CHILDREN VII. GENERATION.

1179. Dorlisca Adelaide, b. Jan. 15, 1845.
1180. Lyman Francis, b. Sept. 18, 1846; d. March 31, 1848.
1181. Elizabeth Rachel, b. Sept. 22, 1848.
1182. Francis Grover, b. Jan. 15, 1851.
1183. Eliza Vinica, b. Dec. 15, 185-.
1184. Amos Edward, b. July 6, 1859.

563.

SOLOMON THOMPSON[6] (Solomon,[5] Jacob,[4] Jacob,[3] Jacob,[2] John[1]), b. September 25, 1791, son of Solomon and Lydia (Murdock) Thompson; m. (1) HARRIET THOMPSON (479), (2) WIDOW MARY SIMMONS. He d. April 2, 1860.

CHILDREN BY FIRST WIFE VII. GENERATION.

1185. Maria L., b. August 13, 1818.
1186. Elvira, b. August 29, 1821; m. William B. Sumner.
1187. Albert, b. Nov. 26, 1824; m. Lucy Coates Hopkins.
1188. James, b. Sept. 5, 1826; m. (1) Abby Faunce, (2) Lucy Bassett.
1189. Harris, b. August 4, 1828; d. Oct. 31, 1849.
1190. Harriet, b. Sept. 30, 1830; m. Joshua T. Faunce.
1190ᵃ. Lydia, } Twins,   { d. August 30, 1833.
1190ᵇ. Lucy, } b. August 13, 1833; { d. August 29, 1833.

565.

CALVIN THOMPSON[6] (Solomon,[5] Jacob,[4] Jacob,[3] Jacob,[2] John[1]), b. October 29, 1796, son of Solomon and Lydia (Murdock) Thompson; m. April 22, 1821, MARGARET RICHARDSON, dau. of Robert Richardson of Boston. Calvin was a carpenter. Moved from Middleboro to North Bridgewater about 1844. She d. June, 1867. He d. June 8, 1853.

CHILDREN VII. GENERATION.

1191. Calvin Murdock, b. May 5, 1823; m. (1) Mary B. Sharp, (2) Helen Badlam.
1192. Edward, b. Oct. 15, 1825; m. Sarah S. Savery of Plymouth, Mass.

1193. Henry, b. Dec. 4, 1827; m. Anne Withington Thayer.
1194. Margaret Smith, b. June 14, 1830; m. (1) August 18, 1872, Noah
      Ford, (2) Jan. 30, 1879, Charles A. Tyler.
1195. George Richardson, b. March 4, 1833; m. Nov. 25, 1857, Mary
      Alice Johnson.
1196. Robert Richardson, b. Jan. 10, 1838; d. Nov. 6, 1849.

566.

JACOB THOMPSON[6] (Solomon,[5] Jacob,[4] Jacob,[3] Jacob,[2] John[1]),
b. October 3, 1801, son of Solomon and Lydia (Murdock)
Thompson; m. (1) NANCY TINKHAM, (2) January 11, 1866,
JOANN BENSON, b. March 23, 1821, dau. of Jonah and Chloe
(Hathaway) Benson. He was captain of militia. He d. Janu-
ary 29, 1879. First wife d. October 20, 1861.

CHILDREN BY FIRST WIFE VII. GENERATION.

1197. Helena, b. Jan. 3, 1832; m. Leander A. Darling, son of Alanson
      Darling. She d. June 21, 1872.
1198. Virgil, b. June 5, 1836; m. (1) Augusta Williams, (2) Nellie
      Williams.
1199. Marian,) Twins,   ⎧ Marian d. young.
1200. Emma,) b. March 9, 1842; ⎨ Emma m. April 7, 1874, Leander
                              ⎩ A. Darling.
1201. Anne Russell, b. Jan. 19, 1844; d. May 27, 1850.
1202. Sophia Tinkham, b. Dec. 21, 1847; d. May 15, 1850.

567.

BETSEY WILD THOMPSON[6] (Benjamin,[5] Jacob,[4] Jacob,[3]
Jacob,[2] John[1]), b. November 20, 1789, dau. of Benjamin and
Mary (Bourn) Thompson; m. HON. WILKES WOOD. He
graduated at Brown university in 1793, was appointed judge
of probate for Plymouth county in 1821, and held the office
until his death. He d. October 1, 1843. She d. December 12,
1822.

CHILDREN VII. GENERATION.

1203. Cornelius Bennett, b. Nov. 5, 1809; m. (1) Lucy Amee Wash-
      burn, (2) Cornelia Burgess Snow.
1204. William Henry, b. Oct. 24, 1811; unmarried. He graduated at
      Brown university in 1834. Was appointed, in 1858, judge of
      probate for Plymouth county, Mass., and held the office until
      his death. He was also representative and senator in the
      legislature of Massachusetts, and one of the Gov. council.
      He d. March 30, 1883.

1205.　Charles Wilkes, b. June 30, 1814; m. (1) Eliza A. Bigelow, (2) Catharine S. Lemist.
1206.　Emily Louisa, b. May 15, 1816; m. Thomas Briggs Crane.
1207.　Joseph Tinkham, b. March 17, 1818; m. Ellen Taylor.——
1208.　Mary Thompson, b. May 28, 1820; m. Russell L. Hathaway.
1209.　Betsey Thompson, b. Sept. 4, 1822; d. Sept. 16, 1829.

571.

Abner B. Thompson[6] (Benjamin,[5] Jacob,[4] Jacob,[3] Jacob,[2] John[1]), b. September 22, 1797, son of Benjamin and Mary (Bourn) Thompson; m. Eliza Williams. Settled in Brunswick, Maine. Was adjutant general of militia.

CHILDREN VII. GENERATION.

1210.　Sarah E., b. Feb. 4, 1823.
1211.　Edward W., b. Oct. 8, 1824; d. Oct. 27, 1828.
1212.　Mary B., b. August 7, 1827.
1213.　Edward W., b. Feb. 28, 1836.
1214.　Eliza S., b. March 14, 1838.
1215.　Ellen M., b. Jan. 7, 1841.

573.

Benjamin Thompson[6] (Benjamin,[5] Jacob,[4] Jacob,[3] Jacob,[2] John[1]), b. November 25, 1803, son of Benjamin and Mary (Bourn) Thompson; m. Margaret Lindley. Settled in Indiana.

CHILDREN VII. GENERATION.

1216.　James A., b. Nov. 27, 1836; d. same day.
1217.　Mary B., b. Feb. 19, 1838.
1218.　Eliza W., b. Nov. 22, 1840; d. Jan. 10, 1841.
1219.　William, b. August 16, 1842.

574.

James D. Thompson[6] (Benjamin,[5] Jacob,[4] Jacob,[3] Jacob,[2] John[1]), b. October 31, 1807, son of Benjamin and Mary (Bourn) Thompson; m. (1) Abigail Kendrick, (2) Louisa H. Farnham. He was a major general of militia in Massachusetts. First wife d. January 15, 1838.

CHILD BY SECOND WIFE VII. GENERATION.

1220.　Abigail K., b. Feb. 1, 1839; d. Feb. 15, 1840.

589.

BARNABAS THOMPSON[6] (Barnabas,[5] Noah,[4] Barnabas,[3] Jacob,[2] John[1]), b. September 24, 1793, son of Barnabas and Sarah (Fuller) Thompson; m. HANNAH SHAW. He held a commission as captain of militia.

CHILDREN VII. GENERATION.

1221. Harrison F., b. Oct. 15, 1815; m. Alzina M. Horton.
1222. Josepha F., b. March 25, 1817.
1223. Florella D., b. June 9, 1819.
1224. James W., b. Nov. 23, 1820.
1225. Miranda R., b. June 8, 1823.
1226. Benoni S., b. August 11, 1825.
1227. Caroline A., b. August 27, 1827; d. August 23, 1834.
1228. Hannah L., b. Dec. 18, 1830; d. March 9, 1833.
1229. Sarah J., b. Feb. 14, 1837.
1230. Henry B., b. May 16, 1838.

590.

ZADOCK THOMPSON[6] (Barnabas,[5] Noah,[4] Barnabas,[3] Jacob,[2] John[1]), b. May 23, 1796, son of Barnabas and Sarah (Fuller) Thompson; m. PHEBE BOYCE. He graduated at the university of Vermont. Author of the Gazetteer of Vermont. Entered into orders in the Episcopal church.

CHILDREN VII. GENERATION.

1231. Harriet F., b. Feb. 1827.
1232. Adaline P., b. March, 1829.

592.

SALMON THOMPSON[6] (Barnabas,[5] Noah,[4] Barnabas,[3] Jacob,[2] John[1]), b. March 11, 1803, son of Barnabas and Sarah (Fuller) Thompson; m. (1) SYLINDA BOYCE, (2) CHARLOTTE A. HUGGINS. He was a captain of militia. His first wife d. November 5, 1826.

CHILD BY FIRST WIFE VII. GENERATION.

1233. Jonathan L., b. Oct. 27, 1826; d. Nov. 5, 1826.

CHILDREN BY SECOND WIFE VII. GENERATION.

1234. Charles O., b. Oct. 22, 1829.
1235. George E., b. July 2, 1837.

594.

ALVINZA THOMPSON[6] (David,[5] Noah,[4] Barnabas,[3] Jacob,[2] John[1]), b. March 23, 1797, son of David and Betsey (Leach) Thompson; m. EMILY SEABURY.

CHILDREN VII. GENERATION.

1236. Mary A., b. May 19, 1828.
1237. Harriet Newell, b. Oct. 20, 1829.
1238. Lucien D., b. March 18, 1831.

596.

EDWIN THOMPSON[6] (David,[5] Noah,[4] Barnabas,[3] Jacob,[2] John[1]), b. August 26, 1800, son of David and Betsey (Leach) Thompson; m. WEALTHY COX. He was captain of militia.

CHILDREN VII. GENERATION.

1239. Amelia J., b. April 2, 1829.
1240. Cynthia A., b. May 14, 1832.
1241. Edwin F., b. August 1, 1837.

598.

OVID THOMPSON[6] (David,[5] Noah,[4] Barnabas,[3] Jacob,[2] John), b. August 27, 1805, son of David and Betsey (Leach) Thompson; m. WAITSTILL SHURTLIFF. He was a member of the legislature of Vermont, also a justice of the peace.

CHILDREN VII. GENERATION.

1242. Noah C., b. Dec. 31, 1831; d. March 13, 1832.
1243. Noah C., b. Dec. 18, 1833.
1244. Alvinza W., b. April 26, 1836.
1245. Betsey E., b. July 31, 1838.
1246. Sarah S., b. July 29, 1841.
1247. Elvira E., b. Jan. 20, 1844.

601.

HOSEA B. THOMPSON[6] (Abel,[5] Noah,[4] Barnabas,[3] Jacob,[2] John[1]), b. August 9, 1803, son of Abel and Polly (Stacy) Thompson; m. SARAH P. BARROWS.

CHILDREN VII. GENERATION.

1248. Abel A., b. May 15, 1837; m. (1) Ruth S. White, (2) Jane E. Burby, (3) Martha A. Burby. First wife d. March 4, 1866;

second wife d. Feb. 24, 1878. About 1884 they adopted from Home for Little Wanderers in Boston, Gertie E. Fairfield, b. Dec. 27, 1875, in Maine. Address, Pawtucket, R. I.

1249. Sarah A. M., b. August 26, 1838; m. (1) Oscar Kennedy, (2) Nelson C. Dimmick.

1250. Ellen R., b. August 25, 1840 ; m. (1) Warren T. Mather, (2) Truman Lewis, (3) Nelson C. Dimmick.

625.

Arioch Thompson[6] (Jabez,[5] Isaac,[4] Barnabas,[3] Jacob,[2] John[1]), b. June 22, 1802, in Plympton, Mass., son of Jabez and Betsey (Wood) Thompson; m. August 23, 1827, Adaline D. Virgin of Plymouth, Mass. He. d. July 10, 1887. She d. March 17, 1887.

CHILDREN VII. GENERATION.

1251. Huldah, b. Feb. 11, 1830, in Plympton; d. Nov. 17, 1852.
1252. Mary H., b. August 6, 1832, in Plympton; d. Feb. 13, 1833.
1253. Velina R., b. Sept. 18, 1835; m. Charles N. Cobb.
1254. Adaline A., b. Dec. 8, 1837, in Plympton.
1255. Arioch A., b. July 20, 1841; m. Hannah Eliza Thompson (1325).
1256. Elva M., b. April 24, 1848; m. John W. Chessman.

628.

Simeon Thompson[6] (Jabez,[5] Isaac,[4] Barnabas,[3] Jacob,[2] John[1]), b. June 13, 1808, in Plympton, Mass., son of Jabez and Betsey (Wood) Thompson; m. (1) September 9, 1833, Abigail W. Churchill, of Plymouth, (2) November 21, 1857, Sarah Faulkner, of Abington. First wife d. August 21, 1853, aged 45 years. He d. May 1, 1860.

CHILDREN BY FIRST WIFE VII. GENERATION.

1257. William Austin, b. July 15, 1834, in Plympton; m. (1) Eliza M. Chase, (2) Emma L. Standish.
1258. Abby Washburn, b. June 24, 1835, in Plympton. Lives in Holbrook, Mass.
1259. Sarah Burgess, b. Nov. 21, 1849, in Abington; m. Charles H. McCarter.

CHILDREN BY SECOND WIFE VII. GENERATION.

1260. Leonice, b. Sept. 15, 1858, in Abington; m. Leonard D. Garfield.
1261. Simeon, b. Nov. 13, 1860, in Abington; m. Elvira C. Reed.

629.

SAMUEL V. THOMPSON[6] (Jabez,[5] Isaac,[4] Barnabas,[3] Jacob,[2] John[1]), b. July 20, 1810 in Plympton, son of Jabez and Betsey (Wood) Thompson; m. October 30, 1833, BETSEY NASH of Abington. Address, Rockland, Mass.

CHILDREN VII. GENERATION.

1262. Samuel Gilbert, b. Dec. 6, 1835; m Elizabeth S. Daniels.
1263. Elizabeth Maria, b. April 14, 1840; d. Feb. 22, 1842.
1264. William Nash, b. Sept. 18, 1841; m. Annie C. Winslow.

630.

JOSIAH THOMPSON[6] (Jabez,[5] Isaac,[4] Barnabas,[3] Jacob,[2] John[1]), b. September 8, 1812, son of Jabez and Betsey (Wood) Thompson; m. JANE ANN SHAW, dau. of Reuben Shaw.

CHILDREN VII. GENERATION.

1265. Eliza J., b. Sept. 5, 1840; m. William Nash. She d. 1873.
1266. Josiah, b. August 1, 1842.
1267. Venus Morton, b. —; d. in the army.
1268. Adelaide, b. —.
1269. Betsey Wood, b. —.

(631 *see* 659.)

632.

SABINA THOMPSON[6] (Isaac,[5] Isaac,[4] Barnabas,[3] Jacob,[2] John[1]), b. May 3, 1801, dau. of Isaac and Phebe (Soule) Thompson; m. MARTIN WILLIS. They lived some time in East Middleboro, later at Eastondale, Mass., where she d. March 21, 1890. She joined the Congregational church prior to 1821; was a cheerful, active woman, full of deeds of kindness to others.

CHILDREN VII. GENERATION.

1270. Huldah, b. Oct. 3, 1825; m. Calvin Done. She d. March 12, 1875.
1271. Cyrus, b. August 20, 1828; d. Oct. 9, 1830.
1272. Martin, b. July 11, 1831.
1273. Cyrus, b. May 16, 1837; m. Orcelia Hayward.

633.

ROXANNA THOMPSON[6] (Isaac,[5] Isaac,[4] Barnabas,[3] Jacob,[2]

John[1]), b. November 15, 1802, dau. of Isaac and Phebe (Soule) Thompson; m. SAMUEL JEWETT. She d. July 31, 1887.

CHILDREN VII. GENERATION.

1274. Sarah A., b. June 19, 1829.
1275. Marietta, b. Nov. 20, 1838; d. August 10, 1885.

635.

CHRISTOPHER C. THOMPSON[6] (Isaac,[5] Isaac,[4] Barnabas,[3] Jacob,[2] John[1]), b. June 5, 1807, son of Isaac and Phebe (Soule) Thompson; m. (1) 1842, ALMIRA DUNLAP, (2) May 31, 1847, MARY A. STRONG, b. June 14, 1821, in Jefferson county, O. In the spring of 1838 he emigrated to the west, stopping first at Winslow, Stephenson county, Ill., later he permanently settled in what is now Thompson township, which town was given his name on account of his public spirit and enterprise. He was its first supervisor and continued to hold this office for five years. Immediately on his arrival he built the second saw-mill in the county, and in 1840 built the first large grist-mill in the county, which supplied Galena with nearly all its flour. He built the first stone schoolhouse in Thompson township, and the first frame schoolhouse in Rush township. He moved to Nora township October, 1874. Owns 931 acres of land. First wife d. October 19, 1846.

CHILDREN BY SECOND WIFE VII. GENERATION.

1276. Hiram, b. Nov. 18, 1848; d. Nov. 20, 1849.
1277. Woodman, b. Jan. 13, 1851; m. Jenefer Eustice.
1278. Winfield S., b. June 16, 1854; d. March 25, 1875.
1279. Whitfield Isaac, b. May 15, 1857; m. Ellen Howard.
1280. Tena E., b. May 21, 1861; m. Jan. 31, 1888, Clarence M. Tinkham, at Lena, Ill.

(636 see 505.)

637.

PHEBE THOMPSON[6] (Isaac,[5] Isaac,[4] Barnabas,[3] Jacob,[2] John[1]), b. April 1, 1811, dau. of Isaac and Phebe (Soule) Thompson; m. NAHUM BAILEY. Settled in Auburn, Maine.

CHILD VII. GENERATION.

1281. Henrietta, b. March 24, 1838; m. Horace N. Johnson.

638.

MARY THOMPSON[6] (Isaac,[5] Isaac,[4] Barnabas,[3] Jacob,[2] John[1]), b. May 17, 1813, dau. of Isaac and Phebe (Soule) Thompson; m. ICHABOD SAMPSON. She d. July 8, 1869. He d. May 6, 1880.

CHILDREN VII. GENERATION.

1282. Columbia, b. —.
1283. Alverado R., b. —.
1284. Melissa T., b. —.
1285. Abby C., b. —.

639.

ISAAC THOMPSON[6] (Isaac,[5] Isaac,[4] Barnabas,[3] Jacob,[2] John[1]), b. July 17, 1815, son of Isaac and Phebe (Soule) Thompson; m. (1) ANNA T. THOMPSON (383), (2) LYDIA R. THOMAS. First wife d. May 11, 1852; second wife d. May 26, 1885.

CHILDREN BY FIRST WIFE VII. GENERATION.

1286. Christiana, b. April 15, 1842; d. April 29, 1842.
1287. Cordelia Thankful, b. March 16, 1844; d. March 6, 1845.
1288. Deborah Anna, b. May 12, 1846; m. Amos B. Paun, M. D.
1289. Hiram, b. Nov. 6, 1848; d. Feb. 3, 1849.
1290. Isaac Edgar, b. Nov. 28, 1849; d. March 30, 1851.

641.

JOSEPH S. THOMPSON[6] (Isaac,[5] Isaac,[4] Barnabas,[3] Jacob,[2] John[1]), b. December 1, 1823, son of Isaac and Phebe (Soule) Thompson; m. MELISSA PINGREY. In 1855 he located on Wells' Creek in Belvidere, Minn. The first birth in the township was that of Ida Thompson. He was a captain in the War of the Rebellion. Has been chairman of board of supervisors. Has held and still holds important office. Owns a large stock farm.

CHILDREN VII. GENERATION.

1291. Ulna Ida, b. June 13, 1856; d. Oct. 27, 1858.
1292. Piva Setta, b. Feb. 21, 1859; m. William W. Thomas. She d. Sept. 19, 1879.
1293. Earl Ettson, b. April 10, 1860; m. Vernie E. Church.

643.

HOSEA V. THOMPSON[6] (Jacob,[5] Isaac,[4] Barnabas,[3] Jacob,[2] John[1]), b. June 23, 1808, son of Jacob and Esther (Shaw)

Thompson; m. January 11, 1837, at Grafton, Mass., SUSAN M. MAYNARD. He died June 9, 1845, in Brighton, Ill. She d. May 2, 1854, in Worcester, Mass.

CHILDREN VII. GENERATION.

1294. Emily M., b. Feb. 16, 1838, at Grafton; d. March 9, 1839, in Boston.
1295. Emily M., b. Feb. 11, 1840, in Middleborough, Mass.; d. August 8, 1847, in Galena, Ill.
1296. Mary Rosaetta, b. April 3, 1842, in Randolph, N. Y. Lived in Pelham, N. H.
1297. Susan Esther, b. May 28, 1845, in Brighton, Ill.; d. August 26, 1846, in Brighton.

644.

JACOB THOMPSON[6] (Jacob,[5] Isaac,[4] Barnabas,[3] Jacob,[2] John[1]), b. August 8, 1809, son of Jacob and Esther (Shaw) Thompson; m. at Lakewell, Mass., ARIADNE V. BOOTH. He d. June 14, 1848, at Dedham, Mass.

CHILDREN VII. GENERATION.

1298. Philander Francis, b. 1847, in Lakeville. Lost at sea in 1863 or 1864, the vessel supposed to have been captured by Raphael Semmes, the rebel, and the crew killed or put in boats to starve to death.

645.

MARCIA V. THOMPSON[6] (Jacob,[5] Isaac,[4] Barnabas,[3] Jacob,[2] John[1]), b. June 22, 1811, dau. of Jacob and Esther (Shaw) Thompson; m. January 1, 1832, at Plympton, Mass., MOSES TITCOMB. He d. February 22, 1879, at Pelham, N. H.

CHILDREN VII. GENERATION.

1299. George H., b. July 18, 1833; m. Abbie E. Champlin.
1300. Warren S., b. Sept. 18, 1837, in Milton, Mass.
1301. Marietta E., b. Jan. 1, 1840; m. Thomas Myers.
1302. Edward M., b. Jan. 17, 1842; m. Laura A. Chipman (1300).
1303. Rhoda Esther, b. Jan. 10, 1844, in Lowell, Mass.; d. March 1 1845, in Boston.
1304. Ben Bill, b. June 6, 1849; m. Augusta E. Cady.
1305. Frederick Charles, b. Sept. 10, 1852, in Norwich, Conn.

646.

SALLY THOMPSON[6] (Jacob,[5] Isaac,[4] Barnabas,[3] Jacob,[2] John[1]), b. February 10, 1813, dau. Jacob and Esther (Shaw) Thompson; m. December 20, 1833. CHARLES CHIPMAN. He d. August 9, 1844.

CHILDREN VII. GENERATION.

1306. Charles C., b. July 4, 1837, in Andover; d. July 6, 1844, at Dracut.
1307. Josiah, b. March 13, 1839, in Andover; d. Nov. 13, 1848, in Lakeville.
1308. Sumner J., b. Dec. 20, 1840, in Andover; m. Feb. 28, 1868, Jane L. Haskins, at Assonet.
1309. Laura A., b. August 9, 1842; m. Edward M. Titcomb (1302).

647.

BETSEY THOMPSON[6] (Jacob,[5] Isaac,[4] Barnabas,[3] Jacob,[2] John[1]), b. August 7, 1815, dau. of Jacob and Esther (Shaw) Thompson; m. July 13, 1840, SIMEON C. CLARK. He d. December 2, 1865.

CHILDREN VII. GENERATION.

1310. Alfred R., b. April 29, 1841; d. March, 1842.
1311. Thaddeus S., b. Jan. 25, 1843; m. Susan F. Smith.
1312. Esther E., b. October 30, 1847; m. David Smith.
1313. Mary F., b. Oct. 15, 1854; m. August 11, 1873, Eugene H. Rogers.
1314. Abbie W., b. July 29, 1858; d. May 26, 1862.

648.

GEORGE MARCUS THOMPSON[6] (Jacob,[5] Isaac,[4] Barnabas,[3] Jacob,[2] John[1]), b. January 22, 1818, in Halifax, Mass., son of Jacob and Esther (Shaw) Thompson; m. July 28, 1844, CAROLINE E. HYDE of Brookline, Mass. She d. November 17, 1884.

CHILDREN VII. GENERATION.

1315. Carrie F., b. June 10, 1845, in Lowell, Mass.; m. August 13, 1865, George Franklin Scates of Randolph, N. H.
1316. George M., b. July 15, 1847, in Lowell, Mass.; m. Feb. 18, 1880, Anna K. Hall of Newton, Mass.
1317. Jacob E., b. June 2, 1849, in Taunton, Mass.
1318. Helen V., b. Jan. 7, 1852, in Taunton, Mass.; d. June 17, 1852.
1319. Henry J., b. Oct. 19, 1854, in Taunton, Mass.; m. Sept. 25, 1879, Rebecca Boothman of Randolph.

1320. Clarence E., b. August 30, 1857, in Taunton, Mass.; m. Nov. 8, 1880, Celia L. Heath of Gorham, N. H.

649.

LEWIS S. THOMPSON[6] (Jacob,[5] Isaac,[4] Barnabas,[3] Jacob,[2] John[1]), b. November 10, 1819, son of Jacob and Esther (Shaw) Thompson; m. June 21, 1840, MARY W. MACOMBER. He d. December 24, 1864, in Portsmouth, Va.

CHILDREN VII. GERERATION.

1321. Asa Lewis, b. March 23, 1841; d. Nov. 10, 1843.
1322. Charles Nathan, b. March 4, 1842; m. Amy Baldwin.
1323. Lydia Augusta, b. June 24, 1844: m. Henry M. Haradon.
1324. Mary Frances, b. Dec. 20, 1846; m. Alexander Irving. Settled in Iowa.
1325. Hannah Eliza, b. Jan. 29, 1849; m. Arioch A.'Thompson (1255).
1326. Asa Lewis, b. Feb. 18, 1851; d. Jan. 16, 1874.
1327. Henry Granville, b. Jan. 5, 1853; settled in Wisconsin.
1328. Sumner Thomas, b. Sept. 2, 1855; m. (1) Mary Hamilton, (2) Anne Hamilton.
1329. Herbert Samuel, b. Jan. 23, 1859.
1330. Willard Carroll, b. Dec. 12, 1860; d. Oct. 28, 1876.
1331. Albert Warren, b. Oct. 4, 1863.

650.

SUMNER SHAW THOMPSON[6] (Jacob,[5] Isaac,[4] Barnabas,[3] Jacob,[2] John[1]), b. April 12, 1823, in Halifax, Mass., son of Jacob and Esther (Shaw) Thompson; m. April 10, 1847, HARRIET STARK WILEY. In 1839 he worked for his brother Hosea, who was a contractor upon the Taunton & New Bedford Railroad; two years later Hosea went west and Sumner took the contract off his hands. From that time, when he was barely 19, until his death, he was almost constantly engaged in the construction and management of railroads. Among the roads which he has built in whole or in part are the Vermont & Canada, the Vermont Central, the New Hampshire Northern, the Atlantic & St. Lawrence, now a part of the Grand Trunk, the New London & Northern, the Boston, Concord & Montreal, the Newport & South Eastern, the Passumpsic, the Frankfort & South Eastern, the Montreal, Portland & Boston, the Woodstock, the Somerset, the Saratoga & Sackett's Harbor, the Eastern, and several of the roads which now form a part of the Old Colony and New York & North Eastern systems. At the time

of his death he was president of the F. & S. E. Railroad, vice
president of the M. & W. R. Railroad, vice president of the
First National Bank of St. Johnsbury, Vt., and director in
several other railroads and financial institutions.

· He was a republican in politics, and was in 1860-61, 1866-67,
a member of the Vermont house of representatives, and in
1876 and 1880 a member of the senate in the same state. In
1880 a presidential elector. While in the house he opposed a
bill to increase the pay of members on the ground that there
had been a virtual contract between them and the people to
serve for the sum then established by law, and upon the
passage of the measure he and one of the senators returned
their surplus pay to the treasury; this, it must be remembered, was several years before a similar measure was opposed
in the national congress upon the same ground, on which
occasion also some of the members returned their back pay.
The records of the senate show that in 1876 he returned to the
treasury the carefully computed portion of his salary paid him
while he was absent from the sessions on a visit to the centen-
nial. In 1876 he was chosen, with an associate, a receiver of
the Montpelier & Wells River Railroad, and the property was
so handled that it was ultimately returned to the parties in
interest with an increased value, forming an honorable excep-
tion to the way in which Vermont railways have been managed
by receivers. This, with the instances cited from his legisla-
tive career, serves to illustrate the method and honorable
character which marked all his business dealings.

He has been liberal to both public and private objects. More
than one young man, with no other claim upon him than that
they were poor, have received from Mr. Thompson the means
of procuring a college education, while he has given freely to
churches and schools, his gifts to the Lyndon (Vermont) Literary Institution alone aggregating more than $30,000.

Fortunes which have been made by their possessors are generally of two classes: those which are attended by production,
which open up new enterprises, give employment to labor and
add to the world's stock of wealth; and those which have
caused no new production or wealth, but which spring out of
the manipulation of property already in existence and from
deals in stocks and securities. Fortunes of the first class are
not usually so large as those of the second, but they are more
honorable to their possessors and generally more enduring.
Mr. Thompson's is emphatically of the class first mentioned,
and its making has called into being enterprises that would

probably not otherwise have existed, and has made the poor happier and less poor than they were before. Being fully six feet in height and thoroughly well proportioned, with clear cut features, eyes large and blue, and a great and noble head, Mr. Thompson was a man of striking appearance. He d. October 24, 1889, at Frankfort, Mich.

CHILDREN V.II. GENERATION.

1332. Ella Esther, b. April 12, 1853; m. Samuel W. McCall.
1333. Hattie W., b. March 26, 1867; m. Charles S. LeBourveau, Jr.

651.

HULDAH V. THOMPSON[6] (Jacob,[5] Isaac,[4] Barnabas,[3] Jacob,[2] John[1]), b. September 10, 1826, dau. of Jacob and Esther (Shaw) Thompson; m. January 16, 1847, SILAS D. NEWCOMB. She d. August 28, 1872.

CHILDREN VII. GENERATION.

1334. Sydney A., b. Dec. 30, 1847; d. Jan. 9, 1850.
1335. Julia A., b. August 17, 1849; m. George Kittridge.
1336. Charles S., b. Dec. 28, 1856; m. —.

652.

CAROLINE M. THOMPSON[6] (Jacob,[5] Isaac,[4] Barnabas,[3] Jacob,[2] John[1]), b. November 7, 1828, in Plympton, Mass., dau. of Jacob and Esther (Shaw) Thompson; m. December 19, 1848, STEPHEN HERSEY.

CHILDREN VII. GENERATION.

1337. Edgar Augustus, b. August 18, 1850, in Lowell, Mass.; d. Oct. 17 1852.
1338. Harriet A., b. March 5, 1854, in Lowell, Mass.; m. Sept. 11, 1878, Loren E. Hilliard.
1339. Adeline J., b. June 19, 1857, in Meriden, N. H.; m. Sept. 12, 1883, John B. Bean.
1340. George P., b. June 5, 1859, in Meriden, N. H.; m. May 26, 1881, Etta M. Bean.
1341. Charles S., b. May 8, 1867, in Meriden, N. H.; m. Dec., 1885, Carrie M. Fadden.

653.

AMASA THOMPSON[6] (Samuel,[5] Adam,[4] Barnabas,[3] Jacob,[2] John[1]), b. September, 1802, son of Samuel and Clara (Sturte-

17

vant) Thompson; m. BETSEY M. EDDY. He d. September 20, 1872.

CHILD VII. GENERATION.

1342. Maria P., b. Nov. 15, 1835; m. Sylvanus R. Fuller. She d. July 2, 1886.

659.

OTIS THOMPSON[6] (Adam,[5] Adam,[4] Barnabas,[3] Jacob,[2] John[1]), b. May 1, 1813, son of Adam and Salvina (Wood) Thompson; m. BETSEY W. THOMPSON (631). She d. October 2, 1888, in Halifax, Mass., aged 73 years 9 months and 18 days.

CHILD VII. GENERATION.

1343. Horace Otis, b. Nov. 5, 1844; m. Heloise Aymar Bourne.

660.

ALBERT THOMPSON[6] (Adam,[5] Adam,[4] Barnabas,[3] Jacob,[2] John[1]), b. October 9, 1815, son of Adam and Salvina (Wood) Thompson; m. CHARLOTTE MARIA WARREN, dau. of Silas Warren. She d. July 12, 1875, aged 53 years 7 months and 11 days.

CHILD VII. GENERATION.

1344. Albert Cranston, b. Dec. 19, 1843; m. Marcia Nickerson. He was a resident of Brockton and a member of Massachusetts legislature in 1887.

661.

SHEPARD THOMPSON[6] (Adam,[5] Adam,[4] Barnabas,[3] Jacob,[2] John[1]), b. November 2, 1820, son of Adam and Salvina (Wood) Thompson; m. PRISCILLA T. WISWELL.

CHILDREN VII. GENERATION.

1345. Alice B., b. Jan. 20, 1848; m. Silas E. Field. He d. March 31, 1881. She d. March 8, 1883.
1346. Salvina W., b. Sept. 15, 1851; d. Feb. 27, 1875.
1347. Austin S., b. April 26, 1855; m. Ellen P. Chase.

663.

WARD THOMPSON[6] (Ward,[5] Adam,[4] Barnabas,[3] Jacob,[2] John[1]), b. May 6, 1826, son of Ward and Molly (Holmes) Thompson; m. MARCIA WRIGHT.

CHILD VII. GENERATION.

1348. Charles, b. Dec., 1849; m. Eunice Washburn.

664.

REBECCA PERKINS THOMPSON[6] (Zadock,[5] Adam,[4] Barnabas,[3] Jacob,[2] John[1]), b. February 29, 1816, dau. of Zadock and Deborah (Bosworth) Thompson; m. SAMUEL S. INGLEE, son of Robert and Lucy (Sturtevant) Inglee.

CHILDREN VII. GENERATION.

1349. Lucy T., b. March 18, 1835; m. Isaac Keith, and had
Stafford I., b. June 13, 1856.
Paulina, b. May 12, 1858; m. Carlos Place.
Louisa M., b. May 30, 1873.
1350. Charles S., b. Dec. 8, 1845; m. Abbie Sturtevant, and had
Robert I., b. March 5, 1887.
1351. Deborah T., b. July 20, 1847; m. George W. Robbins, and had
Walter, b. Nov. 25, 1880.
Florence I., b. Oct. 2, 1882.
Grace A., b. March 17, 1884.
Helen, b. Oct. 10, 1887.

667.

ZADOCK THOMPSON[6] (Zadock,[5] Adam,[4] Barnabas,[3] Jacob,[2] John[1]), b. September 2, 1826, son of Zadock and Deborah (Bosworth) Thompson; m. (1) LYDIA S. POPE, dau. of Henry Pope, (2) MARY E. BOSWORTH, dau. of Martin Bosworth. He d. April 10, 1866, of exposure in the war of the rebellion.

CHILDREN VII. GENERATION.

1352. Rena F., b. Oct. 18, 1857; m. Horace W. French. Lives in Taunton, Mass.
1353. Harry M., b. August 5, 1859. Lives in Taunton, Mass.

668.

SALINA F. THOMPSON[6] (Zadock,[5] Adam,[4] Barnabas,[3] Jacob,[2] John[1]), b. February 20, 1831, dau. of Zadock and Deborah (Bosworth) Thompson; m. SIMEON HORACE WILLIAMS.

CHILDREN VII. GENERATION.

1354. Emma P., b. Nov. 24, 1852.

1355. Ellen F., b. Jan. 7, 1854; m. Curtis S. Oakes, and had
Edna, b. May 17, 1875.
Sarah, b. June 10, 1877.
Horace W., b. Oct. 22, 1880.

670.

JAMES W. THOMPSON[6] (James,[5] Ichabod,[4] Barnabas,[3] Jacob,[2] John[1]), b. December 13, 1805, son of James and Deborah (Washburn) Thompson; m. MARY JAMES. Graduated at Brown University in 1827. Settled in the ministry at Salem, Mass.

CHILDREN VII. GENERATION.

1356. Mary L., b. —.
1357. George J., b. —.
1358. Abby L., b. —.

677.

GEORGE DREW[6] (Sarah,[5] Ichabod,[4] Barnabas,[3] Jacob,[2] John[1]), b. August 28, 1811, son of George and Sarah (Thompson) Drew; m. LUCY LEWIS of Marshfield. He d. August 30, 1884, aged 73 years and 2 days. She d. October 27, 1885, aged 70 years.

CHILDREN VII. GENERATION.

1359. George, b. May 3, 1841; killed May 12, 1864, in the battle of the Wilderness.
1360. Cephas, b. April 30, 1846; m. Emma Damon. Live in Atlantic (Quincy), Mass.

678.

JAMES THOMPSON DREW[6] (Sarah,[5] Ichabod,[4] Barnabas,[3] Jacob,[2] John[1]), b. April 18, 1813, son of George and Sarah (Thompson) Drew; m. GEORGIANA F. TUTTLE. He was a member of the state legislature of 1880. Lives in Halifax.

CHILD VII. GENERATION.

1361. Mary Jane, b. March 23, 1876.

679.

LYDIA HALL DREW[6] (Sarah,[5] Ichabod,[4] Barnabas,[3] Jacob,[2] John[1]), b. February 17, 1815, dau. of George and Sarah (Thompson) Drew; m. November 25, 1841, DR. CYRUS MORTON, son of Dr. Nathaniel Morton (101). Cyrus Morton d. May 18, 1873, aged 76 years and 3 months. Mrs. Morton furnished much valuable information used in the compilation of this work. Resided at Halifax. She d. May 15, 1887, aged 72 years. She had been an invalid for some years.

CHILDREN VII. GENERATION.

1362. Lucy Waterman, b. Feb. 19, 1843; m. Nov. 12, 1860, Harrison D. Packard.
1363. Thomas Drew, b. April 27, 1848. Lives in Halifax. Is town clerk.

680.

STEVEN DREW⁶ (Sarah,⁵ Ichabod,⁴ Barnabas,³ Jacob,² John¹), b. July 16, 1817, son of George and Sarah (Thompson) Drew; m. JANE W. SOULE of Plympton.

CHILDREN VII. GENERATION.

1364. Sarah Thompson, b. Sept. 17, 1853.
1365. Ruth Soule, b. March 31, 1856; m. George Glass of Plympton.

681.

CYRUS DREW⁶ (Sarah,⁵ Ichabod,⁴ Barnabas,³ Jacob,² John¹), b. April 11, 1820, son of George and Sarah (Thompson) Drew; m. December 29, 1844, EVELINA DONALDSON.

CHILDREN VII. GENERATION.

1366. Thomas, b. Nov. 3, 1845; m. July 2, 1868, Ella J. Bourn.
1367. Frank Donaldson, b. July 25, 1849; d. Feb. 15, 1852.
1368. Evelina W., b. Oct. 25, 1853.
1369. Mary Jane, b. July 3, 1857.

683.

JULIA ANN WILLIAMS DREW⁶ (Sarah,⁵ Ichabod,⁴ Barnabas,³ Jacob,² John¹), b. April 21, 1826, dau. of George and Sarah (Thompson) Drew; m. CHARLES LINCOLN WINSLOW of Rockland, Mass. She was a physician of the regular school.

CHILD VII. GENERATION.

1370. Charles, b. Dec. 24, 1855.

684.

LUCY WOOD THOMPSON⁶ (Oakes,⁵ William,⁴ Caleb,³ Jacob,² John¹), b. March 20, 1797, dau. of Oakes and Hannah (Bisbee)

Thompson; m. March 4, 1827, NOAH BOSWORTH of Canton, Maine. He d. January 1, 1864. She d. April 16, 1870.

CHILDREN VII. GENERATION.

1871. Noah T., b. Oct. 24, 1829; d. June 6, 1836.
1872. Oakes T., b. Dec. 13, 1830; d. March 15, 1870.
1873. Erastus P., b. July 28, 1835; un-m.
1874. Abigail F., b. July 6, 1839; d. Sept. 23, 1844.

685.

MARY THOMPSON[6] (Oakes,[5] William,[4] Caleb,[3] Jacob,[2] John[1]), b. March 23, 1800, dau. of Oakes and Hannah (Bisbee) Thompson; m. July 4, 1824, JAMES BROWN of Canton, Me. He d. April 8, 1881. She d. April 19, 1833.

CHILDREN VII. GENERATION.

1375. James Monroe, b. Nov. 15, 1825; m. Eunice Gould Frost.
1376. Arthur, b. Sept. 24, 1827; d. Oct. 15, 1857.
1377. Ira Bisbee, b. April 5, 1829; d. March 12, 1831.
1378. Ira Bisbee, b. June 10, 1831; d. July 19, 1831.
1379. William Thompson, b. Jan. 16, 1833; d. April 28, 1861.

686.

OAKES THOMPSON[6] (Oakes,[5] William,[4] Caleb,[3] Jacob,[2] John[1]), b. October 20, 1802, son of Oakes and Hannah (Bisbee) Thompson; m. December 21, 1834, LIVONIA BANKS, b. January 10, 1813, dau. of William Banks of Hartford, Me. Mr. Thompson succeeded to the homestead and farm of his father at North Hartford, Me., and after an academic education was for several of his earlier years engaged as a teacher in public and private schools, including among his pupils the well-known Washburn family of Livermore, of subsequent congressional distinction. He removed to Boston in 1871. Mr. Thompson relates that when he was a boy there were no roads in that part of Maine where he lived, only trails indicated by spotted trees, and that when but 7 years old he was often sent to Sumner (seven miles) on horse-back to mill, riding on top of the bag of grain which hung over the saddle. He says the first wagon he ever heard of in that locality arrived one Sunday, about the year 1810, and the tithing man stopped the same and entered a complaint against the owner for traveling on the Sabbath. He d. September 14, 1886, in Boston. His wife d. January 7, 1879, in Boston.

CHILDREN VII. GENERATION.

1380. Roscoe Henry, b. May 1, 1836; m. Helen Crafts.
1381. Lucian Bisbee, b. Jan. 29, 1838; un-m. He graduated from Tufts college in the class of 1863, and from Harvard law school in 1867. Held a commission in 1864–5 in the recruiting department in Georgia and South Carolina, where he remained until the close of the war. Address, 35 Congress street, Boston, Mass.
1382. Mary, b. May 22, 1840; d. Nov. 21, 1842.
1383. Cephas, b. August 22, 1842; d. Nov. 2, 1842.
1384. Celia, b. Nov. 22, 1849; m. May 22, 1884, Hubbard L. Hart of Palatka, Fla., owner of Hart orange groves (so-called) and the Upper St. Johns and Ocklawaha river steamers.
1385. Reuel Williams, b. Oct. 22, 1851; un-m. Educated at academy and Bates college, Maine. Address, 35 Congress street, Boston, Mass.
1386. Sarah Banks, b. Sept. 24, 1854; un-m.
1387. Ella, b. April 1, 1856; d. April 19, 1856.

690.

ROXELLANA THOMPSON[6] (William,[5] William,[4] Caleb,[3] Jacob,[2] John[1]), b. March 29, 1803, dau. of William and Susannah (Wood) Thompson; m. HENRY MOULTON in Maine.

CHILDREN VII. GENERATION.

1388. Maryetta, b. —; m. — Storey. Lived in Lewiston.
1389. David Nutter, b. —. Lived in Albion.
1390. Albion Paris, b. —.
1391. Ellen, b. —; m. — Rackley.

691.

FLORINDA S. W. THOMPSON[6] (William,[5] William,[4] Caleb,[3] Jacob,[2] John[1]), b. May 13, 1811, dau. of William and Susanna (Wood) Thompson; m. in Maine, DANIEL TORREY. She d. January 21, 1842, in Payson, Ill.

CHILDREN VII. GENERATION.

1392. William Otis, b. —; m. twice. Was a physician and surgeon in the army. Lives in Hanibal, Mo.
1393. Abner Wood, b. —. Settled in Marysville, Cal. Elected sheriff, also member of city council.
1394. Roscoe E., b. —. Settled on a farm in Missouri.

692.

OTIS THOMPSON[6] (William,[5] William,[4] Caleb,[3] Jacob,[2] John[1]), b. April 17, 1809, son of William and Susanna (Wood) Thompson; m. (1) September 28, 1835, in Maine, CLARISSA A. WING, (2) November 5, 1848, in Iowa, MARTHA LAYCOCK. In 1850 he, with his brother Hiram, brought in wagons some families from Milwaukee to Farmington, Iowa, before there were any railways west of Chicago. Since about 16 years of age it was the aim of Mr. Thompson to live a faithful Christian life. Resided at Bonaparte, Iowa. First wife d. July 22, 1838, in Quincy, Ill. He d. January 26, 1890.

CHILDREN BY SECOND WIFE VII. GENERATION.

1395.   Florinda S., b. Sept. 19, 1849; d. young.
1396.   William Otis, b. Nov. 19, 1852; m. May 29, 1888, Floretta J. Gilbert. He has been town clerk and clerk of the Baptist church for many years, also secretary of several societies; a valuable citizen. Address, Bonaparte, Iowa.
1397.   Judson, b. May 21, 1854; d. young.
1398.   Dana Boardman, b. May 2, 1856; d. young.

693.

HIRAM THOMPSON[6] (William,[5] William,[4] Caleb,[3] Jacob,[2] John[1]), b. May 13, 1811, son of William and Susanna (Wood) Thompson; m. June 18, 1840, at Payson, Ill., ELIZA POTTLE. Address, Bonaparte, Iowa.

CHILDREN VII. GENERATION.

1399.   Susan Clarissa, b. —; m. in Iowa, William P. L. Muir; had one child, d. young. Mr. Muir, b. Dec. 5, 1837, in Philadelphia, Pa. Enlisted August 8, 1861, in Company E, 15th Iowa volunteer infantry. Mustered into United States service Nov. 5, 1861, at Keokuk, Iowa, a private; promoted to first sergeant March 1, 1862. Was in the battle of Shiloh, Tenn., April 6 and 7, 1862; severely wounded in right leg. His regiment was brigaded with the 11th, 13th and 16th Iowa regiments, and known as Brocker's Iowa brigade, and attached to the 17th army corps, Army of the Tennessee. Participated in all the battles and sieges of this army, including battles of Iuka, Corinth, Vicksburg, Jackson and the Atlanta campaign. Oct. 3, 1862, severely wounded in head at battle of Corinth. Feb. 9, 1863, promoted to second lieutenant. Dec. 7, 1863, to first lieutenant. July 20, 1864, breveted captain, and July 22, 1864, major; same day taken

prisoner at battle of Atlanta, Ga., and confined in Macon,
Savannah and Charleston military prisons until exchanged,
Sept. 29, 1864. Detached from his own command during
winter of 1864–5, and served on staff of Brigadier General A.
G. Malloy as assistant adjutant general. Dec. 15 and 16,
1864, was in the battle of Nashville, Tenn., and March 10,
1865, participated in battle of Kinston, N. C. March 16, 1865,
rejoined his own command and assigned to duty on staff of
Brigadier General A. Hickenlooper as assistant adjutant general. July 24, 1865, mustered out of service at Louisville,
Ky., by reason of close of the war.

1400. Hiram, b. August 27, 1845; m. Ellen Brown.
1401. A child, b. —; d in infancy.
1402. George W., b. July 25, 1849; m. Maggie McGaihey.

695.

DEBORAH WOOD THOMPSON[6] (William,[5] William,[4] Caleb,[3]
Jacob,[2] John[1]), b. May 16, 1816, at Livermore, Me., dau. of
William and Susanna (Wood) Thompson; m. February 28,
1841, at Quincy, Ill., BENJAMIN F. CATE of New Hampshire.

CHILDREN VII. GENERATION.

1403. Florinda Torrey, b. August 25, 1842; m. (1) Larson Sylvester
       Stone, (2) John Oatman.
1404. Amanda, b. March 13, 1844; m. William Joseph Ward.
1405. Mary Jane, b. July 1, 1846; m. David Green Bacon.
1406. Roswell, b. April 26, 1848; m. Mary Cordelia Caster.
1407. Ellen, b. Jan. 31, 1850. Address, Quincy, Ill.
1408. Otis Thompson, b. Oct. 23, 1852; m. Nancy Ann Gregory.
1409. Walter, b. Dec. 30, 1855; m. Rosa G. Foote.
1410. Austin, b. May 24, 1858.

697.

ELVIRA S. T. THOMPSON[6] (Cephas,[5] William,[4] Caleb,[3] Jacob,[2]
John[1]), b. July 3, 1804, in Middleborough, Mass., dau. of
Cephas and Olive (Leonard) Thompson; m. September 23,
1824, GEORGE BONNEY, b. May 31, 1796. He d. August 19,
1869. She d. June 5, 1885; both at Rochester, Mass.

CHILDREN VII. GENERATION.

1411. Olivia Cathleen, b. August 3, 1825; m. Dr. Josiah Atkinson.
1412. Juliet Helena, b. April 3, 1828; m. John Eddy.
1413. Anna Leonard, b. July 21, 1837; un-m. Resides in Taunton,
       Mass.
1414. George Bernard, b. March 10, 1839; m. Caroline King Holbrook.

698.

CORDELIA THOMPSON[6] (Cephas,[5] William,[4] Caleb,[3] Jacob,[2] John[1]), b. May 1, 1806, dau. of Cephas and Olive (Leonard) Thompson; m. October 20, 1843, BENJAMIN A. BRYANT of Halifax, Mass., b. May 16, 1822, in Rochester, Mass., son of Azel Bryant. They lived for a time in Georgia. He d. December 26, 1888, in Longwood, Fla. She resides with her son at Longwood.

CHILD VII. GENERATION.

1415. Orville, b. July 4, 1844, in Brunswick, N. J.; m. Alice C. Faroons.

699.

WILLIAM HENRY THOMPSON[6] (Cephas,[5] William,[4] Caleb,[3] Jacob,[2] John[1]), b. November 17, 1807, son of Cephas and Olive (Leonard) Thompson; m. 1834, MARY MILLER of Savannah, Ga., in which place they lived until their death.

CHILDREN VII. GENERATION.

1416. John Cephas, b. about 1836. Was a member of the Black Horse cavalry of the rebellion. He d. 1876, aged 40 years.
1417. Olivia Ann, b. —. Resides at 209 New Houston street, Savannah, Ga.

700.

CEPHAS GIOVANNI THOMPSON[6] (Cephas,[5] William,[4] Caleb,[3] Jacob,[2] John[1]), b. August 3, 1809, in Middleboro, Mass., son of Cephas and Olive (Leonard) Thompson; m. 1843, MARY G. OGDEN, dau. of Col. John Ogden of Ravenswood, Long Island. Cephas inherited a love for art from his father, a well-known portrait painter. He left home when only 18 and commenced his professional career in Plymouth; afterwards went to Providence, where he was very successful in painting portraits of well-known people, and made many valuable friends. He removed to New York in 1837, and was intimately associated with some of our best known writers— Bryant, Longfellow, Halleck, Tuckerman, Hawthorne, and many others. He there painted a large number of portraits of distinguished people, many of which were engraved for publication. Soon after his marriage, in 1843, he returned to his native state to live. Passed a short time in New Bedford, and then settled in Boston for a number of years. Always deeply

engaged in his profession, he had a restless desire to visit
the far-famed galleries of art in England, France and Italy,
and in 1852 he sailed for Europe and remained abroad seven
years, the greater part of the time being passed in Rome. At
first he made a few copies from the old masters—Raphael,
Guido, Correggio and Titian—but very soon rejoiced in the
freedom of being able to devote himself to his own creations,
and there conceived and executed some of his finest works:
St. Peter Delivered from Prison, Prospero and Miranda, The
Mother's Prayer, Angel of Truth, Chastity, and very many
Italian studies from the contadini of the country. In 1859
he returned to America and took up his abode in New York,
where he remained until his death. In April, 1887, he
accepted a position under the United States government as
inspector of life preservers, and, notwithstanding his advanced
age, was able to attend to the duties of his office promptly and
faithfully to within five days of his death, which occurred
January 5, 1888. His widow resides at 239 East Twelfth
street, New York City.

CHILDREN VII. GENERATION.

1418. Anna Cora, b. Oct. 19, 1844, in New York; un-m.

1419. Edmund Francis, b. Oct. 5, 1846: m. Clara Augusta Bisbee.

1420. Hubert Ogden, b. Dec. 14, 1848, in Boston: d. July 26, 1836.
He was educated at the grammar school in New York and
afterward in New York college. He took a clerkship at the
·age of 16 years for a few months, and then became discount
clerk in a well-known broker's office; later was confidential
clerk to another broker for several years. His political
career began about 1873, when he received an appointment
in the department of public works of New York, after holding which for a few months he was made private secretary
to Allen Campbell, then commissioner of public works, and
afterward became his deputy. In 1879 he was appointed
county clerk of the city and county of New York by Governor Robinson, and afterward for several years he held the
office of commissioner of public works. He had large political influence and was for some years next prior to his death
the acknowledged leader of the county democracy.

701.

FLORANTHE THOMPSON[6] (Cephas,[5] William,[4] Caleb,[3] Jacob,[2]
John[1]), b. May 14, 1811, dau. of Cephas and Olive (Leonard)
Thompson; m. GRENVILLE SPROAT. Was for several years
with her husband on a mission among the Indians around

Lake Superior. She d. 1885, in San Francisco, Cal. He d.
prior to 1889, with the Shakers at Lebanon.

CHILDREN VII. GENERATION.

1421. Elvira, b. —; m. — Hutchins of San Francisco; has two or
more children.
1422. Lucy T., b. —; m. — Dodd of Portland, Oregon; has three
sons.

702.

JEROME B. THOMPSON[6] (Cephas,[5] William,[4] Caleb,[3] Jacob,[2]
John[1]), b. January 30, 1814, in Middleboro, Mass., son of
Cephas and Olive (Leonard) Thompson; m. (1) 1839, MARIA
LOUISA COLDEN, b. March 23, 1819, dau. of Caldwalder C.
Colden, grandson of Governor C. Colden of New York, her
mother being daughter of one of the governors of Connecticut;
m. (2) April 19, 1876, MARIE MAY TUPPER, b. December 26,
1837, an artist of merit, dau. of James and Lucretia (May)
Tupper. Mr. Thompson, at an early age, betrayed the genius
within him. His father, a portrait painter of some eminence,
designed an older son for the profession, and, to give
him all opportunity, consigned Jerome to the toils of the
farm, severely discouraging the outcroppings of the artist
talent which he saw the boy possessed in no small degree.
"Where there's a will there's a way," is a true old adage, and
Jerome found time, by stealing away into the garret, to do
much work in his way. When at work in the field his slate
was sure to be hid away in some friendly copse, where it
caught many a visit from the persevering boy. A favorite
sister shared her sympathy with the closely watched boy, and
comforted him much by conniving at and assisting him in his
labors. A good story is told of these stealthy interviews and
hours absorbed by the pallet in the garret. Jerome had at
length succeeded in procuring a real, living sitter in the person of his cousin—since become an eminent minister in the
Episcopal church—and all odd hours possible to be subtracted
from the barn-yard and field were given to the easel. The
picture progressed finely, and was nearly done, when, presto!
in came the angry father, knocking easel, artist and all into
direful confusion, amid which the sitter escaped and the
unlucky boy beat a retreat, first securing his picture, which he
preserved as a relic of the disaster. Such being the decided
bent of his tastes, it is not strange that he deserted farming as
soon as possible. By sign and various ornamental painting he
succeeded in laying up one hundred dollars, and with this

stock in trade, accompanied by his good sister, he "started in
business," opening a studio at Barnstable, where he painted
many portraits, including one of Daniel Webster, who was
thereafter his .warm friend. By such economy as two such
spirits alone could practice, and by dint of perseverance, he
obtained a good living, even in that barren spot. The Barnstable "Patriot" relates this incident as showing the rapidity
with which he wrought: Some gentleman, who had been
abroad, was remarking upon the ease with which some artists
whom he had known would accomplish their work in a very
short time. Thompson offered to bet that in five minutes he
would paint a portrait of any gentleman the party would
select, which might be recognized by any one who knew the
subject. The bet was taken, and one of the gallant landlords
of the Globe Hotel was selected as the sitter. At it Thompson
went, painting upon a piece of smooth pine board, and stopped
on his task the minute the watch had ticked off five minutes.
The result was set upon a post in front of the house, and a
little girl passing on the opposite side of the street named the
original at once. The bet was immediately paid, and the
artist had won a victory. In 1831 the artist and his sister
went from Cape Cod to New York City, to cast their bread
upon that turbulent sea of "noise and confusion." Here he
was not long in winning a position and a handsome support,
while his admirable sister as a miniature painter added much
to her means and repute as an artist. About 1852 he went to
England for study and a wider experience, and there added to
his repute considerably, painting portraits of many of the
nobility of England and France, returning home with money
and added honors. From the time of his return, Mr. Thompson may be said to have found his *forte*. From the study of
Claude Lorraine, and Turner, and Hogarth, abroad, he found
that his strength lay even more in country scenes and rustic
life than in general landscape and faces; and he labored in
the pastoral field with the richest success. Among his pictures
are: "The Apple Gathering," "The Watering Trough,"
"Recreation: or, a Picnic Scene in Vermont," "October
Afternoon." Of the latter Isaac M. McLellan paid a fine
tribute in verse, from which we quote:

> "Rare painter! thanks to thee we tend
> For scenes to nature's self so true ;
> Thanks, that in nature's frostiest time,
> When tempests veil heaven's glorious blue,

> Though hedged by multitudes that swarm
> In splendid square and squalid lane,
> Perennial in thy works we find
> Fair summer's bloom and autumn's wane."

He d. May 1, 1886, at Mount Jerome, his country seat in Glen Gardner, N. J. An abstract from some of the minutes of the National Academy of Design is as follows: "The Council has heard with deep regret of the death of an old friend and fellow member, Jerome Thompson. Mr. Thompson inherited his love of art from his father, himself an artist of merit; his earliest pictorial efforts were in portraiture. * * * He was well known and esteemed by his contemporaries as a painter of ideal and rural landscape subjects, and his name was at one time familiar to the general public through his series of ' Pencil Ballads,' as they have been called, illustrative of popular songs and verses of the time, as: The Old Oaken Bucket, Home, Sweet Home, Scenes of My Childhood, Coming Thro' the Rye, and Woodman, Spare that Tree, compositions which were reproduced by chromo lithography and steel engraving and scattered widely over the land. He was in all ways a most excellent and worthy man, deservedly honored in his life and sincerely mourned in his death."

Dr. Paxton, his pastor and a distinguished Princeton professor, said to Dr. Patten, its president, that Jerome Thompson was the greatest poet, painter, christian and child he ever met. "Truly, an American painter of American scenes and poetic thought." Most of his works were never exhibited by him. Some of his later works are in Paris, sold to their possessors from his studio. During the last winter of his life he painted with greater power, and more pictures, than ever before in a like period of time. During all his life as an artist he kept a "Book of Advice to Myself," dividing his life into epochs of ten years, comparing and compelling advancement—never commending, always severely criticising himself, never looking backward except for the purpose of going forward. He was a great student, always at work, desperately in earnest and enthusiastic. He spent his summers traveling over the country, even amidst the wildest scenery of the far west, not merely sketching, but making studies of nature with fidelity and love. He left a large collection of studies, and several large and important pictures, including his allegorical pictures, "Beulah Land" and "The Valley of Baca." He owned a farm in Minnesota and a home in the Berkshire Hills of his native state. He understood gardening, loved it, and never wearied of its labor. On the morning of the day of his death, when too weak to speak, with an arch smile he drew the attention of his wife to the picture his nurse made standing in the sunlight—and later waved his hand as if forbidding tears, and quickly went to Jesus his Savior, in whom he believed. His first wife d. January, 1874 or 1875.

CHILD BY FIRST WIFE VII. GENERATION.

1423. Jerome C., b. August 11, 1840; m. Lullia I. Wyman.

704.

JULIUS THOMPSON[6] (Cephas,[5] William,[4] Caleb,[3] Jacob,[2] John[1]), b. October 21, 1824, son of Cephas and Olive (Leonard) Thompson; m. January 11, 1848, BATHSHEBA T. WARREN. He practiced dentistry at Taunton, Mass. Residence, Raynham, Mass.

CHILDREN VII. GENERATION.

1424. George Edward, b. Nov. 3, 1848; d. Nov. 19, 1871.
1425. Charles Frederick, b. Dec. 22, 1852; m. Eliza J. Henry.
1426. James Albert, b. August 1, 1857; m. Grace A. Perry.
1427. Lucy Warren, b. Oct. 17, 1861.
1428. Clara Elvira Sturtevant, b. April 18, 1867.
1429. Edith, b. April 1, 1871.

714.

IRA DREW THOMPSON[6] (Ira,[5] William,[4] Caleb,[3] Jacob,[2] John[1]), b. September 25, 1803, in Hartford, Me., son of Ira and Sophia (Drew) Thompson; m. October 6, 1828, LYDIA HATHAWAY. He d. January 11, 1883, in Livermore, Me. She d. January 21, 1869.

CHILDREN VII. GENERATION.

1430. John Q., b. August 1, 1831; m. Rebecca Leslie.
1431. Mandana, b. April 26, 1833; m. (1) David Winslow, (2) Alexander Runyan.
1432. Mary H., b. Feb. 23, 1839; m. Edwin Boothby. Address, Livermore, Me.
1433. Arad, b. Dec. 21, 1840; m. Emma Hilton.
1434. Elbridge G., b. Nov. 3, 1845; m. Nellie Florence Rogers.

715.

SUSAN D. THOMPSON[6] (Ira,[5] William,[4] Caleb,[3] Jacob,[2] John[1]), b. September 25, 1805, in Livermore, Me., dau. of Ira and Sophia (Drew) Thompson; m. February 4, 1828, REV.

CHARLES MILLER, b. October 1, 1794, son of David and Ellen
(Muir) Miller of Auchenbowie, near Stirling, Scotland.
About the age of 21 Mr. Miller took a decided stand as a
Christian, and became by conviction a Baptist. He early
cherished the desire of becoming a missionary, and gave himself
to study for that purpose. Excessive application impaired his
health, to recruit which, he took a sea voyage in 1819 and
landed in Miramichi, N. B. Here he began work as teacher
and preacher, and in 1820 was ordained at Sackville in con-
nection with the meetings of a Baptist association. Four
years, with great zeal and success, he did pioneer work over a
large region where there are now three or four flourishing
Baptist churches. After a three years' pastorate in St. John,
he became, in 1826, the first pastor of the Baptist church in
South Berwick, Me. He was subsequently pastor in Turner,
Me.; Wenham, Mass.; Boston, Livermore, Bloomfield and
Farmington, Me. In 1851 Skowhegan became his home for
the remainder of his life. Twenty years of self-denying missionary labors in the region of the upper Kennebec, and a
brief pastorate in Livermore Falls passed, and Father Miller
closed his public labors in the 81st year of his age and the 56th
of his ministry. His was a glorious sunset; the public official
service closed at 80, but his blessed ministry continued to
the end of life. One who knew him well, writes: "Many
years Father Miller has been in retirement from the active
work of the ministry that he loved so well, but his influence
has been mighty and constant all the while, as his interest has
been unabated. The churches he had served, the ministers
whom he knew, the scattered sheep he had tended so faithfully
and lovingly, as well as his own kindred and loved ones, were
remembered constantly in this good man's prayers." He d.
November 21, 1887, in Skowhegan, in the 94th year of his age.
His widow resides in Skowhegan.

CHILDREN VII. GENERATION.

1435. Abby Seaver, b. Feb. 21, 1829; m. Benjamin W. Norris.
1436. Helen Sophia, b. March 25, 1832; m. Stephen Coburn.
1437. Charles Andrew, b. August 13, 1834, in Wenham, Mass. He
       prepared for college in Farmington and Bloomfield, and
       graduated from Waterville college (Colby university) in 1856.
       Admitted to the bar in 1858, and soon after began the practice
       of law in Rockland, Me., in which he continued until 1863.
       He held the office of assistant clerk of the Maine house of
       representatives during the sessions of 1858 and 1859, and that
       of clerk for four sessions, 1860, 1861, 1862 and 1863. In 1863

he entered the military service of the United States as major
in the second Maine cavalry. Having served in the department of the gulf till the close of the war, he took charge of a
plantation and settled in Montgomery, Ala. He took an
active part in the politics of the state and held the office of
secretary of state of Alabama during 1869 and 1870. He then
became connected with the Alabama & Chattanooga Railroad, as treasurer and director, residing part of the time in
Chattanooga. In 1876 he was chosen a delegate to the republican national convention at Cincinnati, but was taken sick
on his way there and was represented by a substitute. After
a year of failing health he died May 7, 1877, at his father's
house in Skowhegan. He did not marry.

1438. Elizabeth Dodge, b. Dec. 19, 1836, in West Cambridge.
1439. Ann Eliza, b. March 7, 1840, in Livermore; d. March 21, 1842.
1440. Caleb Davis, b. May 28, 1843, in Livermore; m. March 14, 1871,
Arazina K. (Pratt) Steward, b. May 19, 1842, at Newport,
Me., dau. of Jacob and Mary (Burrill) Pratt. Caleb was
postmaster from 1877 to 1838. Residence, Skowhegan.

716.

ELBRIDGE GERRY THOMPSON[6] (Ira,[5] William,[4] Caleb,[3] Jacob,[2]
John[1]), b. June 29, 1807, in Livermore, son of Ira and
Sophia (Drew) Thompson; m. 1833, in Turner, Me., SARAH
BALLOU, dau. of Seth Ballou. She d. July, 1885. Residence,
Foxcroft, Maine.

CHILDREN VII. GENERATION.

1441. Boadicea Aldrich, b. March 25, 1835; m. (1) S. C. Gray, (2) Lemuel F. Dinsmore.
1442. Sarah Abbie, b. Sept. 30, 1838; m. Elliot W. Jameson.
1443. Angelia Constancia, b. 1840; d. in Guilford, aged 19 months.
1444. Elmer Elbridge, b. May, 1845; m. Mary Rollins.
1445. Lelia Mina, b. Nov., 1850; m. William Elliot.

717.

CLARINDA M. THOMPSON[6] (Ira,[5] William,[4] Caleb,[3] Jacob,[2]
John[1]), b. March 16, 1809, in Livermore, dau. of Ira and
Sophia (Drew) Thompson; m. November 15, 1832, JOHN
MONROE of Livermore.

CHILDREN VII. GENERATION.

1446. Charles Frederic, b. July 3, 1834. He was first lieutenant in
company C, eighth regiment, Maine volunteers. He was
killed June 6, 1864, at Cold Harbor, Va.

19

1447. Julia A., b. Sept. 25, 1837; m. A. Russell Swift.
1448. John Pitt, b. Oct. 14, 1848; d. June 15, 1862.
1449. Ira T., b. April 23, 1852; m. Dec. 25, 1875, Ida C. Leach.
       Address, Livermore, Me.

718.

ARAD THOMPSON⁶ (Ira,⁵ William,⁴ Caleb,³ Jacob,² John¹),
b. January 24, 1811, in Livermore, Me., son of Ira and Sophia
(Drew) Thompson; m. (1) February 11, 1844, MARGARET L.
COLE, b. October 19, 1823, at Bucksport, Me., (2) LOUISA M.
BALDWIN, b. May 5, 1831, at Bangor, Me. First wife d. April
10, 1854. In December, 1831, Arad left his home in Livermore and went to Guilford. In 1832 he went to Bangor,
where he has since resided. He was engaged in the dry goods
business for a number of years, being a partner in the firm of
Hatch, Thompson & Co. He occupied the same store for
twenty-five years, building up a large and prosperous business.
In 1868 he disposed of his interest and engaged in other pur-
suits. He was a director in the European & North American
Railroad from its inception until it passed into the hands of
receivers. Was a member of the city government, both as
councilman and alderman, for several years. Was elected
representative to the Maine legislature for the years 1866 and
1867. He was deacon of the First Baptist church for more
than thirty years and church treasurer for same length of
time. Was director in several banks as well as in other organ-
izations. Was also one of the trustees of Colby University.
In 1874 he was chosen president of the Union Insurance Company, which position he still occupies (1888).

CHILDREN BY FIRST WIFE VII. GENERATION.

1450. Harriet M., b. June 20, 1845, at Bangor; d. Dec. 1, 1850.
1451. Margaret C., b. June 26, 1847, at Bangor; m. Frank Dudley.
1452. Joseph Arad, b. Feb. 20, 1854, at Bangor; m. Grace P. Hersey.

CHILDREN BY SECOND WIFE VII. GENERATION.

1453. Louise B., b. June 17, 1860, at Bangor.
1454. Ernestine, b. March 12, 1865, at Bangor.
1455. Grace, b. March 12, 1869, at Bangor; d. May 29, 1870.

719.

BOADICEA L. THOMPSON⁶ (Ira,⁵ William,⁴ Caleb,³ Jacob,²
John¹), b. May 5, 1813, in Livermore, dau. of Ira and Sophia
(Drew) Thompson; m. (1) August 7, 1831, ABNER S.

ALDRICH, (2) October 9, 1851, GEORGE W. PIERPONT. First husband d. April 17, 1848; second husband d. April 19, 1876. She d. June 27, 1873, at Livermore Falls.

CHILDREN BY FIRST HUSBAND VII. GENERATION.

1456. Alpheus Cleander, b. March 6. 1835; d. Sept. 26, 1835.
1457. Alfred Stanley, b. Sept. 5, 1837.
1458. Abner Clarence, b. March 27, 1841.
1459. Sarah Albina, b. April 25, 1845; m. Francis P. Hallowell.

CHILDREN BY SECOND HUSBAND VII. GENERATION.

1460. Georgiana, b. July 18, 1852; m. E. M. Gerrish.
1461. Boadicea, b. August 16, 1853; m. Winfield S. Treat.

720.

ERASTUS THOMPSON[6] (Ira,[5] William,[4] Caleb,[3] Jacob,[2] John[1]), b. April 24, 1815, in Livermore, son of Ira and Sophia (Drew) Thompson; m. (1) June 6, 1843, CATHERINE W. OAKES, (2) October 11, 1877, MARY C. CUMMINGS. He was a boot and shoe merchant and manufacturer in Hopkinton, Mass. First wife d. January 31, 1876. He d. January 23, 1885, in Hopkinton.

CHILDREN BY FIRST WIFE VII. GENERATION.

1462. Charles Erastus, b. Nov. 1, 1845; m. Adelia M. Loring.
1463. Edwin Davis, b. August 26, 1848; m. Mary Bartlett.
1464. Clarence Albert, b. Feb. 17, 1852; m. Mary B. Sayner.
1465. Catherine Sophia, b. July 1, 1855; d. Nov. 5, 1857.
1466. Frank Oakes, b. June, 1858; m. Oct. 10, 1883, Mary Crooks.

721.

ABBY SPRAGUE THOMPSON[6] (Ira,[5] William,[4] Caleb,[3] Jacob,[2] John[1]), b. February 2, 1818, in Livermore, dau. of Ira and Sophia (Drew) Thompson; m. March 4, 1839, JOSEPH SNELLING MONROE of Livermore, b. April, 1812. At one time Mr. Monroe was judge of probate. He d. February 20, 1870, in Abbott, Me. She d. May 13, 1880, at Skowhegan.

CHILDREN VII. GENERATION.

1467. James Augustus, b. April 1, 1840; m. Harriet S. Jackson.
1468. Erastus Thompson, b. Dec., 1843, in Abbott; m. Nov., 1869, Caroline M. Ingalls. Home is Foxcroft, Me.
1469. Mary Frances, b. Oct. 12, 1847, in Abbott; d. Oct. 28, 1851.
1470. Clara Dicea, b. March 15, 1850, in Abbott; m. Jefferson Taylor.

1471. Willis Snelling, b. May 2, 1854, in Abbott; m. Mamie Stewart.
1472. Kezzie Appleton, b. Oct. 7, 1859, in Abbott. Home at Waterville, Me.

722.

JOB DREW THOMPSON[6] (Ira,[5] William,[4] Caleb,[3] Jacob,[2] John[1]), b. March 30, 1820, in Livermore, son of Ira and Sophia (Drew) Thompson; m. March 24, 1844, RUTH W. WINSLOW, b. February 4, 1825. Living on home farm in Livermore.

CHILDREN VII. GENERATION.

1473. Emily B., b. Oct. 17, 1847; m. Geo. C. Wing.
1474. Rose A., b. May 21, 1849; m. Dr. Josiah Dunham.
1475. Fanny, b. Feb. 4, 1853. Address, Auburn, Me.
1476. Charles O., b. May 30, 1855; d. Dec. 18, 1873.
1477. Ezra D.. b. Oct. 11, 1858; m. Myra N. Coolidge.

723.

CHARLES OTIS THOMPSON[6] (Ira,[5] William,[4] Caleb,[3] Jacob,[2] John[1]), b. April 8, 1822, in Livermore, son of Ira and Sophia (Drew) Thompson; m. April 20, 1854, in Chicago, Ill., NANCY MARSH, b. July, 1834, in Dracut, Mass. He left Livermore in 1842; engaged in the shoe trade in Chicago with C. M. Henderson & Co., on Market and Adams streets. His wife d. June 13, 1861, in Chicago.

CHILDREN VII. GERERATION.

1478. Kate Marcia, b. March 2, 1855; m. William Orrington Lunt.
1479. Cora Howard, b. August 9, 1856, in Chicago; d. March 30, 1857, in Chicago.
1480. Mary Alice, b. August 31, 1858, in Chicago; d. May 8, 1864, in Chicago.
1481. Charles Otis, b. Oct. 22, 1860, in Chicago; d. Dec. 30, 1878, in Chicago.

724.

MARY SEAVER THOMPSON[6] (Ira,[5] William,[4] Caleb,[3] Jacob,[2] John[1]), b. June 6, 1827, in Livermore, dau. of Ira and Sophia (Drew) Thompson; m. March 10, 1846, in Livermore, WILLIAM K. WYMAN, b. April 13, 1821, in Livermore. He d. July 8, 1878. Residence, Milltown, Me.

CHILDREN VII. GENERATION.

1482. Martha E., b. Oct. 26, 1847; m. (1) S. Thaxter Bailey, (2) Rev. Wm. Harthorn.
1483. Susan Miller, b. April 18, 1851, in Livermore; d. June 30, 1851.
1484. Drew Thompson, b. Nov. 23, 1852, in Livermore; m. Nov. 3, 1875, at Mt. Vernon, Me., Ida M. Bean of Bradley. Address, West Somerville, Mass.
1485. John Monroe, b. June 22, 1857; m. Minnie B. Haynes.
1486. "Our Baby Sister," b. Oct. 3, 1860, in Livermore; d. Dec. 10, 1860.
1487. David Nutter, b. June 22, 1862, in Livermore; d. July 6, 1863.
1488. Mary Alice, b. March 5, 1865; m. Frank H. Hanson.

725.

SUSAN PORTER THOMPSON[6] (Galen,[5] William,[4] Caleb,[3] Jacob,[2] John[1]), b. October 23, 1807, dau. of Galen and Susanna (Porter) Thompson; m. SOLOMON BEALS. Lives in Middleborough, Mass.

CHILDREN VII. GENERATION.

1489. Solomon Franklin, b. August 30, 1827; m. Abbie M. Stevens.
1490. Clarinda Ellen, b. Jan. 4, 1834; m. Isam Mitchell.
1491. Galen Thompson, b. Oct. 5, 1837; d. April 6, 1840.
1492. Angelina, b. Nov. 3, 1839; m. Wm. Mitchell.
1493. Deborah Thompson, b. July 17, 1842; m. Bradford C. Burgess.

727.

GALEN M. THOMPSON[6] (Galen,[5] William,[4] Caleb,[3] Jacob,[2] John[1]), b. March 23, 1812, son of Galen and Fanny (Marble) Thompson; m. MYRTILLA HARLOW.

CHILDREN VII. GENERATION.

1494. Cephas, b. June 2, 1839.
1494.ᵃ Frances Viola, b. —.
1494.ᵇ Fedora Myrtilla, b. —.
1494.ᶜ Galen Valverd, b. —.
1494.ᵈ Danforth Harlow, b. —.
1494.ᵉ Menden Gerad, b. —.
1494.ᶠ Clifton Everett, b. —.

728.

ALONZO THOMPSON[6] (Galen,[5] William,[4] Caleb,[3] Jacob,[2] John[1]), b. —, son of Galen and Fanny (Marble) Thompson; m. JUDITH P. DOLLEY. Lives near San Francisco, Cal.

CHILDREN VII. GENERATION.

1495.   Rosina Foster, b. —.
1495.ᵃ Rinaldo Forister, b. —.
1495.ᵇ Roxanna Fannie, b. —.
1495.ᶜ Rosellen Florintine, b. —.
1495.ᵈ Eugene Watson, b. Sept., 1853.

730.

LOAMMI BALDWIN THOMPSON⁶ (Galen,⁵ William,⁴ Caleb,³ Jacob,² John¹), b. September 5, 1819, in Jay, Me., son of Galen and Fanny (Marble) Thompson; m. October 11, 1847, in Weld, Me., LAURA JANE DOLLEY. Lives at North Livermore, Me.

CHILDREN VII. GENERATION.

1496.   Davilla Sturtevant, b. July 29, 1848; m. Lizzie E. Hersey.
1497.   Fannie Gertrude, b. April 18, 1851; m. Addison P. Ricker.
1498.   Adelmar Baldwin, b. Jan. 24, 1853, in Jay; m. Feb. 16, 1878, in East Livermore, Ida May Bumpus.
1499.   Willie Augustus, b. Feb. 27, 1858, in Livermore; m. May 17, 1883, in Livermore, Lucretia G. Harmon.
1500.   Laura Boadicea, b. July 23, 1860; m. Ellery May Wing.
1501.   Julia E., changed to Thedia Julia, b. Sept. 15, 1866, in Livermore; m. Irvin A. Thompson (1505).

731.

RODOLPHUS P. THOMPSON⁶ (Galen,⁵ William,⁴ Caleb,³ Jacob,² John¹), b. September 29, 1825, in Jay, son of Galen and Fanny (Marble) Thompson; m. March 24, 1853, ABBIE L. WADSWORTH of East Livermore. Mr. Thompson was born on the old homestead known as "Thompson Fruitland," and where he always lived. He was engaged largely in dairy farming and fruit culture. Had one of the largest farms and orchards in the State. Was classed among the successful farmers of the state and accumulated a handsome property solely by farming. Also noted as a lecturer on agriculture. For many years was one of the directors and president of the Jay Mutual Fire Insurance Company. Was trial justice for many years, doing a large amount of business. Was one of the selectmen of Jay for ten years, and a large part of the time chairman of the board. Was master of his grange several years; also deputy state master. Several times he was a candidate for representative in the legislature and twice candidate for state senator, but unfortunately he was a member of the party that was largely in the minority in Maine, and yet at one time he lacked but six votes of an election. As a public speaker, he was very pleasing and popular, his graceful, winning ways and eloquent words placing him in the front rank of public speakers. He d. April 20, 1889, at Jay; funeral April 23. The remains were placed in the Thompson family cemetery on the farm where he was born. He was widely known as a man of enterprise and integrity, beloved and respected by a large circle of friends.

CHILDREN VII. GENERATION.

1502. Christopher R., b. July 16, 1854; d. May 10, 1858.
1503. Clarence M., b. August 21, 1856; m. Alice L. Richardson.
1504. Clifford R., b. August 18, 1858; m. Alice M. Kyes.
1505. Irvin A., b. Sept. 28, 1860; m. (1) Rosetta R. Goding, (2) Thedia Julia Thompson (1501).
1506. Costella A., b. Jan. 9, 1863; m. Ardean M. Allen.
1507. Flora G., b. August 25, 1869. Has much talent as a poet; also as a writer of prose. Her writings are marked with great tenderness and pathos as well as grandeur and sublimity, and show much originality and strength, and are eagerly sought for publication. She has delivered lectures, standing in the pulpits of full churches and crowded halls. She is an eloquent speaker and her lectures everywhere elicit most hearty commendation.

732.

DON CARLOS D'VAUDRILLE THOMPSON[6] (Galen,[5] William,[4] Caleb,[3] Jacob,[2] John[1]), b. July 4, 1833, son of Galen and Fanny (Marble)Thompson; m. September, 1853, ELMIRA A. ATWOOD of Livermore. Lives near San Francisco, Cal.

CHILD VII. GENERATION.

1508. Arthur D. V., b. Sept. 22, 1855.

734.

ELLEN THOMPSON[6] (Arad,[5] William,[4] Caleb,[3] Jacob,[2] John[1]), b. January 9, 1821; dau. of Arad and Mercy (Bourne) Thompson; m. June 15, 1841, NATHAN KING of Middleboro. While in the Massachusetts senate, it was at the instance of Mr. King that the Plymouth Colony Records were published. ~

CHILDREN VII. GENERATION.

1509. Ellen Frances, b. May 3, 1842.
1510. Ida F., b. July 20, 1844; d. April 15, 1862.

1511. Mary J., b. Jan. 6, 1847.
1512. Sarah E., b. March 21, 1849.

735.

LUCY ANN THOMPSON[6] (Arad,[5] William,[4] Caleb,[3] Jacob,[2] John[1]), b. October 23, 1822, dau. of Arad and Mercy (Bourne) Thompson; m. June 23, 1844, WILLIAM A. KING.

CHILDREN VII. GENERATION.

1513. Alice Maria, b. August 21, 1847; d. Jan. 25, 1854.
1514. Horace T., b. Jan. 9, 1857; d. Feb. 20, 1877, in New York.

736.

WILLIAM ARAD THOMPSON[6] (Arad,[5] William,[4] Caleb,[3] Jacob,[2] John[1]), b. June 21, 1835, son of Arad and Mercy (Bourne) Thompson; m. ELLA MASON WILLIAMS, dau. of James M. Williams of Taunton, Mass. Mr. Thompson graduated at Yale college in 1857. Studied law and practiced law in Boston. He d. September 5, 1876, in Newton. His wife was author of a book entitled, "Beaten Paths: or, a Woman's Vacation in Europe," published by Lee & Shepard, Boston; she also wrote for several popular magazines. She d. March 21, 1875.

CHILDREN VII. GENERATION.

1515. Alice King, b. Feb. 24, 1868. Residence, Middleborough, Mass.
1516. Virgil Williams, b. May 27, 1870. Residence, Middleborough.

738.

RACHEL STONE LEONARD[6] (Boadice,[5] William,[4] Caleb,[3] Jacob,[2] John[1]), b. May 31, 1819, dau. of Simeon and Boadice (Thompson) Leonard; m. DEXTER MARVEL. Residence, Taunton, Mass.

CHILDREN VII. GENERATION.

1517. Theodore L., b. —; m. —.
1518. William D., b. —; m. —.
1519. Joseph B., b. —; m. —.
1520. Alice, b. —; m. —.
1521. Sarah L., b. —; m. —.
1522. Amos, b. —; un-m.

739.

FANNY LEONARD[6] (Boadice,[5] William,[4] Caleb,[3] Jacob,[2] John[1]), b. March 19, 1821, dau. of Simeon and Boadice (Thompson) Leonard; m. THOMAS KENT,[*] owner of several woolen mills and other real estate near their residence at Clifton Heights, near Philadelphia, where he d. about 1885.

CHILDREN VII. GENERATION.

1523. Hannah, b. —.
1524. Henry Thomas, b. —.
1525. Louisa, b. —.
1526. Samuel Leonard, b. —.
1527. Mary, b. —.

750.

JULIET HARLOW WARREN[6] (Irene,[5] William,[4] Caleb,[3] Jacob,[2] John[1]), b. June 23, 1827, dau. of Daniel and Irene (Thompson) Warren; m. May 6, 1849, ALANSON C. KEEN of Marshfield.

CHILDREN VII. GENERATION.

1528. Ida Janet, b. May 2, 1850; d. Feb. 4, 1851.
1529. Frederick Warren, b. Oct. 26, 1851.
1530. Juliet Irene, b. June 16, 1856; d. Jan. 26, 1857.

(772 see 526.)

774.

HARRIET THOMPSON[6] (Alfred,[5] Caleb,[4] Caleb,[3] Jacob,[2] John[1]), b. January 13, 1812, dau. of Alfred and Fear (Thompson) Thompson; m. (1) ASEL THOMAS, (2) RUEL EATON.

CHILDREN BY FIRST HUSBAND VII. GENERATION.

1531. George E., b. —; killed in battle in the war of the rebellion.
1532. Ruth E., b. —; m. Henry Whitman.

CHILDREN BY SECOND HUSBAND VII. GENERATION.

1533. Laura H., b. —; m. Alexander Cushman. She d. —.
1534. Asel T., b. —; m. Hannah Atwood.
1535. Alexander, b. —; m. Lizzie Alden.

775.

ISRAEL T. THOMPSON[6] (Alfred,[5] Caleb,[4] Caleb,[3] Jacob,[2] John[1]), b. February 6, 1814; son of Alfred and Fear (Thomp-

son) Thompson; m. JOANNA TOWN.   Husband and wife both
dead.

CHILDREN VII. GENERATION.

1586.   Charles, b. —.
1537.   Francelia, b. —: d. —.

779.

MARY ELIZA THOMPSON[6] (Alfred,[5] Caleb,[4] Caleb,[3] Jacob,[2]
John[1]), b. October 12, 1826, dau. of Alfred and Fear (Thompson) Thompson; m. DAVID WILDER.   He d. 1887.

CHILDREN VII. GENERATION.

1538.   John C., b. —; m. Helen Carr.
1539.   Eliza, b. —.
1540.   Ruth, b. —; m. Horace Kendrick.

784.

SARAH THOMPSON[6] (Frederick M.,[5] Caleb,[4] Caleb,[3] Jacob,[2]
John[1]), b. June 17, 1823, dau. of Frederick M. and Susanna
(Cheesman) Thompson; m. December 4, 1845, JOHN WALES,
b. July 14, 1812, in Randolph, Mass.

CHILDREN VII. GENERATION.

1541.   Mary Elizabeth, b. June 1, 1853.
1542.   Frederick Atherton, b. May 5, 1857; d. August 26, 1874.
1543.   John, b. Jan. 25, 1865.

786.

CHARLES PERKINS THOMPSON[6] (Frederick M.,[5] Caleb,[4]
Caleb,[3] Jacob,[2] John[1]), b. July 30, 1827, son of Frederick M.
and Susanna (Cheesman) Thompson; m. January 10, 1861,
ABBY HERRICK, b. November 19, 1840, dau. of Josiah Herrick
of Gloucester, Mass.   Charles P. has lived in Gloucester since
May 8, 1857; engaged in the practice of the law.   In 1871 and
1872 was a member of Massachusetts house of representatives.
Was a member of the forty-fourth congress from the then
Massachusetts sixth congressional district.   Was elected over
Gen. Benjamin F. Butler, who was the republican candidate.
Was candidate for governor on the democratic ticket in 1880
and 1881.   Was appointed in October, 1885, by Gov. George
D. Robinson to the office of associate justice of the superior
court, which office he now holds (1890).

CHILDREN VII. GENERATION.

1544. Grace, b. Sept. 27, 1865.
1545. Franklin Hallett, b. Sept. 15, 1869.

787.

CALEB THOMPSON[6] (Frederick M.,[5] Caleb,[4] Caleb,[3] Jacob,[2] John[1]), b. February 18, 1832, son of Frederick M. and Susanna (Cheesman) Thompson; m. SARAH JANE WAITE, b. June, 1837, in Hallowell, Me. He represented the towns of Braintree and Holbrook in the Massachusetts legislature in 1886.

CHILD VII. GENERATION.

1546. Arthur Burnham, b. June 6, 1864; d. June 1, 1877.

789.

ANDREW THOMPSON[6] (Reuben,[5] Andrew,[4] Reuben,[3] Thomas,[2] John[1]), b. July 24, 1791, son of Reuben and Eunice (Whitman) Thompson; m. (1) MERCY TILSON, dau. of Ephraim Tilson, (2) ———.

CHILDREN BY FIRST WIFE VII. GENERATION.

1547. William E., b. —; m. Eliza N. Gardner.
1548. Josephus T., b. April 26, 1822; m. Mary Vining.

CHILDREN BY SECOND WIFE VII. GENERATION.

1549. Henry, b. —.
1550. Charles, b. —.
1551. Mary Ann, b. —.
1552. Henrietta, b. —.

791.

REUBEN THOMPSON[6] (Reuben,[5] Andrew,[4] Reuben,[3] Thomas,[2] John[1]), b. Oct. 24, 1795, in Halifax, son of Reuben and Eunice (Whitman) Thompson; m. SALLY WASHBURN. He moved to Plympton about 1833. He d. March 30, 1875. She d. June 25, 1877.

CHILDREN VII. GENERATION.

1553. Henry Davis, b. April 29, 1830; d. April 21, 1861.
1554. Elmira Morton, b. March 15, 1832; m. Timothy R. Weston.
1555. Charles Lewis, b. Feb. 19, 1836; m. Mary Ann Tribou, Oct. 19, 1865. He was ordained to the Baptist ministry.
1556. Walter, b. Nov. 25, 1837; m. Julia Peterson.

1557.   Josiah Whitman, b. Jan. 1, 1841; m. Isabella O. W. (Phinney) Eldridge.

797.

GILES THOMPSON[6] (Abel,[5] Andrew,[4] Reuben,[3] Thomas,[2] John[1]), b. June 2, 1794, son of Abel and Elizabeth (Leach) Thompson; m. FANNY WATERMAN, dau. of Isaac Waterman.

CHILDREN VII. GENERATION.

1558.   Joseph W., b. Nov. 25, 1819; m. Fidelia Sherman.
1559.   Daniel S., b. Dec. 25, 1822; m. Phila D. Wheelock.
1560.   Abigail, b. Oct. 1, 1825.

799.

DEXTER C. THOMPSON[6] (Nehemiah,[5] Asa,[4] Thomas,[3] Thomas,[2] John[1]), b. April 11, 1800, son of Nehemiah and Experience (Curtis) Thompson; m. HARRIET BOSWORTH, b. March 4, 1807, dau. of Joseph and Deborah Bosworth. He was a justice of the peace. He d. December 2, 1880. She d. July 13, 1878, aged 73 years.

CHILDREN VII. GENERATION.

1561.   Nehemiah, b. Oct. 7, 1835; m. Adeline Gibbs.
1562.   Harriet Dexter, b. April 14, 1841; m. — Wright; no children.

800.

JOSHUA C. THOMPSON[6] (Nehemiah,[5] Asa,[4] Thomas,[3] Thomas,[2] John[1]), b. December 26, 1801, son of Nehemiah and Experience (Curtis) Thompson; m. LUCY C. WESTON. He d. August 26, 1882.

CHILDREN VII. GENERATION.

1563.   Joshua C., b. —; d. Nov. 7, 1829, 3 days old.
1564.   Clarissa C., b. June 15, 1833.
1565.   Joan C., b. Feb. 3, 1836.

801.

EXPERIENCE C. THOMPSON[6] (Nehemiah,[5] Asa,[4] Thomas,[3] Thomas,[2] John[1]), b. February 16, 1806, dau. of Nehemiah and Experience (Curtis) Thompson; m. CAPT. GEORGE WATERMAN. She d. May, 1885.

CHILDREN VII. GENERATION.

1566. George H., b. —.
1567. Leander, b. —.

804.

LEARNED HALL THOMPSON[6] (Asa,[5] Asa,[4] Thomas,[3] Thomas,[2] John[1]), b. September 24, 1807, son of Asa and Hannah (Thompson) Thompson; m. January 22, 1843, HANNAH P. WOOD. She d. January 20, 1864, aged 57 years 6 months.

CHILD VII. GENERATION.

1568. Morton, b. May 29, 1844: m. Katie D. Standish.

807.

ICHABOD THOMPSON[6] (Asa,[5] Asa,[4] Thomas,[3] Thomas,[2] John[1]), b. April 27, 1813, son of Asa and Hannah (Thompson) Thompson; m. LUCY STANDISH, dau. of Josiah and Deborah Standish. He d. February 21, 1862. She d. August 22, 1861.

CHILDREN VII. GENERATION.

1569. Sarah, b. March 26, 1845; m. — Carver.
1570. Asa Carver, b. March 4, 1849: d. June 3, 1863.

832.

ALLEN DINSMORE THOMPSON[6] (Stephen H.,[5] Loring,[4] Thomas,[3] Thomas,[2] John[1]), b. October 26, 1817, in Cornish, N. H., son of Stephen H. and Sarah (Allen) Thompson; m. April 10, 1844, LOUISA BANCROFT. He d. in Windsor, Vt.

CHILDREN VII. GENERATION.

1571. Charles, b. —.
1572. George, b. —: d. in 1880.
1573. Henry, b. —.
1574. John, b. —.
1575. Etta, b. —.

833.

MARSHALL ELLERY THOMPSON[6] (Stephen H.,[5] Loring,[4] Thomas,[3] Thomas,[2] John[1]), b. April 27, 1820, in Croydon, son of Stephen and Sarah (Allen) Thompson. He was a physician at Lowell, Mass., and inventor of several useful medicines; m. November 23, 1854, at Lowell, HATTIE J. BEMIS.

CHILDREN VII. GENERATION.

1576. Ella Josephine, b. June 3, 1856; m. G. H. Lewis.
1577. Anna May, b. May 20, 1866.

835.

LAFAYETTE THOMPSON[6] (Stephen H.,[5] Loring,[4] Thomas,[3] Thomas,[2] John[1]), b. May 14, 1824, in Windsor, son of Stephen H., and Sarah (Allen) Thompson; m. ALICE CLAY in Boston. He d. May 20, 1864, at St. Louis, Mo., in the army.

CHILDREN VII. GENERATION.

1578. Arthur, b. —.
1579. Ella, b. —.
1580. Ida, b. —.

839.

EPHRAIM BRIGGS THOMPSON[6] (Jabez P.,[5] Ebenezer,[4] Ebenezer,[3] Thomas,[2] John[1]), b. November 11, 1813, son of Jabez P. and Sally (Briggs) Thompson; m. ELIZA R. SOULE, b. September 25, 1817, dau. of Jabez and Susanna Soule. He was a member of Massachusetts house of representatives in 1843 and 1844, captain of a volunteer company, assistant internal revenue assessor from 1862 to 1869, and a justice of the peace thirty-five years. He contributed a paper on "Historical Recollections of John Thompson" for the New Bedford Mercury of September 24, 1879. Residence, Halifax. He d. September 8, 1889.

CHILDREN VII. GENERATION.

1581. Ellen A., b. Jan. 3, 1837; m. Henry S. Pope.
1582. Sarah B., b. July 22, 1838; m. Edward M. Baine.
1583. Lucy M., b. May 12, 1840; m. Harrison D. Packard.
1584. Susan Richmond, b. Oct. 20, 1846; d. Jan. 22, 1854.
1585. Jabez P., b. July 24, 1853; m. Abby P. Wood.

840.

DEBORAH PRIOR THOMPSON[6] (Jabez P.,[5] Ebenezer,[4] Ebenezer,[3] Thomas,[2] John[1]), b. February, 1815, dau. of Jabez P. and Sally (Briggs) Thompson; m. October, 1842, GEORGE HART of New Bedford, Mass. He d. May 25, 1863, aged 51 years.

CHILDREN VII. GENERATION.

1586. Cornelia T., b. July 4, 1845; d. August 2, 1878.
1587. George S., b. Nov., 1850. Lives in New Bedford.

842.

CLARA S. THOMPSON[6] (Zebadiah,[5] Zebadiah,[4] Zebadiah,[3] Thomas,[2] John[1]), b. October 27, 1806, dau. of Zebadiah and Martha (Briggs) Thompson; m. REV. THOMAS A. SPILMAN of Hillsborough, Ill. He d. February 12, 1858. She d. April 11, 1840.

CHILDREN VII. GENERATION.

1588. Clarinda Morton, b. —; m. Geo. W. Raugh.
1589. Thomas A., b. July 23, 1834; d. 1834.
1590. Thomas E., b. —; m. Rose M., dau. of Rev. Geo. Inglis of Mendota. He is a Presbyterian minister. Lives at Nokomis, Ill.
1591. Mary, b. March 22, 1838; d. Dec. 24, 1848.
1592. James H., b. —; m. Mary Hutchinson.

844.

MARTHA BRIGGS THOMPSON[6] (Zebadiah,[5] Zebadiah,[4] Zebadiah,[3] Thomas,[2] John[1]), b. September 6, 1809, dau. of Zebadiah and Martha (Briggs) Thompson; m. JOHN B. ATWOOD of Plymouth. He d. 1864.

CHILDREN VII. GENERATION.

1593. Alexander P., b. Sept. 20, 1827; m. 1859, Mercy A. Bartlett. He d. Feb. 2, 1883. She d. Sept. 8, 1882
1594. Rebecca Waterman, b. Dec., 1830; m. Josiah A. Robbins.
1595. Martha Briggs, b. April 2, 1832; m. Amory T. Skerry.

845.

JOHN THOMAS ZEBADIAH THOMPSON[6] (Zebadiah,[5] Zebadiah,[4] Zebadiah,[3] Thomas,[2] John[1]), b. September 3, 1811, son of Zebadiah and Martha (Briggs) Thompson; m. SAGIE BAILEY TILDEN, b. September 4, 1819, dau. of Dr. Calvin and Catharine H. Tilden of Hanson. He was member of Massachusetts house of representatives in 1872. He lives on the old Thompson homestead, Halifax, Mass.

CHILDREN VII. GENERATION.

1596. Clara Spilman, b. Sept. 1, 1842.
1597. Zebadiah, b. Oct. 14, 1844; m. May 10, 1869, Maria Smith of Halifax, dau. of James and Susan (Hall) Smith.
1598. John Thomas, b. July 10, 1846; m. Irene L. Sturtevant.
1599. Mary Sheldon, b. Dec. 10, 1848; m. Lorenzo Augustus Tower.

1600. Christopher Tilden, b. April 9, 1853; m. Eva M. Carpenter.
1601. Charles Briggs, b. Nov. 17, 1859; m. Anna W. Shepard.

857.

JOHN THOMPSON[6] (William,[5] John,[4] Joseph,[3] Peter,[2] John[1]),
b. July 17, 1799, son of William and Belinda (Reeve) Thompson; m. November 20, 1828, at Shoreham, Vt., RUTH BATE-
MAN JOHNSON, dau. of William and Mary Bateman Johnson.
Mr. Thompson fitted for college with Rev. Elisha Yale, D. D.,
pastor of the church at Kingsborough. Graduated from Middlebury college in 1826. Spent two years at the theological
seminary at Princeton, N. J. Licensed to preach September,
1828; soon after appointed missionary; devoted a few years
to work among the Indians in Georgia. The last six years of
his life he was in Winchester, N. H., where he was pastor of
the Congregational church.

CHILDREN VII. GENERATION.

1602. Mary Eliza, b. Dec. 1, 1829, in Georgia; m. Solomon B. Saxton.
1603. William Johnson, b. August 16, 1831, in Georgia; d. August
       18, 1831.
1604. Edwin Johnson, b. Oct. 7, 1833; m. Ella Phelps Armstrong.
1605. George Bates, b. Jan. 12, 1839: m. Mary E. Avery.

SEVENTH GENERATION.

868.

DEBORAH THOMPSON[7] (John,[6] Thaddeus,[5] John,[4] John,[3]
John,[2] John[1]), b. March 28, 1809, dau. of John and Margaret
(Robinson) Thompson; m. SYLVANUS R. BOSWORTH. She d.
October 10, 1877.

CHILDREN VIII. GENERATION.

1606. Arvilla, b. —.
1607. Lucy Ann, b. —.
1608. Mary Elizabeth, b. —.
1609. Cynthia Augusta, b. —.
1610. Margaret Thompson, b. —.

869.

HANNAH THOMPSON[7] (John,[6] Thaddeus,[5] John,[4] John,[3] John,[2] John[1]), b. April 8, 1811, dau. of John and Margaret (Robinson) Thompson; m. EPHRAIM B. GAMMON. She d. September 5, 1851. Address, Mechanic Falls, Me.

CHILDREN VIII. GENERATION.

1611. Sophia, b. —.
1612. Julia Sarepta, b. —.
1613. Edee Malora, b. —.
1014. Rendall Tallman, b. —.
1615. Horatio Hackett, b. —.
1616. Ephraim Adron, b. —.
1617. Nathaniel, b. —.
1618. Cleora Celinda, b. —.
1619. Hannah, b. —.

870.

AMMIEL THOMPSON[7] (John,[6] Thaddeus,[5] John,[4] John,[3] John,[2] John[1]), b. February 12, 1815, son of John and Margaret (Robinson) Thompson; m. (1) HARRIET HOLMES, (2) LYDIA J. THOMPSON, dau. of Jonathan and Phebe (Ellis) Thompson, Scotch descent, (3) MARTHA A. RECORD. First wife d. May 30, 1844. Second wife d. February 16, 1865. Address, East Sumner, Me.

CHILD BY FIRST WIFE VIII. GENERATION.

1620. Leonard White, b. Sept. 6, 1840; m. Lucinda Berry.

CHILD BY SECOND WIFE VIII. GENERATION.

1621. John Elmer, b. June 5, 1849; m. Margaret T. Bosworth (1610).

871.

ABIGAIL ROBINSON THOMPSON[7] (John,[6] Thaddeus,[5] John,[4] John,[3] John,[2] John[1]), b. December 19, 1818, dau. of John and Margaret (Robinson) Thompson; m. AMERICA BONNEY. He d. —. Address, Norway, Me.

CHILDREN VIII. GENERATION.

1622. Delmar, b. —.
1623. Clara Hortense, b. —.
1624. Rosalthe Joanna, b. —.
1625. Benjamin Harris, b. —.
1626. Lumira Thompson, b. —.

21

872.

LYDIA THOMPSON[7] (John,[6] Thaddeus,[5] John,[4] John,[3] John,[2] John[1]), b. December 24, 1822, dau. of John and Margaret (Robinson) Thompson; m. THOMAS BONNEY. He d. —. Address, East Sumner, Me.

CHILDREN VIII. GENERATION.

1627. Anna Rebekah, b. —.
1628. John Thomas, b. —.
1629. Henry Wilson, b. —.
1630. John Henry, b. —.
1631. Thomas Wilson, b. —.

873.

JOHN THOMPSON[7] (John,[6] Thaddeus,[5] John,[4] John,[3] John,[2] John[1]), b. November 23, 1827, son of John and Margaret (Robinson) Thompson; m. MAHALA J. A. BURNHAM. Address, Hartford, Me.

CHILDREN VIII. GENERATION.

1632. Sarah Jane, b. —.
1633. Dorah Margaret, b. —.
1634. Hattie Geneva, b. —.
1635. Grace Cleora, b. —.

875.

WILLIAM HASTINGS THOMPSON[7] (John,[6] Thaddeus,[5] John,[4] John,[3] John,[2] John[1]), b. August 1, 1833, son of John and Margaret (Robinson) Thompson; m. CORNELIA A. FULLER. Address, North Livermore, Me.

CHILDREN VIII. GENERATION.

1636. Estelle Cornelia, b. —.
1637. Charles Hastings, b. —.

876.

LUCIUS THOMPSON[7] (Ammiel,[6] Thaddeus,[5] John,[4] John,[3] John,[2] John[1]), b. July 23, 1819, son of Ammiel and Fear (Tilson) Thompson; m. LYDIA RYDER, b. December 9, 1808, dau. of Samuel and Lydia Ryder.

CHILDREN VIII. GENERATION.

1638. Josephine Augusta, b. Dec. 19, 1841; d. July 23, 1843.
1639. Josephine, b. —.

886.

EDWIN THOMPSON[7] (Eliab,[6] Eliab,[5] Peter,[4] Thomas,[3] John,[2] John[1]), b. June 23, 1829, son of Eliab and Lydia (Thompson) Thompson; m. April, 1854, OLIVE S. PRATT, b. June 22, 1831, dau. of Ebenezer and Olive (Wood) Pratt. He d. June 19, 1868.

CHILDREN VIII. GENERATION.

1640. Cora Clifton, b. March 22, 1857; m. —.
1641. Eliab, b. Oct. 8, 1858; d. Oct. 8, 1862.
1642. Elmer Loring, b.·July 2, 1868.

887.

ASAPH P. THOMPSON[7] (Eliab,[6] Eliab,[5] Peter,[4] Thomas,[3] John,[2] John[1]), b. January 2, 1832, son of Eliab and Lydia (Thompson) Thompson; m. (1) 1858, LYDIA C. ATWOOD of Nantucket, (2) 1863, BETSEY ANN BARKER. First wife d. March, 1861. He d. June 18, 1868.

CHILDREN VIII. GENERATION.

1643. Alexander Prescott, b. Jan. 10, 1865; d. July, 1883.
1644. Lottie Barker, b. Oct. 14, 1866.

889.

FRANKLIN S. THOMPSON[7] (Venus,[6] Thomas,[5] Francis,[4] Thomas,[3] John,[2] John[1]), b. September 15, 1825, son of Venus and Jane (Southworth) Thompson; m. LUCY M. PUTNAM.

CHILDREN VIII. GENERATION.

1645. William B., b. Sept. 15, 1864.
1646. Helen F., b. Sept. 15, 1869.

890.

VENUS THOMPSON[7] (Venus,[6] Thomas,[5] Francis,[4] Thomas,[3] John,[2] John[1]), b. June 29, 1832, son of Venus and Jane (Southworth) Thompson; m. GEORGIE SAWIN.

CHILDREN VIII. GENERATION.

1647. Edward C., b. —. Lives in New York.
1648. Jennie, b. —. Lives in New York.

894.

PHILANDER WILLIAMS THOMPSON[7] (Philander,[6] Thomas,[5] Francis,[4] Thomas,[3] John,[2] John[1]), b. November 30, 1840, son of

Philander and Eliza (Giles) Thompson; m. Lucy A. T. Cushman.

CHILDREN VIII. GENERATION.

1649. Leslie Irving, b. Jan. 13, 1870.
1650. Bessie Allen, b. Feb. 28, 1875.

895.

Charles Lawton Thompson[7] (Philander,[6] Thomas,[5] Francis,[4] Thomas,[3] John,[2] John[1]), b. July 7, 1842, son of Philander and Eliza (Giles) Thompson; m. Lillian Lines.

CHILDREN VIII. GENERATION.

1651. Charles Bennett, b. —.
1652. Lillian Esther, b. —.

(896 see 907.)

898.

Ellen Whitmore Thompson[7] (Philander,[6] Thomas,[5] Francis,[4] Thomas,[3] John,[2] John[1]), b. October 13, 1847, dau. of Philander and Eliza (Giles) Thompson; m. Amasa Gray, Jr.

CHILDREN VIII. GENERATION.

1653. William Southwick, b. Jan. 8, 1870.
1654. Eliza Giles, b. Jan. 28, 1876.
1655. Wealtha Emma, b. Jan. 23, —.

902.

Elvina W. Thompson[7] (Israel W.,[6] Reuel,[5] Francis,[4] Thomas,[3] John,[2] John[1]), b. September 10, 1844, dau. of Israel W. and Betsey W. (Perkins) Thompson; m. William H. Bennett.

CHILD VIII. GENERATION.

1656. Horace P., b. August 17, 1870.

904.

Arabell Thompson[7] (Israel W.,[6] Reuel,[5] Francis,[4] Thomas,[3] John,[2] John[1]), b. June 18, 1850, dau. of Israel W. and Lydia (Lyon) Thompson; m. Samuel S. Bourne.

CHILDREN VIII. GENERATION.

1657. George F., b. September 12, 1875.
1658. Charles A., b. July 31, 1878.

906.

REUEL FRANCIS THOMPSON[7] (Reuel,[6] Reuel,[5] Francis,[4] Thomas,[3] John,[2] John[1]), b. August 20, 1842, son of Reuel and Sarah T. (Wood) Thompson; m. ELIZA SHAW.

CHILD VIII. GENERATION.

1659.   Cora Frances, b. Dec. 19, 1869.

907.

ALFRED WOOD THOMPSON[7] (Reuel,[6] Reuel,[5] Francis,[4] Thomas,[3] John,[2] John[1]), b. March 19, 1844, son of Reuel and Sarah T. (Wood) Thompson; m. ANNIE ELIZA THOMPSON (896).

CHILDREN VIII. GENERATION.

1660.   Alfred Percival, b. April 10, 1871.
1661.   Florence Emerson, b. Feb. 21, 1875; adopted.

909.

LUCIA ANN THOMPSON[7] (Reuel,[6] Reuel,[5] Francis,[4] Thomas,[3] John,[2] John[1]), b. July 20, 1847, dau. of Reuel and Sarah T. (Wood) Thompson; m. ALANSON WASHBURN.

CHILD VIII. GENERATION.

1662.   Reuel Winfred, b. August 22, 1875.

910.

RHODA ELLA SPARROW THOMPSON[7] (Reuel,[6] Reuel,[5] Francis,[4] Thomas,[3] John,[2] John[1]), b. December 2, 1849, dau. of Reuel and Sarah T. (Wood) Thompson; m. ALBERT J. WOOD.

CHILD VIII. GENERATION.

1663.   Grace Evelyn, b. April 4, 1881.

917.

HENRY CLINTON LYON[7] (Priscilla W.,[6] Reuel,[5] Francis,[4] Thomas,[3] John,[2] John[1]), b. May 17, 1838, in Halifax, son of Henry C. and Priscilla W. (Thompson) Lyon; m. WEALTHA GILMORE of Turner, Maine.

CHILDREN VIII. GENERATION.

1664.   Leovis Velma, b. March 27, 1868.
1665.   Nellie Gilmore, b. Nov. 16, 1874.
1666.   Florence May, b. Oct. 23, 1881.

919.

ALGERNON SIDNEY LYON[7] (Priscilla W.,[6] Reuel,[5] Francis,[4] Thomas,[3] John,[2] John[1]), b. October 3, 1843, son of Henry C. and Priscilla W. (Thompson) Lyon; m. LOUISE FRANCES COPELAND of West Bridgewater.

CHILDREN VIII. GENERATION.

1667. Louisa Evelyn, b. Nov. 7, 1875.
1668. Harold Sidney, b. August 10, 1883.

922.

DAVID W. THOMPSON[7] (Benjamin F.,[6] Reuel,[5] Francis,[4] Thomas,[3] John,[2] John[1]), b. November 26, 1846, son of Benjamin F. and Sarah (Wood) Thompson; m. CLARISSA B. FINNEY.

CHILD VIII. GENERATION.

1669. Clara Annie, b. June 3, 1880.

926.

HORACE G. THOMPSON[7] (Martson,[6] Reuel,[5] Francis,[4] Thomas,[3] John,[2] John[1]), b. June 8, 1850, son of Martson and Mary Ann (Wilbur) Thompson; m. December 25, 1881, ANNIE E. STAPLES.

CHILDREN VIII. GENERATION.

1670. Herbert F., b. Oct. 13, 1873.
1671. Henry K., b. Jan. 18, 1878.

932.

ISAAC THOMPSON BABBITT[7] (Sarah,[6] Sarah,[5] Nathan,[4] Thomas,[3] John,[2] John[1]), b. December 21, 1806, son of Isaac and Sarah (Phinney) Babbitt; m. May, 1838, ANN PACKARD, dau. of Ebenezer Packard. Lives in Fitchburg, Mass.

CHILDREN VIII. GENERATION.

1672. Willard, b. 1839; m. Lodicie —; had two children, Herman and Annie.
1673. Ann Zenah, b. —; d. young.
1674. Sarah Ann, b —; d. young.
1675. Charles, b. 1850; m. —; had three children; two d. Lives in Fitchburg.

933·

IRENE ADELINE BABBITT[7] (Sarah,[6] Sarah,[5] Nathan,[4] Thomas,[3] John,[2] John[1]), b. April 30, 1809, dau. of Isaac and Sarah (Phinney) Babbitt; m. CYRUS LOVELL. She d. September 9, 1855. He lived the last four years of his life at Strawberry Point, Clayton county, Iowa.

CHILDREN VIII. GENERATION.

1676. William, b. —; un-m.; d. of wounds received at battle of Gettysburg.
1677. Sarah Adeline, b. Oct. 20, 1840; m. James M. McKinlay.

934.

HARRISON W. BABBITT[7] (Sarah,[6] Sarah,[5] Nathan,[4] Thomas,[3] John,[2] John[1]), b. March 31, 1812, son of Isaac and Sarah (Phinney) Babbitt; m. September 7, 1826, MARILLA T. CONVERSE. He d. July, 1885.

CHILDREN VIII. GENERATION.

1678. Clara Frances, b. June 5, 1849; m. Lauman Holcomb of Granby, Conn.; had one child.
1679. Edwin Converse, b. Nov. 26, 1850; m. Addie —; had one daughter. Lives in Fitchburg, Mass.
1680. Frank Allen, b. July 15, 1853; d. about 1875; un-m.
1681. Mary Alice, b. Nov. 19, 1855; m —; had two children. Lives in Nashua, N. H.
1682. Kate Maria, b. Oct. 7, 1860.
1683. Alfred Lincoln, b. Nov. 11, 1862.
1684. Milton Peck, b. Jan. 2, 1867.

935·

PLINY H. BABBITT[7] (Sarah,[6] Sarah,[5] Nathan,[4] Thomas,[3] John,[2] John[1]), b. June, 1818, son of Isaac and Sarah (Phinney) Babbitt; m. June 19, 1839, LYDIA PERRY.

CHILDREN VIII. GENERATION.

1685. Deborah, b. Feb. 5, 1841; m. Dr. Seth L. Chase of Colchester, Conn.
1686. Caleb Henry, b. 1843; m. —; had several children; d. 1885.
1687. George W., b. —. Member of board of health, Boston, Mass.
1688. Marianne, b. —; m. Theodore Bemis. Lived in Providence, R. I.
1689. Charles, b. —; m. —; had one child. Lived in Orange, Mass.

1690. Lizzie, b. —; m. Harding Jenkins; had two children. Lived in Barre, Mass.

947.

SUSAN HADASSAH TUCKER[7] (Woodward,[6] Susanna,[5] Nathan,[4] Thomas,[3] John,[2] John[1]), b. March 28, 1844, dau. of Woodward and Elizabeth (Cressy) Tucker; m. JOHN W. PICKETT. Lived in Beverly, Mass.

CHILDREN VIII. GENERATION.

1691. John Frederick, b. June 24. 1870.
1692. Mary Susan, b. July 19, 1872.
1693. Elizabeth Tucker, b. Sept. 29, 1876.
1694. William, } Twins.
1695. Edward, } b. March 24, 1879.

954.

JAMES T. ESTEE[7] (Ansel,[6] Abigail,[5] James,[4] Thomas,[3] John,[2] John[1]), b. March 11, 1821, son of Ansel and Olive (Tyler) Estee; m. June 21, 1849, MARTHA TEFFT, dau. of Patta (Hall) Tefft, dau. of Hannah (Cutler) Hall, wife of Azor Thompson (164). Lived many years in LeRoy, N. Y. In April, 1881, moved to Aurora, Ill.

CHILDREN VIII. GENERATION.

1696. Frederick P., b. March 26, 1850, in LeRoy, N. Y.
1697. Clara, E., b. 1851, in LeRoy. Lived in Aurora, Ill.
1698. William C., b. 1854, in LeRoy.
1699. James T., b. 1856, in LeRoy; d. 1878.
1700. Henry M., b. 1859, in LeRoy.

956.

WILLIAM CLARK ROOT[7] (Elvira,[6] Cyrus,[5] James,[4] Thomas,[3] John,[2] John[1]), b. August 17, 1831, in Verona, N. Y., son of Joseph and Elvira (Thompson) Root; m. June 23, 1856, MARY A. WILLIAMS of Pembroke. Lived for many years in Clarendon, Orleans county, N. Y.; d. March 14, 1879.

CHILDREN VIII. GENERATION.

1701. Welden William, b. July, 1857; d. March 1864.
1702. Elvira A., b. —.
1703. Gertrude J., b. —.
1704. Bertha M., b. —.
1705. Cora B., b. —.
1706. Ernest, b. August, 1873.

957.

LUCY E. ROOT[7] (Elvira,[6] Cyrus,[5] James,[4] Thomas,[3] John,[2] John[1]), b. February 9, 1835, in Clarendon, dau. of Joseph and Elvira (Thompson) Root; m. (1) November 4, 1857, GEORGE W. CLARK, son of Nelson Clark of Carlton. George W. d. December 10, 1867, m. (2) May 29, 1885, NATHANIEL ATWELL of Lawton, Mich.

CHILD BY FIRST HUSBAND VIII. GENERATION.

1707. Arthur Burnham, b. Dec. 18, 1866; m. Tillie A. Marvin.

958.

MARY EUSEBIA ROOT[7] (Elvira,[6] Cyrus,[5] James,[4] Thomas,[3] John,[2] John[1]), b. July 5, 1841, dau. of Joseph and Elvira (Thompson) Root; m. April 29, 1862, CHAUNCY BURNHAM youngest son of William Burnham of Murray, Orleans county N. Y. Lived for several years in Van Buren county, Mich.

CHILDREN VIII. GENERATION.

1708. Albert D., b. Oct. 7, 1864. in Clarendon; d. Nov. 10, 1865.
1709. Howard C., b. Sept. 4, 1889, in Ridgeway; d. July 17, 1870.

959.

DANIEL THOMPSON ROOT[7] (Elvira,[6] Cyrus,[5] James,[4] Thomas,[3] John,[2] John[1]), b. September 19, 1844, son of Joseph and Elvira (Thompson) Root; m. in Barry county, Mich., ETTIE REYNOLDS, dau. of John Reynolds. Daniel enlisted August 30, 1862, in company G, 151st regiment, New York volunteers, under the President's second call for 300,000 men to put down the great rebellion. He was in Baltimore the first winter; in West Virginia and Maryland the most of the summer of 1863. Joined the Army of the Potomac in time to take part in the Mine Run campaign in November, 1863, being in third division, third corps. Was in camp near Brandy Station, Va., in the winter of 1863-4. When General Grant reorganized the army in March, 1864, his regiment was attached to third division, sixth corps, and took part in the battles of the Wilderness, Spottsylvania C. H., North Anna, Hanover C. H., Cold Harbor and the first attack on Petersburg. Was sent to protect Washington when Early started on his raid in Maryland and Pennsylvania. Fought Early at Monocacy, Md., July 9, where one-third of his regiment was killed or wounded. Was taken prisoner, but escaped and went to the hospital at Frederick City, Md. Being sick, did not rejoin the regiment until a few days before the battle of Cedar Creek, where Sheridan made his famous ride. Was at Petersburg during the winter of 1864–5. Was in battle of Fort Steadman, capture of Petersburg. Went in pursuit of General Lee, capturing General Ewall with 6,000 prisoners at Sailor's Creek, April 6, and wound up at Appomattox, April 9. Mustered out June 26, 1865, near Alexandria. Removed from New York to Nebraska —returned to New York. Later removed to Van Buren county, Mich. Was made commander of a G. A. R. post. Address, Lawton, Mich.

CHILDREN VIII. GENERATION.

1710. Percy D., b. about 1869, in New York.
1711. Libbie Elvira, b. —, in Michigan.
1712. Cyrus Adelbert, b. —, in Nebraska.
1713. Charles R., b. —, in New York.
1714. Lucy Eusebia, b. —, in Nebraska.
1715. William Clark, b. about 1879, in Nebraska.

960.

IRVING MEAD THOMPSON[7] (Cyrus,[6] Cyrus,[5] James,[4] Thomas,[3] John,[2] John[1]), b. March 15, 1831, in Verona, N. Y., son of Cyrus and Charlotte H. (Mead) Thompson; m. September 13, 1865, MELISSA M. WARNER of Albion, N. Y., b. March 24, 1832. He read law with Judge Benjamin L. Bessac at Albion; was admitted to practice in September, 1856. He was first lieutenant in seventeenth New York battery of light artillery for nearly three years of the latter part of the war of the rebellion, and was mustered out of the service at the conclusion of the war. Received a somewhat severe gunshot wound in the thigh in July, 1864, while unmasking a piece in front of Petersburg, Va. When able for duty he was detailed by the secretary of war as an assistant to Brig. Gen. Joseph Holt in the bureau of military justice at Washington, D. C., and remained on duty in that bureau till mustered out of service. Was district attorney of Orleans county, N. Y., for three years from January 1, 1866, and was postmaster of the village of Albion in said county for four years, receiving the appointment from Gen. Grant while president. Has been a member of the school board of Albion for several years. Has been engaged in the practice of law since 1856, except while in the military service.

CHILDREN VIII. GENERATION.

1716. Edith R., b. July 28, 1866, in Albion, N. Y.; m. Oct. 23, 1889, Fred. S. Taylor.
1717. Warner, b. Dec. 22, 1867, in Albion.
1718. Fred M., b. Nov. 20, 1869, in Albion.

961

MARY AURORA THOMPSON[7] (Cyrus,[6] Cyrus,[5] James,[4] Thomas,[3] John,[2] John[1]), b. April 14, 1833, dau. of Cyrus and Charlotte H. (Mead) Thompson; m. January 8, 1854, in Carlton, N. Y., EMERY H. SIMPSON. She was a contributor to several papers under the *nom de plume* of "Kate Woodland," and wrote many poems of merit. In 1863, with her husband, removed to Hartford, Van Buren county, Mich., where they located on a farm. Mr. Simpson was a practical and successful farmer. He was supervisor of his township, also a representative in the Michigan legislature during the sessions of 1873, 1874, and 1887.

CHILDREN VIII. GENERATION.

1719. Ellen May, b. March 31, 1856, in Carlton; d. August 30, 1861.
1720. Clara Bell, b. Sept. 1, 1857, in Carlton.
1721. Wendell Lee, b. August 10, 1859; m. Marion O. Wood.
1722. Ada May, b. January 25, 1861, in Carlton; m. November 28, 1888, Alva Sherwood of Three Oaks, Mich. An excellent school teacher.
1723. Nathan Fish, b. Oct. 12, 1862; m. Harriet A. Duncombe.
1724. Frank Glenn, b. Sept. 25, 1864, in Hartford; m. Dec. 10, 1889, Leona Johnson. Taught school successfully; is a farmer.
1725. Fred Lynn, b. June 10, 1869.
1726. Mary Maude, b. Dec. 31, 1871; d. Feb. 22, 1888. "Bright, joyous and unselfish, she carried sunshine wherever she went; even her last days were characterized by the same cheerfulness, and every day, as long as her strength permitted, she would lie and sing in her own sweet, happy way. No fretfulness, no pining, no grieving, her young life closed like the sunset of a beautiful summer day, without a cloud in the sky."

963.

LLOYD GARRISON THOMPSON[7] (Cyrus,[6] Cyrus,[5] James,[4] Thomas,[3] John,[2] John[1]), b. February 5, 1837, son of Cyrus and Charlotte H. (Mead) Thompson; m. (1) May 19, 1860, MARY L. THOMPSON (1006), m. (2) ELLEN EASTER. First wife d. March 29, 1863. He enlisted in the war of the rebellion

August, 1863, in Company F, 76th New York volunteer infantry.
Was in the army of the Potomac over two years under General
Rice, brigade commander; General Wadsworth, division commander; and General Meade, corps commander. He was
taken prisoner May 5, 1864, in the battle of the Wilderness;
was imprisoned at Danville, Andersonville, and Florence;
paroled March 6, 1865, a mere skeleton, a physical wreck. In
early life he lived in Orleans county, N. Y.; about 1860, in
western Michigan. After the war he again lived in Orleans
county; later at Fair Haven, Conn. Is a writer of merit.

CHILD BY FIRST WIFE VIII. GENERATION.

1727. Mary Lillian, b. Nov. 15, 1862.

964.

ELLEN E. THOMPSON[7] (Cyrus,[6] Cyrus,[5] James,[4] Thomas,[3]
John,[2] John[1]), b. December 16, 1838, dau. of Cyrus and Char-
lotte H. (Mead) Thompson; m. February 13, 1861, EDWARD
MOSHER, b. October 12, 1835. Lives in Eagle Harbor, N. Y.

CHILDREN VIII. GENERATION.

1728   Gertrude, b. Nov. 8, 1861; m. Washington Simmons.
1729. F. Harvey, b. May 22, 1869.
1730. Ralph, b. Sept. 2, 1874.

974.

FREEMAN LUCIUS THOMPSON[7] (Theophilus Waterman,[6]
Cyrus,[5] James,[4] Thomas,[3] John,[2] John[1]), b. August 16, 1843,
in Brooklyn, Mich., son of Theophilus W. and Ruth M. (Watkins) Thompson; m. November 6, 1867, THERESA M. MINTON,
dau. of Michael Minton. Lived in Montague, Mich., many
years; after the death of his father, returned to the old farm
in Brooklyn, Mich.

CHILDREN VIII. GENERATION.

1731. Minnie May, b. Sept. 12, 1871.
1732. Edward Watkins, b. Jan. 24, 1879.
1733. Burt L., b. March 27, 1880.

983.

CHARLES HUTCHINSON THOMPSON[7] (Nathan,[6] Cyrus,[5] James,[4]
Thomas,[4] John,[2] John[1]), b. November 29, 1838, in LeRoy, N.
Y., son of Nathan and Clarissa E. (Hutchinson) Thompson;

m. March 26, 1862, at Lawton, Mich., by Rev. T. T. George, ELIZABETH GILES SUTTON, b. February 24, 1842, in Bridgeport, Conn., later removed to Poughkeepsie, N. Y., dau. of Luman Sutton and Janet (McDonald) Sutton, whose parents came from Scotland. In 1845 Charles went from Orleans county, N. Y., to Jackson county, Mich.; returned to Orleans county about 1847, attending school, working at farm and other employments in Wyoming county until 1856, when he returned to Michigan and worked on a farm in Van Buren county until December, 1857; was then appointed porter in the state offices at Lansing. In 1861 worked in the office of secretary of state on United States census of 1860. In 1863 engaged in mercantile business a short time. In October, 1863, received the appointment of a clerkship in the auditor general's office, and a few years later was placed in charge of the work of extra clerks in the tax department. In 1889 was made assistant chief clerk, which position he still holds (1890). A prompt, particular, and thorough workman. He united with the M. E. church in 1856 and has occupied many positions of trust and responsibility in the church and Sunday school, especially as steward, treasurer, and chorister for many of the years since 1856. He is compiler of this work. Residence, 312 Capitol avenue south, Lansing, Mich.

CHILDREN VIII. GENERATION.

1734. Allan Sutton, b. May 26, 1866; m. Katie Hatchel.
1735. Ada Bell, b. Dec. 25, 1868.

987.

NATHAN I. THOMPSON[7] (Nathan,[6] Cyrus,[5] James,[4] Thomas,[3] John,[2] John[1]), b. August 1, 1850, son of Nathan and Clarissa E. (Hutchinson) Thompson; m. March 21, 1876, in Keeler, to ELLA AIDA TUTTLE, dau. of Hiram Tuttle. Nathan is a farmer, and correspondent for several papers. Address, Keelersville, Mich.

CHILDREN VIII. GENERATION.

1736. Nellie Lorinda, b. Jan. 18, 1877.
1737. Irma Gertrude, b. July 13, 1880.

990.

CLARA GERTRUDE THOMPSON[7] (Nathan,[6] Cyrus,[5] James,[4] Thomas,[3] John,[2] John[1]), b. August 25, 1858, dau. of Nathan and Clarissa E. (Hutchinson) Thompson; m. January 13, 1883, WILLIAM E. BASS of Lawrence, Mich. Address, Lawrence.

CHILDREN VIII. GENERATION.

1738. William W., b. Dec. 8, 1883, in Lawrence.
1739. Lucille, b. May 15, 1886, in Lawrence.
1740. Nathan T., b. April 11, 1890, in Lawrence.

998.

JAMES D. THOMPSON[7] (Jason K.,[6] Bela,[5] James,[4] Thomas,[3] John,[2] John[1]), b. January 7, 1832, son of Jason K. and Eliza Ann (Frisbie) Thompson; m. April 30, 1855, MARION E. WEBSTER. Lives at Berlin Heights, Ohio.

CHILDREN VIII. GENERATION.

1741. Arthur Clinton, b. Oct. 29, 1858.
1742. Clifford Webster, b. Oct. 13, 1868.

1000.

FRANKLIN D. THOMPSON[7] (Jason K.,[6] Bela,[5] James,[4] Thomas,[3] John,[2] John[1]), b. December 13, 1835, son of Jason K. and Eliza Ann (Frisbie) Thompson; m. November 27, 1862, ABBY N. PRICE, in Nevada, Story county, Iowa, where they live.

CHILDREN VIII. GENERATION.

1743. Kate E., b. Nov. 22, 1863.
1744. Frank L., b. March 22, 1867.
1745. Sylvia L., b. July 10, 1869.
1746. Cora A.,   } Twins.
1747. Clayton A.,   } b. March 30, 1874.
1748. Olive E., b. May 20, 1876.

1001.

FREDERICK FRISBIE THOMPSON[7] (Jason K.,[6] Bela,[5] James,[4] Thomas,[3] John,[2] John[1]), b. September 18, 1838, son of Jason K. and Eliza Ann (Frisbie) Thompson; m. October 22, 1865, GEORGIA PRICE of Nevada, Iowa. He d. January 24, 1885. Residence, Bailey, Pulaski county, Mo.

CHILDREN VIII. GENERATION.

1749. George Morris, b. August 8, 1866.
1750. Emmett Gardner, b. Jan. 10, 1868.

1751. Ormsby Courtney, b. Sept. 11, 1869.
1752. Fred Courtland, b. Jan. 29, 1872; d. Oct. 14, 1872.
1753. Jay Price, b. Oct. 25, 1873.
1754. Gertrude, b. Sept. 3, 1877.

1002.

AMOS FRANCIS THOMPSON[7] (Jason K.,[6] Bela,[6] James,[4] Thomas,[3] John,[2] John[1]), b. March 10, 1846, son of Jason K. and Eliza Ann (Frisbie) Thompson; m. July 2, 1867, CLARA DANIELS. He d. March 20, 1873.

CHILDREN VIII. GENERATION.

1755. William Sherwood, b. June 10, 1868. Address, 1011 Fifth avenue, Eau Claire, Wis.
1756. Effie Alice, b. Jan. 4, 1872.

1003.

ELLEN AMELIA THOMPSON[7] (James A.,[6] Bela,[6] James,[4] Thomas,[3] John,[2] John[1]), b. May 20, 1840, dau. of James A. and Eunice Ann (Benedict) Thompson; m. March 6, 1860, ALBERT STRONG. She d. April 20, 1861.

CHILD VIII. GENERATION.

1757. Nellie A., b. April 20, 1861; m. James Harvey Rodebaugh.

1004.

CELIA BENEDICT THOMPSON[7] (James A.,[6] Bela,[6] James,[4] Thomas,[3] John,[2] John[1]), b. June 5, 1843, dau. of James A. and Eunice Ann (Benedict) Thompson; m. (1) March 11, 1862, ALBERT STRONG, (2) January 20, 1875, DAVID POWELL. First husband d. May 20, 1868. Address, Perry Center, N. Y.

CHILDREN BY SECOND HUSBAND VIII. GENERATION.

1758. Bertie Lincoln, b Feb. 12, 1878; d. April 24, 1879.
1759. Floyd M., b. Jan. 30, 1880.

1005.

IRVING GRAHAM THOMPSON[7] (James A.,[6] Bela,[6] James,[4] Thomas,[3] John,[2] John[1]), b. January 29, 1845, son of James A. and Eunice Ann (Benedict) Thompson; m. January 15, 1868, MARTHA E. BUTLER.

CHILDREN VIII. GENERATION.

1760. Lottie E., b. Feb. 17, 1870.
1761. Eva Belle, b. Nov. 27, 1874.
1762. James Allen, b. March 24, 1876.
1763. William Irving, b. May 20, 1883.

(1006 *see* 963.)

1019.

ERNEST D. R. THOMPSON[7] (Dennis R.,[6] Bela,[5] James,[4] Thomas,[3] John,[2] John[1]), b. June 18, 1857, at Oconomowoc, Wis., son of Dennis R. and Maria H. (Knight) Thompson; m. October 9, 1884, CARRIE L. STREETER. He received a common school and academic education. Taught a district school when 18 years of age. In 1877 began the study of law in the office of Col. Warham Parks at Oconomowoc. In December, 1879, was admitted to the bar of Waukesha county and commenced the practice of law at Oconomowoc. In the spring of 1880 was elected city clerk and filled that position four years. In September, 1882, he formed a law copartnership with Col. Parks, which was not dissolved until November, 1886, at which time he was elected, on the republican ticket, to the office of district attorney for Waukesha county. In April, 1889, he removed to Salt Lake City, Utah.

CHILD VIII. GENERATION.

1764. Donald H., b. Oct. 12, 1885.

1025.

BURDETTE L. JOHNSON[7] (Diadamia,[6] Bela,[5] James,[4] Thomas,[3] John,[2] John[1]), b. October 22, 1849, in Fentonville, Mich., son of Dexter C. and Diadamia (Thompson) Johnson; m. 1871, JANNETT MCMILLAN. Lives in Milwaukee, Wis.

CHILDREN VIII. GENERATION.

1765. Herbert, b. —.
1766. Daisy, b. —.
1767. Robert, b. —.
1768. Edwin, b. —.
1769. Edna, b. —.
1770. Maggie, b. August 24, 1886.

1034.

MARY J. HEATH[7] (Caroline,[6] Nathan,[5] James,[4] Thomas,[3] John,[2] John[1]), b. August 31, 1835, dau. of Daniel and Caroline (Thompson) Heath; m. October 1, 1855, ATTILA G. WILSON of Ronald, Mich.

CHILDREN VIII. GENERATION.

1771. Agnes Louisa, b. Sept. 14, 1856, in Ronald.
1772. Frank P., b. May 12, 1861, in Ronald.
1773. John D., b. Feb. 14, 1866, in Ronald.
1774. Ida Amarilla, b. Jan. 5, 1875, in Ronald.

1035.

NATHAN T. HEATH[7] (Caroline,[6] Nathan,[5] James,[4] Thomas,[3] John,[2] John[1]), b. October 1, 1836, in Clarksfield, Ohio, son of Daniel and Caroline (Thompson) Heath; m. November 8, 1860, in Ronald, Mich., MARI WHITE, b. August 30, 1838, in Peru, N. Y.

CHILDREN VIII. GENERATION.

1775. Albert I., b. Sept. 8, 1861.
1776. Carrie A., b. Nov. 29, 1866.
1777. Daniel J., b. May 27, 1869.
1778. Orrie M., b. April 12, 1873.

1036.

AMARILLA O. HEATH[7] (Caroline,[6] Nathan,[5] James,[4] Thomas,[3] John,[2] John[1]), b. March 14, 1838, in Clarksfield, Ohio, dau. of Daniel and Caroline (Thompson) Heath; m. November 9, 1860, WELLINGTON C. PAGE of Ionia, Mich., b. in Whitestown, Oneida county, N. Y. Address, Ionia.

CHILDREN VIII. GENERATION.

1779. Rufus L., b. Feb. 2, 1866, in Ionia.
1780. Mary A., b. May 30, 1876, in Ionia.

1037.

DANIEL F. HEATH[7] (Caroline,[6] Nathan,[5] James,[4] Thomas,[3] John,[2] John[1]), b. January 2, 1855, in Manchester, Mich., son of Daniel and Caroline (Thompson) Heath; m. ANN NORTH of Palo, Mich.

23

CHILDREN VIII. GENERATION.

1781. Virgil, b. —, in Bushnell, Montcalm county, Mich.
1782. Ben, b. —, in Bushnell, Montcalm county, Mich.
1783. Paul, b. —, in Bushnell, Montcalm county, Mich.

1045.

ABBIE ROOT⁷ (Malinda,⁶ Rebecca,⁵ James,⁴ Thomas,³ John,²
John¹), b. —, dau. of Nathan and Malinda (Shearer) Root; m.
October, 1855, URI MASON, a Methodist minister of the Michigan conference.

CHILDREN VIII. GENERATION.

1784. Elma L., b. Oct., 1857.
1785. Mertie May, b. May, 1872.

1054.

ALBERT CUSHMAN⁷ (Thomas,⁶ Bethiah,⁵ Thomas,⁴ Shubael,³
John,² John¹), b. October 12, 1827, son of Thomas and Lucy
(Pratt) Cushman; m. September 12, 1852, MARY ANN
JEFFERY, dau. of George and Mary (Hall) Jeffery. Address,
76 State street, Boston.

CHILDREN VIII. GENERATION.

1786. Mary Lucy, b. Nov. 22, 1853.
1787. Elizabeth, b. May 30, 1856.
1788. Florence, b. Oct. 21, 1858.
1789. Martha Anna, b. May 7, 1861.
1790. Bertha Frances, b. Sept. 28, 1863.
1791. Alice Reed, b. Aug. 27, 1869.

1055.

CHARLES CUSHMAN⁷ (Thomas,⁶ Bethiah,⁵ Thomas,⁴ Shubael,³
John,² John¹), b. January 20, 1829, son of Thomas and Lucy
(Pratt) Cushman; m. December 18, 1853, ELIZA JANE
KELSEY, dau. of Robert and Abigail (Bennett) Kelsey.

CHILDREN VIII. GENERATION.

1792. George Hawley, b. Jan. 17, 1855. Settled near Chattanooga,
       Tenn., as a civil engineer; m. Marie L. Stabler and had Cora
       Jennie, b. March 7, 1887.
1793. Charles Abram, b. June 22, 1857. Went to Berlin, Germany,
       to complete his education as music teacher; while there mar-

ried a German girl; returned to New York; had Charles
Thomas, b. Sept. 5, 1887.

1794. Cora Jane, b. July 19, 1859; d. Feb. 10, 1862.

1056.

DARIUS CUSHMAN[7] (Thomas,[6] Bethiah,[5] Thomas,[4] Shubael,[3]
John,[2] John[1]), b. July 21, 1830, son of Thomas and Lucy
(Pratt) Cushman; m. (1) September 19, 1859, ELVINA THOMP-
SON (1124); m. (2) May 10, 1868, JANE FRANCES (FULLER)
PRATT, widow of Silvanus Pratt, dau. of Alfred Fuller of Hali-
fax. First wife d. January 2, 1867.

CHILD BY FIRST WIFE VIII. GENERATION.

1795. Albert, b. Nov. 14, 1866.

CHILDREN BY SECOND WIFE VIII. GENERATION.

1796. Alfred Thomas, b. August 20, 1869; d. July 15, 1884.
1797. Joseph Augustin, b. Jan. 31, 1881.

1057.

BETHIAH CUSHMAN[7] (Thomas,[6] Bethiah,[5] Thomas,[4] Shubael,[3]
John,[2] John[1]), b. December 15, 1831; dau. of Thomas and Lucy
(Pratt) Cushman; m. (1) April 13, 1854, ABRAM G. J.
SPOONER, son of Nathaniel and Hannah Spooner, m. (2) April
6, 1864, PHILANDER PRATT, son of Ebenezer and Olive (Wood)
Pratt. First husband sailed in the whaleship Mocktazuma, of
New Bedford, and lost in the Japan sea June 26, 1855.

CHILD BY SECOND HUSBAND VIII. GENERATION.

1798. Lucy Olive, b. Nov. 24, 1868.

1073.

JOSEPH ROBINSON THOMPSON[7] (Cyrus,[6] Isaac,[5] John,[4] Shubael,[3] John,[2] John[1]), b. November 21, 1804, in Hartford, Me.,
son of Cyrus and Rebecca (Robinson) Thompson; m. September 20, 1830, MARTHA CAROLINE ROGERS of Portland, Me.
He was a cornet player in the militia, and for many years was
a manufacturer of tombstones, monuments, etc., in Portland;
also held a position in the custom house at Portland for some
years. He d. November 21, 1883.

CHILDREN VIII. GENERATION.

1799. Henry Francis, b. August 28, 1831; m. Luella A. Gilman.
1800. Maria Caroline, b. Jan. 28, 1833; m. Cornelius D. Maynard.

1801. Ann Meacom, b. Oct. 12, 1835, in Portland; unmarried.
1802. John Edward, b. May 4, 1837, in Portland; d. April 28, 1840.
1803. Joseph Alfred, b. Feb. 25, 1839, in Portland; d. May 8, 1840.
1804. Mary Ellen, b. April 11, 1841, in Portland; unmarried.
1805. Enoch Morse, b. Jan. 19, 1843, in Portland; unmarried.
1806. Charles Rogers, b. Jan. 17, 1845, in Portland; d. Oct. 18, 1849.
1807. William Drake, b. Dec. 21, 1846; m. Alice Turner.
1808. Sumner Cummings, b. Nov. 13, 1848; m. Katie M. Connolly.
1809. Fred Irving, b. Dec. 4, 1850, in Portland.
1810. Stephen Emmons, b. June 23, 1853; m. Addie Ella Jordan.
1811. George Herbert, b. July 20, 1855; m. Hattie M. Hicks.

1074.

CYRUS THOMPSON[7] (Cyrus,[6] Isaac,[5] John,[4] Shubael,[3] John,[2] John[1]), b. December 24, 1805, son of Cyrus and Rebecca (Robinson) Thompson; m. MARENDA PITTS of Livermore, b. December 10, 1810. He was a cornet player in the militia; was a marble worker in Hartford, Me. In September, 1855, he went to Dunkirk, N. Y.; at this place he owned a third interest in a large flouring mill, with his son, Joseph, for miller. In March, 1864, he disposed of his interest in the mill for a farm in Byron, Fond du Lac county, Wis.; farmed it for two years, then moved to the city of Fond du Lac, where he has since resided. His wife d. April 8, 1882.

CHILDREN VIII. GENERATION.

1812. Hiram Pitts, b. Feb. 12, 1833; m. Julia Ellen Blossom, b. June 13, 1835. She d. Dec. 30, 1867. He enlisted in 1862 as private in 112th New York volunteer infantry; served nearly a year in this regiment, then went into 1st United States colored troops, and was mustered out as captain at the close of the war. Is an architect; has business in New York city. Address, Fond du Lac, Wis.
1813. Joseph Robinson, b. Feb. 2, 1835; m. Ellen Bond Fuller.

1076.

MARTHA SPAULDING THOMPSON[7] (Cyrus,[6] Isaac,[5] John,[4] Shubael,[3] John,[2] John[1]), b. April 30, 1814, dau. of Cyrus and Rebecca (Robinson) Thompson; m. July, 1835, STILLMAN REED of North Livermore.

CHILDREN VIII. GENERATION.

1814. Theron, b. August 30, 1836; m. H. Lizzie Eustis.
1815. Cyrus T., b. Jan., 4, 1839; m. Pulepha R. Butler.
1816. Clara, b. Sept. 12, 1841; d. May 5, 1851.

1817. George E., b. Feb. 3, 1843; killed in battle August 25, 1864.
1818. Frederick, b. June 15, 1852; m. Mary E. Dodge.
1819. Carrol, b. August 31, 1854; m. Etta B. Starr.
1820. Charles A., b. Nov. 16, 1857.

1085.

MARY ANN THOMPSON[7] (Uzza,[6] Isaac,[5] John,[4] Shubael,[3] John,[2] John[1]), b. May 8, 1810, dau. of Uzza and Abigail W. (Elliott) Thompson; m. September 18, 1831, HIRAM HALL of Buckfield, Maine, b. September 29, 1806. In 1854 Mr. Hall moved to Dunkirk, N. Y. In October, 1858, to Rockford, Ill. In October, 1859, to Kingston, Minn., where he lived till 1882. She d. October 15, 1868, in Kingston. He was killed in November, 1883, on Michigan Central railroad, at Battle Creek, Mich.

CHILDREN VIII. GENERATION.

1821. Cleora Elmore, b. July 22, 1832; m. George A. Nourse.
1822. Francevilla Valencia, b. Sept. 18, 1834; m. Atwood T. Irish.
1823. Charlotte Thompson, b. Sept. 29, 1836, in Buckfield; m. Charles K. Miner. She d. in Dunkirk.
1824. William H., b. July 9, 1841; m. Ella M. Campbell.
1825. Helen Frances, b. April 24, 1845; m. Ephraim Briggs.
1826 Mary Elva, b. June 7, 1850; m. Granville De Coster.

1086.

LOUISA THOMPSON[7] (Uzza,[6] Isaac,[5] John,[4] Shubael,[3] John,[2] John[1]), b. March 12, 1814, dau. of Uzza and Abigail W. (Elliott) Thompson; m. November, 1837, VERANUS DE COSTER of Buckfield, Me., a farmer; he d. January, 1888.

CHILDREN VIII. GENERATION.

1827. V. Francisco, b. —; m. (1) Ellen Torrey of Turner, Me. He moved to Kingston, Minn.; had one child, a dau. Mother and dau. dead. He m. (2) Emerette Campbell of New Haven, Conn. Was a merchant in Litchfield, Minn. Has one child, Esther L.
1828. William B., b. —. A volunteer; d. in the service of his country.
1829. Georgia, b. —; m. Stephen Morrill of Strong, Me. He is a commission merchant on Main street, Lewiston, Me.
1830. Louisa Victoria, b. —; d. young.
1831. Virgil P.,) Twins. (Virgil is an enterprising farmer.
1832. Virginia,) b. —. (Virginia is a successful school teacher.
1833. Cleora H., b. —; is a school teacher.

1089.

ABIGAIL E. THOMPSON[7] (Uzza,[6] Isaac,[5] John,[4] Shubael,[3] John,[2] John[1]), b. June 3, 1821, dau. of Uzza and Abigail W. (Elliott) Thompson; m. (1) August 19, 1855, ALANSON BRADFORD of Turner, Me., (2) February 25, 1885, WILLIAM ROBIE FRENCH of Canton Pt., Me., a lineal descendant of Edward French of Salisbury, Mass., 1640. First husband d. April 30, 1882.

CHILDREN BY FIRST HUSBAND VIII. GENERATION.

1834. Ella M., b. —.
1835. Flora A. b. —.

1091.

ISAAC H. THOMPSON[7] (Uzza,[6] Isaac,[5] John,[4] Shubael,[3] John,[2] John[1]), b. July 3, 1831, son of Uzza and Abigail W. (Elliott) Thompson; m. HATTIE E. BRAY of Portland, Me. He is a merchant and runs a flour mill in LeRoy, Minn.

CHILDREN VIII. GENERATION.

1836. Frank G., b. —.
1837. Minnie A. b. —.

1100.

MARSHAL THOMPSON[7] (Charles,[6] Ezra,[5] Jacob,[4] Jacob,[3] John,[2] John[1], b. February 13, 1811, son of Charles and Sarah (Darling) Thompson; m. LURANIA HOWARD, b. August 21, 1812, dau. of Cyrus and Deborah Howard or Hayward. He d. October 23, 1880.

CHILDREN VIII. GENERATION.

1838. Georgiana, b. Nov. 5, 1839; m. 1858, Charles F. Snow, son of William Snow of Raynham.
1839. Charles Henry, b. April 3, 1843.
1840. Roland Freeman, b. Sept. 28, 1845.

1102.

CHARLES THOMPSON[7] (Charles,[6] Ezra,[5] Jacob,[4] Jacob,[3] John,[2] John[1]), b. December 7, 1813, son of Charles and Sarah (Darling) Thompson; m. MARY ANN CURTIS, dau. of Marlborough and Lupira (Bisbee) Curtis of Hanover. He d. September 13, 1875.

CHILDREN VIII. GENERATION.

1841. Susan A., b. March 10, 1837.

1842. Lorenzo M., b. Jan. 7, 1841; d. Jan. 25, 1841.
1843. Mary E., b. Oct. 5, 1843.

1107.

JAMES THOMPSON[7] (Abraham,[6] Ezra,[5] Jacob,[4] Jacob,[3] John,[2] John[1]), b. May 15, 1813, son of Abraham and Mary (Sampson) Thompson; m. May, 1836, POLLY SIMMONS, dau. of Peleg Simmons of Kingston.

CHILDREN VIII. GENERATION.

1844. James Henry, b. July 14, 1837; m. Jenny Thayer.
1845. Robert Hervey, b. Sept., 1838; d. April, 1840.
1846. Laura Ann, b. —; m. Stephen Foster.
1847. Mary Wales, b. —; m. Charles Reid.
1848. Vernon H., b. —; drowned on his birthday, aged 18 years.
1849. Frederick Marion, b. —; m. Adelaide Lobdell.
1850. Daniel Webster, b. —.
1851. Webster Leroy, b. —.

1109.

HENRY LEWIS THOMPSON[7] (Abraham,[6] Ezra,[5] Jacob,[4] Jacob,[3] John,[2] John[1]), b. February 19, 1828, son of Abraham and Mary (Sampson) Thompson; m. MARY SIMMONS, dau. of Charles Simmons of Kingston.

CHILDREN VIII. GENERATION.

1852. Mary Eliza, b. May 13, 1863; d. Jan. 19, 1880.
1853. Charles Simmons, b. Sept. 20, 1876.

1123.

LEWIS HENRY THOMPSON[7] (Lewis,[6] Jacob,[5] Jacob,[4] Jacob,[3] John,[2] John[1]), b. November 23, 1826, son of Lewis and Huldah (Wood) Thompson; m. (1) HANNAH HOLMES, dau. of Charles and Hannah (Conant) Holmes, m. (2) MARY HOLMES (no relation of first wife). First wife d. September 14, 1852. Address, New Bedford, Mass.

CHILD BY FIRST WIFE VIII. GENERATION.

1854. Hannah Justina, b. Sept. 4, 1852; d. May 15, 1862.

CHILDREN BY SECOND WIFE VIII. GENERATION.

1855. Frederic Louis, b. Nov. 5, 1868, in Middleboro'. Designer and artist, employed at Pairpoint's silver manufactory, New Bedford, Mass.

1856.   Grace Wilbur, b. July 11, 1872, in Middleboro.

(1124   see   1056.)

1135.

LYSANDER MENDALL THOMPSON[7] (Lysander,[6] Isaac,[5] Isaac,[4] Barnabas,[3] Jacob,[2] John[1]), b. September 2, 1834, son of Lysander and Abigail (Thompson) Thompson; m. (1) MARI-ETTA HATHAWAY, dau. of Seabury C. and Sally (Porter) Hathaway, m. (2) SARAH A. HATHAWAY. He d. February 28, 1887.

CHILDREN BY SECOND WIFE VIII. GENERATION.

1857.   Marietta H., b. July 5, 1867.
1858.   Frederick W., b. May 27, 1870; d. Jan. 27, 1872.
1859.   Loretta M.,   ) Twins.
1860.   Lorentha M.,) b. Feb. 17, 1873.
1861.   Harry M.,   ) Twins.
1862.   Sarah A.,   ) b. June 18, 1874; Sarah A. d. Nov. 30, 1874.
1863.   Josie P., b. July 9, 1878.

1136.

SORANUS THOMPSON[7] (Lysander,[6] Isaac,[5] Isaac,[4] Barnabas,[3] Jacob,[2] John[1]), b. November 12, 1836, son of Lysander and Abigail (Thompson) Thompson; m. LUCINDA SEARS, dau. of William and Mary (Wood) Sears.

CHILD VIII. GENERATION.

1864.   Edgar Porter, b. July 4, 1863; m. Lottie Robinson.

1138.

SIDNEY HERBERT THOMPSON[7] (Lysander,[6] Isaac,[5] Isaac,[4] Barnabas,[3] Jacob,[2] John[1]), b. February 27, 1850, son of Lysander and Abigail (Thompson) Thompson; m. MARY E. CHURCHILL.

CHILD VIII GENERATION.

1865.   Abby May, b. March 8, 1881.

1146.

FRANCES MARIA THOMPSON[7] (Seth,[6] Nathaniel,[5] Ebenezer,[4] Jacob,[3] John[2], John[1]), b. October 8, 1835, dau. of Seth and

Bethiah (Benson) Thompson; m. March 30, 1857, Albinus O. Hamilton, a Methodist clergyman.

CHILD VIII. GENERATION.

1866. James Cunningham, b. June 2, 1858.

1153.

HARRIET TABER[7] (Bathsheba,[6] Ephraim,[5] Ephraim,[4] Jacob,[3] John,[2] John[1]), b. —, dau. of John B. and Bathsheba (Thompson) Taber; m. (1) WILLIAM HESTED, m. (2) JOSIAH G. CHILDS.

CHILDREN BY FIRST HUSBAND VIII. GENERATION.

1867. Nellie B., b. —; d. young.
1868. Ella F., b. —; d. young.
1869. Clara C. C., b. —; m. Joseph C. Davis; had Florence W. and William H., who d. in infancy; the mother d. 21 years old.
1870. Eddie T., b. —; d. young.

1154.

JOHN H. THOMPSON[7] (Abner,[6] Ephraim,[5] Ephraim,[4] Jacob,[3] John,[2] John[1]), b. December 4, 1824, son of Abner and Nancy H. (Gifford) Thompson; m. HARRIET ROBERTSON.

CHILDREN VIII. GENERATION.

1871. Abner, b. —.
1872. Asa, b. —.

1156.

PARDON G. THOMPSON[7] (Abner,[6] Ephraim,[5] Ephraim,[4] Jacob,[3] John,[2] John[1]), b. July 3, 1836, son of Abner and Nancy H. (Gifford) Thompson; m. THERESA GIFFORD.

CHILDREN VIII. GENERATION.

1873. Joseph, b. —; d. young.
1874. Nancy, b. —; d. young.

1157.

REBECCA F. THOMPSON[7] (Alva,[6] Ephraim,[5] Ephraim,[4] Jacob,[3] John,[2] John[1]), b. October 31, 1829, dau. of Alva and Lydia (Chase) Thompson; m. GEORGE DAVIS.

CHILDREN VIII. GENERATION.

1875. Clara, b. —; m. John Records and had two daughters.
1876. Harriet, b. —.

1158.

EVELINE C. THOMPSON (Alva,[6] Ephraim,[5] Ephraim,[4] Jacob,[3] John,[2] John[1]), b. September 16, 1831, dau. of Alva and Lydia (Chase) Thompson; m. AARON BESSE.

CHILDREN VIII. GENERATION.

1877. Lydia, b. —.
1878. Herbert, b. —; m. — Howland.

1167.

SUSAN SHERMAN[7] (Lucy,[6] Ephraim,[5] Ephraim,[4] Jacob,[3] John,[2] John[1]), b. —, dau. of Obed and Lucy (Thompson) Sherman; m. SYLVESTER CRANDALL.

CHILDREN VIII. GENERATION.

1879. Lucy E., b. —; d. young.
1880. Elizabeth, b. —; d. young.

1171.

MARY C. THOMPSON[7] (Jeremiah,[6] Ephraim,[5] Ephraim,[4] Jacob,[3] John,[2] John,[1]), b. June 13, 1835, dau. of Jeremiah and Sarah Ann (Case) Thompson; m. JOHN CORNELL.

CHILD VIII. GENERATION.

1881. Elmer J., b. —; m. Annie Reynolds.

1186.

ELVIRA THOMPSON[7] (Solomon,[6] Solomon,[5] Jacob,[4] Jacob,[3] Jacob,[2] John[1]), b. August 29, 1821; dau. of Solomon and Harriet (Thompson) Thompson; m. WILLIAM B. SUMNER.

CHILD VIII. GENERATION.

1882. Frank W., b. —.

1187.

ALBERT THOMPSON[7] (Solomon,[6] Solomon,[5] Jacob,[4] Jacob,[3] Jacob,[2] John[1]), b. November 26, 1824, son of Solomon and

Harriet (Thompson) Thompson; m. Lucy Coates Hopkins, a direct descendant of Stephen Hopkins of the Mayflower. Mr. Thompson was a large leather dealer in Boston. He d. September 9, 1882.

CHILDREN VIII. GENERATION.

1883. Albert H., b. Sept. 2, 1851. Address 39 S. St., Boston, Mass.
1884. Frederic E., b. April 8, 1853; d. April 6, 1874, in Paris.
1885. Carrie M., b. 1855; d. March 8, 1862.
1886. Nellie L., b. Sept. 2, 1860.

1188.

James Thompson[7] (Solomon,[6] Solomon,[5] Jacob,[4] Jacob,[3] Jacob,[2] John[1]), b. September 5, 1826, son of Solomon and Harriet (Thompson) Thompson; m. (1) Abby Faunce, (2) Lucy Bassett.

CHILDREN BY SECOND WIFE VIII. GENERATION.

1887. Harris, b. —.
1888. Nellie, b. —.
1889. Frank, b. —.

1190.

Harriet Thompson[7] (Solomon,[6] Solomon,[5] Jacob,[4] Jacob,[3] Jacob,[2] John[1]), b. September 30, 1830, dau. of Solomon and Harriet (Thompson) Thompson; m. Joshua T. Faunce.

CHILDREN VIII. GENERATION.

1890. Robert, b. —.
1891. Abbie, b. —.
1892. Lucy, b. —.

1191.

Calvin Murdock Thompson[7] (Calvin,[6] Solomon,[5] Jacob,[4] Jacob,[3] Jacob,[2] John[1]), b. May 5, 1823, son of Calvin and Margaret (Richardson) Thompson; m. (1) June, 1847, Mary B. Sharp of Dorchester, Mass., m. (2) Helen Badlam. He d. September, 1874. First wife d. November, 1856.

CHILDREN BY FIRST WIFE VIII. GENERATION.

1893. William Murdock. b. Oct. 10, 1848; m. Julia B. Hayward.
1894. Clifton Sharp, b. Jan. 2, 1852; m. Nellie Putnam of Neponset.
1895. George Badlam, b. 1855.

CHILD BY SECOND WIFE VIII. GENERATION.

1896. Charles Badlam, b. —.

1193.

HENRY THOMPSON[7] (Calvin,[6] Solomon,[5] Jacob,[4] Jacob,[3] Jacob,[2] John[1]), b. December 4, 1827, in Boston, son of Calvin and Mary (Richardson) Thompson; m. January 23, 1856, ANNE WITHINGTON THAYER, b. September 22, 1839, dau. of Asa W. Thayer of Randolph. Mr. Thompson was a carpenter. His wife d. October 1, 1881. Residence, Pleasant street, Boston.

CHILDREN VIII. GENERATION.

1897. Edward Murdock, b. Dec. 31, 1856.
1898. Annie Newell, b. April 12, 1862; m. Horace Richmond.
1899. Susan Emma, b. June 14, 1864.

1203.

CORNELIUS BENNETT WOOD[7] (Betsey W.,[6] Benjamin,[5] Jacob,[4] Jacob,[3] Jacob,[2] John[1]), b. November 5, 1809, son of Wilkes and Betsey W. (Thompson) Wood; m. (1) October 13, 1835, LUCY AMEE WASHBURN, (2) October 14, 1858, CORNELIA BURGESS SNOW. His first wife d. December 8, 1854. He d. March 23, 1885.

CHILD BY SECOND WIFE VIII. GENERATION.

1900. Nettie, b. August, 1861; d. Sept., 1861.

1205.

CHARLES WILKES WOOD[7] (Betsey W.,[6] Benjamin,[5] Jacob,[4] Jacob,[3] Jacob,[2] John[1]), b. June 30, 1814, son of Wilkes and Betsey W. (Thompson) Wood; m. (1) September 30, 1841, ELIZA A. BIGELOW, m. (2) July 27, 1847, CATHERINE S. LEMIST. First wife d. May 24, 1846.

CHILD BY FIRST WIFE VIII. GENERATION.

1901. Charles Henry Wilkes, b. Jan. 1, 1843; m. July 21, 1864, Mary Whitman. Had two children: Florence, Mary Winifred; the latter d. 1887.

CHILDREN BY SECOND WIFE VIII. GENERATION.

1902. Edward Clark, b. Feb. 19, 1849; m. Oct. 21, 1879, Mrs. Emma Hutchins.

1903. Emily Catherine, b. May 16, 1851; m. May 2, 1877, Charles H. Bates. Had three children: Harry Milton, Roy Melville, Infant.
1904. Caroline Melville, b. Sept. 19, 1855.

1206.

EMILY LOUISA WOOD⁷ (Betsey W.,⁶ Benjamin,⁵ Jacob,⁴ Jacob,³ Jacob,² John¹), b. May 15, 1816, dau. of Wilkes and Betsey W. (Thompson) Wood; m. June 13, 1856, THOMAS BRIGGS CRANE. He d. May 19, 1882.

CHILDREN VIII. GENERATION.

1905. Mary Louisa, b. March 11, 185–.
1906. Emma, b. —; d. —.

1207.

JOSEPH TINKHAM WOOD⁷ (Betsey W.,⁶ Benjamin,⁵ Jacob,⁴ Jacob,³ Jacob,² John¹), b. March 17, 1818, son of Wilkes and Betsey W. (Thompson) Wood; m. November 6, 1844. ELLEN TAYLOR. Address, Middleborough, Mass.

CHILDREN VIII. GENERATION.

1907. Charlotte Taylor, b. Sept. 23, 1845.
1908. Betsey Wild, b. May 18, 1850; d. Sept. 2, 1851.
1909. Janette, b. Jan. 30, 1852; m. Sept. 11, 1872, Edward S. Hathaway. Had two children: Miriam, b. Dec. 30, 1875; Joseph Wood, b. May 5, 1885.
1910. Isabella, b. August 12, 1856; d. Oct. 23, 1861.
1911. Gertrude, b. July 12, 1861; d. March 7, 1877.

1208.

MARY THOMPSON WOOD⁷ (Betsey W.,⁶ Benjamin,⁵ Jacob,⁴ Jacob,³ Jacob,² John¹), b. May 28, 1820, dau. of Wilkes and Betsey W. (Thompson) Wood; m. August 23, 1843, RUSSELL L. HATHAWAY. He d. July 18, 1881.

CHILDREN VIII. GENERATION.

1912. Lucy Wood, b. Oct. 9, 1844; m. Dec. 23, 1868, Capt. Jesse M. Lee. Had one child: Maud Hathaway, b. Oct. 31, 1869.
1913. Cornelius Wilkes, b. Feb. 17, 1846.
1914. Charles Russell, b. Jan. 12, 1849; deceased.
1915. Helen Rowena, b. July, 1851.
1916. George, b. Oct. 2, 1853; m. Oct. 4, 1877, Alice McMurtrie.

1917.   Ida, b. Sept. 28, 1857; m. Joseph W. Cooper and had one child, Russell William.

1221.

HARRISON F. THOMPSON[7] (Barnabas,[6] Barnabas,[5] Noah,[4] Barnabas,[3] Jacob,[2] John[1]), b. October 15, 1815, son of Barnabas and Hannah (Shaw) Thompson; m. ALZINA M. HORTON.

CHILD VIII. GENERATION.

1918.   Albert H., b. August, 1844.

1249.

SARAH A. M. THOMPSON[7] (Hosea B.,[6] Abel,[5] Noah,[4] Barnabas,[3] Jacob,[2] John[1]), b. August 26, 1838, dau. of Hosea B., and Sarah P. (Barrows) Thompson; m. (1) OSCAR KENNEDY, m. (2) NELSON C. DIMMICK. First marriage dissolved by the court. She d. July 3, 1875.

CHILD BY FIRST HUSBAND VIII. GENERATION.

1919.   Flora A., b. August 28, 1855; m. Royal B. Perkins.

CHILD BY SECOND HUSBAND VIII. GENERATION.

1920.   Ruth S., b. March 25, 1868; m. Frank L. Copeland.

1250.

ELLEN R. THOMPSON[7] (Hosea B.,[6] Abel,[5] Noah,[4] Barnabas,[3] Jacob,[2] John[1]), b. August 25, 1840, dau. of Hosea B. and Sarah P. (Barrows) Thompson; m. (1) WARREN T. MATHER, m. (2) TRUMAN LEWIS, m. (3) NELSON C. DIMMICK. First husband d. from wound received in battle in war of the rebellion; second marriage dissolved by court. Address, Bridgewater, Vt.

CHILD BY SECOND HUSBAND VIII. GENERATION.

1921.   Warren T., b. Oct. 11, 1870.

CHILD BY THIRD HUSBAND VIII. GENERATION.

1922.   Andrew N., b. Jan. 27, 1879.

1253.

VELINA R. THOMPSON[7] (Arioch,[6] Jabez,[5] Isaac,[4] Barnabas,[3] Jacob,[2] John[1]), b. September 18, 1835, in Plympton, dau. of Arioch and Adaline D. (Virgin) Thompson; m. November 21,

1854, CHARLES N. COBB of North Bridgewater (now Brocton), Mass.

CHILDREN VIII. GENERATION.

1923. Charles H., b. August 8, 1856; m. Bethia Porter.
1924. Esther V., b. Sept. 18, 1863.
1925. Florence A., b. Jan. 10, 1869.

1255.

ARIOCH A. THOMPSON[7] (Arioch,[6] Jabez,[5] Isaac,[4] Barnabas,[3] Jacob,[2] John[1]), b. July 20, 1841, in Plympton, Mass., son of Arioch and Adaline D. (Virgin) Thompson; m. September 24, 1873, HANNAH ELIZA THOMPSON (1325) of Taunton, Mass.

CHILDREN VIII. GENERATION.

1926. Mabel Lewis, b. Feb. 24, 1876; d. May 3, 1886.
1927. Arioch Persis, b. April 1, 1882.

1256.

ELVA M. THOMPSON[7] (Arioch,[6] Jabez,[5] Isaac,[4] Barnabas,[3] Jacob,[2] John[1]), b. April 24, 1848, in Abington, Mass., dau. of Arioch and Adaline D. (Virgin) Thompson; m. April 24, 1872, JOHN W. CHEESMAN of Holbrook, Mass. P. O. box 201.

CHILDREN VIII. GENERATION.

1928. William S., b. Sept. 11, 1875.
1929. Edna V., b. June 2, 1880; d. Dec. 15, 1883.
1930. Everett N., b. May 22, 1886.

1257.

WILLIAM AUSTIN THOMPSON[7] (Simeon,[6] Jabez,[5] Isaac,[4] Barnabas,[3] Jacob,[2] John[1]), b. July 15, 1834, in Plympton, son of Simeon and Abigail W. (Churchill) Thompson; m. (1) October 9, 1857, ELIZA M. CHASE of Turner, Me., m. (2) 1882, EMMA L. STANDISH of Middleboro'. First wife d. January 25, 1874, aged 39.

CHILD BY SECOND WIFE VIII. GENERATION.

1931. Bertram Austin, b. Jan. 19, 1883, in Abington.

1259.

SARAH BURGESS THOMPSON[7] (Simeon,[6] Jabez,[5] Isaac,[4] Barnabas,[3] Jacob,[2] John[1]), b. November 21, 1849, in Abington,

dau. of Simeon and Abigail W. (Churchill) Thompson; m.
July 25, 1871, CHARLES H. MCCARTER of East Bridgewater.
Address, Holbrook, Mass.

CHILDREN VIII. GENERATION.

1932. Frederic William, b. August 30, 1874, in Holbrook.
1933. Arthur Herman, b. April 22, 1876, in Holbrook.

1260.

LEONICE THOMPSON[7] (Simeon,[6] Jabez,[5] Isaac,[4] Barnabas,[3]
Jacob,[2] John[1]), b. September 15, 1858, in Abington, dau. of
Simeon and Abigail W. (Churchill) Thompson; m. February
11, 1880, LEONARD D. GARFIELD of Millburg. Address,
Brocton, Mass.

CHILDREN VIII. GENERATION.

1934. Chester Arthur, b. Jan 6, 1881, in New Bedford.
1935. Walter Thompson, b. Feb. 8, 1882, in Pembroke.
1936. Merton Leonard, b. July 16, 1885, in Pembroke.

1261.

SIMEON THOMPSON[7] (Simeon,[6] Jabez,[5] Isaac,[4] Barnabas,[3]
Jacob,[2] John[1]), b. November 13, 1860, in Abington, son of
Simeon and Abigail W. (Churchill) Thompson; m. ELVIRA
C. REED of Pembroke.

CHILDREN VIII. GENERATION.

1937. William Erwin, b. Sept. 29, 1881.
1938. Ray Forest, b. Sept. 22, 1883.

1262.

SAMUEL GILBERT THOMPSON[7] (Samuel V.,[6] Jabez,[5] Isaac,[4]
Barnabas,[3] Jacob,[2] John[1]), b. December 6, 1835, son of Samuel
V. and Betsey (Nash) Thompson; m. October 31, 1863, ELIZA-
BETH S. DANIELS.

CHILDREN VIII. GENERATION.

1939. Lizzie Maria, b. July 16, 1865.
1940. Lester Gilbert, b. Nov. 27, 1878; d. July 20, 1886.

1264.

WILLIAM NASH THOMPSON[7] (Samuel V.,[6] Jabez,[5] Isaac,[4] Barnabas,[3] Jacob,[2] John[1]), b. September 18, 1841, son of Samuel

V. and Betsey (Nash) Thompson; m. October 12, 1872, ANNIE C. WINSLOW of Parma, Mich.

CHILD VIII. GENERATION.

1941. Samuel Winslow, b. Oct. 13, 1874.

1277.

WOODMAN THOMPSON[7] (Christopher C.,[6] Isaac,[5] Isaac,[4] Barnabas,[3] Jacob,[2] John[1]), b. January 13, 1851, in Jo Daviess county, Ill., son of Christopher C., and Mary A. (Strong) Thompson; m. JENEFER EUSTICE. Removed to Sioux county. Engaged in farming.

CHILDREN VIII. GENERATION.

1942. John C., b. Jan. 18, 1873.
1943. Raymond W., b. Nov. 30, 1874.
1944. Frank L., b. July 12, 1880.
1945. May Pearl, b. Oct. 30, 1885.

1288.

DEBORAH ANNA THOMPSON[7] (Isaac,[6] Isaac,[5] Isaac,[4] Barnabas,[3] Jacob,[2] John[1]), b. May 12, 1846, in Jo Daviess county, Ill., dau. of Isaac and aAnn T. (Thompson) Thompson; m. AMOS B. PAUN, M. D., youngest son of John and Sarah Paun of New Bedford, Mass. Address, Middleboro', Mass.

CHILD VIII. GENERATION.

1946. Edgar Amos, b. Feb. 24, 1882.

1293.

EARL ETTSON THOMPSON[7] (Joseph S.,[6] Isaac,[5] Isaac,[4] Barnabas,[3] Jacob,[2] John[1]), b. April 10, 1860, son of Joseph S. and Melissa (Pingrey) Thompson; m. VERNIE E. CHURCH. He d. June 5, 1887.

CHILDREN VIII. GENERATION.

1947. Nonie Myrtle, b. July 26, 1886.
1948. Meade Ettson, b. Sept. 21, 1887.

1299.

GEORGE H. TITCOMB[7] (Marcia V.,[6] Jacob,[5] Isaac,[4] Barnabas,[3] Jacob,[2] John[1]), b. July 18, 1833, at Canton, Mass., son of

25

Moses and Marcia V. (Thompson) Titcomb; m. October 6, 1855, in Jersey City, ABBIE E. CHAMPLIN. She d. July 12, 1877, in Pelham, N. H.

CHILD VIII. GENERATION.

1949. Addie E., b. Dec. 26, 1876, in Brooklyn, N. Y.

1301.

MARIETTA E. TITCOMB[7] (Marcia V.,[6] Jacob,[5] Isaac,[4] Barnabas,[3] Jacob,[2] John[1]), b. January 1, 1840, in Boston, dau. of Moses and Marcia V. (Thompson) Titcomb; m. February 28, 1858, THOMAS MYERS of Norwich, Conn. He d. February 22, 1878, in Pelham, N. H.

CHILDREN VIII. GENERATION.

1950. Ora L., b. Dec. 19, 1863, in Pelham, N. H.
1951. Marcia M., b. March 1, 1870, in Providence, R. I.; d. May 6, 1886, in Pelham.

1302.

EDWARD M. TITCOMB[7] (Marcia V.,[6] Jacob,[5] Isaac,[4] Barnabas,[3] Jacob,[2] John[1]), b. January 17, 1842, in Dracut, Mass., son of Moses and Marcia V. (Thompson) Titcomb; m. January 1, 1862, LAURA A. CHIPMAN (1309) at Assonet, Mass.

CHILDREN VIII. GENERATION.

1952. Eddie B., b. Feb. 11, 1863, in Jersey City.
1953. Estelle L., b. June 17, 1865, in Assonet, Mass.
1954. Florence S., b. April 29, 1877, in Assonet, Mass.
1955. Sumner A., b. Oct. 9, 1881, in Pelham, N. H.

1304.

BEN BILL TITCOMB[7] (Marcia V.,[6] Jacob,[5] Isaac,[4] Barnabas,[3] Jacob,[2] John[1]), b. June 6, 1849, in Franklin, Conn., son of Moses and Marcia V. (Thompson) Titcomb; m. March 4, 1873, in Jersey City, AUGUSTA E. CADY.

CHILDREN VIII. GENERATION.

1956. Bertie Warren, b. July 10, 1874, in Pelham; d. Sept. 15, 1874.
1957. Sadie, b. Feb. 1, 1880, in Brooklyn, N. Y.
1958. May E., b. Feb. 29, 1882, in Brooklyn, N. Y.; d. Feb. 1, 1885, in New York city.

1959. Irene, b. August 20, 1883, in Brooklyn, N. Y.; d. Feb. 1, 1885, in New York city.
1960. Laura A., b. Nov. 18, 1884, in South Boston.

(**1309** *see* **1302.**)

1311.

THADDEUS S. CLARK[7] (Betsey,[6] Jacob,[5] Isaac,[4] Barnabas,[3] Jacob,[2] John[1]), b. January 25, 1843, son of Simeon C. and Betsey (Thompson) Clark; m. April 5, 1866, SUSAN F. SMITH.

CHILDREN VIII. GENERATION.

1961. Lester F., b. July 11, 1867.
1962. Winifred S., b. July 8, 1870.

1312.

ESTHER E. CLARK[7] (Betsey,[6] Jacob,[5] Isaac,[4] Barnabas,[3] Jacob,[2] John[1]), b. October 30, 1847, dau. of Simeon C. and Betsey (Thompson) Clark; m. April 4, 1866, DAVID SMITH.

CHILD VIII. GENERATION.

1963. Agnes E., b. May 29, 1872.

1322.

CHARLES NATHAN THOMPSON[7] (Lewis S.,[6] Jacob,[5] Isaac,[4] Barnabas,[3] Jacob,[2] John[1]), b. March 4, 1842, son of Lewis S., and Mary W. (Macomber) Thompson; m. 1864, AMY BALD-WIN. He d. October 3, 1887, at his home in Wisconsin.

CHILDREN VIII. GENERATION.

1964. Lena, b. March 15, 1870.
1965. Lewis S., b. March 28, 1872.
1966. Dolly, b. May 5, 1874.
1967. Mary A., b. July 9, 1876.
1968. Charles, b. Oct. 2, 1878.
1969. Edward, b. Jan. 10, 1881.

(**1325** *see* **1255.**)

1328.

SUMNER THOMAS THOMPSON[7] (Lewis S.,[6] Jacob,[5] Isaac,[4] Barnabas,[3] Jacob,[2] John[1]), b. September 2, 1855, son of Lewis

S. and Mary W. (Macomber) Thompson; m. (1) MARY HAM-
ILTON, m. (2) ANNIE HAMILTON.   First wife d. 1876.

CHILDREN BY SECOND WIFE VIII. GENERATION.

1970. Mary Lewis, b. Nov. 16, 1880.
1971. Lottie Hamilton, b. July 20, 1882.
1972. Arthur Herbert, b. Dec. 23, 1884.
1973. Sumner Francis, b. August 28, 1887.

1332.

ELLA ESTHER THOMPSON[7] (Sumner S.,[6] Jacob,[5] Isaac,[4] Barnabas,[3] Jacob,[2] John[1]), b. April 12, 1853, dau. of Sumner S.
and Harriet S. (Wiley) Thompson; m. May 23, 1881, SAMUEL
WALKER MCCALL, counselor at law in Boston.   Mr. McCall
served his district in 1888 and 1889 in the Massachusetts legislature.   In the session of 1888 he was chairman of the committee
on probate and insolvency.   Early in the session he introduced
an order, upon which he subsequently reported a bill, substan-
tially revolutionizing the practice in poor debtor cases.   This
bill passed the house, and, in an amended form, the senate.
It was a most radical measure, completely overturning the old
practice, with its notorious abuses, under which the right to
arrest men was sold at the rate of a dollar a head, and when,
also, in Suffolk county, men were often sent to jail whose only
crime was poverty, and many a rich debtor was enabled to defy
his creditors.   This bill did away with the system of fees for
magistrates and conferred jurisdiction upon an established
and reputable court, and it has been pronounced by excellent
judges to have been the most beneficent and reformatory act
of the whole session.   He supported the proposition to submit
the prohibitory amendment to the people and also all meas-
ures to restrict the power of the saloon and to secure the
enforcement of existing laws.   In the session of 1889 he was
made chairman of the committee on judiciary, which is the
traditional position of leader of the house, and which requires
very frequent participations in debate.   Perhaps the most
important occurrence of the session was the controversy with
the justices of the supreme court.   The house, in the exercise
of what it claimed to be a constitutional power, asked the
opinion of the justices upon certain questions growing out of
the laws relating to the public schools.   The justices replied
declining to give their opinions.   This reply was referred to
the judiciary committee, on behalf of which Mr. McCall made
an elaborate report, maintaining that it was the constitutional

duty of the justices to answer, and embodying this claim in the form of a resolution. After a debate, which was pronounced on all sides to have been one of extraordinary ability, the resolution was passed 168 to 8. Of this action the Boston correspondent of the Christian Union said that it was "a bold and rather startling act," and of Mr. McCall's report, that it was "exceedingly forceful, learned and in parts brilliant." The questions raised by this controversy are receiving a good deal of attention from the law reviews, and are certainly of far-reaching importance. During the presidential campaign of 1888 Mr. McCall served as editor-in-chief of the Boston Daily Advertiser. He was also a delegate from Massachusetts to the national republican convention in 1888, where he made a speech seconding the nomination of Gen. Gresham to the presidency. Address, Winchester, Mass.

CHILDREN VIII. GENERATION.

1974. Sumner Thompson, b. May 30, 1882.
1975. Ruth, b. Jan. 19, 1885.
1976. Henry, b. August 24, 1886.
1977. Catherine, b. August 10, 1889.

1333.

HATTIE WILEY THOMPSON[7] (Sumner S.,[6] Jacob,[5] Isaac,[4] Barnabas,[3] Jacob,[2] John[1]), b. March 26, 1867, dau. of Sumner S. and Harriet S. (Wiley) Thompson; m. 1885, CHARLES STUART LE'BOURVEAU, JR.

CHILD VIII. GENERATION.

1978. Arthur Thompson, b. 1886.

1335.

JULIA A. NEWCOMB[7] (Huldah V.,[6] Jacob,[5] Isaac,[4] Barnabas,[3] Jacob,[2] John[1]), b. August 17, 1849, dau. of Silas D. and Huldah V. (Thompson) Newcomb; m. October 16, 1874, GEORGE KITTREDGE. She d. April 23, 1882.

CHILD VIII. GENERATION.

1979. Albert H., b. April 15, 1882.

1336.

CHARLES S. NEWCOMB[7] (Huldah V.,[6] Jacob,[5] Isaac,[4] Barnabas,[1] Jacob,[2] John[1]), b. December 28, 1856, son of Silas D. and Huldah V. (Thompson) Newcomb; m. June 6, 1877, —.

CHILD VIII. GENERATION.

1980. Maud C., b. Dec. 5, 1878.

1343.

HORACE OTIS THOMPSON[7] (Otis,[6] Adam,[5] Adam,[4] Barnabas,[3] Jacob,[2] John[1]), b. November 5, 1844, son of Otis and Betsey W. (Thompson) Thompson; m. HELOISE AYMAR BOURNE.

CHILDREN VIII. GENERATION.

1981. Horace Preston, b. Jan. 4, 1880.
1982. Ada Carlton, b. June 21, 1882; d. June 3, 1884.

1375.

JAMES MUNROE BROWN[7] (Mary,[6] Oakes,[5] William,[4] Caleb,[3] Jacob,[2] John[1]), b. November 15, 1825, son of James and Mary (Thompson) Brown; m. November 15, 1849, EUNICE GOULD FROST. Resides in Hanover, Me.

CHILDREN VIII. GENERATION.

1983. Emma G., b. March 2, 1852.
1984. Mary Rae, b. August 5, 1857.
1985. Dollie F., b. Oct. 20, 1859.

1380.

ROSCOE HENRY THOMPSON[7] (Oakes,[6] Oakes,[5] William,[4] Caleb,[3] Jacob,[2] John[1]), b. May 1, 1836, son of Oakes and Livonia (Banks) Thompson; m. June 27, 1872, HELEN CRAFTS, a graduate of the female college at Framingham, Mass., a teacher for three years in charge of 1,500 pupils in the North grammar school of Portland, Me. Mr. Thompson was for ten years associate justice in the district court in Boston. Address, 35 Warren street, New York.

CHILDREN VIII. GENERATION.

1986. Carl Crafts, b. June 3, 1875.
1987. Otho Henry, b. March 18, 1877.
1988. Percival Wheeler, b. August 31, 1883.

1400.

HIRAM THOMPSON[7] (Hiram,[6] William,[5] William,[4] Caleb,[3] Jacob,[2] John[1]), b. August 27, 1845, son of Hiram and Eliza (Pottle) Thompson; m. ELLEN BROWN. He was one of the 100 day men in the war of 1861. Lives in Des Moines, Iowa.

CHILD VIII. GENERATION.

1989. Clara, b. —.

1402.

GEORGE W. THOMPSON[7] (Hiram,[6] William,[5] William,[4] Caleb,[3] Jacob,[2] John[1]), b. July 25, 1849, son of Hiram and Eliza (Pottle) Thompson; m. (1) MAGGIE McGAIHEY, (2) EMMA C. KING. Address, Bonaparte, Iowa.

CHILDREN BY FIRST WIFE VIII. GENERATION.

1990. Ira B., b. Oct. 9, 1873.
1991. Edward, b. Oct. 2, 1875.
1992. Lizzie, b. Dec. 4, 1877.
1993. Charles B., b. July 5, 1879.
1994. Mary E., b. March 28, 1883.

1403.

FLORINDA TORREY CATE[7] (Deborah W.,[6] William,[5] William,[4] Caleb,[3] Jacob,[2] John[1]), b. August 25, 1842, dau. of Benjamin F. and Deborah W. (Thompson) Cate; m. (1) April 9, 1861, LORSON SYLVESTER STONE of Vermont, (2) February 15, 1887, JOHN OATMAN. First husband d. October 2, 1878.

CHILDREN BY FIRST HUSBAND VIII. GENERATION.

1995. Mary Ellen, b. March 30, 1862; m. Sept., 1882, Walter Eugene Downing, and had
  Audrey, b. May, 1883; d. August, 1883.
  Van Cadogan, b. June, 1884.
  Vivia, b. July, 1885.
  Hallie Vey, b. August, 1887.
1996. Charles W., b. Oct., 1864; d. in infancy.
1997. Benjamin C., b. Sept. 19, 1866.
1998. Noel Barton, b. August, 1872.

1404.

AMANDA CATE[7] (Deborah W.,[6] William,[5] William,[4] Caleb,[3] Jacob,[2] John[1]), b. March 13, 1844, dau. of Benjamin F. and

Deborah W. (Thompson) Cate; m. September 5, 1863, WILL-IAM JOSEPH WARD of Connecticut.

CHILDREN VIII. GENERATION.

1999. Frederic Smith, b. Sept. 20, 1864.
2000. Cornelia Hamlin, b. May 11, 1867. Loraine, Ill.
2001. Kate Deborah, b. April 9, 1869.
2002. Ira Joseph, b. July 2, 1871.
2003. Loren Otis, b. August 24, 1873.
2004. Charles Franklin, b. April 26, 1876.
2005. George Herbert, b. March 17, 1878.
2006. Clara Ellen, b. Jan., 1882.
2007. Henry William, b. June 17, 1885.
2008. Rolla Amos, b. Jan. 6, 1888.

1405.

MARY JANE CATE[7] (Deborah W.,[6] William,[5] William,[4] Caleb,[3] Jacob,[2] John[1]), b. July 1, 1846, dau. of Benjamin F. and Deborah W. (Thompson) Cate; m. (1) November 10, 1864, DAVID GREEN BACON of Wisconsin. Divorced from him and m. (2) 1882, FRED. LUMMER.

CHILDREN BY FIRST HUSBAND VIII. GENERATION.

2009. William Edmund, b. August 20, 1866.
2010. Maria Thompson, b. Dec. 31, 1868.
2011. Daniel, b. April, 1874.
2012. George, b. March, 1876.
2013. Nancy Marilla, b. Sept. 15, 1878.

CHILDREN BY SECOND HUSBAND VIII. GENERATION.

2014. Fritz, b. July 17, 1883.
2015. Caroline Mabel, b. July 17, 1887.

1406.

ROSWELL CATE[7] (Deborah W.,[6] William,[5] William,[4] Caleb,[3] Jacob,[2] John[1]), b. April 26, 1848, son of Benjamin F. and Deborah W. (Thompson) Cate; m. October 31, 1873, MARY CORDELIA CASTER of Iowa.

CHILDREN VIII. GENERATION.

2016. Mary Alice, b. Jan. 28, 1876; d. April 17, 1876.
2017. Benjamin Franklin, b. Jan. 10, 1878; d. July 28, 1878.
2018. Rosa Deborah, b. Feb. 21, 1879.

2019. Ina May, b. Oct. 19, 1880.
2020. Harvey, b. March 12, 1882; d. August, 1882.
2021. Ira Allison, b. March 28, 1883.
2022. Edward, b. December 15. 1835; d. August 10, 1886.
2023. Minnie Ellen,   } Twins,
2024. William Elwood, } b. Jan. 2, 1887.
2025. Jacob Roscoe, b. August 25, 1888.

1408.

OTIS THOMPSON CATE[7] (Deborah W.,[6] William,[5] William,[4] Caleb,[3] Jacob,[2] John[1]), b. October 23, 1852, son of Benjamin F. and Deborah W. (Thompson) Cate; m. February 22, 1877, NANCY ANN GREGORY of Arkansas. Address, Quincy, Ill.

CHILDREN VIII. GENERATION.

2026. Ellen Cornelia, b. Oct. 28, 1877; d. June 3, 1879.
2027. Rosetta, b. Jan. 8, 1879.
2028. Otis Walter, b. June 5, 1880.
2029. Amanda Frances, b. Nov. 5, 1881.
2030. Herman Benjamin, b. Jan. 14, 1885.

1409.

WALTER CATE[7] (Deborah W.,[6] William,[5] William,[4] Caleb,[3] Jacob,[2] John[1]), b. December 30, 1855, son of Benjamin F. and Deborah W. (Thompson) Cate; m. January 6, 1880, ROSA G. FOOTE of Quincy, Ill.

CHILDREN VIII. GENERATION.

2031. Frank Jefferson, b. Nov. 28, 1883.
2032. Charles Franklin, b. Nov. 2, 1885.
2033. James Walter, b. August 21, 1887.

1411.

OLIVIA CATHLEEN BONNEY[7] (Elvira S. T.,[6] Cephas,[5] William,[4] Caleb,[3] Jacob,[2] John[1]), b. August 3, 1825, dau. of George and Elvira S. T. (Thompson) Bonney; m. June 29, 1848, DR. JOSIAH ATKINSON of Newburyport, Mass. She d. April 8, 1861, at Newburyport. He d. June 21, 1869, at same place.

CHILDREN VIII. GENERATION.

2034. George Bonney, b. March 23, 1849; d. Oct. 20, 1866, in Singapore, India.
2035. Charles Bonney, b. July 29, 1851. Resides in California.

2036.   Edward Ernest, b. May 15, 1853; a minister, residence, Chico-
         pee, Mass.
2037.   Juliet Olivia, b. Oct. 26, 1854; d. Sept. 11, 1855.
2038.   Elvira Thompson, b. July 4, 1856; d. April 5, 1879.
2039.   William Henry, b. May 6, 1859; d. June 13, 1862.

1412.

JULIET HELENA BONNEY[7] (Elvira S. T.,[6] Cephas,[5] William,[4]
Caleb,[3] Jacob,[2] John[1]), b. April 3, 1828, dau. of George and
Elvira S. T. (Thompson) Bonney; m. November 28, 1848,
JOHN EDDY, a lawyer. She d. March 31, 1850. Residence,
Providence, R. I.

CHILDREN VIII. GENERATION.

2040.   Juliet Bonney, b. Dec. 5, 1849; m. Edward P. Haskell of New
         Bedford. She d. April 10, 1879. Her children were:
         Alice, b. Jan. 15, 1875.
         Ernest E., b. Sept. 24, 1876.

1414.

GEORGE BERNARD BONNEY[7] (Elvira S. T.,[6] Cephas,[5] William,[4] Caleb,[3] Jacob,[2] John[1]), b. March 10, 1839, son of George
and Elvira S. T. (Thompson) Bonney; m. April 3, 1872,
CAROLINE KING HOLBROOK of New York city. Mr. Bonney
is a lawyer. Address, 51 Wall street, New York city.

CHILDREN VIII. GENERATION.

2041.   Mary Wright, b. Jan. 24, 1873.
2042.   Frances Holbrook, b. April 5, 1875; d. July 24, 1877.
2043.   George, b. Jan. 26, 1877.
2044.   Anna, b. April 19, 1879.
2045.   Madeleine, b. March 16, 1882.
2046.   Holbrook, b. Dec. 12, 1885.

1415.

ORVILLE BRYANT[7] (Cordelia,[6] Cephas,[5] William,[4] Caleb,[3]
Jacob,[2] John[1]), b. July 4, 1844, son of Benjamin A. and Cor-
delia (Thompson) Bryant; m. January 25, 1868, at Plymouth,
Conn., ALICE C. FAROONS.

CHILDREN VIII. GENERATION.

2047.   Earl B., b. Oct. 30, 1868.
2048.   Guy A., b. Sept. 25, 1874.
2049.   Forest E., b. May 6, 1878.

1419.

EDMUND FRANCIS THOMPSON⁷ (Cephas G.,⁶ Cephas,⁵ William,⁴ Caleb,³ Jacob,² John¹), b. October 5, 1846, in New Bedford, son of Cephas G. and Mary G. (Ogden) Thompson; m. CLARA AUGUSTA BISBEE. In 1864, at the age of 18 years, Mr. Thompson entered the United States army as a private. Was soon appointed lieutenant, and became captain before he was 21. Was kept on duty in the far west. He d. December 16,. 1879, in Arizona. His widow resides with her children in Everett, Mass.

CHILDREN VIII. GENERATION.

2050. Edmund Ogden, b. April 11, 1872.
2051. Ethel Frances, b. July 10, 1873.
2052. Clara Miriam, b. Dec. 29, 1876.
2053. William Bisbee, b. Sept. 24, 1879.

1423.

JEROME COLDEN THOMPSON⁷ (Jerome,⁶ Cephas,⁵ William,⁴ Caleb,³ Jacob,² John¹), b. August 11, 1840, in New York city, son of Jerome and Maria Louise (Colden) Thompson; m. March 22, 1871, LULLIA I. WYMAN. Jerome C. served in the 5th Minnesota volunteer infantry four and one-half years during the civil war. Was in twenty-seven battles; wounded twice; and was in Andersonville prison. Residence, Lake Crystal, Minn.

CHILDREN VIII. GENERATION.

2054. Arthur Colden, b. —.
2055. Stevens Leonard, b. —.
2056. Bertha Louise, b. —.
2057. Grace May, b. —.
2058. Clark Garfield, b. —.
2059. Ethel Blanche, b. —.
2060. Chester Claude, b. —.

1425.

CHARLES FREDERICK THOMPSON⁷ (Julius,⁶ Cephas,⁵ William,⁴ Caleb,³ Jacob,² John¹), b. December 22, 1852, son of Julius and Bathsheba T. (Warren) Thompson; m. June, 1877,. ELIZA J. HENRY.

CHILDREN VIII. GENERATION.

2061. Bertha Bathsheba, b. April 17, 1878.
2062. George Frederick, b. Nov. 10, 1879.

2063. Charles Albert, b. June 21, 1885.
2064. Roscoe Henry, b. Feb. 18, 1887.

1426.

JAMES ALBERT THOMPSON[7] (Julius,[6] Cephas,[5] William,[4] Caleb,[3] Jacob,[2] John[1]), b. August 1, 1857, son of Julius and Bathsheba T. (Warren) Thompson; m. June 5, 1886, GRACE A. PERRY.

CHILD VIII. GENERATION.

2065. Norma Grey, b. May 21, 1887.

1430.

JOHN Q. THOMPSON[7] (Ira D.,[6] Ira,[5] William,[4] Caleb,[3] Jacob,[2] John[1]), b. August 1, 1831, son of Ira D. and Lydia (Hathaway) Thompson; m. REBECCA LESLIE. Address, Newhall, Iowa.

CHILDREN VIII. GENERATION.

2066. John Leslie, b. —.
2067. Hattie H., b. —.
2068. Lottie E., b. —.
2069. Charles Otis, b. —.
2070. Ira D., b. —.

1431.

MANDANA THOMPSON[7] (Ira D.,[6] Ira,[5] William,[4] Caleb,[3] Jacob,[2] John[1]), b. April 26, 1833, dau. of Ira D. and Lydia (Hathaway) Thompson; m. (1) DAVID WINSLOW, (2) ALEXANDER RUNYON. Address, Shellsburg, Iowa.

CHILD BY FIRST HUSBAND VIII. GENERATION.

2071. Edward N., b. —.

1433.

ARAD THOMPSON[7] (Ira D.,[6] Ira,[5] William,[4] Caleb,[3] Jacob,[2] John[1]), b. December 21, 1840, son of Ira D. and Lydia (Hathaway) Thompson; m. EMMA HILTON. Was in the 20th regiment Maine volunteers. Address, Vinton, Iowa.

CHILD VIII. GENERATION.

2072. Robbie Hilton, b. —; d. —.

1434.

ELBRIDGE G. THOMPSON[7] (Ira D.,[6] Ira,[5] William,[4] Caleb,[3] Jacob,[2] John[1]), b. November 3, 1845, son of Ira D. and Lydia (Hathaway) Thompson; m. NELLIE FLORENCE ROGERS. Address, Lewiston, Maine.

CHILDREN VIII. GENERATION.

2073. William Ira, b. April 7, 1876.
2074. George Elbridge, b. Dec. 24, 1877.
2075. Ethel May, b. Nov. 1, 1879.

1435.

ABBY SEAVER MILLER[7] (Susan D.,[6] Ira,[5] William,[4] Caleb,[3] Jacob,[2] John[1]), b. February 21, 1829, in South Berwick, Me., dau. of Rev. Charles and Susan D. (Thompson) Miller; m. January 21, 1851; BENJAMIN WHITE NORRIS, b. January 22, 1819, in Monmouth, Me., son of James and Mary (White) Norris. Mr. B. W. Norris graduated from Waterville college (Colby university) in 1843. Studied law but did not practice. He was land agent for the state of Maine for three years, 1860-63. Going south, he served in the freedman's bureau in Montgomery, Ala., under commission as major. Was representative to the fortieth congress from Alabama in 1867-69. He d. January 26, 1873, in Montgomery. His family reside in Skowhegan, Maine.

CHILDREN VIII. GENERATION.

2076. Helen Amelia, b. Nov. 1, 1851, in Skowhegan; m. June 1, 1882, Edwin F. Fairbrother, b. August 18, 1847, in Skowhegan, son of Reuben and Miriam (Jewell) Fairbrother, furniture dealer. She d. Dec. 1, 1888.
2077. Mary Abby, b. March 26, 1854, in Skowhegan.

1436.

HELEN SOPHIA MILLER[7] (Susan D.,[6] Ira,[5] William,[4] Caleb,[3] Jacob,[2] John[1]), b. March 25, 1832, in Turner, Me., dau. of Rev. Charles and Susan D. (Thompson) Miller; m. June 29, 1853, STEPHEN COBURN, b. November 11, 1817, in Bloomfield, Me., son of Eleazer and Mary (Weston) Coburn. Mr. Stephen Coburn graduated from Waterville college in 1839. Studied law, taking part of a course in the Harvard law school, and was admitted to the bar in 1845. Afterwards practiced law in

Skowhegan, which was always his residence. He was representative to the thirty-sixth congress in 1860–61. His later years were largely occupied with philological studies, and he left a work which has been posthumously published, entitled "The Syntactic Genesis of Words." He was brother to Abner Coburn, once governor of Maine. He d. July 4, 1882, at Skowhegan, where his family resides.

CHILDREN VIII. GENERATION.

2078. Louise Helen, b. Sept. 1, 1856, in Skowhegan. Graduated from Colby university, class of 1877.

2079. Charles Miller, b. June 17, 1860, in Skowhegan. He fitted for college in Skowhegan high school, and graduated from Colby university in 1881, taking the highest rank. He began the study of law under the direction of his father, but without the fixed purpose of making it his profession. His promising life was cut short July 4, 1882.

2080. Susy Mary, b. Oct. 19, 1863, in Skowhegan; d. August 17, 1865.

2081. Frances Elizabeth, b. June 16, 1867, in Skowhegan.

2082. Grace Maud, b. Sept. 10, 1871, in Skowhegan.

1441.

BOADICEA ALDRICH THOMPSON[7] (Elbridge G.,[6] Ira,[5] William,[4] Caleb,[3] Jacob,[2] John[1]), b. March 25, 1835, in Guilford, Me., dau. of Elbridge G. and Sarah (Ballou) Thompson; m. (1) S. C. GRAY, captain company A, 6th Maine volunteers, who fell at Chancellorsville May 3, 1863, m. (2) 1869, LEMUEL F. DINSMORE, who d. 1885. Resides in Brooklyn, N. Y.

CHILD BY SECOND HUSBAND VIII. GENERATION.

2083. Clarence Thompson, b. —; d. 1876, aged 3 years and 5 months.

1442.

SARAH ABBIE THOMPSON[7] (Elbridge G.,[6] Ira,[5] William,[4] Caleb,[3] Jacob,[2] John[1]), b. September 30, 1838, in Guilford, Me., dau. of Elbridge G. and Sarah (Ballou) Thompson; m. July 19, 1871, ELLIOT W. JAMESON. Residence, Greenville, Plumas county, Cal.

CHILDREN VIII. GENERATION.

2084. Jenny W., b. —.

2085. Dicea T., b. —.

2086. Scott, b. —.

2087. Harry B., b. —.

2088. Currie, b. —.

1444.

ELMER ELBRIDGE THOMPSON⁷ (Elbridge G.,⁶ Ira,⁵ William,⁴ Caleb,³ Jacob,² John¹), b. May, 1845, in Guilford, son of Elbridge G. and Sarah (Ballou) Thompson; m. July 19, 1871, MARY ROLLINS of Dover. Lived at Saginaw, Mich.

CHILDREN VIII. GENERATION.

2089. Harry, b. —; d. in infancy.
2090. Fred, b. —; d. in infancy.
2091. John, b. —.
2092. Charles Fred, b. —.

1445.

LELIA MINA THOMPSON⁷ (Elbridge G.,⁶ Ira,⁵ William,⁴ Caleb,³ Jacob,² John¹), b. November, 1850, in Foxcroft, Me., dau. of Elbridge G. and Sarah (Ballou) Thompson; m. July 19, 1871, WILLIAM ELLIOTT. Address, Dover, Me.

CHILDREN VIII. GENERATION.

2093. Lucy, b. —.
2094. George, b. —.
2095. Infant, b. —.

1447.

JULIA A. MONROE⁷ (Clarinda M.,⁶ Ira,⁵ William,⁴ Caleb,³ Jacob,² John¹), b. September 25, 1837, dau. of John and Clarinda M. (Thompson) Monroe; m. March 29, 1861, A. RUSSELL SWIFT. Address, Wayne, Me.

CHILDREN VIII. GENERATION.

2096. Charles Pitt, b. August 15, 1862; m. Oct., 1887, Edith Lord of Wayne.
2097. Clara Mabel, b. April 20, 1864.
2098. Julia Estelle, b. Oct. 1, 1868.

1451.

MARGARET C. THOMPSON⁷ (Arad,⁶ Ira,⁵ William,⁴ Caleb,³ Jacob,² John¹), b. June 26, 1847, in Bangor, Me., dau. of Arad and Margaret L. (Cole) Thompson; m. April 6, 1871, FRANK DUDLEY, b. February 10, 1844, in Bangor.. Address, 169 High street, Portland, Me.

CHILDREN VIII. GENERATION.

2099. Frank T., b. April 2, 1872, in Bangor; d. July 3, 1872, in Montreal.
2100. Fred Cole, b. Nov. 19, 1873, in Montreal.
2101. Arthur Arad, b. August 14, 1875, in Montreal; d. Nov. 1, 1880, in Burlington, Vt.
2102. Charles, b. May 9, 1877, in Burlington, Vt.; d. Nov. 7, 1880.
2103. Herbert, } Twins.
2104. Edward, } b. April 28, 1880; d. August 16 or 17, 1881.
2105. Margaret Louise, b. August 19, 1883, in Portland, Me.
2106. Philip, b. June 9, 1886; d. March, 1887.

1452.

JOSEPH ARAD THOMPSON[7] (Arad,[6] Ira,[5] William,[4] Caleb,[3] Jacob,[2] John[1]), b. February 20, 1854, son of Arad and Margaret L. (Cole) Thompson; m. February 8, 1882, GRACE P. HERSEY, b. December 23, 1863, in Bangor, Me.

CHILD VIII. GENERATION.

2107. Arthur Arad, b. Nov. 28, 1882, in Bangor.

1459.

SARAH ALBINA ALDRICH[7] (Boadicea L.,[6] Ira,[5] William,[4] Caleb,[3] Jacob,[2] John[1]), b. April 25, 1845, dau. of Abner S., and Boadicea L. (Thompson) Aldrich; m. May 15, 1868, FRANCIS P. HALLOWELL.

CHILD VIII. GENERATION.

2108. Mary, b. August 11, 1878.

1460.

GEORGIANA PIERPONT[7] (Boadicea L.,[6] Ira,[5] William,[4] Caleb,[3] Jacob,[2] John[1]), b. July 18, 1852, dau. of George W. and Boadicea L. (Thompson) Pierpont; m. E. M. GERRISH. Residence, Lisbon, Maine.

CHILDREN VIII. GENERATION.

2109. Lester P., b. Nov. 21, 1875.
2110. Harold, b. August 21, 1879.

1461.

BOADICEA PIERPONT[7] (Boadicea L.,[6] Ira,[5] William,[4] Caleb,[3] Jacob,[2] John[1]), b. August 16, 1853, dau. of George W. and

Boadicea L. (Thompson) Pierpont; m. November 23, 1873, WINFIELD S. TREAT. Residence, Livermore Falls, Me.

CHILDREN VIII. GENERATION.

2111. George W., b. July 21, 1875.
2112. Edith Louise, b. Dec. 27, 1886.

1462.

CHARLES ERASTUS THOMPSON[7] (Erastus,[6] Ira,[5] William,[4] Caleb,[3] Jacob,[2] John[1]), b. November 1, 1845, son of Erastus and Catherine W. (Oakes) Thompson; m. October 1, 1868, ADELIA M. LORING. He d. April 30, 1886.

CHILDREN VIII. GENERATION.

2113. Henry Erastus, b. Jan. 19, 1874.
2114. Fred Loring, b. July 28, 1881.

1463.

EDWIN DAVIS THOMPSON[7] (Erastus,[6] Ira,[5] William,[4] Caleb,[3] Jacob,[2] John[1]), b. August 26, 1848, son of Erastus and Catherine W. (Oakes) Thompson; m. December 1, 1874, MARY BARTLETT.

CHILDREN VIII. GENERATION.

2115. Arthur Bartlett, b. Nov. 5, 1875; d. April 19, 1876.
2116. Katharine Bartlett, b. March 4, 1877.
2117. Charles Bronson, b. March 16, 1880.

1464.

CLARENCE ALBERT THOMPSON[7] (Erastus,[6] Ira,[5] William,[4] Caleb,[3] Jacob,[2] John[1]), born February 17, 1852, son of Erastus and Catherine W. (Oakes) Thompson; m. October 18, 1877, MARY B. SAYNER.

CHILDREN VIII. GENERATION.

2118. Florence Bowker, b. Oct. 22, 1878.
2119. Arthur Edwin, b. Feb. 1, 1881.

1467.

JAMES AUGUSTUS MONROE[7] (Abby S,[6] Ira,[5] William,[4] Caleb,[3] Jacob,[2] John[1]), b. April 1, 1840, son of Joseph S. and Abby S. (Thompson) Monroe; m. Dec. 8, 1861, HARRIET S. JACKSON of Abbot. Home, Abbot, Me.

27

CHILDREN VIII. GENERATION.

2120. Sadie Abby, b. March 19, 1864, in Abbot; m. Nov. 28, 1886,
George H. Currier, and had Clifford Newcomb, b. Sept., 1887.
2121. James Snelling, b. Sept. 6, 1875, in Abbot.
2122. Maud Evelyn, b. July 4, 1878, in Abbot.

1470.

CLARA DICEA MONROE[7] (Abby S.,[6] Ira,[5] William,[4] Caleb,[3]
Jacob,[2] John[1]), b. March 15, 1850, dau. of Joseph S. and
Abby S. (Thompson) Monroe; m. August 29, 1877, in Skow-
hegan, JEFFERSON TAYLOR. Home at Waterville, Me.

CHILDREN VIII. GENERATION.

2123. Agnes, b. April 30, 1882, in Skowhegan.
2124. Frank Monroe, b. Nov. 17, 1883, in Skowhegan.
2125. Morris Monroe, b. May 5, 1887, in Skowhegan.

1471.

WILLIS SNELLING MONROE[7] (Abby S.,[6] Ira,[5] William,[4]
Caleb,[3] Jacob,[2] John[1]), b. May 2, 1854, son of Joseph S. and
Abby S. (Thompson) Monroe; m. July 10, 1884, in St. Paul,
Minn., MAMIE STEWART. Lives in St. Paul.

CHILDREN VIII. GENERATION.

2126. Willis Snelling, b. April 7, 1885, in St. Paul.
2127. Edna Moline, b. May 12, 1886; d. Nov. 2, 1886.

1473.

EMILY B. THOMPSON[7] (Job D.,[6] Ira,[5] William,[4] Caleb,[3]
Jacob,[2] John[1]), b. October 17, 1846, dau. of Job D. and Ruth
W. (Winslow) Thompson; m. May 2, 1870, GEORGE CURTIS
WING, b. April 16, 1847, in Livermore, Me. Mr. Wing fitted
for college and studied law with Henry C. Wentworth, at Livermore Falls; admitted to the bar in Androscoggin county April
23, 1868; in May following entered upon the practice of his
profession at Lisbon Falls, where he remained two years; in
March, 1870, he removed to Auburn, forming a copartnership
with the Hon. Nahum Morrill, which lasted six years. He
served on the superintending school committee of Auburn in
the years 1872 and 1873, and as city solicitor for the years
1878, '79, '80, '84, '85 and '87. He was one of the incorpo-
rators of the National Shoe & Leather Bank in 1875, and ever
since has been a director in that institution; was elected
county attorney for Androscoggin county in 1872; elected

judge of probate 1875, re-elected in 1879, and appointed judge of probate by Gov. Robie for the year 1884; chairman of republican state committee in presidential campaign of 1884, and in same year chairman of the state republican delegation to the convention at Chicago which nominated James G. Blaine for president. Is judge advocate general on Gov. Marble's staff.

CHILDREN VIII. GENERATION.

2128. Nahum M.,) Twins; b. May 6, 1871.
2129. Paul,) Paul d. July 2, 1871.
2130. George C., b. Oct. 6, 1878.

1474.

ROSE A. THOMPSON[7] (Job D.,[6] Ira,[5] William,[4] Caleb,[3] Jacob,[2] John[1]), b. May 21, 1849, dau. of Job D. and Ruth W. (Winslow) Thompson; m. DR. JOSIAH DUNHAM, b. July 12, 1847. Address, Hebron, Me.

CHILDREN VIII. GENERATION.

2131. Fanny Agnes, b. June 30, 1872.
2132. Hazel, b. June 6, 1882.

1477.

EZRA D. THOMPSON[7] (Job D.,[6] Ira,[5] William,[4] Caleb,[3] Jacob,[2] John[1]), b. October 11, 1858, son of Job D. and Ruth W. (Winslow) Thompson; m. January 18, 1880, MYRA N. COOLIDGE, b. August 18, 1861. Address, Livermore, Me.

CHILDREN VIII. GENERATION.

2133. Grace M., b. August 31, 1881,
2134. Ruth B., b. Feb. 6, 1883.
2135. Augustus C., b. Jan. 10, 1886.

1478.

KATE MARCIA THOMPSON[7] (Charles O.,[6] Ira,[5] William,[4] Caleb,[3] Jacob,[2] John[1]), b. March 2, 1855, in Chicago, dau. of Charles O. and Nancy (Marsh) Thompson; m. December 16, 1873, in Evanston, Ill., WILLIAM ORRINGTON LUNT, b. February 23, 1850, in Bowdoinham, Me., son of W. H. Lunt, late of Chicago and northwestern Iowa, and nephew of Orrington Lunt of Evanston. W. O. Lunt is in mercantile business in Kansas City, Mo.

CHILDREN VIII. GENERATION.

2136. Mary Alice, b. Oct. 31, 1874, in Evanston, Ill.
2137. Susan, b. June 19, 1876, in Pontiac, Ill.
2138. William Charles, b. Dec. 28, 1878, in Bement, Ill.
2139. Edith, b. Jan. 23, 1883, in Pontiac, Ill.
2140. Margaret, b. Oct. 30, 1886, in Sedan, Kansas.

1482.

MARTHA E. WYMAN[7] (Mary S.,[6] Ira,[5] William,[4] Caleb,[3] Jacob,[2] John[1]), b. October 26, 1847, in Livermore, dau. of William K. and Mary S. (Thompson) Wyman; m. (1.) May 25, 1868, in Livermore, S. THAXTER BAILEY, (2) May 1, 1878, in Livermore, REV. WILLIAM M. HARTHORN. Address, Milltown, Me.

CHILDREN BY FIRST HUSBAND VIII. GENERATION.

2141. Drew Thompson, b. June 1, 1871, in Livermore. Name changed by legal process to Drew T. Harthorn.
2142. Lillian May, b. May 27, 1873, in Dover Me.; d. May 12, 1888, in Calais, Me.

CHILD BY SECOND HUSBAND VIII. GENERATION.

2143. Anna Alice, b. Sept. 7, 1882, in Effingham, N. H.

1485.

JOHN MONROE WYMAN[7] (Mary S.,[6] Ira,[5] William,[4] Caleb,[3] Jacob,[2] John[1]), b. June 22, 1857, son of William K. and Mary S. (Thompson) Wyman; m. June 24, 1884, in Waterville, Me., MINNIE B. HAYNES. Address, Roslindale, Mass.

CHILD VIII. GENERATION.

2144. Eva May, b. Nov. 29, 1886, in Roslindale.

1488.

MARY ALICE WYMAN[7] (Mary S.,[6] Ira,[5] William,[4] Caleb,[3] Jacob,[2] John[1]), b. March 5, 1865, in Livermore, dau. of William K. and Mary S. (Thompson) Wyman; m. June 20, 1885, in West Somerville, Mass., FRANK H. HANSON of Waterville, Me. Address, Newark, N. J.

CHILD VIII GENERATION.

2145. Helen Sophia, b. Oct. 19, 1886, in Atlantic City, N. J.

1496.

DAVILLA STURTEVANT THOMPSON[7] (Loammi B.,[6] Galen,[5] William,[4] Caleb,[3] Jacob,[2] John[1]), b. July 29, 1848, in Jay, Me., son of Loammi B. and Laura J. (Dolley) Thompson; m. July 9, 1871, in Livermore, LIZZIE E. HERSEY.

CHILDREN VIII. GENERATION.

2146. Emma Belle, b. May 2, 1872, in Livermore.
2147. Ida May, b. August 18, 1882, in East Livermore.
2148. Harriet Stone, b. Oct. 9, 1884, in East Livermore.

1497.

FANNIE GERTRUDE THOMPSON[7] (Loammi B.,[6] Galen,[5] William,[4] Caleb,[3] Jacob,[2] John[1]), b. April 18, 1851, in Jay, dau. of Loammi B. and Laura J. (Dolley) Thompson; m. July 5, 1869, in Livermore, ADDISON P. RICKER. She d. May 26, 1888, in East Livermore.

CHILDREN VIII. GENERATION.

2149. Julius Augustus, b. Sept. 9, 1870, in Livermore.
2150. Archie Guy, b. Nov. 2, 1881, in East Livermore.

1500.

LAURA BOADICEA THOMPSON[7] (Loammi B.,[6] Galen,[5] William,[4] Caleb,[3] Jacob,[2] John[1]), b. July 23, 1860, in Livermore, dau. of Loammi B. and Laura J. (Dolley) Thompson; m. January 28, 1878, in Livermore, ELLERY MAY WING.

CHILD VIII. GENERATION.

2151. Willie Ellery, b. July 4, 1880, in New Portland, Me.

(1501 see 1505.)

1503.

CLARENCE M. THOMPSON[7] (Rodolphus P.,[6] Galen,[5] William,[4] Caleb,[3] Jacob,[2] John[1]), b. August 21, 1856, son of Rodolphus P. and Abbie L. (Wadsworth) Thompson; m. November 26, 1874, ALICE L. RICHARDSON.

CHILDREN VIII. GENERATION.

2152. Charlie R., b. Sept. 9, 1875.
2153. Bertha M., b. Sept. 4, 1877.
2154. Gracie M., b. Jan. 29, 1879.
2155. Merle L., b. August 4, 1885.

1504.

CLIFFORD R. THOMPSON[7] (Rodolphus P.,[6] Galen,[5] William,[4] Caleb,[3] Jacob,[2] John[1]), b. August 13, 1858, son of Rodolphus P. and Abbie L. (Wadsworth) Thompson; m. January 1, 1881, ALICE M. KYES of Jay, Me.

CHILDREN VIII. GENERATION.

2156. Eula H., b. July 2, 1882.
2157. Howard C. b. May 12, 1884.
2158. Ernest V., b. April 16, 1886.
2159. Ruth F., b. May 10, 1888.

1505.

IRVIN A. THOMPSON[7] (Rodolphus P.,[6] Galen,[5] William,[4] Caleb,[3] Jacob,[2] John[1]), b. September 28, 1860, son of Rodolphus P. and Abbie L. (Wadsworth) Thompson; m. (1) September 28, 1881, ROSETTA R. GODING of Livermore, (2) May 25, 1884, in Jay, THEDIA JULIA THOMPSON (1505) of Livermore. First wife d. April 4, 1883.

CHILD BY FIRST WIFE VIII. GENERATION.

2160. Mertena A., b. July 11, 1882.

CHILD BY SECOND WIFE VIII. GENERATION.

2161. Mildred Laura, b. July 5, 1886, in North Anson, Me.

1506.

CASTELLA A. THOMPSON[7] (Rodolphus P.,[6] Galen,[5] William,[4] Caleb,[3] Jacob,[2] John[1]), b. January 9, 1863, dau. of Rodolphus P. and Abbie L. (Wadsworth) Thompson; m. January 1, 1886, ARDEAN M. ALLEN of Jay, Me.

CHILD VIII. GENERATION.

2162, Harry A., b. March 15, 1887.

1532.

RUTH E. THOMAS[7] (Harriet,[6] Alfred,[5] Caleb,[4] Caleb,[3] Jacob,[2] John[1]), b. —, dau. of Asel and Harriet (Thompson) Thomas; m. HENRY WHITMAN. She d. —.

CHILDREN VIII. GENERATION.

2163. George, b. —.
2164. Harry, b. —.
2165. Robert, b. —.
2166. Charles, b. —.

1534.

ASEL T. EATON[7] (Harriet,[6] Alfred,[5] Caleb,[4] Caleb,[3] Jacob,[2] John[1]), b. —, son of Ruel and Harriet (Thompson) Eaton; m. HANNAH ATWOOD.

CHILDREN VIII. GENERATION.

2167. Annie, b. —.
2168. Ralph, b. —.

1535.

ALEXANDER EATON[7] (Harriet,[6] Alfred,[5] Caleb,[4] Caleb,[3] Jacob,[2] John[1]), b. —, son of Ruel and Harriet (Thompson) Eaton; m. LIZZIE ALDEN.

CHILDREN VIII. GENERATION.

2169. Laura, b. —.
2170. Nathan, b. —.
2171. Henry, b. —.
2172. Ruth E., b. —.

1540.

RUTH WILDER[7] (Mary E.,[6] Alfred,[5] Caleb,[4] Caleb,[3] Jacob,[2] John[1]), b. —, dau. of David and Mary Eliza (Thompson) Wilder; m. HORACE KENDRICK. She d. —.

CHILDREN VIII. GENERATION.

2173. Edith, b. —.
2174. David, b. —.

1547.

WILLIAM E. THOMPSON[7] (Andrew,[6] Reuben,[5] Andrew,[4] Reuben,[3] Thomas,[2] John[1]), b. —, son of Andrew and Mercy (Tilson) Thompson; m. April, 1841, ELIZA N. GARDNER.

CHILDREN VIII. GENERATION.

2175. Mary E., b. March 4, 1842.
2176. William F., b. Jan. 18, 1846.
2177. Rufus D., b. Dec. 19, 1848.
2178. James F., b. Oct. 15, 1851.

1556.

WALTER THOMPSON[7] (Reuben,[6] Reuben,[5] Andrew,[4] Reuben,[3] Thomas,[2] John[1]), b. November 25, 1837, in Plympton, Mass., son of Reuben and Sally (Washburn) Thompson; m. October 12, 1864, JULIA PETERSON of Duxbury, Mass. He served three years and three months in company E, 29th regiment Massachusetts volunteer infantry, in war of rebellion. Was wounded May 12, 1864, at Spottsylvania, Va. In 1889 he was commander of Stewartsville Post, No. 298, G. A. R., in Missouri. Address, Stewartsville.

CHILDREN VIII. GENERATION.

2179. Charles Henry, b. April 25, 1867, in Duxbury, Mass.
2180. Annie Morton, b. July 12, 1869, in Duxbury, Mass.
2181. Walter Franklin, b. Jan. 3, 1875, in Plympton, Mass.
2182. Willie Clifton, b. May 10, 1876, in Stewartsville, Mo.; d. Jan. 27, 1877.
2183. Ernest Allen, b. Oct. 16, 1830, in Stewartsville, Mo.; d. August 25, 1881.
2184. Harry Melvin, b. May 27, 1884.

1557.

JOSIAH WHITMAN THOMPSON[7] (Reuben,[6] Reuben,[5] Andrew,[4] Reuben,[3] Thomas,[2] John[1]), b. January 1, 1841, in Plympton, son of Reuben and Sally (Washburn) Thompson; m. MRS. ISABELLA O. W. (PHINNEY) ELDRIDGE. He is a member of the G. A. R., Grand Lodge I. O. O. F., and many other fraternal societies. Resides at Milton, Mass.

CHILDREN VIII. GENERATION.

2185. Arthur Clifford, b. Sept. 12, 1871, in Abington, Mass.; d. Sept. 27, 1872.
2186. Grace Aldine, b. April 24, 1873, in Abington, Mass.; d. Oct. 1, 1873.
2187. Elwyn Washburn, b. July 26, 1875, in Plympton, Mass.
2188. Arthur Garfield, b. Nov. 4, 1881, in Plympton, Mass.

1561.

NEHEMIAH THOMPSON[7] (Dexter C.,[6] Nehemiah,[5] Asa,[4] Thomas,[3] Thomas,[2] John[1]), b. October 7, 1835; son of Dexter C. and Harriet (Bosworth) Thompson; m. ADELINE GIBBS.

CHILDREN VIII. GENERATION.

2189. Dexter C., b. —. Lives in Boston.
2190. Nathaniel, b. —. Lives in Boston.
2191. Charles, b. —. Lives in Boston.

1568.

MORTON THOMPSON[7] (Learned H.,[6] Asa,[5] Asa,[4] Thomas,[3] Thomas,[2] John[1]), b. May 29, 1844, son of Learned H. and Hannah P. (Wood) Thompson; m. October 22, 1866, KATIE DELANO STANDISH, dau. of Shadrach and Catharine (Delano) Standish.

CHILDREN VIII. GENERATION.

2192. Morton Standish, b. August 15, 1867.
2193. Hannah Porter, b. Feb. 18, 1872.
2194. Gracie Alice, b. Sept. 21, 1882.

1581.

ELLEN A. THOMPSON[7] (Ephraim B.,[6] Jabez P.,[5] Ebenezer,[4] Ebenezer,[3] Thomas,[2] John[1]), b. January 3, 1837, dau. of Ephraim B. and Eliza R. (Soule) Thompson; m. May, 1862, HENRY S. POPE of Halifax. Now (1887) resides in Marion, Kansas.

CHILDREN VIII. GENERATION.

2195. Mary T., b. Oct. 26, 1863; d. aged 7 years.
2196. Lucy T., b. May 2, 1865; m. 1886, William Nye of Marion, Kan.
2197. Susan E., b. Oct., 1867.
2198. Harry, b. July, 1869.
2199. Ida, b. Nov., 1871.
2200. Inez, b. May, 1873.
2201. Frank, b. —.

1582.

SARAH BRIGGS THOMPSON[7] (Ephraim B.,[6] Jabez P.,[5] Ebenezer,[4] Ebenezer,[3] Thomas,[2] John[1]), b. July 22, 1838, dau. of Ephraim B. and Eliza R. (Soule) Thompson; m. February 14, 1865, E. M. BAINE. Lives in Halifax.

CHILD VIII. GENERATION.

2202. Ellen T., b. Sept. 20, 1867.

1583.

LUCY MORTON THOMPSON[7] (Ephraim B.,[6] Jabez P.,[5] Ebenezer,[4] Ebenezer,[3] Thomas,[2] John[1]), b. May 12, 1840, dau. of Ephraim B. and Eliza R. (Soule) Thompson; m. November 13, 1861, HARRISON D. PACKARD. She d. April 14, 1865.

CHILD VIII. GENERATION.

2203. Charles S., b. Oct. 5, 1863; m. June 1, 1885, Edea J. Dean of Westford. Lives in Brocton.

1585.

JABEZ P. THOMPSON⁷ (Ephraim B.,⁶ Jabez P.,⁵ Ebenezer,⁴ Ebenezer,³ Thomas,² John¹), b. July 24, 1853, son of Ephraim B. and Eliza R. (Soule) Thompson; m. December 19, 1878, ABBY P. WOOD, dau. of Asaph and Abby C. (Parker) Wood.

CHILDREN VIII. GENERATION.

2204. Fred P., b. Sept. 8, 1882.
2205. Clifford Briggs, b. Oct. 2, 1884.
2206. Myron Wood, b. March 5, 1887.
2206½. Helen Loring, b. April 10, 1890.

1588.

CLARINDA MORTON SPILMAN⁷ (Clara S.,⁶ Zebadiah,⁵ Zebadiah,⁴ Zebadiah,³ Thomas,² John,¹), b. —, dau. of Thomas A. and Clara S. (Thompson) Spilman; m. GEORGE W. RAUGH of Normal, Ill.

CHILD VIII. GENERATION.

2207. Charles F., b. —.

1592.

JAMES H. SPILMAN⁷ (Clara S.,⁶ Zebadiah,⁵ Zebadiah,⁴ Zebadiah,³ Thomas,² John¹), b. —, son of Thomas A. and Clara S. (Thompson) Spilman; m. MARY HUTCHINSON. He is a Presbyterian minister. Lives at Bethel, Ill.

CHILD VIII. GENERATION.

2208. Charles H., b. —.

1594.

REBECCA WATERMAN ATWOOD⁷ (Martha B.,⁶ Zebadiah,⁵ Zebadiah,⁴ Zebadiah,³ Thomas,² John¹), b. December, 1830, dau. of John B. and Martha B. (Thompson) Atwood; m. JOSIAH A. ROBBINS of Plymouth. He d. June 27, 1885.

CHILDREN VIII. GENERATION.

2209. William T., b. —; m. Martha Trimble.
2210. Rebecca J., b, —; m. Charles E. Chamberlin of Worcester. Children, Helen R., Bessie R. and John.

2211. John B., b. Jan. 27, 1855 ; d. Feb. 28, 1866.
2212. Josiah T., b. —.
2213. Herbert A., b. —.
2214. Alexander H., b. —.
2215. Charles B., b. —.
2216. Gordon, b. —.
2217. Walter J., b. — ; d. aged 3 years.

1595.

MARTHA BRIGGS ATWOOD[7] (Martha B.,[6] Zebadiah,[5] Zebadiah,[4] Zebadiah,[3] Thomas,[2] John[1]), b. April 2, 1832, dau. of John B. and Martha B. (Thompson) Atwood ; m. AMORY T. SKERRY of Oakham, Mass. She d. July 3, 1887.

CHILDREN VIII. GENERATION.

2218. Walter Amory, b. Feb. 14, 1857; d. March 28, 1862.
2219. Martha Briggs, b. May 28, 1858 ; m. Charles B. Rockwell. Children, Martha, Skerry and June.
2220. Harry Ward, b. July 26, 1860. He graduated at New York University. "Interne" at United States Marine Hospital, Staten Island.
2221. Amory T., b. Nov. 16, 1863. Graduated at New York University, 1884 ; m. Nov. 16, 1887, Emma Gulick of Brooklyn, N. Y.

1598.

JOHN THOMAS THOMPSON[7] (John T. Z.,[6] Zebadiah,[5] Zebadiah,[4] Zebadiah,[3] Thomas,[2] John[1]), b. July 10, 1846, son of John T. Z. and Sagie B. (Tilden) Thompson; m. July 10, 1869, IRENE L. STURTEVANT of Halifax, dau. of Ira L. and Irene (Sherman) Sturtevant.

CHILDREN VIII. GENERATION.

2222. John Larue, b. Oct. 14, 1870.
2223. Elroy Sherman, b. Feb. 19, 1874.
2224. Mary Gertrude, b. Feb. 26, 1878; d. May 15, 1885.
2225. Charles Edward Percy, b. Nov. 5, 1879.

1599.

MARY SHELDON THOMPSON[7] (John T. Z.,[6] Zebadiah,[5] Zebadiah,[4] Zebadiah,[3] Thomas,[2] John[1]), b. —, dau. of John T. Z. and Sagie B. (Tilden) Thompson; m. LORENZO AUGUSTUS TOWER of West Bridgewater.

CHILDREN VIII. GENERATION.

2226. William L., b. —.
2227. Alice B., b. —.
2228. Edith Allerton, b. —.
2229. Walter S., b. —.
2230. Harry Loring, b. —.

1600.

CHRISTOPHER TILDEN THOMPSON[7] (John T. Z.,[6] Zebadiah,[5] Zebadiah,[4] Zebadiah,[3] Thomas,[2] John[1]), b. April 9, 1853, son of John T. Z. and Sagie B. (Tilden) Thompson; m. EVA M. CARPENTER. Lives in Halifax.

CHILD VIII. GENERATION.

2230½. Nina Christine, b. Jan. 3, 1890.

1601.

CHARLES BRIGGS THOMPSON[7] (John T. Z.,[6] Zebadiah,[5] Zebadiah,[4] Zebadiah,[3] Thomas,[2] John[1]), b. November 17, 1859, son of John T. Z. and Sagie B. (Tilden) Thompson; m. ANNA W. SHEPARD of North Pembroke. They live in Dedham.

CHILD VIII. GENERATION.

2231. Arthur Shepard, b. —.

1602.

MARY ELIZA THOMPSON[7] (John,[6] William,[5] John,[4] Joseph,[3] Peter,[2] John[1]), b. December 1, 1829, dau. of John and Ruth B. (Johnson) Thompson; m. September 1, 1852, SOLOMON BURT SAXTON, b. January 31, 1827, in Wilbraham, Mass., son of Gordon Bliss and Philena Fletcher (Leverance) Saxton, a lineal descendant of George Saxton of Windsor and Westfield, Mass.,—1690. Mr. Saxton has lived the most of his life in Troy, N. Y., where he is engaged in the flour business.

CHILDREN VIII. GENERATION.

2232. Mary Lena, b. Dec. 27, 1855, in Troy; m. Dwinel F. Thompson.
2233. John Gordon, b. Nov. 1, 1857; m. June 30, 1885, Hattie Thompson Rowe, b. Nov. 22, 1862, in Auburn, Me., dau. of William Webster and Mary Elizabeth (French) Rowe, and cousin of D. F. Thompson. John G. is in the flour business with his father.

1604.

EDWIN J. THOMPSON[7] (John,[6] William,[5] John,[4] Joseph,[3] Peter,[2] John[1]), b. October 7, 1833, in Middlebury, O., son of John and Ruth Bateman (Johnson) Thompson; m. December 29, 1857, ELLA PHELPS ARMSTRONG of Shoreham, Vt. He was a professor in University of Minnesota for a number of years; afterwards a home missionary in Dakota; removed to Salem, Oregon, and in 1887 settled over a church near Albany, Oregon.

CHILDREN VIII. GENERATION.

2234. George Burt, b. Jan. 9, 1859, in Shoreham, Vt.; m. Edith Wilson.
2235. Clara Ella, b. Nov. 12, 1861, in Shoreham, Vt.
2236. John, b. Feb. 25, 1863, in Chatfield, Minn.
2237. Mary Saxton, b. Aug. 7, 1865, in Preston, Minn.
2238. Anson Wingate, b. July 12, 1867, in Chatfield, Minn.
2239. Annetta, b. Nov. 7, 1869, in Rushford, Minn.
2240. Nellie, b. 1872; d. April 9, 1872, in Minneapolis.
2241. Edith, b. 1881, in Castleton, Dakota.

1605.

GEORGE BATES THOMPSON[7] (John,[6] William,[5] John,[4] Joseph,[3] Peter,[2] John[1]), b. January 12, 1839, in Middle Granville, N. Y., son of John and Ruth B. (Johnson) Thompson; m. April 23, 1863, MARY ELIZABETH AVERY, b. August 14, 1842, in Troy, N. Y., dau. of Lyman Avery. George B. lived in Troy and Lansingburgh, N. Y., the most of his life, where he has been engaged in the flour business. He is very active in Sunday school work.

CHILDREN VIII. GENERATION.

2242. George Lyman, b. Dec. 9, 1864, in Troy; d. June 23, 1866.
2243. Mary Ruth, b. June 16, 1867, in Troy.
2244. Gertrude Elizabeth, b. August 10, 1869, in Troy.
2245. Gracie Mackey, b. Nov. 11, 1871, in Troy; d. March 8, 1872.
2246. Annie Sophia, b. August 31, 1873, in Lansingburg.
2247. Christine, b. Dec. 25, 1874, in Lansingburg.

EIGHTH GENERATION.

1609.

CYNTHIA AUGUSTA BOSWORTH[8] (Deborah,[7] John,[6] Thaddeus,[5] John,[4] John,[3] John,[2] John[1]), b. March 25, 1849, dau. of Sylvanus R. and Deborah (Thompson) Bosworth; m. ALONZO POMEROY.

CHILDREN IX. GENERATION.

2247.[a] Charles Ripley, b. August 3, 1880.
2247.[b] Lula May, b. August 9, 1883.
2247.[c] Nellie Wilma, b. April 28, 1887.

1620.

LEONARD WHITE THOMPSON[8] (Ammiel,[7] John,[6] Thaddeus,[5] John,[4] John,[3] John,[2] John[1]), b. September 6, 1840, son of Ammiel and Harriet (Holmes) Thompson; m. LUCINDA BERRY. He has been township treasurer.

CHILDREN IX. GENERATION.

2248. Harriet Luella, b. —.
2249. Harvey Ammiel, b. —.
2250. Nettie Lucinda, b. —.

1633.

DORA MARGRETT THOMPSON[8] (John,[7] John,[6] Thaddeus,[5] John,[4] John,[3] John,[2] John[1]), b. October 13, 1856, in Hartford, Me., dau. of John and Mahalah J. A. (Burnham) Thompson; m. May 10, 1876, ELLIAN E. FULLER, b. September 4, 1851, in Livermore, Me.

CHILD IX. GENERATION.

2250[a]. Orlestus Conant, b. April 16, 1881, in Livermore.

1634.

HATTIE GENEVA THOMPSON[8] (John,[7] John,[6] Thaddeus,[5] John,[4] John,[3] John,[2] John[1]), b. October 13, 1859, in Hartford, Me., dau. of John and Mahalah J. A. (Burnham) Thompson; m May 21, 1881, RUFUS H. POTTER, b. August 22, 1856, in Oxford, Me. She d. June 1, 1885.

CHILDREN IX. GENERATION.

2250.ᵇ Thompson Augustus, b. Sept. 18, 1884, in Haverhill, Mass.

1677.

SARAH A. LOVELL⁸ (Irene,⁷ Sarah,⁶ Sarah,⁵ Nathan,⁴ Thomas,³ John,² John¹), b. October 20, 1840, dau. of Cyrus and Irene Adeline (Babbitt) Lovell; m. August 29, 1865, JAMES M. McKINLAY, b. February 28, 1826, in Scotland. Address, 108 West Seventy-ninth street, New York city, N. Y.

CHILDREN IX. GENERATION.

2251. Minne Lovell, b. July 24, 1866.
2252. Addie Maud, b. Jan. 13, 1868.
2253. Lulu May, b. May 21, 1870.
2254. James Buell, b. April 15, 1872.
2255. William Henry, b. April 21, 1874.

1707.

ARTHUR BURNHAM CLARK⁸ (Lucy E.,⁷ Elvira,⁶ Cyrus,⁵ James,⁴ Thomas,³ John,² John¹), b. December 18, 1866, in Ridgeway, N. Y., son of George W. and Lucy E. (Root) Clark; m. August 18, 1886, TILLIE A. MARVIN. Lives in Gobleville, Van Buren county, Mich.

CHILDREN IX. GENERATION.

2256. George W., b. June 5, 1887.
2257. Arthur B., b. Sept. 10, 1888.

1721.

WENDELL LEE SIMPSON⁸ (Mary A.,⁷ Cyrus,⁶ Cyrus,⁵ James,⁴ Thomas,³ John,² John¹), b. August 10, 1859, in Carlton, N. Y., son of Emery H. and Mary A. (Thompson) Simpson; m. October 19, 1886, MARION O. WOOD, dau. of William W. Wood of Piqua, Ohio. Taught school several terms. For awhile was a student at Michigan Agricultural college. Following this, he was appointed a cadet at West Point, N. Y., graduating in June, 1880. Was given a lieutenant's commission in the regular army and assigned to service in the west. In 1887 he was assigned to Lansing, Mich., as military instructor at Michigan Agricultural college. A part of the year 1890 he occupied the position of professor of mathematics and engineering in same college.

CHILDREN IX. GENERATION.

2258.   Bethel Wood, b. July 11, 1888, in Lansing, Mich.
2259.   Dorothy Wood, b. May 3, 1890, in Lansing, Mich.

1723.

NATHAN FISH SIMPSON[8] (Mary A.,[7] Cyrus,[6] Cyrus,[5] James,[4] Thomas,[3] John,[2] John[1]), b. October 12, 1862, in Carlton, son of Emery H. and Mary A. (Thompson) Simpson; m. April 13, 1886, HARRIET A. DUNCOMBE, dau. of Charles Duncombe of Keeler, Mich. Before his marriage he taught school a few terms. After his marriage he removed to Nebraska, engaging in farming. Was elected county superintendent of schools. Later returned to Keeler where he now resides.

CHILD IX. GENERATION.

2260.   Frances Fae, b. July 29, 1887.

1728.

GERTRUDE MOSHER[8] (Ellen E.,[7] Cyrus,[6] Cyrus,[5] James,[4] Thomas,[3] John,[2] John[1]), b. November 8, 1861, dau. of Edward and Ellen E. (Thompson) Mosher; m. November 7, 1883, WASHINGTON SIMMONS. Lives in Eagle Harbor, N. Y.

CHILD IX. GENERATION.

2261.   Ethel, b. July 22, 1886.

1734.

ALLAN SUTTON THOMPSON[8] (Charles H.,[7] Nathan,[6] Cyrus,[5] James,[4] Thomas,[3] John,[2] John[1]), b. May 26, 1866, in Lansing, Mich., son of Charles H. and Elizabeth G. (Sutton) Thompson; m. May 16, 1888, in Lansing, by Rev. M. M. Callen, KATIE HATCHEL, b. December 7, 1865, in Cuyahoga county, Ohio, of German parents. Allan graduated in 1886 from Lansing high school; later was a student at Michigan Agricultural college. He has been employed for some time at Lansing wheelbarrow works. An ingenious mechanic. He and his wife are members of Central M. E. church. Address, Lansing, Mich.

CHILD IX. GENERATION.

2262.   Leroy Hatchel, b. March 27, 1889, in Lansing.

1757.

NELLIE A. STRONG[8] (Ellen A.,[7] James,[6] Bela,[5] James,[4] Thomas,[3] John,[2] John[1]), b. April 20, 1861, dau. of Albert and

Ellen A. (Thompson) Strong; m. October 8, 1883, JAMES HARVEY RODEBAUGH.

CHILD IX. GENERATION.

2263. Harvey Strong, b. Nov. 7, 1885.

1799.

HENRY FRANCIS THOMPSON[8] (Joseph R.,[7] Cyrus,[6] Isaac,[5] John,[4] Shubael,[3] John,[2] John[1]), b. August 28, 1831, in Portland, Me., son of Joseph R. and Martha C. (Rogers) Thompson; m. June 23, 1875, LUELLA A. GILMAN of Laconia, N. H. Address, Portland, Me.

CHILD IX. GENERATION.

2264. Lyman Rogers, b. May 3, 1876.

1800.

MARIA CAROLINE THOMPSON[8] (Joseph R.,[7] Cyrus,[6] Isaac,[5] John,[4] Shubael,[3] John,[2] John[1]), b. January 28, 1833, in Portland, Me., dau. of Joseph R. and Martha C. (Rogers) Thompson; m. October 1, 1868, CORNELIUS D. MAYNARD of Portland.

CHILDREN IX. GENERATION.

2265. Joseph Cornelius, b. July 21, 1870.
2266. Sally Durant, b. May 31, 1872.
2267. George Herbert, b. May 15, 1874; d. Dec. 9, 1874.
2268. Ralph Field, b. Dec. 11, 1875; d. Dec. 14, 1875.

1807.

WILLIAM DRAKE THOMPSON[8] (Joseph R.,[7] Cyrus,[6] Isaac,[5] John,[4] Shubael,[3] John,[2] John[1]), b. December 21, 1846, in Portland, Me., son of Joseph R. and Martha C. (Rogers) Thompson; m. October 21, 1873, ALICE TURNER of Portland.

CHILDREN IX. GENERATION.

2269. Lizzie Wallace, b. Dec. 18, 1874.
2270. Charles Harris, b. August 25, 1876.
2271. Ruth Whiting, b. March 12, 1881; d. March 25, 1881.

1808.

SUMNER CUMMINGS THOMPSON[8] (Joseph R.,[7] Cyrus,[6] Isaac,[5] John,[4] Shubael,[3] John,[2] John[1]), b. November 13, 1848, in Port-

29

land, Me., son of Joseph R. and Martha C. (Rogers) Thompson; m. March 3, 1881, KATIE M. CONNOLLY of Portland.

CHILDREN IX. GENERATION.

2272. Martha Rogers, b. Dec. 10, 1881.
2273. Joseph Robinson. b. Sept. 27, 1883.
2274. Gertrude Edna, b. Nov. 25, 1885; d. May 28, 1886.
2275. Sumner Cummings, b. June 15, 1887; d. August 20, 1887.

1810.

STEPHEN EMMONS THOMPSON[8] (Joseph R.,[7] Cyrus,[6] Isaac,[5] John,[4] Shubael,[3] John,[2] John[1]), b. June 23, 1853, in Portland, Me., son of Joseph R and Martha C. (Rogers) Thompson; m. September 25, 1879, ADDIE ELLA JORDAN of Portland.

CHILDREN IX. GENERATION.

2276. Jessie Louise, b. March 9, 1884.
2277. Lillian May, b. Dec. 3, 18:5.

1811.

GEORGE HERBERT THOMPSON[8] (Joseph R.,[7] Cyrus,[6] Isaac,[5] John,[4] Shubael,[3] John,[2] John[1]), b. July 20, 1855, in Portland, son of Joseph R. and Martha C. (Rogers) Thompson; m. October 13, 1884, HATTIE M. HICKS of Portland. Residence, Portland, Me.

CHILDREN IX. GENERATION.

2278. Ella Almena, b. Nov. 16, 1885.
2279. Bertha May, b. May 1, 1887.

1813.

JOSEPH ROBINSON THOMPSON[8] (Cyrus,[7] Cyrus,[6] Isaac,[5] John,[4] Shubael,[3] John,[2] John[1]), b. February 2, 1835, son of Cyrus and Marenda (Pitts) Thompson; m. ELLEN BOND FULLER, b. December 3, 1849.

CHILDREN IX. GENERATION.

2280. Harry Francis, b. July 2, 1861; d. August 11, 1862.
2281. Alice Mary, b. Sept. 9, 1865; m. Edward W. Phelps, b. Dec. 9, 1864.

1814.

THERON REED[8] (Martha S.,[7] Cyrus,[6] Isaac,[5] John,[4] Shubael,[3] John,[2] John[1]), b. August 30, 1836, son of Stillman and Martha

S. (Thompson) Reed ; m. November, 1858, H. LIZZIE EUSTIS. He d. November, 1862, in the service of his country.

CHILD IX. GENERATION.

2282. Clara, b. Jan. 3, 18—; d. Sept., 1880.

1815.

CYRUS T. REED[8] (Martha S.,[7] Cyrus,[6] Isaac,[5] John,[4] Shubael,[3] John,[2] John[1]), b. January 4, 1839, son of Stillman and Martha S. (Thompson) Reed ; m. (1) February, 1867, PULEPHA R. BUTLER, (2) September, 1878, EMMA BEDFORD.

CHILD BY FIRST WIFE IX. GENERATION.

2283. George E., b. Sept. 4, 1871.

1818.

FREDERICK REED[6] (Martha S.,[7] Cyrus,[6] Isaac,[5] John,[4] Shubael,[3] John,[2] John[1]), b. June 15, 1852, son of Stillman and Martha S. (Thompson) Reed; m. January, 1879, MARY E. DODGE.

CHILD IX. GENERATION.

2284. Margaret, b. March 16, 1882.

1819.

CARROL REED[6] (Martha S.,[7] Cyrus,[6] Isaac,[5] John,[4] Shubael,[3] John,[2] John[1]), b. August 31, 1854, son of Stillman and Martha S. (Thompson) Reed; m. May 1, 1878, ETTA B. STARR.

CHILDREN IX. GENERATION.

2285. Gladys E., b. May 8, 1879.
2286. Harold S., b. Sept. 15, 1881.
2287.* Earl E., b. Nov. 26, 1883.
2288. Roy B., b. July 18, 1885.

1821.

CLEORA ELMORE HALL[8] (Mary A.,[7] Uzza,[6] Isaac,[5] John,[4] Shubael,[3] John,[2] John[1]), b. July 22, 1832, in Buckfield, Me., dau. of Hiram and Mary A. (Thompson) Hall; m. GEORGE A. NOURSE of Bath, Me. She d. in California.

CHILDREN IX. GENERATION.

2289. Gussie, b. —.
2290. John, b. —.
2291. Ethel, b. —.

1822.

FRANCEVILLA VALENCIA HALL[8] (Mary A.,[7] Uzza,[6] Isaac,[5] John,[4] Shubael,[3] John,[2] John[1]), b. September 18, 1834, in Buckfield, Me., dau. of Hiram and Mary A. (Thompson) Hall; m. ATWOOD T. IRISH of Buckfield. She and her husband are dead.

CHILDREN IX. GENERATION.

2292. Elmer, b. —.
2293. Hattie J., b. —.; is a music teacher in California; m. — Miller.
2294. Minnie, b. —.

1824.

WILLIAM H. HALL[8] (Mary A.,[7] Uzza,[6] Isaac,[5] John,[4] Shubael,[3] John,[2] John[1]), b. July 9, 1841, in Buckfield, Me., son of Hiram and Mary A. (Thompson) Hall; m. ELLA M. CAMPBELL of Kingston, Minn. He is secretary of medical and surgical sanitarium at Battle Creek, Mich.

CHILDREN IX. GENERATION.

2295. Charles M., b. Oct. 8, 1867.
2296. Alice E., b. —; d. 1869.
2297. William, b. —; d. 1870.
2298. Willie, b. —; d. 1871.
2299. Cleora, b. Dec., 1873.
2300. Ethel, b. Sept., 1875.
2301. Maud, b. 1877; d. —.
2302. Minnie, b. Dec. 9, 1880.

1825.

HELEN FRANCES HALL[8] (Mary A.,[7] Uzza,[6] Isaac,[5] John,[4] Shubael,[3] John,[2] John[1]), b. April 24, 1845, in Lynden, Me., dau. of Hiram and Mary A. (Thompson) Hall; m. EPHRAIM A. BRIGGS of New York. He is a merchant in Kingston, Minn.

CHILDREN IX. GENERATION.

2303. Albert Newton, b. 1867.
2304. Dora, b. 1871.
2305. Connie, b. 1877.

1826.

MARY ELVA HALL[8] (Mary A.,[7] Uzza,[6] Isaac,[5] John,[4] Shubael,[3] John,[2] John[1]), b. June 7, 1850, in Lynden, Me., dau. of Hiram and Mary A. (Thompson) Hall; m. GRANVILLE F. DeCOSTER of Buckfield, Me. Lives in St. Paul, Minn.

CHILDREN IX. GENERATION.

2306. Willie, b. —.
2307. Albert, b. —.

1893.

WILLIAM MURDOCK THOMPSON[8] (Calvin M.,[7] Calvin,[6] Solomon,[5] Jacob,[4] Jacob,[3] Jacob,[2] John[1]), b. October 10, 1848, son of Calvin M. and Mary B. (Sharp) Thompson; m. April 23, 1873, JULIA B. HAYWARD of Brockton, Mass., dau. of Sumner A., and granddaughter of Ira and Sarah (Edson) Hayward, a lineal descendant of Thomas Hayward, who came from England and settled in Duxbury before 1638. Address, Brocton.

CHILD IX. GENERATION.

2308. Edgar Hayward, b. June 10, 1879.

1898.

ANNIE NEWELL THOMPSON[8] (Henry,[7] Calvin,[6] Solomon,[5] Jacob,[4] Jacob,[3] Jacob,[2] John[1]), b. April 12, 1862, dau. of Henry and Anne W. (Thayer) Thompson; m. April 15, 1884, HORACE RICHMOND.

CHILDREN IX. GENERATION.

2309. Alice Newell, b. Sept. 16, 1885.
2310. Edward Avery, b. June 10, 1887.

1919.

FLORA A. KENNEDY[8] (Sarah A. M.,[7] Hosea B.,[6] Abel,[5] Noah,[4] Barnabas,[3] Jacob,[2] John[1]), b. August 28, 1855, dau. of Oscar and Sarah A. M. (Thompson) Kennedy; m. ROYAL B. PERKINS Address, Bridgewater, Vt.

CHILD IX. GENERATION.

2311. Sadie A., b. Oct. 15, 1881.

1920.

RUTH S DIMMICK[8] (Sarah A. M.,[7] Hosea B.,[6] Abel,[5] Noah,[4] Barnabas,[3] Jacob,[2] John[1]), b. March 25. 1838, dau. of Nelson

C. and Sarah A. M. (Thompson) Dimmick; m. FRANK L. COPELAND. Address, Bridgewater, Vt.

CHILD IX. GENERATION.

2312. Leslie W., b. March 24, 1888.

1923.

CHARLES H. COBB[8] (Velina R.,[7] Arioch,[6] Jabez,[5] Isaac,[4] Barnabas,[3] Jacob,[2] John[1]), b. August 8, 1856, son of Charles H. and Velina R. (Thompson) Cobb; m. BETHIA PORTER of Whitman, Mass.

CHILDREN IX. GENERATION.

2313. Irving H., b. Sept. 9, 1877; d. Sept. 22, 1878.
2314. Ethel S., b. Jan. 3, 1880.

2232.

MARY LENA SAXTON[8] (Mary E.,[7] John.[6] William,[5] John,[4] Joseph,[3] Peter,[2] John[1]), b. December 27, 1855, dau. of Solomon B. and Mary E. (Thompson) Saxton; m. January 1, 1880, DWINEL FRENCH THOMPSON, b. January 1, 1846, in Bangor, Me., son of Joel Dwinel and Harriet Newell (French) Thompson, a lineal descendant of James Thompson of Kittery, Me., 1696. D. F. Thompson graduated at Dart college, C. S. D., 1869; was tutor three years. In 1872 he was appointed professor at Rensselaer Polytechnic institute at Troy, N. Y., where he still remains (1888).

CHILDREN IX. GENERATION.

2315. Alice Quimby, b Dec. 17, 1880, in Troy.
2316. Gordon Saxton, b. August 6, 1883, in Lansingburg, N. Y.
2317. Nathaniel French, b. Oct. 16, 1884, in Lansingburg.
2318. Dwinel Burt, b. Dec. 14, 1886, in Lansingburg.

2234.

GEORGE BURT THOMPSON[8] (Edwin J,[7] John,[6] William,[5] John,[4] Joseph,[3] Peter,[2] John[1]), b. January 9, 1859, in Shoreham, Vt., son of Edwin J. and Ella P. (Armstrong) Thompson; m. May 10, 1883, EDITH WILSON, b. June 8, 1862, in Minneapolis, Minn., dau. of Joseph Patten and Mary Pauline (Corbet) Wilson. Resides in Troy, N. Y.

CHILD IX. GENERATION.

2319. Helen, b. Dec. 29, 1885, in Troy.

SUPPLEMENT

Contains correction of some names, also items that came too late to go in the book in regular form. Refer from the number given here to the same number in the body of the work. Full-faced numbers here indicate a family in the regular place.

264. Gains should be Gaius.

471. The children should be vii. generation instead of vi. generation.

869. Hannah Thompson, b. in Hartford, Me.; m. Sept. 12, 1831, in Hartford, Ephraim Bryant Gammon, b. Dec. 4, 1809, in Buckfield, Me.

871. America Bonney, d. April 19, 1885.

872. Lydia Thompson, b. Dec. 24, 1821, in Hartford, Me.; m. Dec. 5, 1847, in Hartford, by Rev. Levi Burnham, Thomas Bonney of Sumner, Me., b. Jan. 27, 1822. He d. April 14, 1882.

873. John Thompson, m. July 4, 1848, Mahalah Jane Augusta Burnham, b. Jan. 9, 1829.

875. William H. Thompson, m. Nov. 3, 1858, Cornelia E. Fuller of Livermore.

982. Claribel, as she was latterly called, d. Feb. 6, 1891, in Pasadena. She was the sunshine of her home; the gradual decline of health, to her last earthly hour, was borne with saintly patience and sweet unselfishness.

1011. Harry Franklin, son of Lottie M. Buckley, b. Nov. 3, 1890, in Glendale, Van Buren county, Mich.

1206. Emily Louise Wood, m. Thomas Briggs Crane June 13, 1854.

1207. Joseph Tinkham Wood, d. Feb. 6, 1890.

1606. Arvilla Bosworth, b. Oct. 2, 1833; d. Sept. 29, 1862.

1607. Lucy Ann Bosworth, b. Dec. 16, 1836; m. John M. Purkis.

1608. Mary Elizabeth Bosworth, b. June 14, 1839; m. Elmer A. Frazier.

1609. Cynthia Augusta Bosworth, b. March 25, 1849; m. Alonzo Pomeroy.

1610. Margaret Thompson Bosworth, b. May 31, 1851; m. John E. Thompson (1621).

1611. Sophia Gammon, b. Feb. 9, 1832, in Hartford, Me.; d. Feb. 20, 1832.

1612. Julia Sarepta Gammon, b. April 25, 1833, in Hartford; m. June 1, 1856, in Abington, Mass., Samuel G. Curtis. Has two children: Marietta Weston and Maria Eugenie. Julia d. May 21, 1867, in Abington.

1613. Edee Malory Gammon, b. Feb. 27, 1835, in Hartford; m. July 12, 1853, in Broomfield, Me., Edward Farnsworth Blake (deceased). Has two children: Alice Aphia and Grace Florence.

1614. Rendall Tolman Gammon, b. July 30, 1838, in Hartford; d. Nov. 17, 1864, in Salisbury, North Carolina.

1615. Horatio Hackett Gammon, b. Oct. 10, 1840, in Hartford; m. (1) 1863, in East Abington, Mass., Julia F. Bonney. Had one child: Myrtie Belle; m. (2) Clara E. Denning.

1616. Ephraim Adron Gammon, b. June 29, 1844, in Hartford; m. Oct. 9, 1866, in Mechanic Falls, Me. Elsada Lamont Thayer (deceased). Had one child: Harry La Harpe.

1617. Nathaniel Gammon, b. Nov. 25, 1846, in Hartford; m. Dec. 21, 1867, in Harrison, Me., Ellen F. Tibbits. Has four children: Arthur Rendall, Maude Gertrude, Guy Norman, and Ralph Nathaniel.

1618. Cleora Celinda Gammon, b. Nov. 2, 1848, in Hartford; d. Feb. 12, 1869, in Poland, Me.

1619. Hannah Gammon, b. June 28, 1851, in Hartford; m. July 31, 1875, in Lisbon, Me., Oliver Conant Bridge. Has two children: Edward Warren and Charlotte Mabel.

1622. America Delmar Bonney, b. July 7, 1847; d. April 7, 1850.

1623. Clara Hortense Bonney, b. Oct. 17, 1849; m. Feb. 20, 1882, Roscoe E. Bradbury.

1624. Rosalthe Joanna Bonney, b. Oct. 13, 1852; m. May 20, 1883, George W. Scribner.

1625. Benjamin Harris Bonney, b. July 21, 1855; m. Oct. 10, 1882, Lizzie A. Rowe.

1626. Lumira Thompson Bonney, b. August 18, 1857; unmarried.

1627. Anna R. Bonney, b. August 17, 1849; d. June 7, 1877.

1628. John T. Bonney, b. Nov. 21, 1853; d. March 22, 1859.

1629. Henry W. Bonney, b. May 27, 1856; d, March 8, 1859.

1630. John H. Bonney, b. Sept. 22, 1860; m. Dec. 17, 1890, at East Sumner, by Rev. S. D. Richardson, Jennie H. Keene of Sumner, b. Nov. 16, 1865.

1631. Thomas W. Bonney, b. Oct. 14, 1865.

1632. Sarah Jane Thompson, b. Nov. 1, 1851, in Hartford, Me.; d. March 15, 1876; unmarried.

1633. Dora Margrett Thompson, b. Oct 13, 1856; m. Ellian E. Fuller.

1634. Hattie Geneva Thompson, b. Oct. 13, 1859; m. Rufus H. Potter.

1635. Grace Ermena Cleora Thompson, b. June 17, 1874, in Hartford, Me.

1636. Cornelia Estelle Thompson, b. Oct. 28, 1865.

1637. Charles G. Thompson, b. Sept. 26, 1870.

1905. Mary Louise Crane, b. March 11, 1855.

APPENDIX.

New Lever Safety (1734) Agent.

APPENDIX.

THE FAMILY OF FRANCIS COOKE OF THE MAYFLOWER.

FIRST GENERATION.

I.

FRANCIS COOKE of Plymouth, Mass., came in the Mayflower in 1620; m. ESTHER — in Holland, who came in the ship Ann in 1623. He was a very old man in 1650; "saw his children's children have children." He d. April 7, 1663.

CHILDREN II. GENERATION.

2. John, came with his father in the Mayflower in 1620; was old enough to be taxed as high as his father in 1634; m. March 28, 1634, Sarah Warren, dau. of Richard Warren.
3. Jacob, b. in Holland, came in the Ann with his mother in 1623; m. 1646, Damaris Hopkins, dau. of Stephen Hopkins.
4. Jane, b. in Holland, came in the Ann with her mother in 1623; m. about 1628, Experience Mitchell.
5. Esther, b. in Holland, came in the ship Ann with her mother in 1623; m. Nov., 1644, Richard Wright.
6. Mary, b. 1626; m. Dec. 26, 1645, John Thompson (1), who d. June 16, 1696, aged 80 years. She d. March 21, 1715.

A Genealogical Line from Samuel Allen of Braintree, Mass., to Abigail Allen, who Married
James Thompson of Halifax, Mass.

FIRST GENERATION.

I.

Samuel Allen of Praintree, Mass., m. (1) Ann, (2) Margaret. First wife d. September 29, 1641. Was made freeman
May 6, 1635.

CHILDREN BY FIRST WIFE II. GENERATION.

2. Samuel, b. 1632; m. Sarah Partridge.
3. Mary, b. —; m. Jan. 24, 1656, Nathaniel Greenwood.
4. Sarah, b. March 30, 1639; m. Lieut. Josiah Standish, son of Capt.
   Miles Standish of the Mayflower.

CHILDREN BY SECOND WIFE II. GENERATION.

5. James, b. —.
6. Abigail, b. —; m. 1670, John Cary.
7. Joseph, b. March 15, 1650.

SECOND GENERATION.

2.

Samuel Allen[2] (Samuel[1]), b. 1632 or '33, son of Samuel
and Ann — Allen; m. Sarah Partridge, b. 1639, dau. of
George Partridge of Duxbury. He settled in East Bridgewater in 1660. He d. in 1703, aged 71 years.

CHILDREN III. GENERATION.

8. Samuel, b. 1660; m. 1685, Rebeckah, dau. of John Cary. She d.
   1697.
9. Essiel or Asahel, b. 1663.
10. Mehitabel, b. 1665; m. 1685, Isaac Alden.
11. Sarah, b. 1667; m. (1) Jonathan Cary; he d. about 1695; m. (2)
    1705, Benjamin Snow.
12. Bethiah, b. 1669; m. John Pryor.
13. Nathaniel, b. 1672; m. (1) 1696, Bethiah Conant, (2) Abigail —.

14. Ebenezer, b. 1674; m. 1698, Rebeckah Scate. He d. 1730.
15. Josiah, b. 1677; m. 1707, Mary Read.
16. Elisha, b. 1679; m. 1701, Mehitabel Byram.
17. Nehemiah, b. 1681; m. 1707, Sarah Wormel.

THIRD GENERATION.

15.

JOSIAH ALLEN[3] (Samuel,[2] Samuel[1]), b. 1677, son of Samuel and Sarah (Partridge) Allen; m. 1707, MARY READ. He d. prior to 1736.

CHILDREN IV. GENERATION.

18. Micah, b. 1708; m. 1737, Hannah Edson.
19. Josiah, b. —; m. 1741, Sarah Orcut. He d. 1745, aged about 35 years.
20. Mary, b. —; m. 1737, Benjamin Vickery.
21. Esther, b. —; m. 1749; James Edson.
22. Sarah, b. —; m. 1742, Japhet Byram.
23. Nathan, b. 1722; m. 1743, Rebeckah Read.
24. Betty, b. 1724.
25. William, b. 1726; m. 1748, Susanna, dau. of Joseph Packard. Moved to Brookfield.

FOURTH GENERATION.

23.

NATHAN ALLEN[4] (Josiah,[3] Samuel,[2] Samuel[1]), b. 1722, son of Josiah and Mary (Read) Allen; m. 1743, REBECKAH READ, dau. of Stephen Read.

CHILDREN V. GENERATION.

26. Abigail, b. 1743; m. 1765, James Thompson (55) of Halifax, Mass.
27. Nathan, b. 1747.*
28. Nathan, b. 1749.
29. Rebeckah, b. 1751; m. Levi Gilbert of Brookfield, whither the family removed.
30. Esther, b. 1753; m. Amasa Ross.
31. Philip, b. 1757.
32. Hannah, b. 1760; m. John Bacheldor.
33. Philemon, b. 1762.

GENEALOGY OF A FEW FAMILIES DESCENDED FROM ELEAZER
HUTCHINSON. SAID TO HAVE COME TO AMERICA,
LANDING AT PLYMOUTH, MASS., AND
FINALLY SETTLED IN LEBA-
NON, CONNECTICUT.

FIRST GENERATION.

I.

ELEAZER HUTCHINSON came to America, landing at Plymouth, finally settling in Lebanon, Conn.; m. —.

CHILDREN II. GENERATION.

2. Eleazer, b. —.
3. Stephen, b. —.

SECOND GENERATION.

3.

STEPHEN HUTCHINSON² (Eleazer¹), b. —; m. —.

CHILDREN III. GENERATION.

4. James, b. —.
5. Paul, b. —; m. Susanna Sprague.

THIRD GENERATION.

5.

PAUL HUTCHINSON³ (Stephen,² Eleazer¹), b. —, son of
Stephen Hutchinson; m. SUSANNA SPRAGUE. Settled in
1790 in New Marlboro, Mass. In 1817 he was still living there.
Their children were all born prior to 1790 in Connecticut.

CHILDREN IV. GENERATION.

6. Jemima, b. —; m. Holland Underwood or a Clark; d. 1840 or '41.
7. Susanna, b. —; m. — Coan.

8. John, b. —; lived near Albany, N. Y.
9. Joel, b. —; lost track of.
10. Zenas, b. Nov. 21, 1770; m. (1) Fanny Tyler Smith, (2) Mrs. White.
11. Elihu, b. —; unmarried. In 1840 was living in New Marlboro.
12. Phebe, b. —; m. Moses Adams.
13. Triphena, b. —; m. a Clark or H. Underwood.
14. Benjamin, b. July 12, 1782; m. 1808; Hannah Ballard.
15. Paul, b. 1784; m. Mrs. Catharine —.

FOURTH GENERATION.

7.

SUSANNA HUTCHINSON[4] (Paul,[3] Stephen,[2] Eleazer[1]), b. —,
dau. of Paul and Susanna (Sprague) Hutchinson; m. — COAN.
Lived in the state of New York for a time. Were in Canada
during the war of 1812, and were suspected of giving aid and
information to the enemy, for which they were about to be
placed in confinement when they escaped to the States. About
1820 they went south and settled in Georgia.

CHILDREN V. GENERATION.

16. Samuel, b. —.
17. Gilbert, b. —.
Two other sons were born to them.

10.

ZENAS HUTCHINSON[4] (Paul,[3] Stephen,[2] Eleazer[1]), b. November 21, 1770, in Lebanon, Conn., son of Paul and Susanna
(Sprague) Hutchinson; m. (1) FANNY TYLER SMITH, from
Westchester county, N. Y., b. September 17, 1780, a niece of
Dr. Knott, president of Union college, m. (2) MRS. WHITE.
He studied medicine and was a practicing physician in the
town of Western, N. Y. He d. in August or September, 1853,
at his son Arthur's in New York city. His first wife d. in
1827.

CHILDREN BY FIRST WIFE V. GENERATION.

18. Mary, b. Jan. 3, 1802; m. John H. Wallace.
19. Harriet, b. May 7, 1804; m. Edward Barber Smith.
20. William, b. Feb. 26, 1806.
21. Paul B., b. Oct. 9, 1807; m. (1) Parnel Seymour, (2) Mrs. Martha
    T. Brown (427).

22. Geraldine A. S., b. Dec. 1, 1809; m. Albert S. Terry, a Methodist preacher—a man of deep piety and one who preached christian holiness or sanctification. Later in his ministry he joined the Free Methodist church. She was a worthy helpmeet for him. She d. June, 1885.
23. Cornelia M., b. Dec. 11, 1811; m. James Sadgebury. Lived in New York city. She d. about 1888.
24. Charles E., b. August 5, 1814; m. Mary Gertrude Sadgebury.
25. Clarissa E., b. April 22, 1817; m. Nathan Thompson (430).
26. Frances A., b. Nov. 15, 1819; unmarried. Lived in New York city and Boston.
27. Arthur B., b. June 6, 1822; m. (1) Frances A. Wilcox, (2) Mary J. Barker.
28. Sarah B., b. Feb. 4, 1826; m. Ichabod Samson.

12.

PHEBE HUTCHINSON[4] (Paul,[3] Stephen,[2] Eleazer[1]), b. —, dau. of Paul and Susanna Sprague Hutchinson; m. MOSES ADAMS, a farmer. Lived in Steuben, Oneida county, N. Y.

CHILDREN V. GENERATION.

29. Son, b. —; went to Indiana.
30. Susan, b. —; m. a Methodist minister.
31. Aaron, b. —; became a Methodist minister.

14.

BENJAMIN HUTCHINSON[4] (Paul,[3] Stephen,[2] Eleazer[1]), b. July 12, 1782, in Andover, Conn., son of Paul and Susanna (Sprague) Hutchinson; m. 1808, HANNAH BALLARD. He d. July 25, 1845, at Elmira, N. Y.

CHILDREN V. GENERATION.

32. Almira, b. March 16, 1809; m. 1835, Edwin Munson.
33. Jane, b. Dec. 5, 1810; d. Nov. 1, 1889.
34. Samuel S., b. Feb. 9, 1814; m. Sept. 28, 1843, Mary Lynch.
35. Edwin P., b. March 2, 1817; m. Oct. 1, 1850, Mary R. Curtis.
36. Lucy, b. Nov. 14, 1820; m. 1845, David Billings.

15.

PAUL HUTCHINSON[4] (Paul,[3] Stephen,[2] Eleazer,[1]), b. 1784, son of Paul and Susanna (Sprague) Hutchinson; m. MRS. CATHA-RINE —. Studied medicine with his brother Zenas in Western.

Later practiced in Watertown, N. Y. Here he was postmaster for several years. Had consumption and went south in 1816. He d. September 9, 1816.

CHILDREN V. GENERATION.

37. Son, b. —; d. young.
38. Julia, b. —; m. — Jones, a lawyer of Buffalo, N. Y., and stepson of Judge Cheever of Albany.
39. Catharine, b. —.

FIFTH GENERATION.

18.

MARY HUTCHINSON[5] (Zenas,[4] Paul,[3] Stephen,[2] Eleazer[1]), b. January 3, 1802, dau. of Zenas and Fanny T. (Smith) Hutchinson; m. JOHN H. WALLACE, a preacher in the Methodist Episcopal church, Genesee conference. They lived some time near Peoria, N. Y. Later removed to Clinton county, Mich., where they lived several years. He d. January 1, 1864, in Illinois. She was insane for many years; d. about 1875.

CHILDREN VI. GENERATION.

40. Martha, b. —; m. Thomas S. Ladue, a preacher in the Free Methodist church. Lived awhile in Brooklyn, N. Y.; later removed to Oregon. They have two or three children.
41. Charles, b. —; d. in Chicago, Ill.
42. John, b. —; went insane; d. in Clinton county, Mich.

19.

HARRIET HUTCHINSON[5] (Zenas,[4] Paul,[3] Stephen,[2] Eleazer[1]), b. May 7, 1804, dau. of Zenas and Fanny T. (Smith) Hutchinson; m. October 6, 1825, EDWARD BARBER SMITH. Lived some years in Western and Lee in Oneida county, N. Y. In 1850 removed to Hillsdale county and same year moved to Kinderhook, Branch county, Mich. She d. August 23, 1880. He d. June 27, 1871.

CHILDREN VI. GENERATION.

43. Mary, b. Oct. 6, 1827; m. April 4, 1852, Alfred Bates.
44. William H., b. June 16, 1829; m. May 4, 1853, Mary Elizabeth St. John.

31

45. Edward Barber, b. Feb. 2, 1831; d. July 14, 1831.
46. Jane Elmer, b. Oct. 28, 1833; m. William B. Gring.
47. Cornelia Maria, b. June 25, 1835; m. Feb. 11, 1855, Samuel Grose.
48. Charles Edward, b. March 2, 1837; m. Clarinda Davis.
49. Harriet Hutchinson, b. July 22, 1838; d. Oct. 25, 1838.
50. Zenas Hutchinson, b. August 25, 1839. Enlisted in 1861 in the
     war of the rebellion; d. Nov. 27, 1862, at Memphis, Tenn.
51. Fannie Tyler, b. Sept. 29, 1841; m. Oct. 18, 1860, Samuel Grose.
52. Lydia Pease, b. July 17, 1843; d. March 19, 1848.
53. Willard Cerollo, b. April 24, 1849; m. —.

21.

PAUL B. HUTCHINSON[5] (Zenas,[4] Paul,[3] Stephen,[2] Eleazer[1]),
b. October 9, 1807, in Western, Oneida county, N. Y., son of
Zenas and Fanny Tyler (Smith) Hutchinson; m. (1) PARNEL
SEYMOUR, b. 1807, (2) MRS. MARTHA (THOMPSON) BROWN
(427). He was an energetic and driving man in business. He
lived awhile in New York city and Orangeville, Wyoming
county. His first wife d. in 1832 in Lee, Oneida county, N.
Y. He d. October 15, 1885, in Jackson, Mich., at his daughter
Fannie's. He died in the christian faith.

CHILDREN BY FIRST WIFE VI. GENERATION.

54. Seymour Arah, b. July 26, 1829, in Western; m. Martha Milican.
55. Fannie Parnel, b. June 21, 1832, in Lee; m. March 27, 1853, Elijah
     Russell Knapp.

24.

CHARLES EDWARD HUTCHINSON[5] (Zenas,[4] Paul,[3] Stephen,[2]
Eleazer[1]), b. August 5, 1814, son of Zenas and Fanny Tyler
(Smith) Hutchinson; m. August 14, 1844, MARY GERTRUDE
SADGEBURY. Lived in New York city. He d. September 25,
1863; buried in Trinity church cemetery, New York. In 1887
she lived in Framingham, Mass.

CHILDREN VI. GENERATION.

56. Gertrude, b. June 3, 1845; d. March 3, 1859.
57. Charles Sadgebury, b. Oct. 15, 1848; m. Mary A. Denby.
58. Franklin, b. August 26, 1853; m. Margaret G. Farmer.
59. Ella Sadgebury, b. August 2, 1855; d. May 2, 1877.

25.

CLARISSA ELMER HUTCHINSON[5] (Zenas,[4] Paul,[3] Stephen,[2]
Eleazer[1]), b. April 22, 1817, dau. of Zenas and Fanny Tyler

(Smith) Hutchinson; m. January 31, 1838, at Pavilion, N. Y., NATHAN THOMPSON (430). She d. March 29, 1887, in Keeler, Mich. He d. February 7, 1877, in Lansing, Mich.; both are buried in Keeler. For more full history of this family see number 430 and other numbers of Thompsons.

CHILDREN VI. GENERATION.

60. Charles H., b. Nov. 29, 1838; m. Elizabeth G. Sutton.
61. Albert C., b. Oct. 24, 1840. Served in war of the rebellion.
62. Geraldine, b. August, 1843; d. Jan. 18, 1844.
63. Arthur E., b. June 20, 1847; became insane.
64. Nathan I., b. August 1, 1850; m. Ella A. Tuttle.
65. Frank Zenas, b. June 6, 1853.
66. Sarah C., b. Nov. 16, 1855; d. Oct. 12, 1856.
67. Clara G., b. August 25, 1858; m. William E. Bass.

27.

ARTHUR B. HUTCHINSON[5] (Zenas,[4] Paul,[3] Stephen,[2] Eleazer[1]), b. June 6, 1822, son of Zenas and Fanny Tyler (Smith) Hutchinson; m. (1) February 14, 1851, by Rev. Dr. Kipp, of the Episcopal Church, FRANCES AMELIA WILCOX of Albany, N. Y., m. (2) October 17, 1854, by Rev. D. Marks, of M. E. Church, MARY J. BARKER. First wife d. May 6, 1852; buried in Albany. Second wife d. March 26, 1886, aged 64; buried in Westchester county. Address, 410 Bleeker street, New York city.

CHILD BY FIRST WIFE VI. GENERATION.

68. Daughter, b. —; d. 4 years of age.

CHILD BY SECOND WIFE VI. GENERATION.

69. Child, b. —; d. at birth.

28.

SARAH B. HUTCHINSON[5] (Zenas,[4] Paul,[3] Stephen,[2] Eleazer[1]), b. February 4, 1826, dau. of Zenas and Fanny Tyler (Smith) Hutchinson; m. January 24, 1849, ICHABOD SAMSON, b. October 26, 1814, in Saratoga, N. Y. He d. December 20, 1884, in Boston, Mass., where he had lived many years. He was a firm believer in the christian faith, a faithful and earnest member of the Congregational church. She removed to Rome, N. Y.

CHILD VI. GENERATION.

70.　Cornelia, b. Jan. 24, 1870.

32.

ALMIRA HUTCHINSON[5] (Benjamin,[4] Paul,[3] Stephen,[2] Eleazer[1]), b. March 16, 1809, dau. of Benjamin and Hannah (Ballard) Hutchinson; m. 1835, EDWIN MUNSON. Lives in Elmira, N. Y.

CHILDREN VI. GENERATION.

71.　Sarah Jane, b. Sept. 23, 1837; d. August 25, 1839.
72.　Amelia, b. —.
73.　Marcus Morton, b, July 9, 1843; d. June 4, 1864, of wounds received ten days before in the battle of Dallas, Ga.

35.

EDWIN P. HUTCHINSON[5] (Benjamin,[4] Paul,[3] Stephen,[2] Eleazer[1]), b. March 2, 1817, son of Benjamin and Hannah (Ballard) Hutchinson; m. October, 1850, MARY R. CURTIS.

CHILDREN VI. GENERATION.

74.　Charles E., b. August 9, 1851; m. Edith Fielding.
75.　James, b. —.
76.　John, b. —; d. —.
77.　Edwin P., b. Sept. 1, 1857; m. July 4, 1880, Clara Veazie. She d. July 9, 1885, of consumption.

36.

LUCY HUTCHINSON[5] (Benjamin,[4] Paul,[3] Stephen,[2] Eleazer[1]), b. November 4, 1820, dau. of Benjamin and Hannah (Ballard) Hutchinson; m. 1845, DAVID BILLINGS. Lives in Elmira, N. Y.

CHILDREN VI. GENERATION.

78.　Edward B., b. July 31, 1846; m. Jan. 25, 1887, Sara May Blades.
79.　Hosmer H., b. May 26, 1848.
80.　Myra, b. —.

SIXTH GENERATION.

43.

MARY SMITH[6] (Harriet,[5] Zenas,[4] Paul,[3] Stephen,[2] Eleazer[1]), b. October 6, 1827, dau. of Edward B. and Harriet (Hutchinson) Smith; m. April 4, 1852, ALFRED BATES. She d. —.

CHILDREN VII. GENERATION.

81. Edward, b. —; d. —.
82. Charles, b. —; went west.
83. George, b. —; m. — Flint in Kinderhook.
84. Mary, b. —; m. Eugene Turner of Gilead, Branch county, Mich.
85. Emma, b. —; m. A. E. Ammerman of Bethel, Branch county.
86. Elda, b. —; m. H. S. Kaiser of Bethel, Branch county, Mich.

44.

WILLIAM H. SMITH[6] (Harriet,[5] Zenas,[4] Paul,[3] Stephen,[2] Eleazer[1]), b. June 16, 1829, son of Edward B. and Harriet (Hutchinson) Smith; m. May 4, 1853, MARY ELIZABETH ST. JOHN, dau. of Rev. Marshall St. John of the Methodist Episcopal Church, Genesee Conference, N. Y. William was licensed in 1858 as a preacher in the M. E. Church; is a member of Rock River Conference, Ill. Was chaplain in the United States infantry service, 75th Illinois regiment, from 1862 to 1864. Present address, Hinckley, Ill.

CHILDREN VII. GENERATION.

87. Willard Marshall, b. Feb. 9, 1854; m. Hannah S. Young of Lasalle, Ill.
88. Ida Zuileme, b. Jan. 2, 1857.
89. Seymour Edward, b. March 3, 1859; m. Olive Lee of Mendota, Ill.
90. Charles Anderson, b. April 23, 1861; d. August 17, 1862.
91. Cornelia Elizabeth, b. May 28, 1863.
92. Harriet Hutchinson, b. Jan. 2, 1865.
93. Morris Simpson, b. Dec. 15, 1868.
94. Albert George, b. Jan. 10, 1870.
95. Grace Clarinda, b. April 15, 1872.
96. Frederick Arthur, b. July 22, 1875.

46.

JANE ELMER SMITH[6] (Harriet,[5] Zenas,[4] Paul,[3] Stephen,[2] Eleazer[1]), b. October 28, 1833, dau. of Edward B. and Harriet

(Hutchinson) Smith; m. W. B. GRING. They lived in Chicago, Ill., awhile. He was in the commission business. She d. June 24, 1874.

CHILDREN VII. GENERATION.

97. Wilbur, b. —.
98. Clara L. B., b. —; deceased.
99. Bertha, b. —.
100. George, b. —.
101. Kearney, b. —; deceased.

47.

CORNELIA MARIA SMITH[6] (Harriet,[5] Zenas,[4] Paul,[3] Stephen,[1] Eleazer[1]), b. June 25, 1835, dau. of Edward B. and Harriet (Hutchinson) Smith; m. February 11, 1855, SAMUEL GROSE. She d. February 11, 1859.

CHILDREN VII. GENERATION.

102. Ida H., b. —; d. August, 1862.
103. William Edward, b. —.

48.

CHARLES EDWARD SMITH[6] (Harriet,[5] Zenas,[4] Paul,[3] Stephen,[1] Eleazer[1]), b. March 2, 1837, son of Edward B. and Harriet (Hutchinson) Smith; m. September 29, 1862, CLARINDA DAVIS. He was a traveling preacher in the Rock River Conference of the M. E. church from October, 1865, to September, 1882. In 1883 he was granted a location at his own request. Lives at Onarga, Ill.

CHILDREN VII. GENERATION.

104. Cora Lavina, b. July 1, 1863; d. Oct. 8, 1878.
105. Hattie Indianna, b. Nov. 26, 1865; d. August 23, 1866.
106. Edward Jacob, b. Oct. 6, 1867.
107. Lillie Maud, b. August 30, 1869.
108. Grace Elizabeth, b. Jan. 31, 1872.
109. Walter Charles, b. April 23, 1873; d. Sept. 9, 1878.
110. Addie Naomi, b. Dec. 4. 1874.
111. Fleda Mary, b. August 14, 1877.
112. Arthur William, b. March 25, 1879.
113. Myrtle Augusta, b. June 22, 1880.
114. Pearl Antoinette, b. Jan. 10, 1882.
115. Laura, b. Nov. 6, 1883.

51.

FANNY TYLER SMITH[6] (Harriet,[5] Zenas,[4] Paul,[3] Stephen,[2] Eleazer[1]), b. September 29, 1841, dau. of Edward B. and Harriet (Hutchinson) Smith; m. October 18, 1860, SAMUEL GROSE, whom her sister Cornelia married in 1855. They lived awhile in Chicago, Ill., Warsaw, Ind., and later in Findlay, Ohio.

CHILDREN VII. GENERATION.

116. Cornelia B. H., b. —.
117. Milo Zenas, b. —.
118. Frederick Charles, b. —.
119. Thaddeus Theodore, b. —.
120. Andy M., b. —.

53.

WILLARD C. SMITH[6] (Harriet,[5] Zenas,[4] Paul,[3] Stephen,[2] Eleazer[1]), b. April 24, 1849, son of Edward B. and Harriet (Hutchinson) Smith; m. —. Lived in Coldwater, Mich.

CHILD VII. GENERATION.

121. Edward, b. —.

54.

SEYMOUR ARAH HUTCHINSON[6] (Paul B.,[5] Zenas,[4] Paul,[3] Stephen,[2] Eleazer[1]), b. July 26, 1829, in the town of Western, N. Y., son of Paul B. and Parnel (Seymour) Hutchinson; m. MARTHA MILICAN. They lived many years in New York city. He d. in 1876 in Yonkers, N. Y.

CHILD VII. GENERATION.

122. Paul, b. —.

55.

FANNIE PARNEL HUTCHINSON[6] (Paul B.,[5] Zenas,[4] Paul,[3] Stephen,[2] Eleazer[1]), b. June 21, 1832, in Lee, N. Y., dau. of Paul B. and Parnel (Seymour) Hutchinson; m. March 27, 1853, at Churchville, N. Y., ELIJAH RUSSELL KNAPP, b. July 25, 1825, in Churchville. They removed to Michigan, living awhile in Livingston county, then in Tecumseh, and later in Jackson, where she d. October 11, 1889, after a long and painful illness. In early life she connected herself with the Baptist church. In July, 1890, the family removed to St. Johns, Mich.

CHILDREN VII GENERATION.

123. Sarah Elizabeth, b. Oct. 12, 1855, in Churchville; d. Oct. 15, 1856.
124. Cornelia Frances, b. Jan. 18, 1859, in Churchville.
125. Seymour Clark, b. Feb. 19, 1862. Is employed by American express company as messenger on Detroit, Grand Haven & Milwaukee Railroad.

57.

CHARLES SADGEBURY HUTCHINSON[6] (Charles E.,[5] Zenas,[4] Paul,[3] Stephen,[2] Eleazer[1]), b. October 15, 1848, son of Charles E. and Mary G. (Sadgebury) Hutchinson; m. September 30, 1868, MARY A. DENBY. He is a minister in the Baptist church; was ordained June 27, 1882, at Matteawan, N. Y.

CHILDREN VII. GENERATION.

126. Ethel, b. —; d. 8 months old.
127. Dolly, b. —; d. 1 week old.

58.

FRANKLIN HUTCHINSON[6] (Charles E.,[5] Zenas,[4] Paul,[3] Stephen,[2] Eleazer[1]), b. August 26, 1853, son of Charles E. and Mary G. (Sadgebury) Hutchinson; m. October 25, 1882, MARGARET G. FARMER. He graduated in June, 1881, from Union Theological seminary, New York city, and June 28, 1882, was ordained a Baptist minister at Framingham, Mass.

CHILDREN VII. GENERATION.

128. Florence Elizabeth, b. August 4, 1883.
129. Charles William, b. March 17, 1885.
130. Helen Simpson, b. Sept. 2, 1886.

74.

CHARLES E. HUTCHINSON[6] (Edwin P.,[5] Benjamin,[4] Paul,[3] Stephen,[2] Eleazer[1]), b. August 9, 1851, son of Edwin P. and Mary R. (Curtis) Hutchinson; m. May 31, 1870, EDITH FIELDING.

CHILDREN VII. GENERATION.

131. Edith, b. June 11, 1873.
132. Ralph, b. Feb. 19, 1875.

INDEX.

INDEX.

I.

TO NAMES OF THOMSONS OR THOMPSONS.

The figures denote the consecutive number in the book at the left of the name, and the family number in the middle of the page, if the person was the head of a family.

33

II.

INDEX TO NAMES OTHER THAN THOMPSONS.

The figures denote the consecutive number at the left margin, or the family number in the middle of the page under or by which a Thompson is recorded who was related to the person named by marriage or otherwise.

III.

INDEX TO NAMES OF HUTCHINSONS IN APPENDIX.

The figures denote the consecutive number at the left of the name, and the family number in the middle of the page if the person was the head of a family.

IV.

V.

COOKE AND ALLEN.

For names of Cooke, see Appendix.

For names of Allen and those with whom they intermarried, see Appendix.